TURNER

WE ARE THE LIGHT
JOIN US

TURNER

WE ARE THE LIGHT
JOIN US

A THRILLER BY
JONATHAN
DE MONTFORT

DE
MONTFORT
Literature

De Montfort Literature Ltd
20-22 Wenlock Road
London, N1 7GU, UK
Registered office: 20-22 Wenlock Road, London, N1 7GU, UK
De Montfort Literature and associated logos are trademarks and/
or registered trademarks of De Montfort Literature Ltd.

First published in the UK by De Montfort Literature Ltd, 2018
This edition published in the UK by De Montfort Literature Ltd, 2018

ISBN 978-1-912770-01-4

A CIP catalogue record is available at the British Library

Typeset in Sabon by Falcon Oast Graphic Art Ltd, www.falcon.uk.com

De Montfort Literature is committed to a sustainable
future for our business, our readers and our planet.

Printed and bound in Great Britain by Clays Ltd, Elcograf S.p.A.

www.demontfortliterature.com

*To my mum and my brother for supporting me
in my many hours of need whilst writing this.*

*To Sarah for changing my path and so without
whom this book would never have been finished.*

*To Fi and Catherine, whose real names
I shall take to the grave, for your
inadvertent inspiration to this story.*

*And finally
To 'D' for teaching me the meaning of pure love.*

Chapter 1

Richard

The rush—that's what he would call it. The rush of incandescent energy into the core of his being, that tangible yet undefinable place so central to who he was.

He was standing at the crest of a gargantuan mountain, the world crouched beneath his feet. Everest? Energy spiralled out of his core through his arms and into his hands, which tingled as if he were holding crystalline globes of energy. Their weight, their power overwhelmed him.

He opened his arms like a cross, allowing energy to stream off his body into the night sky like an inverted aurora borealis. It felt like . . . lightning? He closed his eyes, tilted his head back, and opened his mouth in exhilaration; he wanted to scream to set free such prodigious power.

If I could just reach up, I could touch . . .

Anything was possible.

Someone was speaking to him. He opened his eyes.

He was back in his bedroom, staring up at a stain next to the sleek light fixture where he had flattened a huge moth during the summer. It was imprisoned by pale lines creeping across the ceiling; the morning light had found the tiniest weakness in the black wall of the curtains and was pushing into the room as far as it dared.

Just a dream.

'We are the Light,' a voice whispered into his ear. 'Join us.'

He sat up with a start. A bead of sweat trickled down the side of his face.

It was just the voices of his dream continuing as he woke, but they were fading, fading. *Such madness in my sleep, such serenity in reality. How often it is the other way around.* He took a deep breath, relieved to be back to normality. Whatever that was.

'Time to get up, son.' Dad's disembodied head appeared from around the door. 'Big day today.'

Richard gathered himself into the present and reluctantly swung his feet out of bed.

We are the Light.

He glanced back towards the bed. 'Um, Dad?'

No answer. *He must already be downstairs.*

Well, it wouldn't hurt just to take a look. He got down on his knees and peered under the bed.

'What're you doing, you tart?' James towered in the doorway. He was four years older and a full two feet taller than his brother.

Richard thought quickly, then produced a mischievous grin. 'Looking for monsters, of course. Why? What did you think I was doing?'

If he knew what I really was looking for, it would feed his comedic 'genius' for a lifetime.

'You're weird, you are,' he retorted. 'A word of advice—tone that down for your first day. Better get a move on.'

Phew, got away with it—just.

He thought about it over and over in the shower. He'd dreamed about the rush twice in the past week alone, leaving him tousled but energized the next morning. But the voice was new, and he wasn't certain it was a welcome addition. *We are the Light.* Was that a 'what' or a 'who'? He wrung his hands, twisting his skin painfully, as the idea strengthened like the morning light outside.

Back in his room, he faced his new uniform, a black blazer and trousers with a white shirt, crisp as a newly painted wall—thank God James had learned the dark art of ironing from Mum. The blazer had a badge on it with some innocuous Latin phrase underneath. He fumbled with the black-and-white tie. The knot reminded him of that terrible feeling he always got in his stomach when he worried about what lay ahead. Today, it was new teachers, new subjects, new everything. He had the hopeless sense that the world was changing and there was nothing he could do but put his head down and be a good little lamb.

He looked in the mirror at the lopsided tie. It would have to do. *Will everyone hate me? Or worse, will they think I'm a nerd?*

And girls—he'd never gone to school with girls before. The truth he'd never told his parents was that this was the main reason he'd picked this school over the others—well, that and the fact that James

3

went there too. Somehow, just knowing his brother was nearby soothed him like a cool drink on a summer's day.

Too bad summer was over.

'Come on, tart, get it together,' James shouted as he rushed past on the way to breakfast.

Richard groaned, but knew he couldn't put the day off any longer. Again, his stomach churned. Why did people always use the word 'butterflies' when 'knot' was so much closer to the truth?

'Morning, son.'

Dad was already sitting at the glass-topped table in the centre of the kitchen, deep in his morning routine of reading the *Financial Times* and drinking his first brew of the day. As usual, he wore a blue pinstriped suit with a white shirt and patterned tie. The air was pungent with the greasy, sweet-and-sour smell of bacon, eggs, and coffee.

Richard came around the table and dropped his things at the foot of his chair.

Ah yes, Dad and his pinstriped suits. He's so proud of them—has them tailor-made at Savile Row. He does look good in them, though. I overheard a couple of the mothers saying so at sports day, just after Mum—

'Don't you look smart. Now, come here and let me help you with that tie.' Dad stood up and reached towards the bedraggled snake around Richard's neck. In a clatter of pottery and glass, his coffee cup lurched over the edge of the table.

Richard whipped out his hand and caught the falling

cup like a toad whipping its tongue to catch a fly. Not one drop spilled.

Dad gaped. 'Good catch.'

'Wow, how the f—'

He caught himself almost immediately, but Dad was already instinctively glancing at the door as if at a ghost. Richard knew what he was looking for—or who. He'd seen Dad doing this a few times ever since Mum had left. Ever since she'd abandoned them. Mum hated swearing. She would've been standing there with her 'telling off' face, her eyebrows raised in a V like a cartoon witch.

Dad's face took on a familiar sad look. 'Sad' wasn't really the word for it; 'lugubrious,' a word he'd discovered recently in an old novel of Mum's, was a much better fit. That's what angered him the most about her leaving, watching Dad's normal level of almost childlike enthusiasm fade to a shadow of its former brilliance.

Richard set the coffee cup in the centre of the table and shifted uncomfortably.

What did we do that drove you away, Mum? Was it that time I broke the glass in the conservatory window? Because I was sick all over your favourite rug? Why couldn't you even have said goodbye? You could've at least told us why—why you hated us.

Dad was looking at him again, his eyes glinting in the kitchen spotlights. 'Impressive. Since when have you been able to do that?'

'What do you mean?'

'Never mind. You saved my favourite mug—and more importantly, my coffee. You're Daddy's little hero today.'

5

He choked back the tears and tried to swallow the snooker ball in his throat.

'Ooh, Daddy's little hero,' called James from the doorway.

'I'm not a hero. Don't call me that.'

Dad stood up and wrapped one arm around Richard. His messy hair added even more height from Richard's puny thirteen-year-old perspective. 'Don't be like that, James. You know you're my little hero too.'

James stuck out his tongue. 'Take that! I'm a hero too.'

Dad gulped the remainder of his coffee. 'Right, boys. It's time for me to go and sell some hedges.'

Richard groaned. *I guess he still thinks it's funny that I used to believe he actually sold hedges. I wonder how he came to own a hedge fund, anyway?*

'See you tonight,' Dad called as he disappeared.

Richard moved glumly over to the table, where Dad had left the usual ingredients so he could make sandwiches for lunch. They all had to pull together now that they were only three. It seemed strange now that Mum had once done all the household chores. According to the local girls, that was an antiquated way to live, but Mum had seemed to enjoy it. She'd seen it as her place to look after the home. Out of Mum and Dad, Richard wondered who had the better deal, if either.

But doing the family chores had grown on him, and he now found them therapeutic. He finished the two sets of sandwiches with ham and cheese. Pickle on the inside to ensure bread integrity, as he put it. He pictured himself in a sandwich-making world championship where such things mattered. The commentators would scrutinize his knife skills and bread-arranging technique, giving him marks for speed and style.

'Come on then, Hero,' urged James. 'We'd better get going.'

'Stop calling me that. I'm not a hero.'

'Whatever . . . Hero.'

Apparently, there was nothing he could do. The name had stuck.

James stopped at the hallway mirror and brushed his hair, perfecting his suave, side-parted look.

'Let's go,' Richard said with a groan.

James spun around and presented himself theatrically. 'Gotta look good for the ladies, bruv. And you're gonna need to look cooler than that. Wait there.'

He ran upstairs, where Richard heard him rattling around in the bathroom.

'Right, bruv, let's try this.' He teased a ball of hair wax through Richard's thick black hair, just like his, to make it stand slightly on end. 'There you go. Perfect. They're gonna love you.'

They picked up their bags, slung them over their shoulders, and headed out of the door. They walked in silence for a few minutes.

'First day at Wellesworth College, eh? You excited?'

'Yeah. Kind of nervous, though.'

'Don't worry, bruv, it'll be fine. And anyway, I'm always there if you need me.'

James was an old hand at the quintessentially English private school. He only had one more year to go after this one.

Richard eyed his brother without trying to appear too interested. *Was he as cocky when he first started? Was he ever like me?* He reached up and carefully plucked a strand of waxed hair out of his eyes.

'Thanks, James.'

Chapter 2

Richard

His hands were slimy with a film of grease, his insides as hollow as the Tin Man in the ancient *Wizard of Oz* movie he'd seen as a kid. He wasn't a kid now, though; he was a full-fledged teenager. Right?

He followed James dutifully through the kind of cold, overcast morning that was so common in September. The air was heavy with water; it was about to rain. Now and then, a little whirlwind of red and yellow leaves danced around them. They approached the school gates and made their way across the vast expanse of play-ground tarmac towards a Tudor building with orange brickwork and turrets like a miniature castle. Just inside the gates, a small group of boys and girls were chatting.

One of the boys called across. 'Hey James, how ya been?'

'All good, Andrew, and you?'

'Good. Kinda excited to be back.'

'Hey James, good to see you again,' a dark-haired girl added.

James grinned at her and winked. The others looked at Richard, who'd lagged behind.

'This your brother?' Andrew asked.

'Sure is.'

'Hey, what's your name, mate?'

'His name is Hero.'

Richard stepped forward. 'Stop calling me that. I'm not a hero.'

'Come to save us all from Wellesworth hell? He looks more like a little hedgehog than a saviour, James.' Andrew grinned wickedly and launched the group into a chant: 'Hero, Hero, Hero.'

'Thanks, mate,' Richard muttered. He never should have let James put that stuff in his hair. *I'm doomed. The kids'll never let this go.*

James just laughed as the school bell rang. 'Have a good day, bruv, got to get to class—and so do you.' He hurried away with the others.

Richard sighed and wandered in the same direction before spotting what appeared to be the main entrance: a huge oak door at the top of some concrete stairs. He entered between two long lines of hangers with what must have been hundreds of coats and bags dangling on them. To his right was a corridor filled with pupils, but he dared not enter. The teachers were knotting up around a doorway about halfway down. Eventually one of them broke away and came to where the students gathered. The students began pelting the teacher with questions, none of which made sense to Richard.

'And you? What do you want?'

He snapped out of his trance. 'I don't know where to go. I-I'm new here.'

'Well, what class are you in?'

'I don't know.'

'Do you have the letter that was sent to you about your first day here?'

He pulled out a letter from his bag and handed it over. It smelled a little like fresh sandwiches.

'Ah, you're in Mrs Shah's class. That's one of the temporary buildings. Go through there.' He pointed to a set of double doors. 'Continue down the steps, turn right at the opening, follow the building around, then keep going until you see the playing fields in front of you and the temporary buildings on the right. It's the one straight ahead, right at the end, okay?'

'Er, okay.'

'Off you go, then.' The teacher nodded.

He walked through the double doors, down the steps, and turned right. It had started raining. Plump drops lanced like ice spears against his cheeks. He had to close his eyes to avoid the pain. He would have to make a run for it. But by the time he turned the first corner around the building, he was already wheezing as if he were coming down with a full-on asthma attack.

He slowed to a trot, then a walk. The wax in his hair was melting down his forehead, and his soggy uniform drooped like the cheeks of a basset hound. His shirt was practically transparent.

The temporary building was full of students sitting at modern desks. Every face turned towards him as he stood panting just inside the door, fat droplets of rain dripping down the front of his face and off the end of his nose. A little laugh rippled around the class.

11

He surveyed the room for a spare seat. There was one at the very front next to one of the girls.

The girls.

He slid into the seat as unobtrusively as possible. His stomach tightened, and he swallowed hard. He avoided eye contact with his neighbours as he tried desperately to stifle the burning in his ears.

'You'll need one of these.' Mrs Shah handed him a sheet of A4 paper with his schedule for the coming term. 'We meet here once the bell goes at half past eight. Lessons start at nine o'clock. Do try to be on time.' She raised her eyebrows.

'Sorry,' he replied.

'And maybe bring an umbrella next time.'

He smiled sheepishly, feeling more dry already under the heat of twenty-five sets of eyes and his own burning face.

The morning was a blur of different rooms and subjects and teachers. The teachers seemed to assume that he knew things he didn't, but nothing had stumped him yet. Then came Latin. What a useless subject—an ancient language from Roman times that no one had used for centuries.

Richard hadn't really noticed the two girls sitting in front of him until one of them turned around.

'Hi, I'm Felicity, but you can call me Fi.'

The other girl also swung around. 'I'm Angelina.'

'Hi, er, Fi.' This was intimidating. He'd never really talked with girls before.

'You're James Turner's brother, aren't you?'

'Yes, how did you—'

She smiled. 'You look a lot like him. Did I overhear him calling you Hero earlier, at the gates? That can't be your real name.'

A raging fire consumed his face. 'Oh God, all I did was save my dad's coffee.'

They blinked at him, confused.

'He loves coffee. He knocked it off the table by accident this morning. I caught it and put it back, and he called me a hero.'

He could see their curiosity fading fast.

'It was dumb.'

Fi shrugged apologetically. 'Seems a bit over the top.'

'Exactly.'

'I think you're going to have to get used to the name, though. It seems to have stuck. Anyway, Hero, has anyone taught you the facts of life?'

Surely she couldn't mean—

The fire in his face raged even more fiercely. He had no idea what she was talking about. He studied the desk in front of him.

He was saved by the arrival of another new teacher, a tall grey-haired man wearing a dark suit. Hmm. Unusual for a teacher.

The teacher moved to the blackboard and cleared his throat. 'Class . . .'

Fi gave Hero a final smile. 'You're cute.' She looked at Angelina, giggled, then turned around to face the teacher.

'Good afternoon, everyone, and welcome to Latin class. We work hard here, so let's not waste any time.

We'll start with some basics.' The teacher began to write.

amo: I love
amas: you love
amat: he, she, or it loves
amamus: we love
amatis: you love (plural)
amant: they love

He turned and surveyed the students with a grim but not entirely unfriendly smile. 'Okay, repeat after me . . .'

The lesson seemed to go on for an eternity. The longer it went on, the more the teacher reminded Richard of his uncle, whom he hadn't seen for many years now. The smells of the countryside filtered through to him from beyond the wall of boredom. He could almost smell tangy pine mixing with the sweet scent of sodden grass underfoot. He could almost hear the stream trickling beneath the wind-filled trees. He smiled at the thoughts of the happier times at Mum's cottage in Devon, where he felt at home. Free. He saw Dad and Uncle—what was his name again?—whispering to each other in a way that reminded him of how he and James used to plot in ways that annoyed Mum.

He shook himself from his daydream and checked the clock. Only two minutes had passed. Two minutes of glorious freedom. How did teachers do that, make forty minutes last forever?

Finally the bell rang.

Deo gratias.

He stood up and pulled out his schedule: music in the

main music room. The Latin teacher was already cleaning the blackboard.

'Excuse me, sir?' he asked.

'Mm?'

'Can you tell me where the main music room is, please?'

A hand landed softly on his elbow. 'Come with me,' Fi said. 'I'm going there now.'

'Great, thanks.' He hoped his expression looked more like a casual smile than a panicked rictus.

She led him down the stairs, out of one of the many doors along the side of the school, and across the playground.

'That's the music block.' She pointed at the building directly in front of them.

They marched towards it under an awkward silence.

'So you know my brother?' he finally asked.

'I've heard of him.'

'Really? Why?'

'He's just, I don't know . . . Funny? Handsome? He's Turner.'

'If you say so.' *One for James.*

'You definitely follow in his footsteps,' she added.

'You think so?'

'Of course.'

Their eyes met briefly.

'Thanks,' he mumbled.

They arrived at the music rooms, which were on the top floor of a two-storey block separated from the main school. The teaching room desks were arranged in a semicircle like an amphitheatre; in the centre, a small stage area, and in one corner, a grand piano.

Richard liked music all right, but he loved the piano, perhaps because there was one at home, which Mum had taught him to play from an early age, or perhaps because he'd listened to Mum and James playing so beautifully so many times. He loved the start of Mike Oldfield's 'Tubular Bells' and Ludovico Einaudi's 'Nuvole Bianche', which Dad loved to listen to again and again. Sometimes Dad even teared up, much to the amusement of his sons.

'What a sap,' James would say. 'Seriously though, he's such a girl, isn't he?'

Richard chuckled, then snapped back to the present as the teacher walked in.

'So, music. Let's learn some notes.' The teacher's manner was fast-paced and almost theatrical. 'Well then, there's A, B, C, D, E, F, and G.'

The class sat in compliant silence.

'No?' The teacher raised his eyebrows. 'The best way to learn music—or indeed anything, in my opinion—is to do it. So whilst we will learn more about the theory and history of music in these classes, it's important that you actually play, preferably with an instrument.'

'Does a recorder count?' someone asked.

A quiet laugh fluttered through the air.

'Yes, Billy. In fact, the recorder can be a very charming instrument. Just ask the Pied Piper.'

Another nervous chuckle echoed around the room.

The teacher handed out a list of musical instruments they could learn to play. It seemed too good to be true: the school would provide specialist lessons for whichever instrument each student picked and even loan the instruments, if necessary.

'I don't even know what some of these things sound like,' chortled the boy next to Richard, leaning close and flapping his paper. 'Who'd want to spend time tootling around on a horn when we could be out on the practice fields?'

But Richard already knew what he wanted to learn. He imagined his fingers flying over the black-and-white keys, a prodigy leading the orchestra—a hero, even, painting a symphony of darkness and light. He bent over the selection sheet with a flush of pleasure and ticked the last box on the list: PIANO.

Chapter 3

Richard

That evening, Richard settled in the kitchen as usual to cook the family dinner. Tonight, it was chicken with sage and onion seasoning, a good, satisfying meal to end a good, satisfying day. It used to take him forever to make something from scratch, but after Mum left, Mrs Smith had come over many times to show him how to do it. She loved to talk about her two daughters and how much she enjoyed looking after them—she never tired of that topic— but she never spoke of Mr Smith.

Very odd.

Whenever she helped out, she stayed over and had dinner with them all. She was always very enthusiastic talking with Dad, and James watched her with an intensity that Richard rarely saw in him for anything else.

Hero heard the scratch of a key at the front door. *It must be James; he always did that.* The door swung open, and heavy footsteps made their way down the hall. Richard heard a gym bag collapsing to the floor en route like a miner after a hard day's work at the coalface.

'Wow, that smells delish,' James called.

'Thanks. It's nice to get some appreciation after slaving over a hot stove all evening.'

'All evening,' James echoed with a chuckle, sitting down at the table.

Richard presented him with a plate organised in almost psychotic order, all separated into little portions. The contrast of colours was stunning.

'I think you've outdone yourself this time. Good day at school, bruv?' James shovelled a bite of chicken into his mouth along with an assortment of sweet peppers. His cheeks bulged like a pet gerbil's.

'Yeah, it was in the end, although the beginning was a real horror show.'

'What happened?' He was almost unintelligible through the food.

Richard began designing his own plate. 'Well, I just got pissed on, that's all.'

'What?'

'This morning, it was hammering down, and I didn't even know where my class was. By the time I found my way there, I was absolutely drenched. Naturally everybody laughed their tits off.'

'Knob.'

'I guess you're right.' He pointed at James's plate. 'Oh, by the way, I farted on that.'

James stopped chewing, one side of his mouth turned up in amusement, his nostrils flaring in disgust. Richard burst into an open-mouthed smile like an orange segment.

James moved the ball of food to one side of his mouth. 'Oh, it is *on*, bruv.'

'Yeah? Well, you're the one eating my fart.'

James started chewing again but couldn't help giggling. He held his hand in front of his lips, his face burning as he tried not to spray a kaleidoscope of food across the table.

'Don't laugh,' Richard said. 'You definitely shouldn't laugh. Otherwise, food will go up your nose, and you wouldn't want that, now, would you?'

James's body shook as his laughter forced its way out through his eyes and ran down his bright red face in salty rivulets. Finally, he forcefully swallowed the food. 'So, bruv, what's for dessert?'

'I don't know, just look in the fridge. I'm sure there's some yoghurts in there or something.'

'Hmm, I'm in the mood for something a little more substantial.' He pointed towards his target with one eyebrow raised and a malevolent smile of a Bond villain. 'I think I'm going to get myself some of your chin.'

'We're not playing Touch My Chin.' Richard's voice was more pleading than firm.

'Well, here's the situation. I've just discovered that I've been eating your fart, so now I'm going to try to touch your chin. You can either defend yourself, or you can just sit there and take it like a girl.' James arose majestically, his right arm bent upwards at the elbow as if wielding a sword. '*En garde.*'

Richard sighed. 'Fine. But I'm feeling good. You're getting it this time.'

'I'm shaking in my boots.'

Richard leapt in front of James and met his arm with his own. Like medieval warriors in a bizarre meat-sword

20

duel, they stood staring into each other's eyes, waiting for the other to twitch.

James moved first with a lightning strike to Richard's chin, index finger extended. Richard saw it coming. He sidestepped in what seemed to be slow motion and delivered a strike with his own pointed finger.

Yeees! Take that.

James parried when Richard's finger was just milli-metres from his chin.

Bastard. Thought I had you.

'Well, well. You *are* feeling good.' James took on a Bruce Lee pose. '*Waaadaaah!*' In a flash, he tapped Richard's chin, then opened his arms to an invisible, adoring crowd.

Richard held up his hands in surrender. 'Okay, you got me. You win.'

'Oh, I don't think so. This is far from over. Nobody, and I mean *nobody*, farts on my food and gets away with it.'

'I didn't really fart on your food, mate.'

'That's not the point. You made me think you had. Now take your medicine like a man.' He struck another martial arts pose.

They had watched those old seventies films over and over, resulting in what Mum had called 'the total de-struction of the house'. In the end, the Council of Peace (aka Mum and Dad) had convened and ordered that these films were never to be watched again.

Richard responded with a flourish. '*Hawah!*'

'Now you're getting into the spirit of things, bruv.'

James whipped an open hand towards him. Richard

parried, attacked, and parried again as James flickered past. Richard jumped back, crashing into the table. Pottery clattered, mugs rattled, and tea sloshed everywhere. He glanced back. James whirled in a blur, taking Richard to the floor with a leg sweep, and then cradled his chin in the palm of his hand.

'Now, why are you being cheeky?' he said as if to a small child.

Richard grunted. 'I told you, I'm feeling good.'

'This is more than just feeling good. What happened at school?'

'Nothing. Just a normal day.'

'Okay, have it your way.' James used his first and second fingers to play the tom-toms on Richard's chin. 'Bop-di bop-di bop.'

'Okay, okay, I met a girl.'

The hand lifted. 'Aha, I knew it. What's her name?'

'Oh, come on.'

The fingers wiggled, ready to play the tom-toms again. 'Fi.'

'Fi? What's her full name?'

'Felicity.'

'Felicity . . .?' James asked as if confirming a message on a bad telephone line. 'Ah wait, that's Andrew's sister.' In his best Austin Powers voice, he added, 'Felicity Shagwell.' He released Richard and rose to his feet.

Richard rolled up from the floor. 'What?'

'Just a little joke I have with Andrew. Felicity, eh? She's quite attractive.'

Hey, don't talk like that about my girlf— 'She's also a nice person.'

'And that is, of course, the most important thing.' James sat down and began eating again as if nothing had happened, as if the prior five minutes had been as inconsequential as a fly landing on the wall.

Richard slid into a chair across the table with his own plate. 'So here's something I thought of today.'

James raised an eyebrow.

'Whatever happened to our uncle?'

'Uncle? What are you talking about? Dad's an only child.'

'He came with us to Devon at least once, I'm certain. But I can't remember his name, and I can't remember seeing him at all since—'

Since Mum left. Oh.

James fixed his gaze upon his brother. 'Honestly, bruv, I've no idea what you're talking about.'

He's lying. But why?

The first month at school for Richard—now known everywhere as Hero—passed in a blur. Except, of course, for this particular moment. This endless, torturous moment. His eyes skimmed the text before him.

We've been learning this crap for weeks now. Look at this one: Romeo and Juliet, *supposedly a romantic tragedy. The only tragic thing about this is their stupidity. What kind of plan is poisoning yourself? Perhaps they should've discussed it. It's just too contrived. It should be titled* People Being Stupid—*but then again, isn't that how people always behave?*

He looked up from the book and surreptitiously studied his classmates. Ben, Tom, Charlotte, Oliver,

Angelina. And Fi. Some of them were new friends; some had come with him from his old school. But thanks to all of them, that out-of-place feeling he'd had on day one, standing in front of the class with water dripping from his nose, was a fading nightmare. *Luckily, kids have short memories.*

He realised with a start he was staring at Fi, who was returning his gaze. She was wearing that sweet smile that made him feel as if he'd just drunk the richest, thickest, creamiest cup of hot chocolate he'd ever known on a cold winter's night by the fire. He felt gooey, like the remnants at the bottom of the cup.

The bell rang for lunchtime.

He had zipped himself up and was washing his hands in the washroom when both the basin and his hands began to seem further and further away. His skin turned cold, and goosebumps bristled against his clothes.

'Hero,' a voice whispered.

He glanced in the mirror, but no one was there. He turned slowly, water dripping from his hands onto his shoes. Nobody.

'Do the right thing.'

'Who's there?' he called out.

Nobody answered.

'Come on, stop messing around.'

He walked across to the stalls, three in total. He checked the first one. Nobody. Hesitantly, he moved on to the second and pushed open the door. Nothing. He felt his heart beating in his neck. His head was sweltering; a thin film of sweat formed on his face.

Slowly, he moved towards the final stall. Standing to

one side, fully expecting some kind of prank to explode in his face, he opened the door. His muscles tensed.

Empty.

'We are the Light,' the voice murmured from behind him.

He spun around, but no one was there. Sweat dripped down his face, which was burning like a log fire in winter. He walked back to the basin, where the tap was still running, and splashed some water on his face.

'Join us.' The voice was right next to his ear, as clear and real as a cloudless night sky.

He felt a hand on his shoulder and froze, blinking the water out of his eyes. There was a face, another face, next to his in the mirror.

A flash of fear hammered down his spine and into his legs. He ducked as if he were trying to smash through the floor like a mole burrowing underground to escape a predator.

'What're you doing?'

It was Tom, his childhood friend who'd migrated with him to this school.

'Dammit, Tom,' he exclaimed in relief. 'What're you doing sneaking up on me like that? I nearly shat my pants.'

'That would've been hilarious.' Tom sniggered.

The heat in his face was now more from the rising tide of anger. 'And what's with the whole "do the right thing" and "we are the Light"?'

'What're you talking about? I just asked if you wanted to join us.'

What?

'You know, playing football. In the yard.'

He snatched a couple of paper towels and buried his face to cover his confusion. 'Sure, why not? Let me just dry myself off.'

'Come on, we'll miss it,' Tom said.

'Okay, okay.'

He jogged out behind Tom, tossing the used paper towels in the bin as he passed.

'Hey, Hero.' Fi used that sing-song voice that only teenage girls do, mimicking their favourite film star's sexy tone but getting it slightly wrong. 'What're you doing?'

'We're just going to play football in the yard,' he said.

'Oh.' She deflated like a balloon with a slow puncture. 'It's just, I don't have anyone to have lunch with, and I thought—'

'Ah. I see. Well . . .'

He glanced at Tom. On some unheard channel of male telepathy, a message was transferred, one that all post-pubescent males understood.

Tom gave them a toothy grin. 'Hero, to be honest, I think we've already got too many people. You'd be doing us a favour.'

'Okay, well, have a good game.' He turned to Fi. 'Shall we?'

She shifted her books to the other side and fell in beside him. 'We shall.'

Chapter 4

James

I was on full autopilot on the way home after a decent training session at the gym. Night-time had already drawn in with winter approaching, and the lack of street lamps meant I could hardly see a thing. Training had recently become much more interesting, although sometimes I worried about the master. Other than that, the previous few weeks had been fairly smooth, except of course for the change in Hero's behaviour. It was hard to put my finger on exactly what was different. He seemed withdrawn now even by his usual reserved standards.

And then of course there was Vicki.

The lights in the house were still off as I arrived, making the house more imposing than usual. Hero should have been home by now, and I had the sense that something was wrong. Was it the smell in the air? The way the shadows formed around the porch windows? I really couldn't tell, but having no choice, I pushed my key into the lock.

The house was cold—strange, since I could hear the fizzing and pinging of the central heating. My heart was beating faster, and my lungs were snatching at the air like an overweight hamster running in its wheel. I quietly closed the door behind me, but I could see nothing, so I fumbled towards the light switch on my right.

The hall was empty. There was somebody there, though, in the darkness. I couldn't see them, but they were there. They were in the kitchen. I could feel it.

I padded over to the kitchen but dared not enter. The air was thick. Was it tension? Or could I somehow smell the breath of the intruder? I snaked my hand inside the door, feeling for the light switch. Preparing to duck quickly, I switched it on.

The light hit like a slap to the face.

'What the hell are you doing?' I shouted.

Hero was sitting by himself at the table, the dinner he'd presumably prepared left untouched. After Mum left, all of the clothing-related duties fell to me and all of the cooking to him. It suited him, really; he loved food, always had. He'd always been a little chubby, but in a cute way.

I barged forward. 'What the hell are you doing sitting in the dark on your own? You scared me half to death. I nearly ran in here and slapped you.'

I drew up short before I could smack him upside the head. Maybe he was missing Mum. I think it affected him more than it did me. I missed her too, but I had to remain strong for him. And Dad.

They say your heart sinks when you're sad, but I didn't think that was true. When Dad told us those fateful words that Mum was gone, I don't think either of us realised that we were never going to see her again. We'd expected her to walk back through the door at any moment. We probably still did. But back then, it'd felt as if the world were closing in and I couldn't breathe, as if someone had locked me in a wooden box and buried me alive, and I kept punching and punching, trying to get out, but no matter what I did, it didn't work.

Sometimes I caught myself referring to Mum in the past tense, and it scared me. Maybe we had a link, a biological connection that a son naturally has with his mother, and I knew she was never coming back—and it wasn't because she didn't want to. But I realised that was a stupid idea. Why would Dad lie to us?

I kept telling Hero that it wasn't his fault, but I could see every day in his eyes that he believed Mum had left because of him. That hurt more than anything; I hated to see him in pain. I wished I could just reach into his cells and suck out the distress like a Hoover.

I lay a hand on his shoulder. 'Come on, bruv, I understand. I miss Mum too.'

He glanced up from his meal and then back, staring at the arrangement of broccoli and carrots on his plate, and shook his head slowly.

So it wasn't about Mum. 'Is this about Felicity?'

He looked up and pursed his lips.

'Already? Man, girls are harsh.'

'She's fine,' he mumbled. 'It's just not gonna work out, that's all.'

I slid my arm the rest of the way around his shoulder and gave him an affectionate hug. 'Now, more importantly—where's my dinner?'

He turned to face me, horrified at my inhumanity, but as soon as he realised I was joking, he started to grin.

'See? That's all I was looking for, that smile of yours. But seriously, mate, where's my dinner?'

He started to giggle. They say that it warms your heart when you make another human being laugh. I admit, it made me feel good.

'It's in the oven,' he said when he stopped chortling. 'I guess I'd better do my homework.'

'Okay, thanks.' I plucked the dish out of the oven using a towel. 'Bruv, it'll be okay. These things always work out in the end.'

He nodded and smiled forlornly before going upstairs. I didn't see him again that night. I guess he wanted to get his homework done and think things out for himself.

Whatever those things were.

The next morning at breakfast, Hero was equally sombre. He couldn't have slept much, because he was already in the kitchen when I arrived.

'Morning, James,' Dad said with his usual exuberance. 'Hero's really getting into this cooking malarkey. He even cooked bacon and eggs again this morning and made my coffee. I could definitely get used to this.'

Hero gave him an empty smile. I noticed that he wasn't eating himself, nor was there any sign that he had.

'Not hungry?'

'No.'

'Are you okay, bruv? You normally eat like a horse.'

'Just not feeling great.'

'Shall we go?' I started towards the door.

He hung back. 'I'm feeling really rough. Maybe I'm not well enough to go to school today.'

'Hmm. Well, let's head out, see how you go. If you still feel bad, you can always come back, right?'

'Okay.'

We walked to school in silence. Hero seemed intent on studying the pavement. As we arrived at the school gates, I said, 'Okay, bruv. See you later.'

'Can we have lunch together today?'

'What?' He'd never wanted to have lunch with me before.

'Just be good to spend time with you.'

Liar.

'Maybe you *are* ill?' I reached for his forehead as if to check for a fever.

'It's okay,' he mumbled, pulling away.

Damn it all. Something was definitely wrong. I knew I should work out a way to have lunch with him, if only to find out what was going on—but I couldn't. I was meeting with Vicki. Shit.

'Bruv, I can't today, I've got stuff on. Anyway, you've got your friends to have lunch with, right?'

'I guess.'

Hmm. 'Well, have a good day. I'll see you at home later, okay?'

'Sure.'

The day was the usual mishmash of classes and gym. Oh, and Vicki.

Yes indeed, Vicki. God, she wore a short skirt. Was

that even legal? Fair enough, though—she had great legs. She deserved to show them off.

When I first met her, she'd been standing at the school gates and chatting with one of her friends, who promptly disappeared as I approached. She must've been waiting for me but was trying to be subtle about it. About as subtle as a brick through a window.

'Hey, James,' she purred.

'Hey, how *you* doin'?' That Joey from *Friends* thing really shouldn't work, but it did. Girls were so shallow; it was almost too easy sometimes.

She giggled in that way only teenage girls can, the way that made you feel happy yet on edge. You were never sure if they were mocking you or interested. Most of the time, it seemed to be both. I used to think that they were always mocking me. That had been a waste of a few years. Still, I'd made up for lost time.

'Would you walk me to the tube?' she asked.

'Well, I've got to go to the gym. How far is it?'

'Not far. St James's Park.' She raised her voice at the end as if asking a question.

'That's on my way. Let's go.'

At the tube station, I did the usual trick of putting my hand on her waist as I gave her a goodbye kiss on the cheek. She grabbed my lapel, pulled me back, and pushed her face against mine. Our teeth smacked together with a clatter.

'Ow.' I pulled back slightly, holding her at bay. 'Relax. Let's just take our time.'

I pulled her closer again. As we kissed, I caressed her curves and slid my hand down to her thigh, then back upwards over the thick cotton of her hold-ups until I reached the warmth of her skin.

God, I loved stockings.

She recoiled slightly. 'Not here.'

'Sorry.' I retracted my hand and slowly pushed her back against the wall, pressing myself against her. Her hardened nipples prodded my chest.

'I really want to continue this,' I breathed, 'but I have to get to the gym now.'

'Oh, James.' Her sigh made her disappointment clear.

'It's okay. We'll pick this up again tomorrow.' I caressed her cheek with my fingertips.

She gazed at me the way a doting dog looks up at its owner. Always leave them wanting more—well, at least the first time.

I made my way to the gym, thinking about Vicki and those luscious thighs throughout my session and then more on the way home, imagining what we might have done had I taken her back there.

When I realized I was approaching home, I hastily adjusted my trousers using my hand in my pocket to give myself some room. I didn't want to be showing *that* to the family. All the main lights in the house were off again, but I knew that there were no intruders today. I don't know how I knew. The master told me this sense is part of the training and will only get stronger. That's the part that really scared me, though.

I marched up the steps. What was it with this kid and sitting in the dark at the moment?

The dark. There was something about those words that jumped into my throat and touched the end of my tongue like a jack-in-the-box, then disappeared just as quickly, like a memory of something I'd never done. Not in this life, anyway.

I switched on the main hall light and dumped my bag on the floor. The books and gym kit made a satisfying thud. I noticed a faint glow I hadn't seen before coming from Hero's room upstairs. Time to see what this was all about, then. How was I gonna do this? An indirect approach might be best.

I stood in the doorway. 'Brrr, it's cold out there.'

'It is winter.' There was a stillness to his voice, as if a part of his soul were missing.

'Good day at school, bruv?'

He turned from his computer to face me, smiled, and nodded.

'Don't you want to turn the light on?' I asked.

He shrugged and turned back to his computer.

Don't make it easy for me or anything, bruv.

I thumped a fist rhythmically against the door jamb. I was getting angry because he was in too much pain to talk. *Deep breath, James.* I really was an asshole sometimes.

'Manage to have lunch without me today?'

'Indeed,' he replied. 'How was training?'

'Good as always. Thanks for asking.'

'What do you guys do, anyway?'

What was this? I quietly caught my dropping jaw. 'That's the first time you've ever asked me about my training.'

'Yeah, well, I was never into fighting before.'

'Well, we don't really fight, exactly.'

'So what do you do, then?' He pushed his chair back and looked at me with interest.

Wait a sec. Why was he into fighting all of a sudden? 'Okay, you're right, we do fight a bit. But not hard. You know, we do the usual martial arts sword fighting, a bit of meditation here and there, and obviously fitness training.'

'Fitness? Forget that.'

Yeah, podge boy. I laughed. 'Each to their own, eh?'

I caught a sudden glint in his eyes; perhaps something lit up on the monitor. But I'd seen this in him before. It was so bright, it terrified me.

'How come you're always so calm, James?' he asked.

'What d'ya mean?'

'You know, you're always calm about everything. You're so confident all the time. How?'

'Hmm, I never thought about it, to be honest.'

'Is it your training?'

I felt a shadow extend over my soul. I could not answer that question—must never tell. Everyone had the right to choose freely. 'Well, yes. And because I've lived a thousand lifetimes.'

He snorted. 'You're weird, you are.'

I smiled, my eyes lightening with a new sunrise. 'Maybe, but what I definitely am is stinky.'

'Yeah, I can smell you from here.'

'I need a shower. Hey, have you eaten already?'

'I'm not hungry.'

'Okay, well, after my shower, I'll make something to eat. You should come and join me.'

'I'll see how I feel.'

35

I swung around the corner into the bathroom. Still hadn't got it out of him. Something was definitely wrong, and it wasn't Felicity—or at least, not only her. I'd have to talk to Andrew about her tomorrow, although that was definitely going to be awkward. Awkward indeed.

Hero was sitting up on his bed as I headed back to my room after brushing my teeth. Okay, enough dicking around. I was just gonna have to go for it.

I stopped in his doorway. 'You weren't hungry in the end, eh?'

'No.'

'Are you okay, bruv?'

'I'm fine, mate. I just can't sleep at the moment.' He fidgeted nervously with his hands.

'You've been like this for a while, though. Is everything really okay?'

'It's cool. Don't worry about me.'

'Okay, well, try to get some rest, bruv, eh?'

'Thanks, mate.'

I went to my room and lay down on my bed, looking up at the ceiling, thinking. My blood was pumping hard, making the bed hot and uncomfortable. It was no good. I couldn't just lie here staring at nothing.

I sat down at the computer and typed 'depression' into the search engine. I browsed several related websites, the various symptoms and causes. Some sounded similar to Hero's demeanour, but nothing that really jumped out at me. This couldn't be it. He wasn't depressed.

I was about to turn off the computer when something

in the corner of the screen caught my eye, a single word. I clicked the link. Lo and behold, I had my answer.

I sat, unblinking. Impossible, surely? No one would dare. A small volcano sprouted inside me, seething hot lava.

Oh bruv, why do you never ask for help?

There was a knock at the door. I clicked to BBC News just as the door opened.

'Is everything okay?' Dad asked.

'All good, just wondering what was going on in the world.'

He raised an eyebrow. 'When I was a kid, we had magazines for that kind of thing.'

'I did *not* need to know that,' I said, laughing and shaking my head.

'Have a good night, son.' He started to leave, then turned back. 'Just be careful. There's some very strange people in this world, okay?'

'Sure, Dad. Thanks.'

He closed the door behind him as he left. I shut down my computer and went back to bed. At least the poor kid had me beside him now. Whatever was going on, I was going to find out.

I'm going to be your guardian angel, bruv.

Chapter 5

Hero

Breakfast was quiet, as it had been for some weeks. Hero sat scooping his wet cornflakes up in his spoon, then tipping them back out into the bowl, over and over.

'You really shouldn't play with your food like that— you know, Mum,' James said, then paused with his mouth downturned. 'Sorry. Sometimes it's as if she's still here.'

Hero shovelled a bite into his mouth. It tasted like chunks of cardboard. *Sometimes I just can't hide from James.*

James regarded him with a knowing look, as if fate were now sealed and he knew what the future held. 'Come on bruv, let's get going. I think today's gonna be a great day for both of us.'

He shoved the bowl of tasteless flakes to the centre of the table. 'I'm glad you think so.'

'You'll come around to my way of thinking, trust me.'

They went into the hall and put on their jackets, and James clapped him encouragingly on the back as he opened the door.

'If you say so.' *Only if I find a way to hide away for the rest of my life.*

Hero had been dreading lunchtime all day, as he had for weeks now. He exited the classroom where he'd been learning one of his favourite subjects, maths. He felt safe with numbers; they never lied or tried to hurt him.

The main corridor was dimly lit by the pale light of a few sparse windows. At his locker, he put his books away and took out the packed lunch that he'd habitually made for himself.

'Hey, Hero,' someone cawed.

He opened his mouth, but no words came out.

Martin was a boy in the last year of school, a huge rugby player who had clearly developed early. As if that wasn't enough, he had three of his friends with him, as always.

Without further ado, Martin smashed him backwards into the locker. He slid to the floor. His stomach was a boulder bearing down on his bowels. *Why can't they just leave me alone?*

Martin scooped the books from the cabinet onto Hero's head and bent down to whisper into his ear. 'You know, I could shit in your mouth right now. Maybe I'll do that later today when we see you after school, as usual.'

He laughed, his friends joining in. Then he grabbed the lunchbox from Hero's hand, took out one of the sandwiches, bit into it, and dumped the rest onto the floor.

'Mmm, delicious. Enjoy your lunch.' He threw the

sandwich with the bite out of it at Hero's head. 'See you later, *Hero*.'

The group cackled as they disappeared into the darkness of the corridors.

Physics class after lunch became an exercise in distraction. Hero couldn't get the threat out of his mind. *Would Martin really shit in my mouth?* He retched at the thought, somehow holding down the vomit with willpower alone. Time seemed to slow to a near standstill.

2:30 . . . 2:32 . . . 2:33 . . . 2:33 . . . still 2:33 . . . 2:35 . . .

The idea of being held down while Martin dropped his pants and squatted over him . . . He felt helpless, hopeless. The daymare continued as he imagined Martin grunting as he slowly squeezed.

Hero's stomach heaved. This time he couldn't hold back, and a small amount of vomit jutted into his closed mouth. He grimaced as he swallowed it back down.

Hero hurried the length of the first street on his way home, then took a left into the road. Maybe he'd got away from school ahead of them after all. Just one more corner and then—

'Hey, Hero, we were just talking about you. We didn't think you'd show up today. Thought maybe you'd take a different route.'

Martin and his three friends were lying in wait.

'Oh, bugger off, Martin.'

'"Bugger off,"' Martin said mockingly. His friends laughed. 'Who even says that?'

'I think I heard my nan say it once,' one of the boys answered.

'Are you Dave's nan, Hero? Are you? Are you an old woman?'

They all sniggered again.

Hero pulled himself a little straighter. 'I heard Dave's nan gave birth to his mum by taking a shit.'

Where the hell had that come from? A rush of cold adrenaline prickled his arms.

'Whoa-ho. Did you hear that, Dave? I think Hero's getting a little bit cheeky.'

'Too cheeky,' Dave added.

'And speaking of taking a shit, that reminds me—*get him.*'

The circle of boys closed in, and Hero began to back away. Dave made a grab for him, but he was too slow. Hero legged it around all three of them and bolted for home.

Martin and the boys hurtled after him. Hero heard their feet slapping closer and closer until someone shoved him against a small garden wall. He banged his knee and stumbled to a stop bent awkwardly over the wall, his kneecap throbbing.

Dave yanked his arms behind him in an armlock. Hero's eyes widened as Martin moved in and punched him viciously in the stomach three times. He didn't even have time to breathe before Martin followed up with two more punches to the mouth.

So this is what it's like to get beaten to a pulp. He might've thought it was happening to someone else if it hadn't hurt so much.

Dave released him, and he tumbled to the road. If it hadn't been for the warmth of the blood oozing over his chin, he wouldn't have known his lip had split.

Martin sneered inches from his face. 'You shouldn't've been cheeky, and you shouldn't've tried to run, Hero. Now you're really gonna get it.'

Hands grasped Hero's arms and legs from all sides, while Martin dropped his pants and turned away. Hero saw his bare white cheeks descending from above.

He squeezed his mouth and eyes closed, his nostrils flaring as his breathing quickened to a frenetic pace. He tried kicking, flailing, wriggling—anything to get free—but his assailants were too strong. He couldn't move. His heartbeat boomed in his ears like the World War I guns in the documentaries Dad loved to watch.

He risked opening his mouth for a shout. 'Help!'

Martin laughed. 'I'm gonna shit in your mouth now, Hero, d'ya hear me? Open wide, here it comes— *nnnnnnnnnnn.*'

Hero became heavy and the world around him went hazy. An inner stillness spread to his extremities, like an inverse rush. He stopped struggling, and the world switched off like Mum and Dad's old goldfish-bowl TV. Just a single luminescent pinhole of light remained—but through it came a lifeline.

'Hello, lads, what's going on 'ere? Is that my brother you've got down there?'

Hero's eyes flew open.

James stood just behind the other boys, ready for a showdown. 'If you wanna fight, why don't you pick on someone your own size?'

'Shit, it's Turner.' Dave backed up a step.

Martin rose, struggling to tug his pants up past his knees. 'Piss off, Turner. This is nothing to do with you.'

'Yeah . . . no. I'm afraid I won't be able to do that.' James pointed at his brother. 'You see, that's my brother. You pick on him, you pick on me. Simple enough even for an idiot like you to understand. But even if he wasn't family, the powerful should never be allowed to prey on the weak, especially when they're as ugly as you lot.'

Martin and the boys glanced at each other. The hands holding Hero's hands and feet shifted anxiously. Hero lifted his head from the pavement just a bit to better see what was transpiring above him.

James's face was implacable. 'Well, come on, then, wankers. Or are you all too chicken? The four of you can only pick on one smaller boy? You're pathetic. You know that, right?' He flung one hand towards Martin. 'And pull your pants up, mate, no one wants to see your tiny cock. I mean, seriously, how do you deal with the laughter you must get from every girl who sees it?'

Hero couldn't quite suppress a smile. *How does he think of all this stuff so quickly?*

Slowly, Martin stood up, fastened his pants, and stalked towards James. 'Okay, I didn't want to do this, but you asked for it, mate.'

James smiled as if to say 'Indeed I did' and gazed at Martin with cool, steady eyes.

Martin hesitated.

Hero knew why; he felt it too. Immense power emanated from his brother. And what was wrong with his eyes? They weren't moving—wait, no, they were moving, but they had no colour. That couldn't be right. Hero blinked deliberately and looked again. They looked normal enough—but wow, he was unflinching. Was he even blinking?

He glanced over at Martin. A vein pumped on the ringleader's temple like a caterpillar on speed. *He's afraid. He's actually afraid of my brother.* Warmth like the elixir of life flooded into Hero's chest, arms, and legs. He smiled, choking back tears of joy and relief.

James remained expressionless. Martin, now standing in front of him, clenched his fists, but James stared directly into his eyes.

Martin let loose with a punch. In a blur of speed, James twisted to his right, smashing Martin's nose with one elbow. The sickening crack startled everyone except James, who simultaneously positioned his left leg behind Martin's right, sending Martin flying backwards to the road.

Dark red blood advanced rapidly down Martin's white shirt, reminding Hero of those strange post-war maps of an expanding Communist Russia that he'd seen on videos in history class. The grips on his hands and feet had vanished, and he sat up.

James brought the heel of his shoe down into Martin's stomach. Martin winced, squealed, then threw up over his own face.

James glanced at the other three boys. Hero could have sworn there was the slightest flicker of a smile at the corners of his mouth.

He's enjoying this.

The other three boys approached James.

Now even his eyes are smiling.

They surrounded him, Dave behind, another in front, and the third hanging slightly back and to the right. Dave darted forward but found himself clutching at empty space. He looked ridiculous, like a human mario- nette whose wires had tangled. He jerked in reaction to a whistling near his left ear—a mistake. His nose met with the palm of James's hand, now travelling at high speed. He brought up his hands to protect his face, only to receive a sharp punch to the solar plexus. He collapsed to the ground, gasping for breath as if his life depended upon it. Hero couldn't be certain if it was the light from the street lamp that made Dave's face look so grey, but it was a look that would've kept good company inside a coffin.

The attack had been so fast and clinical that the other two backed away.

'What's the matter, lads? Lost your balls now you're in the big boys' league?' James said.

The boys looked on in horror at their fallen comrades, now covered in blood and puke. Their faces shone with a thin film of sweat, and their pupils had shrunk to the size of pinheads.

Standing under the street light, James looked like an Old West gunslinger, towering imperiously in the moonlight at the O.K. Corral. At any moment, Hero half expected him to say, 'I'm your Huckleberry.'

James pointed at the boys. 'I'm warning you, if I find out that you or any of your friends have so much as looked at my brother in the wrong way, or if you even fart in his general direction, I will hurt you. And to be clear on this, I won't just rough you up like I did today. I'll really hurt you.'

The boys took another handful of steps backwards.

And then it was over.

James walked past them and helped Hero to his feet. 'Let's go home, bruv, and get you cleaned up.'

'How did you know?' Hero whispered, his hands still jittery as he gathered his scattered belongings.

'I followed you around school today. I saw them beating on you earlier, so I followed you home just now.'

How had he managed that? All that peering over his shoulder the whole way from school, and Hero'd never known that James was right behind him, covering his back the whole way. Crazy.

'Well, I didn't see you.' He straightened his shirt and fell into step alongside his brother.

James smiled. 'I'm very good at that.'

Chapter 6

Hero

Blood splattered the bathroom sink where it had dripped from Hero's mouth, forming long rivulets and circling the plughole, the deep red contrasting with the white of the porcelain.

'You know, you make me laugh, bruv. You say you don't want to be a hero, and there you are standing up to four guys much bigger than you. Sounds like a hero to me.'

Hero looked up into the mirror at James, who was standing in the doorway.

'What was it you said? "I heard your nan gave birth to your mum by taking a shit."' James laughed so hard that he had to steady himself against the door frame. 'That's genius, bruv. I'm definitely stealing that one for later usage.'

Hero grinned, then regretted it immediately when his split lip reopened. Blood welled over his teeth, filling his mouth with a warm, metallic taste.

'So why were those guys bullying you, anyway?'

Hero grabbed some loo roll, packed a wad of paper between his lip and his teeth, and began recounting the last few weeks, starting with standing in the music room next to Fi after their first class there.

'Hey. So what instrument did you pick?' she asked.
'Piano,' he replied.
'Can you play?'
'A little.'
'What grade are you?'
He shuffled his feet. 'I took my grade eight last year.'
'Wow. Would you play for me?'
'Sure. What instrument do you play?'
'The violin. I'm not too good, though. So how about tomorrow?'
'Eh?'
She was grinning at him. 'Will you play for me tomorrow at lunchtime?'

'Wait, wait, wait,' James interrupted from behind.
Hero dragged himself back to the present.
'You pulled a girl on your first day at school? Man, you're *my* hero, buddy. Go on.'
Hero grinned tentatively, mindful of his lip, and took a deep breath. 'Well, the next day, lunchtime arrived, and we met outside the music building.'

Fi's hair bounced as she ran over, and Hero's heart seemed to jump in rhythm to it.
'Hey, how's your day going?' he called.
'Boring,' she said with a sigh. 'And yours?'
'Okay. Still seems easy. Shall we?'
Upstairs in one of the practice rooms, he sat down at

the piano and swallowed dryly. The fur on his tongue had absorbed every drop of moisture in his mouth, and the heat in his face was hoovering the energy from his trembling hands.

'So, any requests?' he croaked.

She shrugged. 'Anything.'

'Well then, I think you'll like this.' He launched into Beethoven's 'Moonlight Sonata'.

'Whoa,' she murmured.

He played all of the most famous part, the part he knew she would be familiar with and appreciate.

'You know, Beethoven was losing his hearing when he composed this piece, and you can hear the sadness in his heart all the way through it.' He looked out of the window to hide the rush of emotion. 'Imagine that. You dedicate your whole life to your one true love, your passion, and then through no fault of your own, it's ripped away from you. I don't think I could handle that.'

He glanced back. She was watching him intently with shining eyes.

'This next piece is different.' His smile trembled as he gathered the music in his head. His throat and chest tightened in anticipation. Then deliberately, as the piece demanded, he began 'Meine Freuden'.

The electricity of the music drew her like a magnet to lean closer over the keyboard.

'It's beautiful,' she said.

She moved sideways so that she was looking directly into his eyes.

He could nearly feel the heat from her blushing

cheeks; he was mesmerised. She closed her eyes and pushed her lips against—

'Whoa, bruv.' James leaned back, amazed. 'So your second day at a mixed school, and you got your first kiss? I am so proud of you. C'mere.' He opened his arms for a hug.

Hero obliged, wrapping his arms around his brother.

'Growing up fast, eh, buddy?' James ruffled his hair. 'So tell me—and I'm pretty certain I know where this is going—what did that have to do with Martin?'

'Well, that day after school, I was putting my books back into my locker . . .'

'Hey, Hero.'

There was a little laughter. He turned around to see Martin and his three friends.

'I hear you've been getting it on with Fi,' Martin said.

Wow, good news spread fast. He shrugged and gave what he hoped was a humble, friendly smile.

'Stay away from her. She's mine.' Martin loomed over him, blocking what little light there was in the corridor.

'I'm not sure you can really own people, you know.'

With no warning, Martin shoved him backwards against the lockers and held him there by the throat. Hero struggled for breath. His head felt as if it were going to explode, thumping in time to his heartbeat.

'Don't talk back to me. Just stay away from her, you little shit.'

Martin dropped him to the floor and stomped off with his friends.

'So why didn't you just stay away from her?' James enquired.

'Well, I did. But then Fi asked me why I was ignoring her. She was worried that I didn't like kissing her. So I told her that I really enjoyed it and wanted to do it again, but Martin—'

'As I thought,' James muttered. 'So she told Martin to leave you alone?'

Hero nodded.

'And that made him even more angry?'

He nodded again.

'You're growing up real fast, bruv. Girls will be the end of us all, you know.' James paused for a moment, tapping his finger against his lips. 'Look, from now on, I'll be watching over you. I'll always be there to protect you. But just in case I'm a bit late, remember these rules: Sometimes you stand and fight. Sometimes you do nothing. And sometimes you run, brother.'

Hero dabbed at his lip dubiously. 'I've never seen you run from a fight.'

'I never run from a fight if I know I can win. But trust me, if I was up against four guys who were bigger, stronger, and faster than me, I'd be out of there so fast my knees'd be up by my ears.'

Hero laughed, and his lip burned. 'Ahhh, don't make me laugh. It hurts.' Sick from the warm taste of blood, he began applying antiseptic cream to his cuts.

James pointed to more blood at the edge of one nostril. 'You're lucky they didn't break your nose. You've still got your looks, at least. Are your hands hurt?'

Hero held up his hands and wiggled his fingers. 'All fine.'

'I know what'll make you feel better. Come on.' He motioned Hero to follow him.

They went downstairs to the sitting room, where James sat down at the piano and started playing 'The Entertainer'. Every so often, he deliberately played out of key and looked at Hero quizzically.

Hero burst into laughter.

'Come on, bruv, sit down. Join me.' James scooted to the left side of the piano bench, still playing. Hero took the upper notes, leaving the lower ones to James. They continued playing the song out of key, a task made more difficult by their hilarity.

'You see, bruv? Everything will be okay because we can always laugh together. Let's try something else.'

James began the next song. Hero recognised 'Nuvole Bianche' and joined in. The notes travelled between them like a wind, an energy moving backward and forward, binding them together. Hero felt as if their combined souls were riding on the ebb and flow of the music.

As they finished, James slipped an arm around Hero. He responded in kind.

'I'll always be there for you, bruv,' James said solemnly, 'and you'll always be there for me.'

The pain and terror of the day ground inside Hero like gears forced to shift without a clutch. Tears welled like oil, a beautiful, warm fluidity that slid up into his throat. The dam inside him broke, and the water tore through the valley of his soul and rushed out though his eyes, burning his face, dripping onto the piano keys. The sheer force of it caused him to shake uncontrollably.

James wrapped his other arm around Hero to complete the embrace. 'It's okay, bruv. Everything's going to be okay.'

Finally, the waters subsided. The birds in the valley were still silent with shock, but Hero knew that they would sing again. Soon.

'Go upstairs and lie down. I'll deal with Dad, okay?'

Hero nodded in gratitude and headed for the stairs. What would he do without his brother?

Later that evening there was a knock at the front door. Hero sat down at the top of the stairs, out of sight, as Dad opened it. There was Martin with his father, a man about Dad's age.

'I'm sorry to bother you,' said the man, 'but I believe your son and mine had a fight earlier this evening, and I wondered if we could talk about it.'

'Come in,' Dad replied.

How was he always so calm? James too, for that matter.

Dad led Martin and his father through to the front room. 'Please, sit down.'

Martin and his father sat, with Dad following suit in the armchair to their left.

'I prefer *Love Island* myself.' Martin's father grinned as he nodded towards the TV news programme that was summarising the day's headlines.

Dad switched it off.

Hero scooted into the shadows behind the bannister.

Years of experience had taught him he could watch from here without risk of discovery.

Dad raised his eyebrows to signal Martin's father to proceed.

'This afternoon, your son James attacked Martin and, well, you can see the results.'

Martin was clearly sporting a broken nose. Hero grinned in the darkness.

'Really? That doesn't sound like James.' Dad got up, went over to the door, and shouted, 'James, can you come down here please?'

James thumped Hero on the back of the head as he sauntered past him, down the stairs, and into the lounge. 'Hey, Dad. Ah, Martin, isn't it? You've got some balls showing up here.'

'Don't talk like that, James. Out of respect for her.' Dad nodded apologetically. 'Martin's dad tells me you beat up his son earlier this evening.'

'Well, Dad, before we go any further, I really think you should take a look at this.' James pulled his phone from his pocket, pressed a button, and held it towards Dad. '*Et voilà.*'

Hero's stomach tightened as the sounds of the boys bullying him outside school filtered from the tinny phone speakers.

James looked up at Martin and his dad with disgust. '"I could shit in your mouth right now"?' He overenunciated each syllable as if trying to comprehend the true horror of the words.

Dad cleared his throat. 'Is that really the kind of thing that you teach your son? Does it make you proud that your son behaves like that? It seems to me that James did the right thing in stopping your son from, as he put it, "shitting in Hero's mouth".'

Martin sniggered.

His father elbowed him viciously. 'Shut up. I think kids should work out their own problems, and James shouldn't just be stepping in on behalf of—Hero, is it? What kind of name is that, anyway?'

'My son's name is not your concern.' Dad crossed to the ornate marble fireplace and slid his finger down the side a black-and-white photo of him and Mum on their wedding day on the mantel. Hero had seen him do this before when he was angry and trying to control himself. 'But I have three things to say about this. Firstly, I think that as parents, we have a duty to teach our children morality. We have to show them that violence is not an option and bullying is wrong. You can rest assured that I'll be calling the school tomorrow and explaining the situation to them. They need to protect Hero from your son because, in my opinion, the strong should protect the weak. That's how things work in our society. Otherwise, it ends up in absolute chaos—a complete breakdown of civilisation.'

He began to pace. 'Secondly, it wasn't really Martin against Hero, was it? It was your much older son and his three friends against him. By your ideology, that's unfair.' He held out his palm as if to say 'wait right there.' Dad always seemed to know instinctively when someone might butt in. He was adept at controlling the conversation like this. 'And finally, let's just say for one second that I agree that we should let our children fight.

That does beg the question: what are you doing here in my house right now?'

He looked from Martin to his father. 'I think you two need to leave. Immediately.'

Martin shot up, and his father followed suit.

Hero winced. *This is not going to end well—for me.*

Martin's father sneered as they passed in front of Dad. 'You think you're so clever, don't you? One of these days, I'm gonna give you what's coming to you.'

Dad jerked his head towards him. 'No, you won't.'

'Yes, I will.'

A shadow befell the room. Even the landing grew cold, as if all the heat in the rooms had dissipated.

'I promise you—you won't.' Dad marched ahead of them with an intense visage and yanked open the door, gesturing for the two of them to leave.

The door closed behind them. The shadow was gone.

Dad shook his bowed head and rubbed his fingers in the crooks of his eyes. He turned to James. 'Training going well, is it, James?'

James smirked.

'Let's have a chat, shall we?'

James glanced up at Hero on the landing. Hero scooted further back into the shadows. The springs of the sofa creaked lightly as they sat.

'What was that all about?' Dad sounded pretty serious. 'Why were they picking on Hero, anyway?'

'Apparently there's some girl at school—'

'Stop—'

There was a beat of silence.

'Girls will be the end of us all,' they chanted in unison before dissolving into laughter.

Under cover of their released tension, Hero inched forward again until he could see their faces.

'I understand why you did what you did, but it's a bit scary,' Dad said. 'I mean, gathering video evidence— what made you think to do that?'

'Justification, Dad. Every action in this world needs to be justified. We both know that.'

'Seems I've taught you well.'

'Modest as ever.'

Dad's face flickered with concern. 'Violence is not the answer, son. I know I taught you better than that.'

'These guys don't understand any other language. I gave them a choice.'

'What choice? It seemed to me like you confronted them.'

James's stance changed to utter disdain. 'They've been beating up Hero for weeks now. You must've noticed the change in him.'

Dad bowed his head as if tired of confronting pain. 'I'm not saying that what they did was right, but violence is a last resort. Once you've gone there, there's nowhere else to go, and then it just keeps escalating until one side is completely destroyed. Do you really want to be the kind of person that's willing to do that?'

James rolled his eyes. 'I'm not gonna go out of my way to attack somebody, but if they come after me or Hero, then I'll defend us. We both know the school's not gonna do anything, and neither are the police. The only time they act is when something really serious happens, like someone's put in a coma or dies. Do you really wanna wait till then?'

Dad stroked the stubble on his chin. 'And what're you going to do if—no, *when*—they come back? Are you going to be looking over Hero's shoulder twenty-four hours a day?'

What did Dad mean, 'when they come back'?

'We've got it covered. The teachers will look out for him. I'll walk him to and from school. I've already sorted it with my gym, no probs. If they catch Hero off guard when I'm not around, I've told him to run home as fast as possible. He's quick enough to outrun these guys.'

'And if he isn't?'

'Then I'll send a message to them to explain how disappointed I am with their behaviour.'

Dad made a disapproving noise deep in his throat.

'It would be a meeting that they won't walk away from,' James finished.

'Don't say that. Please don't go down that path.'

'It'll be okay, Dad.' He patted Dad's leg somewhat patronisingly and stood to go.

'You're better than this, James,' Dad called as James took the stairs a cocky two steps at a time.

But James had already passed Hero, disappeared into his bedroom, and closed the door.

I'm causing so much trouble.

Hero crawled back to his room, not daring to lift his head for fear of being seen. He didn't want to see Dad's disappointment in him.

Maybe I can be better?

*

58

At the end of music class the next day, Fi blocked the doorway as Hero went to leave.

'Oh God, what happened to your face?' she asked.

'Martin. Again.' He'd been speaking with Fi less and less as the bullying had become worse. Today had been the first day that he'd felt free enough even to smile at her, but now he didn't want to show her his ugly, broken face.

'I told that guy to stay away from you.' She caressed his split lip with her thumb.

He relaxed. It felt good to feel her touch. 'Well, he didn't.'

'Is that why you've not been around as much lately?'

He felt himself go bright red. 'Sorry. Please don't talk to him again.'

'Don't worry. I'm done with that guy after this. It looked like he came off worse, though.' She grinned.

'That was James. Look, can I make it up to you? I mean, not talking—'

'Yes, you can.' She nodded encouragingly. 'Tea.'

'You mean after school?'

'You told me you live quite close.' Her smile thawed the thick, icy layer of Martin's intimidation.

The rest of the day whizzed by. Hero struggled to focus, not out of fear but anticipation. But as he and Fi approached the gates at the end of the day, he was gripped by nerves. *James is meeting me by the gates to walk me home. This could be awkward.*

James was already waiting and beaming. 'Hey, bruv. Hey . . . Felicity, isn't it?'

Please stop smiling, James—and please, for God's sake, don't pull any comedy routines.

She looked utterly charmed. 'Yes, but call me Fi. You're James, right?'

'The one and only. It's good to see you. You two look good together.'

Relief flooded Hero's limbs. *Wow. Thanks, James— you really came through.*

During the short walk home, James kept silent for the most part. Hero and Fi exchanged glances and smiles in between looking at their feet. Hero's heart was racing.

'Here we are,' James announced at the last corner. 'You can make your way home from here, right?'

'Sure,' Hero replied.

'Enjoy your homework, then.' James sauntered back the way they'd come.

Fi gazed steadfastly ahead. 'Has he gone yet?'

'I think so.' Hero glided one hand around her waist.

Her high cheekbones took on a pale redness, and her lips trembled slightly. He folded himself into her. The beautiful warmth of her soft lips was an electric charge that sent his heart twisting and racing even faster.

She gasped, her lips still against his.

He pulled back and took her hand in his. 'Come on, then. Let's have tea.'

Once they were home, Hero felt as if he might have to cut his hand off to separate himself from her. He focused on making tea, as had become his usual homebound duty. The tea was drunk innocently enough, although it did get cold during their many long pauses.

Fi looked at her watch. 'Oh my God, is that the time? I've got to go.'

The way her hair bounced as she stood up was so

beautiful. He wouldn't be able to wait to get to school to see her again. He walked her to the door. 'Tea and kissing is so much better than tea and biscuits.'

Her eyes widened.

Oh shit. Had he just gone too far?

She smirked and shook her head. 'Don't ever become a comedian, Hero.'

But he didn't think she really minded.

Over the next few days, James came to school with Hero in the morning and accompanied him on his way back home before gym. Although Fi didn't join them again on their homeward journey, the couple were now an official item at school, regarded with jealousy by their friends.

The bell rang at the end of the school day, and Hero made his way towards the gates, where he knew James would be waiting. It was a cold winter's afternoon, and the light was fading fast. James was there already, looking agitated.

Hero felt a twinge. *I never thanked him, did I? I should say something.*

He fell in beside his brother. 'Hey, thanks for being there for me. Thanks for taking me home every day. It's made a really big difference.'

'No worries, mate,' James said with a grin. 'One day, I'm sure you'll return the favour. Anyway, it's the least I can do for my bruv.'

'You're not angry for having to look after me?'

'Not at all. Why on earth would you think that?'

'You just seem a bit pissed off, that's all.'

'It's not you, buddy. There's something in the air.'

James glanced over his shoulder. They'd reached the street where he'd saved Hero a few days before. 'Something's coming. Something's wrong, bruv.'

Hero became aware of the sound of several people running behind them.

James pointed across the road. 'Go now. Run home as fast as you can.'

'What?' He surveyed the area, his eyes darting backward and forward, looking for predators. *They're back—I knew it. They'll never stop, just like James said.*

'Just do it. Now.'

Hero dashed across the road and rounded the corner towards home. Then he stopped and crouched behind a garden wall, peeking over the top to spy on his brother.

James had turned around to face three well-built men jogging towards him. He fixed his gaze on them, emotionless, looking directly into the eyes of the man at the front.

The group stopped in the middle of the road, directly in front of him.

'I heard you beat up my little brother last week,' called the leader. The thug was holding a knife that glinted in the light from the street lamps. One of the others was carrying a wooden baseball bat and the other, a crowbar.

'I assume you're talking about that complete tit, Martin,' James said. 'He and three other brave lads thought it a great idea to beat up my little brother on a daily basis. Now, what big brother could stand by and let that happen? You must be so proud that Martin and all his mates have got such ginormous balls. What did you say your name was, anyway?'

'I'm Warren,' he said, 'and you won't be forgetting it. Now it's your turn to find out what it feels like to be hurt by someone bigger than you.'

James widened his stance. 'I don't think so.'

James had that same look in his eyes that Hero remembered from the previous fight. Was he even blinking? He peered through the dusk, trying to see if James's eyes had any colour.

I don't think they do. What the hell is going on?

A knot formed in his stomach. He looked again, and James's eyes looked normal again. But the knot stayed. His heart was racing, even though he was crouched low and still.

Warren waved dismissively. 'Fuck off, dickhead. Like you said, what big brother could let that go?'

'I haven't got time for this,' James called back. 'You've got weapons. Use 'em or piss off. This is your last chance to walk away.'

'Shut up, mate. We're gonna break you up so bad, you're gonna wish you'd never seen my little brother.' He glanced at the others. 'Ryan, Jack—deal with this prick.'

Hero was transfixed. Ryan raised his baseball bat and edged towards James; Jack did the same wielding the crowbar. Ryan brought the bat towards James, but before he could connect, there was a dull, crunching thud. The weapon had connected with Jack's face instead, which now had a huge dent in it.

Hero recoiled, aghast. James had somehow changed positions with Jack.

Jack staggered a few steps. Then his eyeballs rolled

up to the back of his head, and he dropped to his knees and onto his face.

Ryan and Warren looked on, as amazed as Hero. Warren pivoted deliberately towards James. His advance was cut short by a wrenching, tearing sound. He stumbled and let out a burbling scream that seemed to pierce its way out of the side of his throat. His leg was no longer straight; there was a strange, V-shaped angle at the knee. Blood began to spread outwards from the joint, and Hero realised that the leg was broken. He imagined what it must look like under Warren's jeans, cartilage and bone crawling through the broken skin like blood-soaked maggots.

The knot in Hero's stomach exploded, and he fell to all fours. With one hand on the wall to steady himself, he vomited a pool of carrot-and-blueberry porridge onto the pavement. The intense sour cheese aftertaste caused him to retch a second time. Somehow, he choked it back, leaving only the emission of a foul burp. He panted as a bead of sweat ran down the length of his nose and dripped off the end.

He heard another dull thud and then, after a long silence, a voice above him. 'I thought I told you to run home.'

He looked up at James, who held out his hand to help. 'Come on, bruv, let's go.'

James pulled him up and set off briskly towards home. Hero craned his neck to see the scene they'd left behind.

'Don't look back,' James ordered. 'Just keep going.'

He snuck a look at his brother, whose grim face remained focused on the pavement ahead.

Oh, James. What have you done?

Hero pondered the afternoon's events as he, Dad, and James ate dinner at the kitchen table. In the corner, the TV was blaring out the news.

What happened back there with James and those men? How did he stop them?

With the sickening thud and deathly silence of the fight echoing in his mind, Hero gradually became aware that the reporter was talking about what'd happened today.

'. . . significant gang violence in Westminster earlier today as police and ambulances were called to a scene of absolute carnage. Three men brutally bludgeoned each other to death using a variety of blunt weapons, including a baseball bat and a crowbar. Police are looking for a fourth man who they think might be a primary witness and are appealing for him or anyone else who may have seen the incident to come forward with any information at this time . . .'

Hero glanced anxiously around the table. Dad was glaring at James, nostrils flared. James refused to meet his eyes.

James couldn't've done it. He's a good person. I'm sure he'll tell the police what really happened.

James methodically folded his napkin, set it next to his plate, and left the table.

Won't he?

Chapter 7

Hero

Images of the day buzzed over and over in Hero's mind like shocks controlled by torturers who wouldn't let up until he told them what they wanted to hear.

It's no use. He sat up in bed, staring at the shard of moonlight coming in through the crack between the curtains. *I'll just read for a bit. That usually sends me to sleep.*

He reached to his right, fumbling like a blind man looking for his cane. He nearly knocked his alarm clock to the floor, catching it at the last second. *There.* He switched on the lamp and swung his legs over the edge of the bed, planting them firmly on the plush white carpet. His bare skin prickled in the cool air as he levered himself out of bed, reached into his schoolbag, and pulled out *Nineteen Eighty-Four.*

Now, where was I? Ah yes, Room 101.

A light knock at the door echoed in the silence of the night. He crept towards the door like a saboteur on a mission.

'You okay, bruv?' James whispered.

'Yeah, fine, just can't sleep.'

'Wanna talk?'

'I prefer to whisper,' he said with a grin. 'Come in.'

James wore the melancholy smile of a victorious soldier coming off the battlefield. He patted Hero on the shoulder and sat down at the computer desk. 'It's good to see you happy again, bruv.'

Hero closed the door and perched on the edge of the bed.

'So what's keeping you up?' asked James.

'Just restless, I guess. Can't stop thinking about earlier.' He glanced down at his hands. 'What happened back there today? To those guys, I mean.'

'Listen, bruv, there're some very bad people in this world. They never stop, until they're stopped.'

Hero smirked. 'Like the Terminator?'

'Worse, mate, because these people really exist—and they're everywhere. You'll understand one day.'

Hero's head snapped up, and he regarded James. He was serious.

I have to ask.

'But was it you? Did you hurt them?'

James blinked silently.

Please don't be angry. 'D-did you *kill* them?'

'They killed each other.'

Hero let out a gust of breath. *I knew it. He is a good person. He could never have killed anybody.*

James picked at a cuticle. 'Maybe I helped them get to where they needed to be, but I didn't lay a finger on them.'

Or could he? Why's he always so cryptic? 'But still, they died. I can't get it out of my head. I feel really bad about that.'

'Bruv, being bullied is not your fault. Don't keep blaming yourself. Those dickheads got what was coming to them.'

Hero reflexively smoothed his Luke Skywalker duvet cover with one hand. 'What does Dad think of all this?'

'He thinks the whole situation could've been avoided. He doesn't understand—and he should.'

Whatever. Dads never really remember what it's like, do they? 'Do you think they'll leave me alone now?'

James raised his eyebrow.

Hero rolled his eyes. 'I didn't mean the ones today, James, obviously. I mean Martin and his friends.'

'They will.'

He wanted to believe it. He wanted to believe it was all under control, just like James said. Just like James always made it so. 'You know, you really were amazing today. And the other day. I never really said thank you, but thank you.'

'Cheers, bruv. But as I said, I'm sure you'd do the same for me.'

'But would I, mate?'

'I'm sure you would, if you could.'

Was Fi right? *Could I follow in his footsteps? Could I make people leave me alone like James could?* 'How come you're so calm all the time?'

'I've told you before—because I've lived a thousand lifetimes.'

More word games. Always playing at something. 'Yeah, yeah, you always say that. What does it even mean?'

'Sometimes I wish you knew. But maybe that's not your path.'

Hero snorted. 'Ooh, Master Yoda, your path it is.'

They stifled their laughter so as not to wake Dad. Hero jiggled his leg, full of nervous energy. *I'm gonna ask him.*

'James? You know how you train every day?'

'Nyeees . . .'

'Would it be okay if . . . if I came with you? To see? Maybe to, you know . . .?'

James's face lit up. 'Okay? It's more than okay. Ah, bruv, this is gonna be great. You and me. Team Turner.'

The door opened. 'Boys?' Dad peered around the corner as if he'd just caught them with a couple of girls or having a party. He seemed disappointed when he realised they were just talking. 'What are you doing out of bed?'

'Sorry, Dad, couldn't sleep,' James replied. 'It's been a difficult couple of days. A difficult couple of months, actually.'

Dad's expression changed. He looked down at the floor. 'Oh, boys. Come here.' He opened his arms, and the boys came into his embrace. 'You mustn't blame your mum. She'd be here if she could.'

Would she? Then, where was she? And why wasn't she here now?

Hero hung on a little longer than James, trying to choke back the snooker ball of sadness in his throat. But it was no good. He couldn't bottle up his tears for Mum any longer. As he let the floodgates open, he felt James reach over his head and put a hand on Dad's shoulder in the way that male family members do when one of the pride is hurt.

And they all pulled together.

'Hey, bruv. Are you ready?'

Hero nodded nervously. 'I think so.'

'Excited?'

He nodded again.

James set a brisk pace to the gym. They'd been walking about ten minutes when James stopped cold. 'Hold up, bruv.'

Hero frowned.

'Don't panic, but we're being followed.'

Those guys are never going to leave us alone. Hero's stomach tightened into the knot, spraying acid into his throat.

'Don't worry, bruv, it's just your girlfriend, Fi.' He slapped Hero's shoulder. 'Very slowly, look out of the corner of your eye. Don't make it obvious.'

Hero did as he was commanded and carefully studied the scenery behind them without moving his head. James pretended to straighten Hero's clothes to make their situation appear more natural.

'You see? Over there, right by the hedge on that corner.' James nodded imperceptibly.

There she was, doing a good job of hiding but not good enough. He could clearly see her peering out every so often.

'Good to know that someone loves you, eh, bruv?'

Hero grinned, trying desperately not to burst into nervous laughter.

'We're gonna have to do something about this. Here, hold my hand.' James hurried around the next corner into an alleyway, Hero in tow. 'Follow me.'

They finished the fifteen-minute journey to the gym in eerie silence. It seemed as if everything had died yet somehow was still alive. *Must be more nervous than I thought.*

James let go of Hero's hand outside the door to the gym and looked up and down the street. 'Good. We lost her.' He ducked inside.

Hero followed him into a large martial arts hall with mats surrounded by a wooden walkway. In the centre of the mat stood a tall African American man with white hair and a greying beard. Nobody else was in the gym.

James slipped off his shoes. Hero followed suit.

'This is the master,' James said, tugging Hero onto the mat.

Hero was finding it hard to breathe, his whole body yearning to bounce in time to his heartbeat. Everything around him glowed with perfect clarity like polished crystal. His grin was insuppressible.

'Hello, James,' the master replied.

Hero grinned. 'The master—what, like on *Doctor Who*? Isn't he, you know, really evil?'

James gave him a little shove. 'Don't be cheeky, bruv.'

The master waved James away. 'It's okay.' He turned to Hero with a smile as slow and warm as the tones of his accent from the American Deep South. 'That's very quick, son, and I'm glad you asked. You should always ask about someone's intentions, especially if they're going to be your teacher. There definitely are masters out there who are like the guy in *Doctor Who*, but I'm not one of them. You can think of me as the Light Master.'

'The Light Master?'

'Well, I used to be called a Master of the Light, but it's too . . .'

'Poncey?' Hero sniggered.

'Oi, bruv, cut it out,' James snapped.

'James, it's all right. It's understandable that your brother's a little nervous. I was going to say too flamboyant or grandiose, but poncey will do.' He squinted at Hero. 'I don't believe we've been formally introduced.'

'Sorry,' said James. 'This is Hero, my brother I told you about.'

'Ah, Hero.'

The stupid nickname was a punch in the stomach. He'd been excited all day, only to be greeted like this. 'I'm not a hero.'

'I've been waiting a while to meet you,' said the master. 'James tells me you stood up to four big kids beating on you. Sounds heroic to me—although looking at you, perhaps "stupid" might be a better word?'

Hero startled. 'Eh?'

'Don't worry, son. We'll make sure that doesn't happen again, okay?'

'Er, okay.' He looked the master up and down: scruffy black T-shirt, faded blue sweatpants. He was just . . . some guy. 'So what makes you a master?'

'I'm old.'

Was this guy for real? He glanced at James.

'Some people think I'm also quite good. But it's mostly that I'm old.'

'He's the best martial artist I've ever seen,' James added.

Hero shrugged and looked around the empty room. 'So where is everybody?'

'Interesting,' the master responded. 'Very few people notice that. Actually, the others are meditating.' He pointed towards the closed door on the left. 'I imagine all of this is quite scary.'

Hero smiled sheepishly. 'A bit.'

'I understand, son. I remember my first day in a training school like this. Didn't know what to expect, worried I might get hurt, didn't know what I was doing. Sound familiar?'

He nodded.

'Well, let's start off with something that you *are* good at. Tell me, do you and James play any games with each other? Anything physical and fun? Do you boys wrestle around in front of the sofa?'

Hero and James exchanged a smile.

Hero took a step back. 'No, no, it's embarrassing.'

'There're no silly games here,' the master said reassuringly.

He took a deep breath. 'Well, James and I play a game called Touch My Chin that—oh, it's too embarrassing.'

James pointed theatrically at Hero and laughed. 'It's a great game. You're just embarrassed 'cos you never win.'

The Light Master smiled. 'And what does Touch My Chin involve?'

'Simple, really,' Hero said. 'You just have to touch the

other player's chin to score a point. Naturally, you also need to defend yourself against being touched.'

'And don't forget the fly-by,' James said.

'The fly-by?' the master asked.

'You can deliberately not touch the other player's chin when you have a clear shot and instead do a fly-by. Then you score ten points—'

'—for nobility,' Hero and James chorused.

The master chuckled and shook his head. 'Okay, James, Hero.' The smile faded from his face, and he backed away towards the edge of the mat. 'Show me.'

Hero took up a position opposite James in the centre of the mat.

'One arm or two?' James asked.

'One,' Hero answered flatly.

'Left or right?'

'Right.'

'Okay.'

They positioned themselves with their right arms crossed like swords in a fencing match.

'*En garde*,' they cried simultaneously.

And then they were lost in the game. Occasionally, one of Hero's thrusts would slip past James's parry, but James would quickly move his head out of the way to prevent a touch.

'That was a close one, buddy,' James said. 'You're getting better at this.'

James blocked a strong attempt from Hero, then jumped into the air, rotating three hundred and sixty degrees to give himself a clear shot at Hero's chin. He deliberately swiped past it instead.

'Fly-by!' He landed behind Hero, raising his arms as if saluting an invisible crowd. 'For nobility.'

'For nobility.' Hero turned to the Light Master and sighed. 'You see? I told you I'm not a hero.'

'You have raw talent, son,' the Light Master said encouragingly. 'You're the fastest natural I've seen.'

Hero wiped a trickle of sweat from one cheek. 'Clearly, not fast enough. I only lasted ten seconds.'

'Almost everybody I know who has fought your brother lasts about two or three seconds at most.'

Hero glared at James accusingly. 'You play Touch My Chin here?'

The master chuckled. 'We do a different type of fighting here. But I do find it interesting that your game is very like sword fighting. Anyway, Hero, you're sweating. I guess that was quite a workout?'

He swiped his forehead with the back of his arm. 'It always is whenever I play with James.'

'Shall we get a drink? Tea? Coffee?'

'I'd prefer a hot chocolate.'

'I'd love a coffee,' James chimed in.

'Just like Dad,' Hero said mockingly.

James scowled.

The master led them out of the gym and across the road to a busy coffee shop. The smooth, almost sweet smell of freshly ground coffee set his nose and brain dancing. The place was packed, mostly with teenagers leaning back on the mahogany chairs, playing with their phones while chattering over the whooshes of steam from the milk foamer. Others focused on their laptops, doing their most important work. Luckily there were a couple of open spots left.

'Take a seat.' The master gestured towards a vacant table. 'I'll get the drinks.'

The boys squeezed in next to a trio of ladies excitedly talking about a friend who was getting married.

The master brought their drinks back on a tray. Hero couldn't wait; it had been a while since he'd had hot chocolate, and this had whipped cream on top. As the Light Master reached to hand James his coffee, the steaming cup slipped and tumbled towards the lady sitting next to them. She shrieked and jerked back in anticipation of being scalded.

And then Hero was holding the cup by its rim. Not a drop had spilled.

'It's okay,' he announced. 'I've got it.'

The woman gasped and lifted up her hands, unscathed. 'Did you see that? Unbelievable.' She turned to everybody in the shop. A few of the other customers started to clap.

Hero shrugged. 'Anyone can do that.'

'I've never seen *anyone* do that before.' She turned to the master with a frown. 'And sir, could you be more careful? If it wasn't for the young man here, that would've gone all over me.'

'Sorry, ma'am. Getting a little clumsy in my old age.' He turned back to the boys. 'We'd better leave.'

They picked up their drinks and headed back to the gym.

'That's not the first time that's happened, is it?' the master asked Hero as James held the door. 'You saved your dad's coffee, right?'

Hero glanced at James. 'You told him about that?'

The master lay a warm hand on Hero's arm. 'That's why I set up another accident just now. I had to check. I had to see it for myself.'

Hero felt pinned beneath that light touch.

'When you saved your dad's coffee, that was when your brother knew you had a talent, the same one he has.'

'What talent? James? What's going on?'

James nodded as if to say 'just listen'.

Hero wilted. Was he different? Was it obvious? How many other people knew? He didn't want to be different; he just wanted to be like everyone else. But 'a talent'— something strong? Maybe he could defend himself at last.

The master drew back his hand. 'If I told you that I could teach you to beat your brother at Touch My Chin and defend yourself against those bullies, would you be interested?'

Hero nodded. 'That's why I'm here. Well, I'm not so bothered about Touch My Chin, but I do want to be able to defend myself.'

'What you have is natural ability,' the Light Master said. 'It's linked to your emotional state. That's why you're able to catch that cup without thinking, but you weren't able to outrun those kids. To do it all the time, when you want to, you need to come and train here with us every day.'

Hero couldn't hide his grin. 'Okay.' He turned to James to ask when he—

James was looking at him with a strangely sober expression. And so was the Light Master, for that matter. Hero blinked.

'Listen to me,' the master said. 'This is a big commitment that will last five years. That's a long time for a young man your age. Are you sure you can do that?'

If James could do it . . . He nodded. 'Yes.'

'We might have a problem, though, master,' James said, one hand thoughtfully on his chin.

'Which is?'

'There's a girl at school. She's obsessed with Hero. She was following us this evening.'

Hero shifted uneasily, glaring at James. What business was this of anybody's?

'Ah, that *is* a problem,' the master said. 'I'm sorry, Hero, but you can't train while your attention is on things like girlfriends. You can't have a girlfriend.'

Hero looked from the master to James and back again. His brother had chosen not to have a girlfriend? Seriously? 'Why not? What is this, a cult?'

'Not a cult, son, but the training we do here is very dangerous. And because it's linked to your emotions, you mustn't have close ties with anyone until you've mastered it. Otherwise, you could hurt them, maybe even kill them.'

Hero studied the mat as he absorbed the implications of what he was hearing. He looked up at James. 'I really like her.'

James raised both hands and let them drop again to his sides. 'Sorry, bruv. You can't—not and be one of us. You need to drop her.'

He stood rooted to the spot, the last droplets of sweat evaporating from his red face. He looked back at the master. 'How long?'

'That depends on you, son. But in all likelihood, about two to three years.'

He shook his head again. 'I really like her.'

James squeezed his arm gently. 'I know, bruv. And I'm sorry, I really am. I wish it were different. But there's no choice on this.'

'How am I going to do this?' He looked at James again.

'Don't worry, bruv, we'll sort it all out together.'

'This part is very important,' the master said. 'You mustn't tell anyone about this training. Only you and other invitees can come here. No one may come who's not invited.'

Hero frowned.

James leaned closer. 'Bruv, what he means is you can't tell *her* why. In fact, you can't talk to her again at all.'

The master nodded in agreement.

Hero's face burned as he thought through all the different scenarios. He felt as if the ground were crumbling beneath his feet.

'Any questions, son?' the master asked.

Hero shook his head, still dumbstruck. Still confused. He stood motionless, a shadow of the person he'd been just minutes before. 'Actually, yes. Just one. What is this talent you're talking about?'

The Light Master smiled. 'All in good time, Hero, all in good time. That's it for today. I'll see you tomorrow, same time.'

Hero nodded, left speechless by the entire proposition. He followed James home in silence. What was his talent? He just couldn't understand what the Light

Master might be talking about. At least James respected his need to ponder the future. He'd figure it out.

Eventually.

'Thanks for taking me today, James.' Hero plodded up the stairs to their bedrooms behind James.

'It's cool, bruv. Did you enjoy it?'

'I really like the master. There's something about him. I don't know.'

'He's a good guy.'

They stopped at the top of the stairs.

'I love you, James. You know that, right?'

'Don't be a sap, mate.'

'I'm just saying.'

'And I'm just saying don't be a sap.'

They went into their own rooms.

'I love you too,' James whispered across the hall.

'I heard that!' Hero cried, sticking his head back into the hall.

James poked his head out of his room. 'What? You've got bloody bat ears, mate.'

'Don't be a sap, mate.'

'What was that?' James swaggered over to Hero's room.

'You're being a sap, mate.'

'I see. Well, I disagree—and you know what this means?'

Hero closed his eyes wearily. He loved his brother, sure, but he was worn out after all this business of the Light Master and giving up Fi. 'Nooo . . .'

'Oh yes.' James pointed at Hero's chin, wibbling his finger.

'No, no, nooo.'

'I'm touching your chin, buddy,' James said gleefully.

'You've touched my chin once today already.'

'But I haven't, though, have I? I took the noble path, remember?' He strode towards Hero. 'No need for nobility now, I think.'

Hero leapt for the far side of the bed, but James wrestled him to the mattress.

'Touch, touch, touch,' James exclaimed, repeatedly poking Hero's chin. He released Hero from under his weight. 'Okay, bruv, I've gotta get on.'

Hero uncrumpled himself from the mattress. 'I'm gonna get you one day.'

'Yeah, sure you will, bruv. Sure you will.'

Chapter 8

Hero

Even though only a day had passed and Christmas was far from arriving, Hero felt that the depth and darkness of winter had passed and a new year was underway. It was as if the new shoots of spring were showing their pale green tips to the world, a new hope. Perception changed everything. Whereas before, every day at school had been a torturous eternity in hell, now every lesson flashed by in an instant. The joy expanded within his throat, aching to burst out in song and dance: *Da da de da de da*. He burned through every lesson at school, his mind hungry, starved from the months when all he could think about was the bullying.

The only fly in the ointment was Fi. He could feel her eyes on him in every class they shared, burning into the back of his head.

Don't look. Don't encourage her.

His heart was a soft peach being crushed by an iron fist.

But I want to. I want to look. I want to encourage her.

The wonderful feeling of her lips pressed into his

mind. He hesitated, caught somewhere between the head and the heart. He turned his head towards her but stopped halfway.

I can't. The training. It's bigger than her, it's bigger than me, and it's bigger than all of this. I know it. I don't know how, but I know it.

The final bell rang. He fumbled trying to put his books away in his bag and dropped them all over the floor. *Less haste, more speed.* He hustled to the school gates, but James wasn't there yet.

He paced up and down inside the open gates.

Come on.

He waited.

Come on.

Finally, he saw his brother in the distance with a dark-haired girl. James had his arm around her and was whispering in her ear. He kissed her on the cheek, his hand lingering on her arm a moment longer than necessary.

Why does he get to do this and I don't? God, I miss Fi, and it's only been one day.

Hero looked on with envious eyes.

I guess he must've mastered the ability, whatever it is.

Finally, James sent the girl on her way and sauntered across to meet Hero.

'What took so long?' Hero asked.

'Bloody hell, bruv, you're keen today. It's only five past four,' James said, tapping his watch.

'You don't know what you've started.'

If only James realized how true that was, Hero

thought as they strode through the chilly streets. He didn't even mind getting out of breath; he was in training now, and he had things to do and places to go.

As quickly as they got there, the Light Master was already standing in the centre of the mat, as if he'd been waiting for them to arrive. Hero scurried along the wall, a little out of breath, towards the spot where they'd left their things last time.

'Okay, Hero, you're fast,' called the Light Master. 'We can agree on that, right?'

He wondered if he should put down his book bag, join the master on the mat, or something else. 'If you say so.'

'I do say so,' the master said with a smile. 'But you need to be faster. We need to get you to use all of your talent. You need to be as fast as you can be.'

Hero didn't know what to say.

'You don't believe me?'

He finally decided to put down his things and sit to unlace his shoes. 'It's just that I don't even think I'm fast. Nothing seems fast to me.'

'Yes, son.' He regarded Hero in a fatherly way, with his head tilted to one side. 'You can be a lot faster. Come with me.'

The master walked Hero to the back of the gym and unlocked a door to a room lined with rows of black leather chaise longues. To the side of each chair was a small table holding a video monitor, a set of headphones, and what appeared to be a pair of sunglasses.

'Sit down, son. Relax.'

Hero picked a chair and tentatively reclined, resting his back and head. The seat was comfortable. Was this a dentist's chair? What was he gonna do? He tried to control his breathing, but he was still huffing from the walk over.

The master handed him what looked like a high-tech helmet. A dangling wire ran inside to two LCD screens. 'Put this on.'

He did as he was told. 'What is it?'

'A VR helmet.'

Hero turned it over in his hands.

'Our abilities as humans come from our brains' perception of the world around us,' the master said. 'So we need to train ourselves in a way that allows our brains to perceive the world more effectively. The helmet works to train your perception.'

He slipped on the helmet and leaned forward so the master could connect the wire. 'Okay, but how?'

'The lights and sounds cause your brain to go into a meditative state that help you focus. They'll make it easier to take on board the training we do here.'

He was a little worried about that, actually. Exercise hurt—like other things that happened in a dentist's chair, for that matter. His skin felt tight, his muscles like stone, reminding him of that woman with the snakes in her hair. What was her name? Medusa.

I wonder if that's where they got the idea.

'Will it hurt?'

'Not at all. In fact, you'll probably enjoy it. Close your eyes and relax. Ready?'

He closed his eyes, struggling to look more relaxed than he felt. 'Yes.'

The Light Master switched on the device. Multicoloured light exploded like fireworks in front of Hero's eyes, and pulsating sound filled his ears. The sound seemed to be outside his head, even though he was wearing a helmet.

Then the rain came, the sound pouring around him. It was so relaxing that he felt a little dizzy. Gentle words floated through the water from an angel in a faraway forest: *The relationship between the world and people is a simple one . . . Inside the world beat the hearts of every person, and inside every person beats the entire world . . . The love of every person has the capacity to bring the whole world together as one or to tear it into fragments that would be lost in a cosmic instant in the infiniteness that is the universe and time.*

Colours folded in on themselves, creating a tunnel of light that he was speeding through. The angelic voice melted into the sound of the rain.

The lights and sounds had stopped. Hero breathed quietly. His body was like jelly, and his head pulsed with an echo of the light and sound. He was alone in the room, a single spotlight creating a pool of illumination around his chair. Through a window, he saw that night had drawn in.

The main lights flickered on when he stood up, extinguishing the spotlight. He slipped off the helmet and walked into the main gym. The Light Master was training James and two girls in sword fighting. Hero leaned against the door jamb and watched as their swords popped in and out of hazy focus as if caught by a low-speed camera.

'Forward and rotate, forward and rotate,' the master called. He turned his attention towards Hero. 'How do you feel?'

'Good. Really good,' Hero replied.

'Step into the ring. Let's practise.'

Hero joined the others in the centre of the mat. James and the girls stowed their swords in a rack, then rejoined Hero and the Light Master.

'Okay, let's do the short form together.'

He picked his teeth. He had no idea what was going on. His mouth felt as if he'd been eating sand.

'But what do I do? I've never done this before.'

'Follow me. Trust me, you'll get it.'

The master took up the opening pose. In silence and slow motion, he led the traditional t'ai chi short form practice of thirty- four moves. Hero copied the beautiful, arcing shapes as closely as he could. It was almost too easy. From Parting the Wild Horse's Mane to Fan Through the Back, the moves seemed natural, as though he'd done them before.

I even know the names of these moves. This is freaking me out.

They closed the sequence with the Crossing Hands and then returned to the stance.

'What did you think of that, Hero?' the master asked.

'It felt good, as if I'd actually done it before.'

'In a way, you have.'

He frowned. 'I don't think so. I'm sure I'd remember, if I had.'

The master smirked. 'Not only does the meditation open your mind, it trains you in our ways.'

Who were these people? *This is like something on one of those conspiracy theory shows. Except it's real.*

'You could think of it as reconfiguring your brain to insert knowledge.'

'I didn't even know that was possible.'

'One of our greatest discoveries, actually.'

Hero glanced at James. 'Why don't they do this at school, then?'

The master moved away from the centre of the mat. 'The rest of the world hasn't caught up with us yet, son. And we should all be thankful for that.'

'You don't know the half of it, bruv.' James was grinning at him.

He did his best not to look as self-conscious as he felt.

'Let's take a look at how you did your first time,' the master said. 'Come on.'

The Light Master beckoned Hero to the video monitor at the edge of the gym and pressed Play.

Hero watched for a moment and shrugged. 'Looks like it's stuck on fast forward.'

'No, Hero, it isn't.'

'Eh?'

'It's not on fast forward.'

He peered at the video playback. 'It can't be. That's impossible.'

'Look closely. You can see the dust moving away from your body.'

The master was right. Shock waves rippled away from him with every motion.

'That is how fast you move. And in time, you'll move even faster.'

88

Hero stared at the recording. He thought he'd performed the short form as precisely and accurately as a brain surgeon, but in fact, he'd been moving so fast that his image blurred as the video struggled to keep up.

'But I wasn't even trying.'

'Exactly. It's taken us many years to work out that it takes no effort at all. Once we realised that, we managed to even the balance a bit.'

'Balance? What do you mean?'

The Light Master and James exchanged glances. The air became thick, and for a moment it seemed as if time had paused.

'Tell me, Hero, has anything unusual happened to you recently?' the Light Master asked.

Hero was silent, still trying to digest what he'd seen. There was something else at work here. 'Well, apart from being bullied . . . Although I'm not sure that's unusual, exactly.'

The Light Master returned his tentative smile, then became sombre. 'I think you know what I mean.'

Hero nervously glanced between the people on the mat.

'The voices,' he said at last.

'And what do those voices say?' the master asked.

'They say, "We are the Light. Join us."'

Everyone in the gym was staring at him now.

'I heard them earlier, during the meditation. They were saying something about the beating heart of the world. I can't really remember.'

The master nodded. 'We call it the voice. Although it does sound like there are many, it is in fact only one voice.'

The hairs along the back of Hero's neck stood up. 'Wait—you've heard it too?'

'Of course. We all hear it, and it seems to say the same thing. It's particularly strong during meditation because your mind is open.'

'I thought I was going mad. But what does it mean?'

'The voice instructs us on the right thing to do. But come on, Hero, you're an intelligent guy. Let's see if you can work it out.'

Hero rubbed his temples. 'Well, if you're the Light Master—and obviously there're other people, so you're not the only one—so . . . The Light isn't a thing? It's a group?'

'And?'

'We're connected? We've all got something in common?'

'And what do you suppose that might be?'

He already knew the answer. 'We're all fast? Really fast?' His eyes widened. 'We've all got the same ability.'

But the Light Master's expression suggested he was expecting something else.

'It's more than that, isn't it?'

'Yes.'

'What?'

The master had begun to pace up and down the edge of the mat. 'Our ability. It's not that we're fast. It's that we can all slow down time.'

Hero glanced at James then back at the Light Master. *They're having me on.* He started to smile. It got broader and broader until laughter bubbled over. The master blinked at Hero, unmoved, but James was smiling as if sharing the joke. This was one of James's cheeky gags.

'You're not serious.'

'I'm deadly serious, son.' If this was a joke, then the master was not part of it.

'But I don't slow down time,' Hero said. 'Nothing goes slower for me.'

'It doesn't seem faster or slower to you because you actually change time. You've done it your whole life—you've just never noticed it before. But after training with us, you will notice it. You'll notice it a great deal.'

Hero looked away uncomfortably. The man was daft.

'I'm not a fan of parlour tricks, but let me convince you,' the master said quietly.

And then he was gone.

'Behind you,' a voice whispered in Hero's ear.

Hero whipped around. The Light Master was just behind him, his mouth to Hero's ear.

James cackled. 'Don't worry, bruv, I nearly shat my pants when he did that to me.'

Hero giggled, mostly with relief.

The master circled around and retook his position in front of Hero. 'Now, can you understand why you can't be close to anyone during this very delicate time?'

Hero shook his head.

'Think about it, son. If you slowed down time like I did just then, how fast would you be moving? I've told you that this happens when you get emotional. Imagine if you got emotional while you were kissing that girl. What do you think would happen?'

Hero's hand flew to his mouth and nose to cover his shock.

'That's right, son. You could smash her face right off—and the worst part is you wouldn't be hurt yourself.'

He squinted. Theoretically, he was following this. But in practice?

'When we slow time, there's an energy field that protects us,' the Light Master said. 'We can extend it around others, but that takes control you don't have right now.'

'But you'll teach me, right?'

The master nodded.

'And then I could—for example—go back to Fi?'

James burst out laughing. 'Subtle, bruv.'

The master grinned, shaking his head. 'Yes, Hero, you could.' He became serious again. 'But you might want to think that through.'

Hero frowned.

'Hurting someone accidentally is not the worst thing that can happen.'

'It's hard to imagine how that could be true,' Hero muttered.

'Really?' James stabbed a finger towards him. 'What do you think would happen if someone like Fi found out you had a superpower like this? Do you think she'd hang around? You know what kids are like. She'd scream "freak" at the top of her voice.'

James was right. Hero felt powerless to do anything but stare.

'And that's why it's important that nobody sees us jump in and out of the time dilation,' the master said.

'Why would they even see that?'

'Because as you change time, there's a point at which, from other people's point of view, you'll appear to be jumping erratically from place to place. I disappeared right in front of your eyes, remember?'

Hmm, he hadn't thought about that. 'But who cares? So what if people know that we're different?'

'Can you imagine what a government would do with one of us?'

He shrugged.

'There'd be people that would come for you, put you in a lab, and dissect your brain so fast your feet wouldn't even touch the floor. Then they'd hound the rest of us to the ends of the earth. They'd never stop, ever.'

That was probably true. *They'd want to understand us, if only to send us—but wait, no no no.*

'Even if they did find us, so what?' Hero asked. 'We could dilate time and walk right past them, surely.'

The master gave him a disdainful look. 'Do you really want to live a life where you're constantly looking over your shoulder into the shadows? And forget the government—what do you think regular people would do if they found out about us?'

Hero's skin tingled as he tried to take it all in. *Looking over my shoulder—that's exactly the life I don't want. That's why I'm here.*

The master kept pressing. 'Have you heard of the Spanish Inquisition? Or the Witchfinder General, burning people at the stake?'

'People aren't like that anymore.'

'Really? So, you don't think there's any stigma attached with being a Muslim, then? Or homosexual?'

'Oh.'

'Sure, the target group changes every so often, but

one thing you can guarantee is that if you're different, you're going to be in that group. And no one is more different than we are.'

He knew this was all true. He'd seen how kids treated boys who were a little effeminate, or shy, or different in some other way.

'I can't tell you how many times I've had to relocate my gym. That's why I sleep in this place. I daren't go outside often, in case I'm recognised.' The Light Master breathed out heavily as if he were exhausted. 'I'm talking about people with pillowcases over their heads and torches in their hands. Burning torches. I really don't want to have to move again, Hero. I like it here.'

'Are you sure you're not just seeing the worst of humanity?'

The Light Master smirked. 'Don't worry, Hero, you'll see things this way too.'

Chapter 9

James

God, you're bad at this, bruv. I'm clearly going to have to give you a hand.

Hero sped towards me down the path between the ageing tennis-cum-netball courts and the even older science block. He couldn't see me, of course. Behind him, there she was, as expected.

Felicity Shagwell. What are we going to do with you?

My brother hurtled past me and through the double doors towards the lunch hall. I stepped out from my hiding place, and the red-faced Fi sprawled over me.

'Oh, I'm so sorry,' she squealed, dropping the book she was carrying.

'Not at all. It's not every day that I'm accosted by a beautiful girl,' I said with a gallant smile.

Her face became an even darker red, almost purple.

You girls really are so shallow.

'James,' she said. 'Where did you come from? I didn't see you.'

'Don't worry about it. I'm always in the place you least expect me.' I bent down and picked up the book she'd dropped, *Pride and Prejudice*.

'What do you think of it?' I asked, slowly handing it back to her. Needed to buy him more time to get ahead of her.

'It's good.' She snatched it from me.

'Who's your favourite character?'

'Mr Darcy.'

As expected. So shallow. When she returned my gaze, she had that hazy, faraway look of the lovelorn. I was taken aback by the intensity of it.

Hmm, I'm going to need a long-term plan for you. What the hell have you done to this girl, bruv?

'I'm sorry, I'd love to chat, but I'm in a hurry.' She squeezed past me.

'For lunch?'

'I'm hoping to meet someone.'

Hopefully not.

'Who? Not Hero? Tell him I said hi if you do see him.'

She scurried away like a dog chasing a rabbit.

I continued on my way to the library. A blond boy about Fi's age in a white lab coat was standing at the windows which ran the entire length of the chemistry lab, watching my every move. He slowly twisted a conical flask in his hands as he glowered at me. From the size of him, I guessed he must be in the rugby team. I returned his glare until he averted his eyes. One must never back down.

I smiled with satisfaction. A handsome athlete for the lovely young lady.

Well, well, well, Mr Blonde, you might be exactly what I'm looking for.

Chapter 10

Hero

'You're going to need to get fit. Very fit.'

Hero tried to look confident, but he was so nervous he'd barely slept the previous night.

'Why?' he asked.

'There're many reasons,' said the Light Master. 'Firstly, because the mind and body are linked. The healthier you are, the more you can focus and the faster you'll be. Secondly, because your body needs to be able to handle this pace. Your bones need to be able to cope with being able to move very fast without breaking, and you need to be very flexible. You'll need to do yoga to stretch your muscles, tendons, and ligaments. And last but not least, everyone loves a guy with a good body. Now you're not going to tell me that doesn't motivate you at least a little bit, are you, son?'

Hero laughed nervously.

'Okay, well, let's get started, then. James?'

'Come on, bruv. Let's take a short run.'

Hero was silent. His chest tightened as memories of past attempts at running during PE zipped through his mind.

I feel sick.

He sat down next to James to put on his trainers. James opened a cupboard and took out two watches and two elastic straps with a black box in the centre.

'What're those?' Hero asked.

'Heart rate monitors. Put the watch on. The strap goes around your chest like this.' James demonstrated.

Hero followed suit and, sure enough, his heart rate was soon showing on the watch.

'Right, then. A 10K should be good for starters,' James announced.

'What?'

'Only joking, bruv. Let's start with two miles. An easy one.'

Two miles? An easy one? For you, maybe. I'm carrying around a lot more extra padding than you, mate.

'Seriously, I don't think I can run a hundred yards.'

'Come on, stop being a tart.'

The cold night air was sharp on his tongue, invigorating to his lungs. James looked so loose and svelte that it was difficult not to admire his elegance. *I hope I don't see anyone I know, especially Tom. He'd be laughing his tits off tomorrow.*

Before they'd reached the first corner, his trainers were grating against his heels and his shins were crying out in terror of the pavement. The air stabbed cold daggers into his lungs.

He slowed to a walk, coughing and trying not to vomit. 'James. Got to stop. Can't do this.'

'Yes, you can, bruv.'

'I can't. It hurts.'

James put his arm around his shoulders. 'Bruv, everybody hurts the first time. Do you think I didn't collapse in a heap on my first run?'

Hero raised his eyebrows incredulously.

'It always hurts the first time, but the pain goes away. That's why we're going to take it easy. Every time it hurts, we'll stop and walk. Then when you feel better, we'll jog again. Soon you'll be running 10K before breakfast.'

He can't be serious.

'Do you trust me?'

No. 'Of course.'

'I promise you, it *will* happen. You're going too hard at the start. Everyone does that. Keep your heart rate between one fifty and one seventy. If it goes higher, slow down. If it goes lower, speed up. Simple. Now come on, bruv, stop titting around, and let's do this.'

Hero started to jog again, one eye on his wrist monitor. His brother was right. At one hundred and seventy-two, his legs and lungs started to burn. He slowed down and felt better almost immediately.

So that's it, then. I really can do this. Why did no one ever tell me this before?

It was the rush again, only this time it was no dream. Hero felt it every time he came here, every time he trained. It was as if it was meant to be. His heart had started to open, and he realised he was exactly where he was supposed to be at this point in his life. Lightness, acceptance, and joy burst through him like high-pressure water into a previously uncharted network of pipes.

The one hundred and twenty-eight moves of the t'ai chi long form took a while to move through, but it gave him time to think. The term 't'ai chi' always made him laugh. *Trust the Chinese to label a martial art 'the supreme ultimate fist'. They're always so literal.*

What'd been almost impossible over the first few weeks now felt easy and natural, as though he'd been doing it forever. It had become so natural that sometimes he imagined meeting up with Fi again. She would put his hand on his chest. Her eyes would widen, and her lips would moisten a little. He would pull her closer in his strong, manly arms—

He opened his eyes as he finished the forms. The Light Master stood in front of him wearing an enigmatic smile.

'Let me introduce you to our special room, Hero,' he said.

What now? He scratched the back of his hand as if he were trying to scrub out a stain.

He followed the master towards the back of the gym, and they stepped inside what appeared to be an empty broom closet. The door closed behind Hero. There was a set of buttons on the right-hand wall. The master pressed one, and the room jolted. Hero realised that it was in fact a lift.

'I won't lie, this part of the training is quite intense.'

The elevator lurched to a stop, and the master opened the door.

The cold, dry rush of conditioned air on Hero's face smelled stale and sweaty, like week-old laundry. There was a constant whoosh of air from a large inflow pipe on the ceiling. The nervous knot in his stomach clenched as he realised he was looking at another gym—an advanced, ultra-high-tech gym. Mirrors down the front wall faced a row of bikes and, behind that, a bank of running machines. It was a strange contrast with the old-fashioned gym upstairs, giving him the impression of moving forward in time.

'Ooh, the infamous Hero,' called Emma from one of the training bikes.

Jane waved from a running mill.

'In here, we keep the oxygen level lower, simulating training at three thousand metres of altitude,' the Light Master said.

'Why?' he asked.

'It stimulates your body to be more efficient with oxygen. When you're at virtual sea level, you'll find you're capable of a lot more, both physically and mentally.'

The air had a strange tinge, as if all the colours were more vibrant than normal. Every surface seemed to have a sharper edge, as if he were at the very edge of needing sleep, but without any sense of tiredness.

Maybe that's why they call it 'getting high'.

'Get on one of the bikes,' said the master.

Hero climbed gingerly onto the nearest bike.

'Put your feet in the straps.'

The bike beeped then whirred, and the saddle height and distance from the handlebars adjusted by themselves. Hero sat up nervously.

'It automatically fits itself to the perfect riding position.' The master turned and walked to a box in a corner of the gym.

A projector screen descended from the ceiling.

Emma looked across, drawing air through her teeth, and grinned. 'I'm sorry, Hero. This is gonna hurt.'

He swallowed hard. He hated being sick, especially all over the floor. He'd have to clean it up then, and that would be even worse.

The master returned with a heart rate monitor and gave it to Hero. 'It's just base level one, Emma.'

'Still tough the first time,' she said.

'Don't listen to her, Hero. You'll be fine. Now, you see this panel?' The master pointed at the LCD screen between the handlebars. 'This is your heart rate, this is your power output when you're peddling, and this is your cadence. You'll want to keep that at around ninety.'

Hero nodded. His heart rate was already ninety-eight.

'When the session starts, the bike will automatically change its difficulty to fit what you're seeing on the video screen. Occasionally, it might give you instructions about your cadence. Try to follow the instructions as closely as possible.'

'Are you sure you don't want to fetch a bucket for him?' Emma said.

'Emma.'

Hero gulped.

The master patted him on the shoulder. 'Don't worry, son, it detects if you're struggling and will adjust the programme to suit you. But it will keep you right on the edge.'

A countdown popped up onscreen, and music began playing from unseen speakers, the beat somehow conveying a sense of urgency, as if something were about to happen.

'Okay, start pedalling. I'll see you in an hour.' He crossed back to the lift and left.

Hero spun his legs faster and faster. The LCD display told him his cadence was 89 RPM. This wasn't so bad. The countdown finished with a LET'S GO! superimposed over a group of riders on the screen. It looked like something from the Tour de France.

The resistance ramped up immediately. So did his heart rate, now 121 and climbing. His legs warmed to a low burn, and his lungs rasped a little as he tried to fill them. As his heart levelled at 137, Emma dismounted, ran to the back, and returned with a water bottle and a bucket.

'Just in case. It can get a bit crazy in here.'

The screen started a new countdown: WARM-UP OVER. HERE COMES LEVEL 1.

Oh shit.

The resistance jumped, and the music took on the frantic tick-tock of dance music. Hero dug in with a greater sense of urgency. Every five minutes, he discovered, CADENCE: 120 would flash across the screen and the music would go crazy. His lungs and legs burned, his head thumped along with his heartbeat, and the room grew distant. He started to eye up the bucket.

I'm gonna puke.

His upper lip had started to wobble when the resistance let up completely and the screen began to flash.

Traffic lights! What the—

All the riders in the video piled up at a red light. He

slowed to a stop as well, the acidic volcano inside his stomach simmering down.

He looked across at Emma. 'That was close.'

'I told ya. It's relentless.' She reached out and cupped Hero's shoulder in her hand. 'Don't worry, it gets easier.'

She glanced towards the running machines, then got off her bike. 'Come on, let's take a quick run.'

'Now? I'm not sure this thing is over yet.'

'Oh, don't worry. You'll get plenty more workout over here.'

He slid down onto wobbly legs and staggered towards the running machines.

I hope Fi appreciates my body when all is said and done here.

Chapter 11

Hero

The Light Master unsheathed the sleek silver scimitar and handed it Hero. This was the moment he'd anticipated since he'd first seen sword practice more than a year ago.

He hefted it gingerly. 'It's a lot lighter than I'd expected. It looks so big.'

'You can thank Hollywood for that,' the master said. He disappeared into a side room and returned carrying a wooden sculpture, which he placed in the middle of the training mat.

'What's that?' Hero asked.

'A training dummy. You'll start with this, and eventually you'll move up to fight with a real person.' The master smiled encouragingly. 'Now, the best way to survive a sword fight is to make yourself a hard target to hit. Turn sideways on and keep moving. If you can hide, even better.'

Hero tentatively swished the sword backward and forward, crackling through the air.

'Unfortunately, there's no guarantee that there'll be

anything to hide behind,' the master continued, 'so we need to work on your movement and positioning. The good news is that you're very fast.'

Hero grinned.

'The bad news is the other guy may also be fast.'

His smile faded. 'So what do I do?'

'Move, block, and attack. You get that right, you live. Of course, if you get it wrong, you die.'

What the hell is he talking about? I just want to defend myself. Then again, what about that time with James and those—

'Remind me, why am I fighting to the death again?'

'If someone runs at you with a weapon, you can assume it's a fight to the death.'

This is not a game anymore.

'Don't worry, Hero, I'll teach you everything I know. You'll understand how to attack, parry, and feint with the best of them.'

'Faint?'

'Feint. It means to do a fake move. I have a two-year course on feinting. Once you've finished it, you'll be able to throw somebody off balance just by wiggling your shoulder.'

Hero raised one eyebrow.

'By the time you leave this gym, you'll even have defeated me.'

'I'm going to fight you?'

'Oh yes.' The master grinned. 'Now, are you ready?'

Hero forced himself to nod.

'Then, *en garde.*'

He lifted his sword towards the dummy. He wondered

if Fi would be impressed if she could see him now. With a sword! His hands tingled at the thought.

Of course she would.

It was a bright Saturday morning outside. James and Hero were limbering up for a mammoth session, as had become their routine now that Hero's strength and fitness were developing. The puppy fat, as James called it, had gone. Hero liked how he looked. He'd even taken a bit after his brother and started admiring his 'guns' in the mirror—nearly getting caught a couple times.

'Hey, James,' he said.

James looked across coolly, as if expecting him to do something inappropriate. As if that were still an issue after nearly a year.

'I'm gonna punch you,' Hero said with a huge grin.

'Uh-huh.'

'Wait there.' He made a stop sign with one hand and clenched the other to a fist by his side. Then, with the slow, deliberate pace of t'ai chi practice, he sent his clenched fist towards his brother. 'No really, wait there.' He grinned, miming the intense effort of propelling the slow-motion punch closer and closer to his brother's face.

James was not amused. 'I wouldn't do that if I were you.'

'Hang on, nearly there.' He grit his teeth in a dramatic grimace.

'So you're unimpressed with our training methods, Hero?'

The boys snapped to attention.

The Light Master was watching from the far end of the room. 'You think it's no good? Have you stopped to consider what would happen if we combined our training with our speed?'

Oh God. I bet he thinks I'm a right idiot. Hero felt the heat rise in his face.

'How about I show you? Then we can stop this nonsense. Perhaps you might even take it seriously.' The master walked to the centre of the training floor and took up the usual starting stance.

'Brace yourself, bruv,' James warned under his breath.

Hero grinned. *What's he gonna do from over there? Blow on me?*

The master moved into the first position, left hand in defensive position above and in front of his head, with such incredible speed that Hero barely saw the movement.

Wow.

A supersonic bang filled the room. Hero cringed as the windows at the top of the gym blew outwards with the shock wave. Glass tinkled to the floor beneath them.

The master rotated to face them.

James turned and dropped to a crouch, bringing his hands over his bowed head.

The Light Master made a small circular motion in front of his body with his left hand whilst his right traced a larger arc above his head. Then he brought his hands together in front, accelerating towards them in a blast of compressed air that knocked Hero off his feet.

Hero could barely breathe. He rolled to his side, ribs aching.

'So how do you feel now, son?'

'Embarrassed,' he croaked.

'And so you should, young man.'

James stood up. 'I told you to brace yourself, bruv. You really should learn to listen to me.' He held out his hand. 'Come on, let's do this.'

Hero took James's hand, rose to his feet, and snuck a glance at the Light Master.

'You two get busy. I'm going to have to replace those windows again.' The master sighed as he turned and trudged back to his office.

Chapter 12

Hero

It'd taken almost a year for Hero to stop passing out in these meditation sessions. Even after three, he found that his senses still pulsated for a few minutes after he'd finished.

He opened his eyes to the darkness of the room, save for the single spotlight on his chair.

'Welcome back, Hero,' the Light Master whispered. 'Don't get up. Tonight, you're going to take your first lesson in controlling time.'

Electric motors hummed as Hero's lounger erected itself into an armchair. The master swung out a table from the side that reminded Hero of one of those miniature tables on an airplane. The candle the master set there flickered in unseen currents.

'Now, Hero, I want you to focus on the flame. Close your eyes. Imagine it in your mind: how it flickers, the warmth. Open your heart to the flame. Open your soul to it.'

Relaxing came more naturally after the meditation, but that didn't seem to be saying much. Hero closed his eyes and tried to visualise the candlelight bobbing above the wax. His mind snatched at patches of light, but nothing would stick.

Then the candle flame flashed crisply into his mind's eye. *Join us*, the voice whispered in his ear. *Do what you say you'll do. We are the Light.*

His shoulders tensed; the voice seemed so close and real.

'Relax,' the master said. 'Let the flame flow through you. Feel its energy.'

Time seemed to slip away, more so than he'd ever felt before. He started to feel as one with his environment, with the fire; it seemed to be within him. His soul was tissue paper burning from the inside out.

We are the D—

His breath caught as energy writhed the length of his body. His brain lit up with ideas.

I can do anything I want. No one can stop me! I can put the fear of God into every bully at school. I can make Fi stay with me forever. I can be the one who calls the shots, the one who's in control. I don't have to be the Light—I could control the Light. I could extinguish the Light, extinguish the Light M—

He gasped as if resurrected from the dead and bolted from the room.

That was all he could remember until the master found him cowering in a corner, hands over the back of his head, rocking back and forth. There was an itch in his brain too deep to scratch. *No one can stop me!* His nerves crawled like ants, their tiny legs scraping and tearing at his skin.

A warm hand closed on his shoulder. 'What happened, son?'

He whispered through parched lips. 'The voices.'

'The voice? What did it say?'

'Not one voice. There's more than one.'

James approached, his eyes widening as the master turned to him. It looked for all the world as if they were silently conversing.

'How many?' the master asked Hero.

'A different voice. At least one.'

'What happened? What did it say?'

'It's not what it said, it's how it said it. How it made me feel.'

James leaned in. 'How did it feel?'

He didn't want to tell them. *You can do anything. No one can stop you!*

He couldn't help the smile that burst across his face. 'It felt good, like the first time I kissed Fi.'

He turned his face away. It had felt good, but it shouldn't have. *This isn't me.*

They were silent, puzzled.

He spoke into the wall. 'And then it was as if I was being burned, and everything inside me was empty. And then I felt numb.'

Tell them.

No. It isn't me. He scratched frantically, trying to get to the itch.

The gym had gone quiet, like one of those westerns where the out-of-town gunslinger walks into a bar, the music stops, and everyone turns to look.

'But I enjoyed it. I enjoyed being numb. It felt good, like I wasn't human anymore—but for a moment, I wanted that. There's a word in my mouth: dac . . .

112

dah . . .' He scrunched his face, straining for something just beyond his grasp. 'I don't know. Sorry, it's gone.'

'Interesting,' the master said, kneeling down beside him.

He looked up. 'You know what it is, don't you?'

'You really are fast, aren't you?' the master replied. 'But I'm not sure you're ready to hear all of this. We normally don't tell people until they're older.'

'If the voice thinks he's old enough, we have to tell him,' James said.

'He's too young. No one's ever been told at his age.'

'We have to tell him something.' James came over and tapped Hero on the arm.

I knew this was all too good to be true. Hero glanced back and forth between them nervously.

The master rubbed his balding head with a pained expression. Then he relaxed. 'Hero, do you remember when you first came here, we told you that you couldn't use your ability? You couldn't be noticed.'

Hero nodded.

'Do you remember why?'

It seemed obvious. He was different—they all were—and they had to hide it. People didn't like difference. But there was more, wasn't there?

'You said that people would come for me, try to hurt me.'

'That's right, and they will. I've seen it happen. But there's more to it than that.'

Hero's heart accelerated. *I knew it! Too good to be true.*

'There're another group of people who'd come for you, and they're far more dangerous.'

'Who?'

The master glanced at James. 'People who have our ability—and they're very interested in newcomers like you. It's their voices you can hear, and you need to learn to ignore them.'

Hero frowned. 'But who are they? I need to know. I need to be sure I'm doing the right thing.'

The master and James gasped together.

The Light Master dropped his head and sighed. 'I've been waiting a very long time to meet someone like you. Do you trust me, Hero?'

Hero looked searchingly at James. 'I guess,' he said finally and shrugged.

'I promise you, son, you're doing the right thing. When the time is right, I'll tell you everything. But right now, you need to listen to me. These people, the ones like us, they're looking for people like you. You mustn't even think about controlling time unless you're in this gym. Do you understand?'

Hero nodded. Anything to make them leave him alone. He'd had enough of this bullshit, this pain, and now the numbness. It was too much.

Chapter 13

Hero

Hero lay on his bed with the lights off, resting his eyes. Things were better in the dark because no one could see him. The insatiable itch was getting worse. A flicker of joy like the flicker of that God-damn candle flame. *I could even kill someone. Who'd stop me?* The master had said to ignore the voices. *Don't make me laugh.* He'd tried everything, even dunking his head into ice-cold water at break time right after physics class. Tom had walked in and laughed his head off. Hero had lifted his head, and something about his face had shut Tom up in a hurry. He'd put his hands up and backed away.

He couldn't go back. No more gym, no more itch. Simple. It wouldn't be a problem. He'd been meeting James at the gym ever since James left school a year ago. He was more than competent enough to look after himself now, and James had his own place. He said Dad was getting in the way. Of what, Hero wondered. Girls, probably. *So many girls, I could devour—*

Fi, please help me. I need you. I need you to hold me. Hold me down. He arched his back, trying to force the avalanche of thoughts from rumbling through his mind.

He didn't want to face the master, anyway. How could he, when only yesterday he said he would come back? He had enjoyed going to the gym. It had made such a difference in his life. And he liked the master; he was a good guy. It was a shame he'd never see him again, that it would end it like this . . .

He snapped to consciousness hours later when the lights flicked on.

'Where were you tonight? The master was asking about you.' James was at the bedroom door.

'I don't feel good. I didn't want to go.'

'Everything okay?'

'Fine.'

'Okay. Well, will you come tomorrow?'

Hero's eyelids sank shut. *What do you think? Something burned my insides out, and now I have this terrible itch in my mind. And I can't tell him. I can't let him down like that.* 'I'll see how I feel.'

James nodded and left.

The next day was the same. The terrible numbness, the idea that he could do anything to anybody. Who would stop him? Who would care?

The answer made him choke. No one.

He lay on his bed, alone, in the darkness.

'Coming tonight, bruv?'

Hero nearly jumped out of his skin. 'Where did you come from?'

'I told you many times, I'm very good at hiding.'

'Well, anyway, no. I can't. Sorry, I still don't feel good.'

'I see.' James nodded and walked out of the room.

Hero sank back into his pillow and let oblivion over-take him again.

'Hello, son.'

Hero sat up. 'Master, what're you doing here?'

The master smiled as he approached the bed. 'I thought I'd come see how you were. I'm always worried when a student doesn't come to the gym, especially one as promising as you.' He knelt down and placed a hand on Hero's shoulder. 'You need to face this, son.'

'I can't. I'm sorry.'

'Talk to me. What happened?'

'It hurt. It really hurt.'

The master nodded.

'It burned me from the inside out, but then—but then it was nice. And I wanted the pain, and . . .' Hero's eyes flooded, and he sniffed and bobbed as tears dripped onto the duvet.

The master snaked his arms around him. 'It's okay, son, let it out.'

When the flood dried up, Hero sat back.

'Feel better?'

He nodded.

'You were saying.'

'I wanted to hurt people—no, that's not quite it. I was okay if they got hurt, so long as I felt good.' He looked at the master squarely in the eye. 'It was horrible. I'm sorry, master, but I can't face it again.'

The master nodded. 'And how do you feel now?'

'Sad. I feel like I've let myself down, let you down . . . James . . . everybody.'

'I understand, son. We've all been there. But if you

don't face this, you'll always remain here in this moment. You'll feel like this for the rest of your life.'

Hero bowed his head. He didn't want that, but why did the master care so much?

'Do you want that itch for the rest of your life?'

Hero jerked his head up. How did he know?

The Light Master gave a small smile. 'Like I said, we've all been there. You can either face this or spend the rest of your days tearing your skin off—and hating yourself for it. You're a good kid. I don't want that for you.'

Something inside Hero loosened. *He really understands this? He really cares?*

'Listen to me, son, you can do this. You don't have to face this alone. I'll help you—we'll all help you—every step of the way.'

'You promise? You'll always be there?'

'I promise. We'll get through this together.'

I think he does. The darkness was already lifting away from his soul. The horrible itch had dulled a little too; perhaps it was afraid of the Light Master. In that moment, he knew that with the master's help, he could beat this. And that was more than enough.

He swung his legs over the side of the bed. 'Okay, then. Let's go.'

The Light Master led the way out into the hallway. Only the moon's dim luminescence through the skylight penetrated the darkness of the entire house.

A disconnected face appeared in front of Hero, the body consumed by the shadows. *Is that Dad?* Hero's mind felt full of buzzing bees, as if he'd got up too quickly. He was sure he hadn't.

118

'How you doing?' Dad's voice came softly, gently. 'I hear you've been having some problems.' He put his hand on Hero's shoulder.

Hero opened his mouth to speak, but Dad continued. 'It's okay, son. Facing your demons is always hard.' Dad turned to the Light Master. 'He's a special one, this one. You'll take good care of him, right?' It sounded almost like a threat.

'Yes, of course'—the master stepped aside—'Mr Turner.'

The master kept those promises. Each day during the meditation, he sat on a stool next to Hero's reclined chair and held his hand as Hero meditated with the candle flame. It was like being a little kid again, when he'd had nightmares and Mum's soothing touch had let him relax. Her watchful eye would catch the bad dreams, and he suffered no more. Whenever Hero heard the malevolent voices now during meditation, he would tense up, and the master would calmly say, 'It's okay. I'm here. You're not alone.' He would place a hand on Hero's shoulder, and the voices would shy away. Even the itch dulled to a niggle. Were they scared of the master?

As the days went by, the malevolent voices came less and less often, until all he could hear was the one and only voice.

One evening, Hero took off the headgear after the light and sound show had finished and settled in ready for the hard part. The flame.

The master was there as usual. 'Ready?'

Hero nodded cautiously. Something felt different today, and he couldn't quite put his finger on it. He sat back and stared at the candle flame, opened himself to it, felt its warmth. His sight zoomed in and for a moment, he was inside the flame looking out.

His hand flew to his mouth. The itch was gone—not even the niggle remained. The relief was better than going to the loo after triple maths. He returned to the flame, but it was frozen as if caught within an ice block.

'Can you see this?' he asked the master.

But the master too was frozen mid-breath. Hero moved the table aside, got up, and peered at him. The whole world seemed to have gone silent in a silence that infused his skin and his bones.

He involuntarily moaned in terror and reached out to the master. The master grabbed his wrist with a speed that made him jump with fright. In the master's steady grip, the world seemed to normalize again.

'Yes!' the master cried. 'You did it. You controlled time! James, come in here. Hero did it—he's mastered time.'

James burst into the meditation room and skidded to a halt like a cartoon character. 'Yes, bruv! Who da man?' He threw his arms around Hero, then stepped back and raised his hand in the air. 'Up top!'

Hero obliged with a high five. *And all it took was three years of my life. Three years of pain I won't be getting back.*

He felt as if he'd just finished a marathon and was sat down, covered in foil and having a massage, hot tea in hand. *What an accomplishment. I really can do it. I can*

*be like James. And actually, it wasn't even that painful.
I do look good now. I feel good.*

'This is only the first step to becoming ready, but well done,' the master said.

It was like the first time he rode a bike without stabilisers and he knew he'd never need them again.

'Ready for what? I can control time. That was the whole point of this. That was the reason I've had to keep away from people, wasn't it?' He bolted upright. 'Wait a second—so I could go back to Fi now?'

The master chuckled. 'You've just learned to control the most incredible power in all the world, and the only thing you can think about is this girl? She must be very special, son.'

'She is.'

Fi had never left his mind, not since the day he'd met her. She instinctively understood him; he felt alone without her. And that didn't have to be the case anymore, if he could only win her back.

Chapter 14

Hero

Maybe she'd be in the lunch hall. It had been months since he'd been there, ever since he'd begun spending all his lunches hiding.

Well, no need to hide anymore.

Hero's heart had been gradually picking up pace since the morning, and now it was racing. His cheeks were flushed and his skin glimmered with sweat as he made his way towards the hall.

What will I say?

He scratched around for suggestions. Nothing. His bowels liquefied, and he hurried to the toilet and dived into one of the stalls, trying to catch his breath.

What will I say?

His stomach churned. He took small, shallow breaths, trying to keep his breakfast down.

Just be natural, James would say. What does that even mean? I wish I had his swagger. I'd just go on in there and say something charming, and it'd all be okay. He trembled as he mentally played through various different scenarios. *What if she's with her friends? Then sit down and say, 'Mind if I join you?' How weird would that look?*

His stomach twisted into a knot. He squeezed his eyes shut, trying to push the offending images out of his mind and find something positive to focus on. Warmth infused his limbs as he imagined her lips pushing against his, their gentle heat melting into his soul.

The all-too-familiar knot in his belly was gone. *I'll make it up as I go along. Let's do this.*

He stumbled backwards as soon as he stood up. His right foot felt three inches thick; it'd gone numb from sitting on the edge of the seat. He rubbed and jiggled his leg frantically. He was still hobbling slightly as he made his way through the maze of darkened corridors towards the lunch hall. The sound of the chattering pupils grew louder and louder as he approached the side entrance.

Here we go.

He swallowed hard, opened the double doors, and walked inside. Dozens of munching faces were all ignoring the 'don't talk with your mouth full' rule of British politeness. He picked his way towards the main entrance at the other end of the hall, concentrating on groups of girls, seeing if he could pick out Fi or any of her friends.

Maybe she's not here. Perhaps it's for the best. Maybe it's not meant to be.

He sighed, partly from disappointment, partly from relief.

But there—the face he was looking for. She was facing him, concentrating on her conversation with her lunch-time partner. Whoever it was had blond hair. Angelina, no doubt.

Maybe I can make a quick quip that I finally have the answer to her question about the facts of life.

No, don't be stupid.

He froze halfway to their table. It wasn't Angelina at all. It was Bran, smeghead extraordinaire. The knot in his stomach returned full force. *What is it with these girls and rugby lads?*

He wanted to hide—under the tables, anywhere. Trying to look natural, he put his chin down on his chest and kept heading for the main door. His heart felt as if it were filling with hot black oil.

Hold it in, you must hold it in.

The moment he turned the corner into the corridor, salty tears began to spill down his face, darkening the wooden floor beneath his feet. He stumbled along the long corridor, wondering how it'd been made—anything to prevent thinking about her. He ended up shuffling about in front of a blue door, ancient with neglect, the paint peeling from its edges.

Curious, he tried the doorknob. The smell of fresh paint and canvas invited him inside; art had always been a mystery to him. He'd have loved to be able to do it. Sketches and paintings lined every wall from top to bottom. More stood on easels, many only half finished. He saw paintings of people, animals, land, and seascapes, as well as dreamlike images that even Dali would've thought crazy. His eye caught a selection of paintings whose breathtaking beauty leapt off the canvas, almost mathematical in their construction, as if Escher had painted them through Picasso's eyes. What he read in the corner of the first sent his heart diving: *Felicity.*

'Can I help you?'

He turned to find a teacher wearing dungarees covered in paint blotches and a cardigan coat made from thick brown wool. She had short hair and thick, NHS-style glasses, but her face was kind and welcoming despite her steely tone.

'I doubt it. I was looking at these paintings. They're beautiful. Stunning.'

'Felicity is very talented.' She regarded him with a wistful smile. 'I thought I recognised you when I came in.'

'I'm sorry, but I don't think so. I don't do art.'

Her smile grew. 'I know, but I'd like to show you something.' She went across to a filing cabinet and began digging through one of the drawers. 'I probably shouldn't show you this, but somehow it seems wrong not to.'

She pulled out an A3 painting. 'This is one of hers.'

It was Hero, dressed completely in white. Behind him streamed wondrous light from an unseen source. There was a look in his eyes as if he were seeing into some beautiful, peaceful future in the distance—yet at the same time, an imperceptible darkness at the corners of his mouth, in the gleam of his eyes.

'She said it came to her in a dream, but now I see you before me, I don't think it was a dream at all. This painting captures you perfectly—your very essence.'

Hero put his hand over his mouth, gritting his teeth. Tears blurred his vision.

'Oh no, what's the matter?' The teacher opened her arms. 'Come here.'

Instinctively, Hero surged into her arms.

She held him tightly, stroking his back. 'What happened between you two?'

He gathered himself as much as he could. 'Nothing,' he squeaked finally, like a church mouse.

'Of course. And that's the problem.'

He nodded.

'It's okay.' She caressed his hair maternally, stood him back, and looked him in the eye. 'Some things just aren't meant to be.'

'I know, but it doesn't make it any better.'

'No, it doesn't.'

His eyes were drawn back to Fi's painting. 'You're right, she has captured my essence. You can even see the shadow with its hand on my shoulder.' He pointed at the right side of the painting.

'Really? I can't see it.'

'It's there. You just have to look hard enough.'

She studied the painting.

He bobbed his head. 'And thanks. For just now.'

'Anytime.'

He started towards the door.

'I mean it. Come back anytime.'

'Thanks, I will. Oh, err, please don't tell her.'

'Don't worry.' She smiled. 'I won't.'

Chapter 15

Hero

The sun beat down from the cloudless, blue sky, warming Hero's arms and legs. The freshly cut grass of the sports field was almost luminescent green, and its smell was invigorating. A small crowd of pupils, teachers, and family members had gathered at the side of the racetrack to see the final of the one-hundred-metre sprint.

He glanced sideways at his competitors. *They look so out of shape, this'd be an easy win even without my ability.* His training had pushed him to new limits.

He remembered the moment that had changed everything in both his training and his life. He had wept. He had run ten kilometres without stopping for the first time in his life, and he had wept. Then his legs had buckled under him, and he'd held onto the front door frame to prevent himself from dissolving into a human puddle. How long ago that seemed now. Since then, he'd run to school, raced to the gym, cycled across town to see friends.

Anything's possible.

He smiled, heartened by the confidence that he'd built.

No one can stop me. He enjoyed the thought now. *But in a good way.*

'On your marks . . . Get set . . .'

Bang. He got away from the starting line first, as always. His heart accelerated as hard as his legs. He felt the hardness of the ground against the soles of his feet as he pounded towards the finish line with ease, but he put a look of strain on his face. For the crowd. He peered out of the corner of his eye and eased up enough to let Manmeet sprint past him in lane three. He grimaced and crossed the finish line in second.

He picked out his brother in the crowd. James smiled knowingly and winked.

The Light Master had repeated again and again what had to be done in these situations. For a long time, Hero had argued on every occasion.

'It's important that you don't stand out,' the master explained. 'With your speed, you'll easily beat the other boys in sports. But you must not do this. You don't want that kind of attention, son, trust me.'

'What's the point of having a skill if you can't use it?'

'If you start breaking records, people are going to notice you. I believe we've already had a conversation about that, haven't we?'

He'd glowered at the master.

'I know it's hard, bruv,' James added. 'I used to want to show off more than anything—you know me.'

He smiled in spite of himself. 'Show-off.'

James and the master both chuckled.

'But we both know it's for the best, right?' James said.

'I guess you're right,' he said.

'Listen, bruv, you don't need to show off to pull girls,' James said. 'It took me a long time to realise that. In fact, the opposite is almost always true.'

That was easy for him to say, he was so good-looking—and besides, Hero still only wanted one girl. 'Really?'

'All you have to do is be amazing and know that you are.'

At the time, Hero had simply shaken his head slowly. *There really doesn't seem to be any upside to this so-called superpower.*

And yet here he was, pulling races.

'Manmeet!' he called, wiping his brow theatrically and jogging to catch up with the winner. 'Good race, mate. One of these days, you'll have to show me that superpower you activate right at the end.'

Chapter 16

Hero

'Hey, Fi!'

Hero glanced up at the shout from above as he scuttled across the main courtyard.

Oh shit, Bran.

Bran was leaning out of a top-floor window—must have been the Latin room—waving excitedly at someone behind Hero in the courtyard. Hero followed the wave downwards to where Fi stood gesticulating at Bran in horror.

'Stop being an idiot—you're going to fall,' she cried. 'Get back inside.'

Bran waved with both hands, laughing hysterically. 'It's fine, see? No hands.'

As Hero's eyes were drawn back to her anxious face, Fi recoiled and shrieked.

Instinctively, he dilated time with all his might, cutting her scream short. Everything around him went still and dead. He crossed the courtyard, stopping inches from Fi, her face a contorted waxwork of fear.

He flicked his eyes up towards Bran, whose face was frozen grotesquely aghast. His torso, now fully out of the window, had begun a fatal journey towards the asphalt beneath.

Oh Bran, you total idiot. Hero squinted at the playground below Bran. There would be no surviving that fall, not head first. But if he wasn't supposed to use his ability . . .

Keeping time dilated, he jogged up to the Latin room, weaving between the statuesque pupils along the way. He entered the room to see Bran toppling over the windowsill, pupils in the room staring at him, horrified.

He couldn't simply let Bran die. *How am I going to do this? I don't want to kill him by accident.* Something about that idea made him feel warm. *But I would get Fi back if I did. No one can stop me.*

He remained frozen amongst the other motionless students for five seconds that stretched over an eternity. Then he rolled his shoulders, approached Bran, and eased time ever so slightly. He took hold of Bran's legs and tugged until the bottom half of him was once again safely on this side of the window. Making his escape down the stairs, he relinquished time.

The school erupted with noise.

Hero smirked at getting away with something so brazen, so easily. It felt a little bit naughty, like stealing sweets from a shop. He turned the corner to exit quietly by one of the back doors and crashed into someone wheeling through at top speed. They reeled apart.

Fi stood glaring at him with a deep frown. He wanted to reach out and take her tightly in his arms and feel her warmth against his. Instead, he bowed his head to hide his reddening face, pushed past her, and went back outside.

As he reached the back of the school, the hairs on the back of his neck prickled. Someone was following him. *Maybe there's a chance this time—maybe she broke up with Bran?*

He turned around, smiling broadly. No one was there. A gentle breeze whisked leaves across the car park. Something caught his eye—or rather, the presence of nothing did. The shadows on the building seemed darker and longer than normal. The wind picked up pace, and the leaves rustled frantically.

Join us, came a whisper on the breeze.

The shadows continued lengthening and darkening, reaching out towards his feet. He didn't feel threatened at all; in fact, he wanted to step into them. The darkness drew him in with a welcoming embrace.

Join us, if you dare, the voices murmured.

I'd like that. No one can stop me.

He took a step backwards. Pulling away felt like peeling chewing gum from the sole of his shoe. Cold dread descended on him.

I used my power right out in the open. This is it—this is what they warned me about.

He cried out in terror and backed further away.

'I'm sorry, I won't use my power again,' he moaned.

But the shadows continued to leak towards him. Shadowy fingers reached out to grab him. A part of him wanted to let them. He stumbled backwards a few more paces, eyes glued to the darkness, then turned and ran around the end of the school hall.

He pulled to a halt in the midst of a knot of other students, who looked perplexed and annoyed at his sudden arrival.

Tom flagged him down with a wave. 'Are you okay? You look like you've seen a ghost.'

Hero shrugged and tried a tentative smile. 'Good, thanks.'

'You're weird, you are,' Tom said. '"I won't use my power again."'

Hero's stomach knotted. 'You heard that?'

Tom grinned.

Play it off. He yawned and stretched melodramatically. 'Maybe I'm too powerful for you muggles. Or maybe I *am* weird. I think that's why no one likes me— well, no one except you, eh?'

'Much to my own detriment,' Tom said with a smirk.

Hero dropped his game face. 'Sometimes I feel so alone, Tom, I don't know where I'd be without you.'

'You know, you could just be more sociable.'

He digested that, then nodded. 'Lunch?' He raised his eyebrows.

'I thought you'd never ask. I'm starving.'

Sword training nights were long, sweaty, and brutal. As was the routine, they warmed up using wooden scimitars, gradually working their way up and down the length of the mat, each step carrying them into a new attacking or defensive pose. Next came the same moves, one on one, with Emma or Jane, and they finished off with a practice fight.

It'd taken Hero a long time training with the dummy

before he'd been trusted with a wooden sword. He drove forward with complete focus, sending Emma staggering backwards. Behind him, James battled against Jane.

'You're looking good tonight, Hero,' the master called from the sidelines as Emma stepped back into range and bowed in concession.

'Is he?' James grunted as he fended off a lunge from Jane. 'He should prove it, then.'

The master glanced at James. 'Why not? Everybody—stop.'

James and Jane lowered their weapons. Hero wiped his forehead on his sleeve and bent forward to catch his breath.

'Gentlemen, take your positions on the mat.' He gestured at Hero and James.

Hero stood up and turned towards the centre with a frown. *Thanks, bruv.*

'*En garde!*' James raised his sword and grinned.

Silently, he reciprocated with his own. His frown deepened.

'Bruv? Focus.' James waggled his eyebrows.

They eyed each other up, slowly circling the mat.

James sliced his sword down the inside of Hero's blade, knocking it sideways and leaving him defenceless. Just like that, he tapped Hero on the shoulder with his blade, then flashed it downward and tapped him again on the chest.

Hero stared dumbly at his chest. Had this been a real fight, he would have lost his arm—and his life.

James glanced at the master and shrugged in disappointment.

The master crossed to the sword cabinet, humming quietly to himself. Hero and James glanced at each other nervously. The master pulled out two razor-sharp metal scimitars and extended them towards the boys. 'Put down your practice weapons and use these.'

Hero swallowed a snooker ball of saliva. He gingerly took a weapon, holding it at arm's length, keeping the edge as far away as possible.

'These are real?' he asked, wobbling the blade up and down.

The master nodded. 'You're going to need to be a lot faster, son, if you don't want to get hurt.'

Oh shit! We could really hurt each other with these. We could even—

'Bruv?'

He faced James, who was already poised in the centre of the mat, and moved dazedly into position.

Metal clanged as they met. They broke apart and James lunged again immediately, his blade tearing through the fabric of Hero's T-shirt, only millimetres away from doing the same to his skin.

'Jesus, James, you could've killed me!'

James's eyes were empty as a shark's.

Electricity arced between them. James moved left. As if a light had switched on in his mind, Hero reached for his ability. He slowed time more than he'd ever done before. James's face was scrunching with effort; Hero saw the vibrations of his sword as it moved through the air towards his shoulder. He rotated his sword upwards and smashed it against James's, then continued towards his brother's throat.

The two fighters roared. James's blade lay against Hero's neck, with Hero's centimetres short of its own mark.

'Half an inch, James—that's all it is,' Hero cried. 'I should've had you.'

'The master was right: you *are* looking good.' James lowered his arm and turned towards the Light Master, nodding sagely. 'He *is* looking good.'

Hero slid onto the piano bench in his favourite lunch-time hideout, the music room. He'd been working on this song in his head one bar at a time, every time he thought about Fi. Now, he'd almost finished it.

Today's the day.

His fingers hovered above the keys as he brought the wistful minor-key melody to the front of his mind. With them came a wave of emotion, a heart-wrenching, breath-squeezing sickness in his chest. Then he began to play. The notes wove a rolling, repeating melody in a minor key, floating to a harmonic higher key near the end. The rush began to move through him, electrifying every sinew. Ever since he'd learned to control time, he'd found it easier and easier to channel his emotions too, and music was one of the most powerful channels.

As the last notes faded away, he heard heavy breathing behind him. Fi stood peeping at him from the door, tears running down her face, mascara smudged around her eyes.

'It's beautiful,' she managed after a moment. 'What is it?'

He stood up. 'It's nothing, just a song I hear in my mind when I think about—'

A new droplet ran down her face. She swiped it away hastily.

'When you think about what?'

'Nothing. It was nothing.' He looked at the floor.

'I don't know why I'm crying.'

He looked into her soul through her eyes. 'You know, it's okay to cry. You should be proud that you can. Some people can't be so bold with their emotions.'

'Your music, it's so beautiful. I always love to hear you play.'

'But it's been ages since—' He blanched.

She adjusted the books in the crook of her arm, avoiding his eyes. 'I come up here at lunchtime and listen to you sometimes. I never . . .'

'I'd have thought you'd be spending your time with Bran.'

Her face flushed.

This conversation was not headed anywhere good. He walked towards her. She gasped as he gently gripped her shoulders and slowly moved her out of the doorway, and they locked eyes. He couldn't let go. He longed to snake his arms around her and hold her.

I won't be that guy.

He tore his eyes away, released her shoulders, and stepped into the hall. He glanced back over his shoulder in time to see her press her lips as if breathing in a final kiss.

Chapter 17

Hero

Dread and excitement mixed into finality as Hero walked to the gym. Today was the end of an era. His eighteenth birthday was coming up, and school would soon be over. In September, he'd be on his way to university, and that meant he'd no longer be coming to this gym, which had been his second home for so long.

He wanted the training, the gym, the Light Master—everything—to go on for the rest of his life. He was going to miss all of this; in a way, he'd already begun. He'd been thirteen when he walked into the gym with his brother that first time, a complete mess. Now he was focused, disciplined, top of his class. Perhaps more importantly, no one bullied him anymore. He got into scraps at times, as all boys did, but he commanded a healthy respect, not because of his brother but because of the person he'd become. His training had given him back the dignity that he'd lost during that first year at Wellesworth. There was a cool calmness about him now that a lot of people thought he'd got from James. Not surprising.

But it hadn't all been good. His habit of constantly

hiding himself had led him away from friendships. He continued to be a loner, even though he knew that the few friends he'd made, like Tom, would stay with him his whole life.

Now he understood why James had always seemed so mature for his age. When you could slow down time, you learned faster, thought faster, and reacted faster than everyone else.

Well, almost everyone else.

But James had been right. You really did live a thousand lifetimes.

Hero pulled up short inside the door of the gym. The centre of the floor had been sunken beneath ground level. The Light Master and James were standing near a ladder leading down into the pit.

'It's time, Hero,' the master called. 'We think you're ready.'

Hero stared, trying to hide his awe.

'Today is your qualification.'

James nodded as if to say 'It's all okay, bruv.'

The master continued. 'As you can see, the floor has been lowered. The pit is designed to test your reflexes in all of the disciplines that you've learned.' The Light Master gestured for him to climb down. 'Please.'

He tentatively made his way to the edge. Each rung had a hand-hold built into it. At the bottom, he looked up a bit breathlessly at the master and James, his legs feeling hollow inside his tracksuit bottoms.

'This is the first test, not the last,' the master said paternally. He pulled a remote control from his pocket. 'Get yourself set.'

Hero turned to the centre of the pit, where a scimitar lay in the middle of a painted red circle. He assumed that the master had pressed a button somewhere overhead as he became surrounded by whirring and clicking noises. Panels slid open along the three facing walls at random heights, revealing small ports of some sort underneath. More holes opened up in the floor, and he heard further panels sliding open behind him.

'Stand on the circle to start the test,' the master said. 'And pick up that sword—you'll need it.'

The edge of the scimitar glinted in the gym's panel lighting. Hero picked up the weapon.

The whirring noise of an engine warming up filled the pit, and the ground vibrated. A bird outside took flight from the windowsill, disturbed by the vibration and noise. He was watching its escape with some degree of envy when it seemed to freeze in mid-air. Its wings were moving like one of those slow-motion sequences in the wildlife documentaries Mum used to watch.

Something else caught his eye, a small orange ball moving slowly towards his head. He swivelled to the right, moving back enough to allow the ball to pass in front of his eyes, and found himself looking down the length of a wooden stick at the dark port from which it'd been fired. He flinched, ducking his head and shoulders like a tortoise retracting into its shell.

A few feet away, a metal post shot out of the floor. Wooden arms flicked out on hinges and spun. Instinctively, he brought the sword up and sliced off the outstretched wooden arms.

Behind him, another windmilling post popped up

from the floor, followed by more orange balls and sticks all coming at him from different angles. He catapulted himself through the air to avoid the projectiles, slicing off the artificial rotating arms on the post as he tumbled over the top of them.

After that, it was pure reaction for five minutes or more, with balls, sticks, and posts emerging at different heights and angles. At some point, he realised he was trapped. The machine had conspired against him: no movement he could make would allow him to escape without being hit. He relaxed and closed his eyes, hoping that it wouldn't hurt too much.

But no pain came.

No pain, no noise, nothing. He opened his eyes, and a smile of relief spread across his face. Nothing had happened, quite literally. The flying objects were frozen in mid-air. He could even see a flick of sweat, presumably his own, frozen like a glass bead on an invisible wire. James and the master stood above him motionless, trapped in an eternal moment, James's hair swished upwards by the power of Hero's movements.

Hero was drawn to the immense smile on his brother's face, a grin that would have made a Cheshire cat jealous. But he saw something more in James's expression. His eyes glistened, and his jaw and fists were clenched. Hero's eyes fixed upon the goosebumps on James's skin. *He's trying not to cry. He's proud of me. He's really proud of me.*

His heart twanged with inspiration.

With one finger, he nudged two of the balls and three of the sticks aside, then slipped carefully between them.

141

Crouching defensively, he eased time back to normal.

And then he braced for the reaction.

He felt the shock wave first, followed quickly by a sonic boom, and finally, blackness. Then the world unfroze.

'—at the hell was that?' James was shouting.

'Redemption, James,' the Light Master replied. 'That, son, was redemption.'

Hero heard footsteps walking away in the darkness above him, then the heavy clunk of the emergency lighting switch. He stood and turned slowly to the centre of the pit. All of the balls, sticks, and posts had been destroyed. The shock wave had continued upwards, smashing the unprotected main lights.

The master peered over the edge. 'Well, well, Hero. As we suspected, you're more than ready. Come with me.'

Hero grinned and began scrambling up the ladder.

'Okay, guys, I'll see you later,' James announced.

'You're leaving? Where're you going?' asked Hero.

But he was already on his way out. 'I've got a few things to do,' he called over his shoulder. 'I'll be at my place later if you need me.'

The door slammed behind him.

When Hero looked back, the Light Master was already on the way to his office. He jogged to catch up. The master sat down in his chair behind his old, functional wooden desk. It was completely clear except for a sticky notepad and a biro.

'Please.' He gestured to Hero, who sank into the seat nearest the door. 'Now that your training has almost ended, son, we need to talk. Have you ever wondered why you and others have this gift?'

Always secrets. Just when I think it's over, there's something more.

'Is there a reason?' he said flatly, but he knew there would be something—of course.

'Yes, and it's a very serious one. Can you keep a secret?'

He couldn't be serious. 'Like the one I've been keeping for the last five years, that I can slow down time?'

The master chuckled. 'Everyone who has the ability has a choice about how they might use it. Have you ever thought about it?'

'To defend myself, of course. That's why I came here, remember?'

'Is that it? You'd never use it any other way? What if you saw someone being attacked by a gang? Like your brother did with you?'

Hero resisted the urge to jerk upright in his chair. 'Well, no. Obviously I'd help them.'

'Of course you would. In fact, you did. Why did you help that boy at the window?'

He blanched. 'You know about that?'

'Of course.'

'I don't know. I remember thinking that it seemed like the right thing to do.' His throat contracted as he remembered what had happened after he saved Bran.

The master gave him a sharp look. 'And afterwards, something happened, didn't it?'

He knows. He knows everything. He shivered as the memories flooded back. *The shadow—what was that?*

'I found out about what happened that day because I was curious as to why you suddenly stopped arguing with me about using your ability.'

Hero's tongue felt glued to the roof of his mouth.

'Do you remember your first meditation experience all those years ago?'

He nodded.

'There was a word in your mouth, wasn't there?'

He reached, and reached farther, then started as the oncoming truck of knowledge barrelled into sight. 'The Dark!'

The master shifted in his seat.

'Why couldn't I remember that before? It's like the whole thing slipped from my mind.'

'They're very, very good at hiding, son. Sometimes they can be right in front of you and you can't even see them. They're just like us.'

'What do you mean, just like us?' *I'm sure he told me about this. Why can't I remember?*

'There're two types of people who have an ability like ours. Those that use it to help others are called the Light. Those that use it to help only themselves are—'

'The Dark.' He couldn't help his nervous laugh.

The Light Master didn't react.

Hero continued to titter. 'Oh come on, don't you mean the Dark and the Jedi? Doesn't that make you Master Yoda? You know, you're a little taller than I imagined, and a lot less green.'

'This isn't funny, son. You're three days away from your birthday. After you turn eighteen, you'll have to make a Decision. You can join the Light, you can go

144

Dark, or you can stay clean. But if you use your ability to help someone even once, even by accident, the Dark will most assuredly come for you.'

His laughter died away, and he nervously wiped his mouth. 'What does that even mean, "the Dark will come for me"?'

'I think you know.'

He was going to have to ask. 'The shadows . . . One time, I swore the shadows were reaching out to me . . . It was after I saved Bran. Was that the Dark?'

'And you were alone, right?'

Hero nodded rapidly.

'They always come when you're alone. They'll arrive within twenty-four hours from the moment you use your ability.'

'Twenty-four hours?'

'Those're the rules.'

More rules. Who made this up? At any rate, the solution seems simple enough. 'Well, what if I'm not alone?'

'You will be.'

'But I could be with someone.'

'You won't.'

He sat back, stymied.

'Have you ever wondered why you don't see us on TV?' the master asked.

'We're all really careful, like you said. We're good at hiding.'

'But even so, someone would be bound to slip up eventually, wouldn't they?'

'I guess.'

'So why're we never on TV?'

Nothing came to mind.

'We think reality changes when we use our ability,' the master said. 'So if someone tries to record us, they can't. They can see us and remember us, but not record us. Not even a painting.'

Not buying it. 'That's kind of weird though, isn't it?'

'It is, but that applies to a lot of what we do.'

Hero sighed, shifted, and rubbed his hands up and down his thighs. 'So I'll be alone. And nothing I do can change that?'

'Exactly. When the Dark comes, the first thing you'll notice is that your clothes will have changed. You'll be wearing all white. Just like you've already experienced, the shadows around you will lengthen—but this time, they'll catch you, and the world will fade out. You'll be pulled into the darkness.'

He didn't like the sound of this. It sounded like bollocks, but he knew it wasn't. He'd seen it.

'It's a dark place with no walls, no ceiling, and a floor that you cannot see. You'll be lit up, as will the Dark, but that's the only light there. You'll both be holding a sword, and only one of you will come out.'

'You mean—' He couldn't bring himself to say it.

The master nodded.

'With swords?'

He continued nodding. 'Somewhat sickeningly, the Dark refer to the fight as the Game, but its official term is "Justification". The good news is that if you win, you're clean again. You get to make a new Decision to go light, dark, or clean.'

Hero crossed his arms tightly. His eyes felt as if they

were going to pop out of their sockets and roll onto the floor. All this time—the swords, the t'ai chi, the meditation—and the training, the endless running, the puking on a regular basis in the high-altitude gym. All for this? He didn't know what was worse, being bullshitted like this or the possibility that it was true. And if it was true, then that meant—

'So everything you made me do was to turn me into a soldier for you—sorry, the Light. Whatever.'

He wanted to storm out, but having come this far, he may as well end things politely.

The master remained stoic. 'It's understandable that you don't believe me.'

Hero burst out in nervous laughter. *I'm not getting trapped in some kind of cult.*

'But to be clear, you are not a soldier. You came to me, I didn't come to you, remember?'

He had a point. *And what about James? He seems okay.*

'In the end, if you had not come to me, you would have used your ability accidentally to help someone. The Dark would have come, and you would have been totally unprepared. And that, as they say, would have been that.'

'So I suppose I should thank you, despite the fact that you sound completely nuts?'

The master laughed raucously. 'I know how I sound. But you don't need to thank me. You made some choices that brought you here, and later, you'll make some more that will take you somewhere else. But if you think that the training has been hard, then you've totally misunderstood the point of this conversation.'

He believes this. He really believes this. 'This is insane. Why did you wait until now to tell me?'

'We've found that if we tell someone about the Decision too early, before they're ready, the burden of knowledge becomes too great for them. They leave, and then—well, the Dark always gets them in the end.'

Hero leaned back in his chair. He couldn't believe this. 'I'm sorry, but this is just too insane.'

The Light Master narrowed his eyes. 'Son, I like you, but you are trying my patience. I'll say this one more time. If you use your ability after you turn eighteen to help somebody, the Dark will come for you. You can choose to be prepared or not, but if you're unprepared when the Dark come, you will die.'

He'd never seen the master get even remotely angry before. Images of all of the crazy things that had happened skipped through his mind, from James's strange and timely appearances right through to Bran and what happened afterwards. Like a bottle filling with water, he began to fill with belief, and as the water arrived at the bottle's neck: *It's true, isn't it?*

'Why eighteen?' he asked, still grasping for technicalities. 'I wouldn't have thought that the Force or whatever would care about the legal drinking age in Great Britain.'

The master snorted. 'Very funny—a lot funnier than you might think. But you've got that the wrong way round. Actually, almost everyone is ready by about the age of sixteen. You remember when you first controlled time?'

He nodded.

'You were ready then. Many years ago, the Dark and

the Light agreed to a hiatus of approximately two years in length so that we wouldn't start fighting too soon. Before that, it had been total carnage, blood and terror like you wouldn't believe. Killing children—babies, even. In the end, both sides agreed to give each other enough time to gain the maturity to make Decisions in good conscience.'

Am I ready to decide what kind of person I want to be? Am I a good person?

The master rested his elbows on the desk. 'The reason you finish school no later than eighteen and the reason eighteen is the age of majority in most countries is because of us, the Light and the Dark. Almost every society is structured around us.'

'But that's huge!'

'It's quite natural that people like us would rise to the top of virtually every endeavour we took on. You've done it yourself, haven't you?'

Hero stared down at his feet, thinking of the way he'd manipulated time at his exams.

'Exactly. And that brings me to my final piece of advice: be careful about how you use your ability. Up until eighteen, you get a free pass. But from now on, every time you use your ability to help yourself, you let the Dark into your heart a little bit more, until finally you find yourself celebrating joining them.'

I'd never join them.

A flash of anger flared up from his chest. 'And James knows about this? Have the Dark come for him?'

'Any conversation about James's Decision you need to have with him, not me.'

149

His voice grew higher, louder. 'How can I be prepared when I don't know when they'll come?'

'No one is ever truly prepared for the Dark to come. You do get used to it, though. If you survive.'

Hero started for the door.

'Hero.'

He swung around.

The Light Master looked into his eyes. 'If it's any consolation, you're the best I've ever seen. But that's not enough to win, son.'

He let the door swing closed behind him, maybe too emphatically.

And so that's it, the end of an era. That's how we leave it. He'd expected it would be different. He felt empty, forlorn. A new chapter would follow, but that didn't console him. He apparently had a huge Decision to make, one that would affect the rest of his life, and he didn't know what to do.

So he did what he always did when he didn't know what to do. He called James.

'Hey, bruv, what's up?'

'Are you free right now?'

'Sure.'

'You at your place?'

'Yep.'

'Okay, I'm coming over.'

'Is anything—'

'Of course something's wrong, and you know exactly what it is.'

There was silence on James's end of the call, and then Hero heard him take a deep breath. 'Come on, buddy, I've been saving some special whisky for this conversation.'

They sat in the front room, Hero on the sofa and James in an armchair, and looked at each other in silence. Hero kept opening his mouth with an intake of breath as if to say something, then closing it again.

'I don't know,' he said eventually. 'What do I do?'

'I can't tell you whether to be selfish or helpful, mate,' James replied.

'Come on, man, you know I'm not gonna go dark. It's light or clean.'

'You know you'll never stay clean, bruv. You like helping people too much. It's who you are.'

Hero tilted his head. 'And what about you?'

'What about me?'

'Which way . . .?'

'Oh.' He picked up his whisky and took a sip. 'I stayed clean.'

Hero sat forward. 'No way—you? You're joking, right?'

James set his glass carefully back on the table and wiped at a few drops of moisture there. 'Not at all. But I'm pleased you think I'd be such a man of action.'

'You helped me without thinking.'

'That was before I was eighteen.'

'Right.' Hero picked up his whisky and stared at it thoughtfully.

'Once I turned eighteen, I discussed it with the master,' James said. 'We decided that it would be better if I was around to help you through your first fight. The

151

only way to be certain of that was for me to stay clean.'

'Why did you think it'd be necessary?'

'I handle the fights easily, due to my aggressive side— but you, you're not like me. You'll have more difficulty. You've never been in a proper fight before. I have, and I can tell you, nothing can prepare you for that first time. So I'll be here for you, brother. I'll wait until you've gone through your first fight, at least.'

'What if I decide to stay clean like you?' He took a cautious sip of the whisky. It caught like a hot match in this throat, but he was damned if he would let James see that.

James grinned and pointed at Hero's glass. 'In the end, you won't be able to resist. You know it and so do I. Just call me after your first fight.'

'What if I don't make it?' He took another painful taste.

A look of disgust fluttered across James's face. 'Don't be a tart. You're the best the master's ever seen. I'll be expecting that call from you—so don't disappoint me, bruv.'

Chapter 18

Hero

Hero paced outside the main dining hall, his heart beating hard.

Relax. Breathe.

He filled his lungs to capacity, but even that somehow stopped short of satisfying his need. He slowly exhaled.

He would miss this place once he'd gone, even though he was a relative outcast here with few friends. He'd always expected the soul-crushing pain of glimpsing Fi and Bran together to subside over time, but it hadn't. Everyday things, like making a cup of milky tea, still reminded him of her. Sometimes he thought about her painting of him and felt a surge of hope, but the book had closed on that chapter, leaving nothing more than a placeholder to be referred to at times like these, again and again.

Hero turned and paced another length. Tom sat against the wall in one corner, head buried in a book, skimming each page whilst talking to himself. Hero's lip curled in half a smile. *Cramming won't help you, Tom.*

Either you did the work and you know it by now, or you didn't and you don't.

He scanned the room. There—Fi talking with a group of her friends. *I wonder what they talk about at times like this? The exam? How much they studied? Or something inane like the latest fad diet or boys? Bran. Why would she choose Bran after . . .*

He smiled forlornly.

But Bran. That's a cereal that helps you go to the toilet. An appropriate name for a complete douchebag.

His smile broadened.

And then he realized Fi was looking at him and nervously returning his smile.

The buzzer sounded, and the large double door was opened inwards by two teachers. This was it: the last fight for a place at Cambridge.

'Fight?' As if. This is going to be a slam dunk.

When the exam began, Hero dilated time just enough that he could read through and understand every question on the paper. Ten minutes to him was one by anyone else's watch. When he was certain he had everything just so, he eased back into normal time, mindful not to use his ability ostentatiously.

He set aside his pencil and allowed himself to let his mind wander: things past, alternate futures. Wishes granted, wishes lost, heartaches and heart melts.

He thought back to that first day at the gym when James and the master had told him to forget about Fi. He relived the moment when he'd finally been free to go to her, but when he got to the dining hall, she was already with Bran. Yet over all the days since, he'd felt her eyes burning into him in class. When they passed in the corridor, although they never looked at each other, an invisible energy passed between them.

We were supposed to be together. I wonder what would've happened if I'd ignored James? His hopes imploded like a Coke can crushed under a boot. *I wish I had. I wish I'd ignored him, just so I could hold her near me one more time. Feel her lips against mine. Smell her perfume, and feel her heart beating against my chest.* He was floating away, dizzy with the idea of a final encounter with Fi.

'And pencils down.'

He crashed back to earth like a rocket that had spent its fuel. Then he felt it, focused on the side of his face.

Fi was watching him, a slight smile on her trembling lips.

She looks nervous.

He returned the smile with a nod, and she grinned in response.

As everybody got up, packed their things, and left the hall, Hero made his way back through the double doors to pick up his bag.

'How was it for you?'

He straightened up and beamed at Fi. 'It was good, thanks. And you?'

'I think it went well.' She smiled, a little stiffly. 'So that's it, then?'

'That's it for the summer.' He pursed his lips. 'That's it forever. Now I guess we wait around and poo our pants until results day.'

'I need some air.' She looked at him expectantly.

Am I missing something?

She looked at her hands and played with her fingers. 'Would you join me? I know it's been a long time since we . . . since we spoke, but I don't want to leave things like that.'

She wants to be friends! He'd always thought she hated him for having stopped talking to her. *So maybe that's why she went off with Bran?*

He shook himself back to the present. 'Sure. I'd really like that.'

They stepped outside. It was a beautiful June day, the deep blue sky scattered with wispy clouds a seemingly touchable distance from the rooftops. The sun thawed fingers and limbs stiff from the frigid air-conditioning of the hall. It was the perfect day for a stroll with a long-lost love.

'So you're going to be a Cambridge boy, I hear?' she asked.

'Yes, indeed. I've always been a proper toff, as you well know,' he bantered in his favourite faux-posh voice. 'And you?'

'I'm going to Bournemouth, studying art.'

'I guess that makes sense. I always loved your paintings.'

'You've seen them?'

'I used to go up to the art room—'

'Oh my God! How many did you see?' She sounded panicky.

'They were beautiful.' He smiled, transported by the sweet memory. 'I don't know how you do it.'

She chuckled.

'What?'

'It's just that you're going to Cambridge, doing some ridiculous degree, and here you are complimenting me on my art degree at Bournemouth.'

'I'm not doing a ridiculous degree,' he said. 'I'm doing economics and computer science.'

She giggled.

'What?'

'You really have no idea, do you?'

His brow wrinkled in perplexity.

'About how many people look up to you.'

He shrugged and kept his eyes on the path as they strolled. *Is she actually admiring me?*

'You play piano, you're really smart in every subject, you're going to Cambridge. Is there anything you can't do?'

'Well, I can't draw to save my life, and I'm crap at sports.'

'That's not true, you're as fit as anything. Sure, you've never won anything in the sports day, but I always got the impression you were deliberately losing or something.' She shot him an intense look.

Oh Christ. Does she know? He smiled gamely. 'Don't be stupid. Why would I deliberately lose?'

'Yeah, I know—it was just an impression,' she muttered, reddening. Then her expression hardened again. 'But you conduct yourself with such maturity, as if nothing in the world could faze you, then you go on and help all those people. I mean, you did all those speeches for the years below and even help them with their homework. Who does that?'

157

She took a deep breath. 'And I know you saved Bran that day. I don't know how you did it, but I know you did.'

His panic rose to nuclear threat levels.

Go on the attack, bruv.

The echo of his brother's advice broke his inertia, and he waved one hand in what he hoped was humble dismissal. 'I know you want me to be a hero, but you're wrong. Hero's just a stupid, ironic nickname made up by my brother.'

'No, Hero, it's you who's wrong. People stopped calling you Hero ironically ages ago. The reason you're lonely at school's not because they don't like you—it's because they're afraid of you.'

How did she know that I'm lonely?

'Tom told me what you said, you know,' she said.

'He told you what?'

'About being alone. About not using your powers.'

He sputtered before he could put a lid back on his emotion. 'Who would take that seriously? And anyway, *you're* not afraid.'

'That's because I know you. I tried to explain to everyone about you, but they teased me about—'

Her face flushed.

Go on the attack.

As he cast about frantically for ideas, he realised they were standing in the exact spot where they'd kissed so many years ago. He drew to a stop and smiled.

'Brings back memories, doesn't it?' she asked.

She remembers. 'Yes, it does.'

'Isn't your house quite close to here?'

He nodded. 'Well remembered. Just around the corner.'

'Can we go there? For old times' sake?'

Old times' sake? He had no idea where this was going. 'Sure.'

She beamed. 'Good. Because I've got some questions for you.'

Chapter 19

Hero

They walked the short journey to the house.

She knows. That's the only explanation. I haven't been careful enough. This is what James warned me about.

They went straight through to the kitchen.

'Can I get you tea? Coffee?' Hero asked, walking over to the sink area.

'Water, please.' Fi sat down at the table.

She's going to grill me. She's going to scream 'freak' at me. There're going to be thousands of people in masks with torches, hunting me down forever more. I must put her off somehow. That's it—I'll question everything she saw. No one will believe her.

He brought the glass of water and gave it to her with trembling hands.

'So, what questions?'

'Well, it's just one question, really.'

Here we go.

She set the glass on the table untouched. 'Why?'

'What do you mean, why?'

'Why did you suddenly stop talking to me?'

He contemplated every possible answer, every truth, and every falsehood.

Never lie, Hero, the voice whispered from nowhere.

He went rigid, trying to hide his reaction.

Oh, just tell her.

'I've regretted it,' he said. 'More than you know.'

She leaned closer. 'So why, then?'

Never lie, the voice came again.

'It was the training,' he said sombrely. He slid into the chair next to her. 'After I was beaten up by Martin and then our kiss in the street, some more people came. They wanted to kill me. I ran and hid. I didn't see what happened exactly, but the police said that they turned on each other.'

Her hand floated to cover her mouth.

'I decided that I needed to be able to defend myself, and I asked to train with my brother. They told me I could train but that I couldn't talk to you again until I'd completed the first part.'

'But why?' she exclaimed.

It wasn't her fault. It was mine, we could have been together, but for—

His throat felt a mile wide. 'Because you followed us. They said the training is so intense that if I talked to you before I was advanced enough, you might die.'

'Oh my God.'

He was aching to take her hands in his. 'But the training, it changed me. Much as you realized that you don't know how I saved Bran but you know that I did it all the same, I realized that the training was bigger than me, than you. It's bigger than anything we understand.'

161

'What training? What happened? Why would it kill me?'

He sat back in his chair. 'You know, I know you know about me.'

She tilted her head questioningly, but there was a glint of knowledge in her eyes.

'I saw your painting of me in the art room. The man in white with a shadow on his shoulder—you captured me perfectly.'

Her expression darkened. 'You know, that picture is strange. You can see the shadow, and I can see the shadow, but no one else can—and the weird thing is, I never actually drew it.'

His skin bristled. Her eyes seemed panicked as if she was trying to say more but couldn't.

He scooted forward, leaning urgently towards her. 'I didn't mean to hurt you. I was trying to protect you.' His throat was so tight that his next words squeaked like a mouse. 'But I did hurt you, Fi, and I shouldn't have.'

'You did hurt me, and you're right, you shouldn't have.' She sounded stern, but she leaned closer still, just inches away.

'I'm sorry. I'm so, so sorry,' he murmured as tears burned paths on his face.

She brushed his tears aside with her thumbs as she rested her fingers on his face. 'It's okay. It's going to be okay.'

Her soft, pink lips met his. Their tender warmth made him gasp. He cupped her face with one hand, his fingers slowly urging her closer. They kissed harder and harder, devouring every ounce of each other. She moaned and grasped him tightly, desperate to intensify the feeling.

She drew back at last. 'I want you. I've always wanted you.'

Hero felt as if he were standing next to himself, staring at the two of them.

'Please,' she whispered. 'I know you want me too.'

I can't fight this. I can't fight my own heart. I just can't.

'It's true. I always have, since that first day you spoke to me. I felt a connection with you, as if we were supposed to be together and what I was doing was wrong.' He stood up and held out his hand. 'Come on.'

They held hands as they climbed the stairs to his bedroom. He spun around, snaking his hand around her waist, then pulled her towards him, kissing her hard. He unbuttoned her blouse, revealing a lacy white bra. She undid her cuff buttons and let the blouse slide down her back to the floor. He reached around with both hands to undo the bra, fumbling with the unseen hooks.

'I've never done this before,' he breathed.

'Me neither,' she replied, unbuttoning his shirt.

'What about . . .?'

'I was saving myself.'

He pulled back and looked into her eyes.

'For you, Hero. I always wanted it to be you.'

Forgetting about the bra, he put both his hands on her face, feeling every angle and curve as he kissed her. He pulled his shirt off by the arms, letting it fall in an untidy heap behind him.

'Wow, you have been training.' She ran her fingers

over his hairless pecs and between the ridges of his six-pack.

Then she reached behind herself and undid the clasp, letting the bra slip between their naked bodies.

He trailed his fingers over her face and down the side of her body. His thumb gently brushed her nipple on the way over the flawless skin of her waist before coming to a rest. He leaned in and kissed her neck, focusing on a small dark freckle near her collarbone. The warmth of her body radiated into his.

'God, you feel good,' he gasped.

She breathed in slowly and led him to the bed. They sat down on the edge and, after an awkward pause, took off their shoes and socks. He removed his trousers, and she slid out of her knee-length skirt, revealing long, smooth legs that shone in the afternoon sun.

What do I do now?

They looked at each other and giggled. Hero put his hand on her thigh, sliding it slowly upwards.

'Wait,' she said, getting up and searching through her clothes. She pulled out a small, shiny packet. 'Here, put this on.'

'I don't know how.'

'Really?'

'Yes, really. I don't sit at home practising rolling it on and off, you know.'

I'm starting to sound like James. That's no bad thing, he'd say.

She smiled. He put the packet to one side and grabbed his boxer shorts.

'Together,' she said.

They faced each other for a moment, staring curiously. He felt naked, and not just physically; exposed, vulnerable, but safe.

'So you really do find me attractive, then.' She grinned and sat back on the bed as Hero opened the packet. 'I think you're supposed to hold that bit whilst you roll it on, to make sure air doesn't get in.'

He struggled to follow her instructions precisely. 'Well, it's lucky I'm so excited—otherwise, this would be impossible.'

She turned his head and kissed him. He slowly pushed her back so that she was lying on the duvet, her black hair splayed in high contrast against the white cover. As he looked down on her, she appeared so small and helpless. He knew she wasn't, she'd wanted this for as long as he had.

They both gasped as he gently pushed forward and her warm body enveloped him. She slid her fingers down to his hips, pulling him in as tightly as she could. Electricity arced around his body, and his face flushed. He kissed her deeply, as if kissing beyond her lips, beyond her mind. The heat of his face slowly slid into the rest of his body like hot lava, popping and fizzing as it expanded to every nerve. It was as if the energy of the sun had melted their two souls together, like the melding of copper and tin to make one body of bronze.

The sun exploded with brilliant heat, a shock wave expanding through the inner universe. And then it was gone, leaving nothing but empty space as the remnants of their energy trails fizzled and vanished. His soul retreated back to the safety of his body like a turtle into its shell. He felt complete and yet tragically alone. His eyes burned.

Fi started to cry.

'I'm sorry, did I do something wrong?' His voice quivered as he desperately tried to regain some semblance of manliness.

She sniffed. 'No, it was beautiful. It was perfect.' She turned onto her side, her back towards him. 'Hold me. I don't want to be alone.'

He put his arm around her, and she pulled it tightly in to herself. They stayed like this for some time. Their pulsating bodies continued their silent communication, even though they were once again separate.

'That was really lovely. I'm glad we took this last chance,' Fi said, straightening her skirt as she prepared to descend the stairs. 'It's a shame we waited five years.'

Hero grinned. 'Really? You'd be doing that at thirteen?'

'True.' She grinned right back. 'But it's still a shame, isn't it? All that time, we could've been together.'

Hero pulled her to him, and they kissed, holding each other tightly. He never wanted to let her go.

She gently pulled away, caressing his face, and led him to the front door. 'I'll never forget you.'

'Wait—won't I see you again?'

'I'd like that—if you want to.'

'Of course I want to.'

She paused expectantly.

'I'll probably need your number, then,' he mumbled.

She giggled. 'I thought you were never going to ask.'

She wrote the number on a small pad atop the mahogany telephone table by the door.

How long should I wait to call? I heard there's a three-day rule, but I can't wait that long. I want to call tonight—would that make me look desperate? If I wait, maybe she'll think I'm not interested.

His head began to thump as if his skull were fractured.

Never play games. The voice echoed around him.

'I'll call you tonight,' he squeezed out, 'if that's okay? I don't like to play games. I really like you.'

She smiled. 'You're very different, but in a good way.' She gently touched his face again and pecked his cheek. 'Talk to you later, then.'

He closed the door behind her and breathed out heavily.

James cawed behind him. 'Well, well, bruv, what an afternoon that was.'

Hero started and spun around.

'"I'll never forget you,"' James mocked in a high-pitched voice. '"But wait! I wuuuv you."'

Hero folded his arms over his chest. 'How long have you been here?'

'Long enough. Should've closed the door, bruv.' And then back in the high-pitched voice, '"I was saving myself."'

'Oh, don't. I can't handle this right now. I'm feeling a little fragile.' He moved to the kitchen and collapsed into the chair in front of Fi's glass of water.

'I warned you,' James said gently, 'didn't I?'

'You did.' He squeaked like a rusty gate, the emotion of the afternoon finally overcoming his resistance. He puffed out his cheeks and gave a nervous laugh.

'Come here, bruv.'

Hero took his hand, and James pulled him to his feet. They threw their arms around each other, and James slapped him on the back.

'I'm really pleased for you, bruv. I know how much she meant to you, how long you waited.' He stood Hero back, holding him by the arms. 'I didn't want to deny you the joy of love, but you know now. You know how difficult this is for people like us. We have so much going on in our heads. I wanted to protect you from all that. That's what family's for, to look out for each other.'

'Thanks, mate,' Hero whispered. 'It's good to know you'll always be there for me.'

'I don't mean just you and me.'

'I know.'

James broke into a grin. 'And now, I've got to say— high five, bruv.' He raised his hand above his head.

Hero recoiled. 'You really are disgusting sometimes.'

'No, seriously, bruv! I clearly don't have to teach you anything about sex. I've never heard a girl scream like that before. What the hell were you doing to her?'

Hero's scowl turned into a guffaw.

James shook his upraised hand. 'Seriously, bruv, high five.'

'High five yourself, *bruv*,' Hero mocked as he slapped the proffered palm.

James winked. 'Already have.'

Chapter 20

Hero

Hero groaned. His old friend the knot was back, digging a hole in the pit of his stomach. Today was supposed to be a celebration. He was finally eighteen, and James had promised 'a great night, bruv.'

Knowing him, that involves lots of whisky and even more girls.

Hero chuckled, but his mirth was short-lived.

All I want is Fi.

They'd just finished their first proper date. He'd called her as promised, and they'd met at Oxford Circus for civilised tea, coffee, and cakes before Hero ran off the rails with his brother this evening. He already missed her. She was like crack cocaine— instant withdrawal symptoms.

His thoughts wandered on to what sort of party James had planned, who'd be there, what presents he might get.

Maybe Dad's bought me one of those new iPhones. That'd be so great.

The sounds of shouting and giggling children invaded his warm thoughts. Several boys were playing football in the park across the road, none of them older than ten or so. Two ample women were half watching the game but mostly chatting from the sidelines. One of them rocked a pram, occasionally cooing to its occupant. As Hero looked on, half of the players erupted in shouts, jumping up and down in celebration of a spectacular goal.

I guess that's what it feels like to be free, not a care in the world and a summer of playing Jumpers for Goalposts football. Still, university is supposed to be a carefree place. Why shouldn't I enjoy it like everyone else? I'll stay clean—that's what I'll do, to hell with the Game. To hell with James and the Light Master. They don't know me.

The kids' football bounced its way towards Hero, and one of the kids barrelled after it, running as fast as he could. Hero had already glanced away—the kid would get it—when one of the mothers screamed, a shrill, burbling cry that caused the birds in a nearby tree to take flight. The squealing of brakes and tyres joined the mothers in chorus.

The ball smacked off the car's bumper and sailed down the road. The driver sat in stunned silence, hands on the wheel, so stiff he seemed to be almost standing inside the car. The boy was nowhere in sight. The mother ran towards the car, whilst the one with the pram wrenched away and covered her eyes. The street had fallen silent; even the birds had nothing to say. The driver opened his door and got out, shaking, forcing himself to look at the carnage.

An astonished voice rang out from between two parked cars. 'It's okay, Mum. That man saved me.'

The driver placed both hands on the bonnet of his car to steady himself and dissolved into nervous chuckles.

The mother scooped up her son, holding him tightly in her arms. 'Never do that again! Never go into the road without looking first.'

'That's exactly what the man said.'

'What man?' She looked up and down the street.

'He was just there.' The boy pointed into the deserted street.

'There's no one there, honey.'

'I'm not lying. He was right there.'

She shushed him and stroked his hair. 'Well, you're safe, thank God.'

Hero continued walking down the tight alleyway, certain the smile on his face would never leave him. *Maybe they do know me after all.*

He honestly couldn't think of a time he'd felt better. The exhilaration, the fulfilment, the warmth when the little boy had thanked him. But then the terror of the moment itself: the football resting against the bumper of the car. The boy's hands on the ball. The driver's face frozen, contorted. The startled birds. The mother's scream cut short.

He hadn't thought about it at all. He'd turned instinctively, strolled across the road, and plucked the boy from the maw of the vehicle.

'What're you doing?' the boy had asked.

'Saving your life, I suspect.'

The boy looked around, seeing how close the car was and how still everything was around them, like a 3D freeze-frame. 'Wh-what's going on?'

'I told you, I'm saving your life.'

'Did you do that? Everyone, everything is frozen.'

'That's me, all right.'

'H-how?'

'Listen, kid, there's a reason why you're taught to look both ways before walking into the road.'

The boy looked down, reddening.

'You're lucky I was there,' Hero said with a smile. 'You've been given a second chance, kid. Use it. Live a long and happy life.'

Hero put him down.

'Wai—'

The boy's protest was cut off as he let go. Hero had ambled up the street and turned right to take the usual shortcut. The singing birds and hum of the traffic returned as he normalized time.

I'm on my own now. He brought his arm up to wipe his brow and froze.

His sleeve was pure white.

So soon?

The knot took its place in his gut as he saw that the rest of his clothes had changed too. The shadows in the alley began to lengthen, and he braced against a strong gust of wind carrying a strange, low-pitched murmur.

Shit.

The shadows stretched towards him. He looked up at the sky, but all he could see was an unsettling wave of darkness. The wave accelerated towards him and then past. As it rushed by, he felt it stretching away to infinity, pulling his body and mind away into nothingness. For a single moment, in the darkness, he felt infinitely large yet infinitely small, a sensation that very nearly overpowered him.

A man was screaming somewhere in the distance beneath the sound of the rushing wind. Hero's mind and body started to return like an incoming tide on a barren beach, and then he snapped back to normality. The scream echoed around him, and he realised it was his own.

'First time's a bitch, isn't it?' asked a voice with an American accent.

In front of him stood a man not unlike himself dressed in a tight-fitting black suit and shirt. He was standing in darkness, just as the Light Master had explained. The effect was strange, the two of them in a blackout lit by unseen spotlights.

The man smirked. 'The good news is you won't experience it again.'

The black suit against the darkness made the man difficult to see, but Hero glimpsed real malevolence in his smile. The man raised his sword, rotating it in a gratuitous display of speed and skill. Hero looked down and found what he expected: a scimitar in his own hands. The weapon looked different than it had at the gym. It was sharp. Very sharp.

Hero limbered up by slowing down time and swishing his weapon. The American took a step back. His face had lost its smugness.

A lifetime of Touch My Chin had taught Hero to be confident at times like this. He sensed that he had an advantage.

'That is good news, isn't it?' he replied.

173

The American's mouth twitched almost imperceptibly.

The two men edged towards each other.

'Don't worry, I'll make this quick—but it won't be painless,' Hero said.

The American flinched.

He's as nervous as me. He felt lighter just knowing that. *Don't float away. Focus.*

The duellers swished their swords to the *en garde* position, sparks scattering as the metal clanged together. The Dark flickered, and his weapon crackled menacingly as it sliced along Hero's sword and thrust towards his neck.

Hero slipped sideways, avoiding the skewer. His nerve pulses bolted along their neural pathways at light speed.

The Dark hammered his sword against Hero's again and again, changing his angle and direction of attack each time. Hero easily rotated his sword into position to defend the blows.

He's so slow.

The next crackle came right next to his ear, bringing piercing pain. A sliver of skin and cartilage flew through the air like a lifeless worm from a bird's beak.

He got me.

The Dark pressed on, teeth gritted, lips snarling.

The master's drills echoed in Hero's mind: *Constantly defending is a sure-fire way to die.* He focused his concentration, and his vision shifted. He saw the two of them from above, one in white, one in black. They danced around each other, swords flailing.

It's chess. I need to outmanoeuvre him.

He dilated time further as he put together a strategy,

observing the different angles and moves, calculating the Dark's weakness.

Here we go.

His brain was on high alert; every sense in his body was triggered. Step by step, he executed his plan. He could smell the sweat on the American's face. He manoeuvred his opponent, slowly widening the defensive zone. Even in that dark place, he could see the redness of his cheeks, the individual pores perspiring. The man knew it was checkmate.

As simply as he could possibly have conceived, he nudged his opponent's sword to one side and drove his blade through the Dark's lung and into his heart. The man's pupils contracted. The resistance made Hero think of cutting through a Sunday roast, the meat giving way like a sponge.

Blood spurted from his conquered opponent's mouth; Hero felt its warmth trickling down his face. The Dark's knees wobbled then collapsed under the weight of his body. Hero looked into the man's eyes and slowly eased him to the seamless, unseen ground, his arms shaking.

The American was moving his lips, trying to say something, but all Hero could hear was the gurgling of blood in his throat. The man screwed up his face and opened his jaws wide with the pain of drowning, and a gasping, burbling scream escaped. He stiffened with a jolt, and Hero noticed a change. The Dark's eyes were brighter than before, and his open mouth was lit from within.

The Dark began to shudder. There was an unexpected smell like the sizzling bacon that Dad used to cook every morning. Their faces now inches apart, Hero watched the man's eyes and mouth grow brighter and brighter. He jerked back—that was fire. The Dark was burning inside.

The Dark's jaw tensed as he tried to cry out. He gargled and coughed up more blood, pouring over his chin and running onto his suit. His eyes were black dots on a field of white, his face a mask of terror, pain, and confusion. The candle behind his eyes flickered, then went out. Perhaps the Dark was gone, but the shell was very much alive.

The body screamed as the fire escaped its prison. The barbecue aroma was joined by the rancid, chemical smell of burning fabric and hair. Hero retched. Transfixed by this horrific beacon of light in the raven blackness, he stumbled backwards. The black suit had mostly burned away, exposing the man's sizzling, melting skin and fat, dripping in flaming clumps into small islands of fire on the ground.

The sound of rushing air broke Hero's trance. The Dark's body began to shake faster and faster until he was vibrating. Sensing danger, Hero turned to run.

The concussion knocked him off his feet and slammed him against the alleyway wall. He gagged and coughed for breath. The cacophony of exploding flesh behind him faded as he slid down the bricks onto his face and was enveloped by a different kind of blackness.

Chapter 21

Hero

Hero became aware of a buzzing both inside and outside his head. His mind was buzzing, his tongue was buzzing, his teeth were buzzing.

Is that a fly about to land on my face?

Silence.

Thud.

He opened his eyes and saw a blurry dirt track beyond translucent wings. He scrunched his lids closed and open a few more times, and the alleyway came into focus. The fly made its escape as he pulled himself onto his hands and knees.

Need some ibuprofen.

He was back in the alleyway he'd been in before the fight. The Dark had evaporated, and he was wearing his original clothes. Steadying himself against the wall, he rose to his feet.

Was that real? Did I imagine—

His hand jerked involuntarily to a stabbing pain in his ear. He drew his hand away; it was wet. His fingers were covered in blood.

Real.

The blood was an incredible red. Everything around him seemed vibrant with colour, more real than anything he had ever seen before.

'I won,' he shouted triumphantly. 'I won!'

He punched the air, his whole body ablaze with euphoria. He reeled a few steps as the reality set in. Then he corrected his course and resumed his journey towards home. His legs wobbled as he walked down the alleyway. The stench of bacon and roast beef clung to the tiny hairs in his nostrils, ready to choke him when he least expected it.

Like carving a Sunday roast. That's what it felt like to run my sword through someone's heart.

His stomach somersaulted.

So easy to kill.

The burbling scream of the Dark as he choked on his own blood echoed in his ears.

To murder.

A golf ball formed in his throat until he could hardly breathe, hardly swallow. He cried out in pain. In his mind, he saw the fire melting the fat away from the man's body. The knot clamped down on his stomach. He dropped onto all fours and retched again and again until everything he'd eaten that day was deposited onto the dirt and nothing but air tasting of goat's cheese was coming up.

He fumbled for his phone. It tumbled to the ground, just missing the mess. He picked it up with shaking hands.

'Hey bruv, what's up?' James answered on speakerphone. Hero heard the shower running.

'James, help. I just . . . I just . . .'

The water cut off, and James's voice zoomed into the phone mic. 'Where are you?'

'In the alleyway, near home.'

'Go to the Kings Arms. You know it?'

'Uh-huh.'

'Get yourself a whisky. Actually, get me one too. I'll meet you there.'

Hero stuffed the phone back into his pocket and stumbled to the pub. Thank God it was close. The unoiled door squeaked open. The place was completely empty save for a couple of elderly gentlemen in one corner who eyed him suspiciously as he shuffled to the bar.

The barman came across to meet him. 'Have you got ID, young man?'

He nodded numbly. 'I just turned eighteen.' His hands trembled as he pulled out his driving licence.

The barman studied it. 'Okay, what can I get you?'

'Two Glenmorangies, please.'

'Doubles or singles?'

'Doubles.' He sat staring into the distance as the barman put two tumblers in front of him and poured the whisky.

'That'll be ten pounds, please.'

He took a tenner out of the wallet still clutched in his grasp and placed it on the bar. His hand was now visibly shaking.

'You okay? You look like you've seen a ghost.'

Hero refocused on the man's face and nodded slowly.

'And you seem too young to have Parkinson's,' said a familiar voice from behind.

James wasn't smiling; he looked caring, almost paternal. He reached up and touched Hero's ear gently. 'Didn't move fast enough, eh?'

Hero sluggishly shook his head.

'Does it hurt?'

'A little. Not too bad.'

James sat down on the bar stool next to Hero, reached into his pocket, and pulled out some ibuprofen. 'Thought you might need a couple of these.'

'Thanks. How did you know?' He threw a couple of pills into his mouth and helped them down by finishing his whisky in a single gulp.

James nodded at the barman, who refilled Hero's glass.

'We're celebrating,' he said as he handed over a credit card.

'I'd hate to see you two at a funeral, then.' The barman put the card behind the bar and handed a tab key back to James.

Hero drained his refill and stared blankly at the wall ahead of him. 'It was too easy. Too easy to kill him— and it's impossible now. It's not like it is in the movies, where people prance around, killing without a care in the world. It's bollocks, James, total bollocks.'

James signalled the barman to pour another one. 'Keep drinking, mate. It'll get easier.'

'The price of saving someone is that I kill someone—I murder someone,' he whispered hoarsely. 'It's fucking insane.'

James wrapped his arm around his shoulder. He threw back another whisky. James said it would get better soon. Surely it would be soon.

The room was moving left and right even though he was still lying down. Slowly, Hero sat up on the couch and took a deep breath that morphed into a yawn.

'Afternoon,' James said from the door. 'How're you feeling?'

'I'm okay, thanks,' he replied, blinking in the light from the full-length windows.

'That'd be the ibuprofen and water. I told you you'd thank me.' James grinned and sat down in the armchair opposite the couch. His smile faded. 'How're you really feeling?'

Hero's lips began to tremble. 'I just killed a guy. How do you think I'm feeling?'

'Still wanna talk about it?'

He shook his head silently.

'Coffee?'

He nodded.

James considered him pensively. 'You should call Fi. I'm sure she'd love to hear from you, and I think she'd be good for you right now. Take your mind off everything.'

It was a good idea. He tried to nod and smile, but his face felt frozen. He shuddered as burbling noises emanated from his mouth.

James threw his arms around him. 'It's gonna be okay, bruv, it's gonna be okay.'

James held him until the shuddering stopped and his stomach growled loudly.

'Let's get that coffee, eh, bruv? And some breakfast.'

Hero sat down at the circular wooden table whilst James poured the coffees and put some bread in the toaster, blathering nonsense about all manner of things, none of which Hero really listened to. All he could think of were those eyes. Those panic-stricken eyes, fading into the darkness, and the feeling of the sword plunging into the man's heart.

Like carving a Sunday roast.

His stomach somersaulted again.

'Are you okay, bruv?'

He gulped hard, trying to keep down his breakfast. James resumed his inane chatter. Eventually, the knot shoved off or at least took a tea break, and he was ready to face the world once again, albeit barely.

He stood up from the table. 'Okay, James, I'm gonna head off now. Thanks for breakfast and . . . everything.'

'No worries. I'll come with you outside—I want to show you something.'

'Okay.'

They took the lift to the ground floor. Outside the big plate glass front doors, James walked over to one of the bushes. The whole place had been newly built in that bright red brick and pale yellow stonewall that was so popular before styles changed for the better; it had originally been white, of course. But it was nice to have so much greenery right outside the front door, especially as someone else was looking after it all. The hedges were neatly trimmed, and the trees were perfect spheres like big green lollipops.

'Here,' James called.

Hero followed him.

'You see this rock?' James lifted it up to show him two keys. 'I always keep the keys here in case I lock myself out. Anytime you want to come over, if I'm not in, just use the key. It's fine, buddy.'

'Not sure why I'd come over if you're not in.'

'Well, maybe you want to get away from Dad—or if you're with Fi.'

He couldn't help but smile. 'Oh, okay. Of course.'

But James had gone sombre again. 'Give her a call. You need her. And she needs you.'

Chapter 22

John Turner

John walked his usual route to work that morning, savouring the freshness of his crisp, newly ironed shirt against his skin. Today, he was wearing his favourite dark black suit from Savile Row, made in the finest Italian wool.

As he walked down the steps onto Birdcage Walk to cross to St James's Park, he noticed a blond girl in her twenties watching him somewhat surreptitiously. Her piercing blue eyes, almost wolf-like, gleamed above her elegant white blouse and dark, knee-length skirt. John admired the sheer black stockings that continued down to shiny black Louboutins, just glimpsing the red soles.

You must be old enough to be her father, ya perv.

He kept his head forward as if oblivious to anything outside a narrow corridor on his side of the pavement, an important trick he'd learned in his youth. He studied her in his peripheral vision, allowing himself to wonder what it might be like with a blond, blue-eyed girl in her twenties, flesh firm to the touch and—

A pang of guilt exploded in his gut like a nuclear bomb. His heart took the express elevator to hell.

I miss you. I miss you so much.

His mind snatched at fleeting images: her jet-black hair, her pale, freckly skin. He was so engrossed in remembering every detail of her face that he didn't notice the dark Mercedes pull up at the kerb ahead.

He was startled by the clunk of the back doors opening on either side of the car. Two men got out, both in black suits as expensive as the one he was wearing. He wondered if they used the same tailor.

He smiled assertively. 'Morning, gents. What can I do for you?'

'Good morning, Mr Turner.' The darker-haired man gestured towards the car. 'Please, sir.'

'I don't know what your mother taught you, but mine always told me not to get into a car with strange men. I'm way out of your league, anyway.'

'Very droll, Mr Turner.' The man's tone was almost regal. 'You know why we're here. He wants to see you.'

'Well, tell him to get off his arse and come and see me, then.'

'Mr Turner, if you force this issue, you know what's going to happen.' The man tilted his head patronizingly.

John's gaze flicked between them as he considered their position, both physically and strategically. Then he dropped his head, stepped towards the car, and bent to get in.

The two suits breathed a sigh of relief and visibly relaxed. It was a mistake they would never make again.

Chapter 23

Hero

Hero ambled aimlessly from James's place. Everywhere he looked, he saw those eyes, their light fading in the darkness. They reminded him of the cartoons he'd watched as a kid where you could see the villain's eyes blinking from the dark. But this wasn't TV; this was real.

Cartoons and movies made it look so easy to take someone's life. The evil ones, the baddies, deserved to die. *He was evil. It's fine.* But the thought didn't sit well. The sickness in his stomach soured, pushing acid upwards into his mouth. And then a thought entered his head, spreading like a drop of black paint in a tin of white. *What if he wasn't evil? What if he was just some guy like me?*

The world seemed further away than ever, as if he were walking at the bottom of a well. Everyone else carried on, oblivious to his pain. He responded by allowing an icy numbness to weave itself into his skin.

Why can't I be normal? Do normal things, like spending time with Fi? The thought rescued his soul from the shroud that was trying to suffocate it. He wondered if his heart might crawl out through his throat and try to hop its way to her door.

The house was cold and seemed emptier than usual. He went through to the kitchen to make himself a tea. And maybe a biscuit. On the table sat a letter; it was addressed to him. He recognized Dad's handwriting.

His phone buzzed in his pocket.

'Are you at home?' asked James.

'Yes.'

'Do you have a letter there? From Dad?'

'Yes.'

'What do you think?'

He turned the letter over on the table. 'I haven't opened it yet. I just got here.'

'Open it. Call me back.' James hung up.

He opened the letter.

To my youngest son, Richard 'Hero' Turner,

Sorry for the formal start. I never know how to address these things—too many years in business, I guess. Firstly, I want you to know that I love you and I'm immensely proud of you and your achievements. I'm certain that you'll get all your A's and go to Cambridge as you've always dreamed. I've set aside a special account for you; the details, cards, etc. are in the envelope. There's enough money in there to see you through the early years of your life, especially through university. I've also made provisions for accommodations in Cambridge and here in London. I know you'll do well and get everything you desire. Finally, I've left you a car. It's in the Covent Garden NCP. I know you'll like it.

I want you to know that your mum loves you very much too. She didn't leave because of you. I can't tell you the actual reason, but I can say that there are some very dark forces in this world, darker than you can possibly imagine. I thought I'd cleaned my hands of them, but it's obvious to me now that this is impossible and they'll never leave your mum or me alone unless I stop them. I'll be gone for some time, but I will see you again.

You're a man now. You're capable, and you're ready to face the world without me. My only advice to you is this: love is the only thing that makes the darkness of this world bearable. Cleanse yourself of this darkness. Go out into the world, my son, and find your love.

Love,
Dad

Hero stared at the paper, motionless but for his heartbeat. His phone buzzed again.

'So?' James asked.

'I . . . I don't know. What's happened?'

'I'm not sure, but Dad's gone.'

'Do you know where?' Hero looked around for Dad's things, for any clue where he might have gone.

'No, but I'm sure he'll be back. He said it was something to do with finding Mum.'

'You spoke to him?'

'No. He sent a letter to me too.'

'Oh.' He listened to their breath in the phone receivers on either side of the call. 'Do you think he knows about us?'

'Us?'

'The Light, the Dark.'

'I don't think so. I don't know. Why do you ask?'

'Nothing, really. Something Dad wrote.'

'Can you come to the gym at seven o'clock tonight?' James asked. 'The Light Master called, and he wants to see us both. I think he's planning something.'

'What did he say to you?'

'The Light Master?'

'No, Dad,' Hero said. 'In his letter.'

'Not much. Look, can we discuss this later at the gym? I've got quite a bit on right now.'

'Sure, see you later.'

James hung up.

Hero looked down at his phone and selected Recent History, Dad.

'This is John Turner.' Voicemail.

He hung up and selected Dad Office.

'Good afternoon, Turner Capital.'

Thank God. 'Hi, Zoey, it's Richard. Is my dad there?'

'Hey, Hero, long time no speak. How's things?'

'Good, thanks. And you?'

'Great. Getting married next month.'

'Congratulations.' He tried to sound light-hearted. 'About my dad, though—is he there?'

'I haven't seen him today. Let me just check.'

Automated Muzak played for a minute before she came back on the line.

'No, no one's seen him today.'

Tension mounted in Hero's chest. 'Does anyone know where he is?'

'I already asked. There's nothing in his sche—ah, wait. What's that?'

He heard low voices in the background, and then Zoey came back to the phone. 'Okay, apparently he called earlier and said he's going away on business for a while. He's assigned everything to one of the senior guys here.'

'Does he know where Dad is?'

'He doesn't. No one does. Actually, I'm surprised *you* don't.'

It was nothing compared to the shock Hero felt. He swallowed dryly. 'Yes, well, thanks anyway, Zoey.'

'Good luck for Cambridge. I've got my fingers crossed for you.'

'Thanks. Bye.'

He ended the call and stared out of the kitchen window into the colourful back garden. *What the hell is going on? Why is this happening to me?* He was engulfed by impending dread. He paced around the kitchen for a few moments, then pulled out his phone again.

This time, the name he selected was Fi.

Chapter 24

Hero

The evening air was thick. It'd been a humid day, and the summer heat lingered like a warm, wet towel against the skin.

The afternoon had been long. Luckily, Fi had been in high spirits and chatted away for over an hour whilst Hero listened, curled up on the sofa and smiling gratefully. After that, he'd flitted between making coffee, reading his book in the garden, and watching mind-numbing daytime TV, flicking from channel to channel—anything to distract his mind. The knot was ever-present.

Every so often, the dam broke and his mind flooded with thoughts of what might have happened to Dad. And then the real horror came: the screams of that man. *Not the Dark. He was a man.*

He switched off the TV and sat staring at the blank screen, its darkness pierced only by the memory of those fading eyes.

Now, as the sun faded, it was time to walk the familiar route in anticipation of learning more. The gym and the Light Master were the only beacons of light in his otherwise dim world. *What did James mean that the Light Master was planning something? Why so cryptic? Why not just say?*

Everyone was already there at the gym: James, the master, and the two girls. There were tables laid out with a couple of champagne bottles on one side and flutes already fizzing.

'Here he is,' the Light Master exclaimed. 'Champagne?'

'What's going on?' Hero asked.

The master raised a flute. 'To our new hero!'

He scowled. 'Don't call me that. I'm not a hero. Especially not now.'

'Why do you say that?'

'Because I just killed somebody.'

'No, Hero, you've Justified yourself.'

'I don't feel Justified.'

Cleanse yourself of this darkness.

The master set his glass down on a table and stepped closer. 'What did you do before you Justified?'

'I saved a kid.'

'How?'

'He ran out in front of a car. I stopped time and pulled him out from under the bumper.'

There was an incredulous intake of air around him.

'Impressive,' Jane said.

'Yep, that'd do it,' the master said. 'How long was it before you were Justified?'

'About a minute.'

'Oh my God,' Emma whispered.

'What?'

'It's not normally that fast,' James said.

Hero shrugged.

The master looked him in the eyes. 'It means they're watching you.'

Hero felt coldness wrap around his heart. 'How? I've not seen anybody.'

'Like I said, they're good at hiding, and they're able to move in the shadows.'

He couldn't catch his breath.

'In the same way they bring you into the darkness,' the master continued, 'they're able to move around between places. If there's shadow in the room, they can watch you from within it.'

His hands drifted to his throat in horror. 'So they've been watching everything I've been doing?'

'Don't worry, bruv. They wouldn't have seen any of your more personal moments.' James elbowed him in the side.

'But that's kind of a big deal. I mean, that's practically a superpower.'

'Not really. They can't use it whenever they want. Only when they're on specific business—like watching us.'

'But why? What do they want with me?'

'Other than your soul, you mean?' James asked mockingly.

Hero gaped back at him.

'Because you're the best that we've ever seen,' the master said. 'They've probably been watching you since you first joined this gym.'

He was probably right. Hero recalled the day he saved Bran—the overextended shadows, the ice lightning that shot down his spine. Through his soul.

'But of course, you *have* seen them, haven't you?'

Hero looked up sharply.

'After you helped that guy at school,' the master continued.

Words stuck in his throat. *He really does know everything.*

'You saw them?' James said incredulously. 'Why didn't you tell me?'

'I don't know, it kind of slipped my mind.'

'What was it like?' Jane demanded.

'Unpleasant, but pleasant.' Hero suppressed a shudder.

'How did it feel, saving the kid from the car?' the master asked.

He brightened in spite of himself. 'Amazing. The best feeling I think I've ever known.'

'Better than sex, eh, bruv?' James said with a grin.

Hero shot him a look. 'Well, I don't really have much to go on.'

'Based on what I heard the other day, it must be a very close call.' James began laughing.

'Oh come on, man,' Hero pleaded, turning his face from the girls.

'Okay, boys, calm down.' The master gestured with his hands. 'So Hero, want to do it again? You can't stay clean forever.'

Cleanse yourself of this darkness.

Hero took a sharp breath. Mum. Dad. Would they be looking at him disapprovingly right now?

Find your love.

And then it became clear. He relaxed; he hadn't even realized he'd been tense, he'd been that way for so long.

'I can't do this,' he whispered.

'What was that?' James barked.

'I can't do this.'

'What do you mean?' Emma asked.

He raised his voice. 'This. All of it. Killing people—no, murdering them. Maybe they have made bad choices, but they're still people. They don't deserve to die.'

James looked aghast. 'You're joking, right, bruv? Don't you understand? These people are monsters. Manipulating their way through the world, turning us all into slaves. We have to stop them.'

Hero shook his head vehemently. 'Sure, we have to stop them, but there has to be a better way. No one deserves to die like that. No one deserves to die. Full stop.'

'There's no other way, Hero,' the Light Master said gravely. 'You have to remember, we didn't make the rules. They did.'

He took a step backwards. 'Then, I'm sorry, but I can't accept these rules. I can't play this Game.'

'You dick,' James shouted. He looked ready to launch a fusillade of punches in Hero's face.

'I'm sorry.'

James made a shooing motion. 'Don't "sorry" me, you asshole. You're supposed to be the hero. You're supposed to be the best. Do you know what I've given up for you? Do you, asshole? No? Well, I'll tell you. I've been sitting in the wings babysitting you—and for what? So you can turn around and act like a total girl? All these years, I've been wasting my time. Wasting my life.' He glared at the master. 'He's supposed to be the one that was gonna save us from the Dark, but he doesn't even have the balls to face up to what needs to be done. This is the best we've got? You must be joking. If this is the best we've got, then we've got nothing.' He wiped his mouth with the back of his hand, then pointed at the Light Master. 'No, *you've* got nothing.'

The Light Master lifted a hand, but James backed away towards the door.

'You're pathetic, you're all pathetic,' he shouted. 'You're not worth my time. You're not worth fighting for.'

Hero took a few steps after him. 'James. Please don't be like this. I want to fight for you, but I can't kill.'

'No, Hero, it should've been me— I should be the one, the hero,' James snarled. 'I'm done with this, and I'm done with you.'

He turned and barged through the exit into the night.

'Come back!' Hero ran after him, smashing the doors open as he went.

It was strangely cold and dark outside for such a beautiful day earlier. A gust of wind bounced a solitary Coke can down the road. The street lamps poured their yellow light in isolated pools along the pavement. One of the lamps flickered and buzzed before switching on fully.

'James! Please come back.' Hero's voice fluttered and echoed in the breeze. He looked up and down the street, but there was no sign of James. He dropped to his knees. 'Mum, Dad . . . James . . . Come back.'

His cry cut like the howl of a hungry baby through the silence of the night.

But it found no ears.

Chapter 25

James

I walked out of the gym. My time there was done. As pure as he was, Hero was never going to fight for anyone, not even the Light. I heard him screaming my name, but I ignored him.

What a sap.

As I looked up and down the street trying to decide which way to head now, a low-pitched murmuring approached behind me. There was a loud clunk, like an electrical breaker switching off. My skin bristled.

I spun around, and for the first time in my life, I froze. I'd never seen anything like this before. At the end of the block, the street lights were switching off with a clunk, two at a time, one on each side of the street. It created the strange effect of a wall of darkness accelerating towards me.

My stomach seemed to be clenching all of my muscles together into a ball.

Brace yourself, bruv.

I snapped out of my trance and crouched on one knee, protecting my face with my arms.

Oh f—

As the dark wall hit, the groaning wind dragged me backwards for a moment.

And then, nothing.

'Hello, James.' A woman's soft voice rang out behind me. She had an American accent. 'I've been wanting to meet you for a while.'

I turned around. I noticed her fine, straight blond hair first. It fluttered on her shoulders against the darkness and her black suit. I tried not to step backwards. You never wanted to be too obvious with girls like her.

She smiled with smooth, scarlet lips that glinted in the unseen light of that place. What was it the master had called it? The Dark.

'Not what you were expecting?' Her hips swayed unnecessarily as she walked towards me. She must've been doing that deliberately, but my God.

I struggled for an effective comeback. 'No, but then I wasn't expecting anything at that moment. Except maybe a long walk home.'

'You should always expect something.'

'Well, it's a pleasant surprise, anyway.'

'Really? What makes you so sure?'

Something caught my eye, a glint of metal from an unseen light. She dragged my gaze back with her bright blue eyes. I found myself staring at her neck, imagining her wondrous pale skin in my mouth, and I felt any morsel of resistance leave me. If she asked me to get on my knees, I'd do it and pray that it wouldn't hurt.

'This?' she said with a laugh, holding up the sword in her perfectly manicured hand. 'This isn't for you, so calm yourself.'

Black fingernail polish, my favourite.

'I notice I don't have one,' I replied defiantly.

There was a glint in her eye as if to say 'so what?'

'Not exactly fair,' I continued.

'Whoever said this was fair?'

I chuckled. Hard to argue with that.

'We always carry a sword into a first meeting. Sometimes we make a mistake, and you guys get violent. But I can tell you're okay.'

'Who are you?'

'I'm Sophie, and I'm here to ask you to join us.'

I raised an eyebrow.

'We are the Dark . . .' she continued.

'. . . Join us, if you dare,' we finished in unison.

'So you do remember, James.' She laughed.

'How could I forget? You've been with me my whole life.'

'I take it that you're on board, then?'

'How can you be so sure?'

'We've been watching you for some time. You know, you've really impressed us.'

I had to keep calm. Not give anything away. 'I have that effect on people.'

'I'm sure you do.'

'So why should I turn dark? What's in it for me?'

She fixed me with an unwavering gaze. I was transfixed by her lips. For a moment, I imagined what she might do with them.

Focus, James.

'Focus, James,' she ordered, snapping her fingers in front of my face.

Whoa. Had she read my mind? A pang of anxiety shot from my stomach into my balls.

'Really? What's in it for you?' she asked incredulously.

I held her stare as best as I could.

'Why did you kill those guys, James?' She sounded so relaxed.

I felt my face start to burn. 'What guys?'

'James, please. You remember, with your brother. No one's judging you. We're all as dirty as each other here.'

I'll bet. 'I don't really know.'

'I know. The same reason I kill people.'

She seemed so fragile—how could she possibly be a killer?

'Because we enjoy it.'

How the hell—

'How the hell did I know that?' This girl was scary. Then her tone changed. 'You've been one of us for as long as you can remember, haven't you?'

Her words hung in the tense air.

'Yes, I have.' In that moment, I felt I'd given myself to them. I'd given myself to her.

'Welcome to the Dark, James.' She smiled. 'We'll be in touch soon.'

The darkness turned grey, and objects began to emerge from behind a dusky silk sheet. Everything looked so familiar. Then I realized it was my own apartment fading into view as the sheet melted away like tissue paper in water. Somehow I was back home. Weird. I'd known about the Dark Corridor, but I didn't know they could transport like that. I thought it was business only.

Unless I was business.

'I know you're still listening,' I said to no one. 'Just one thing you need to do for me.'

I went to the sink and poured myself a glass of water. I drained it in one gulp.

'Call me Turner.'

The reply whispered in my ear so closely that it sent a tingle down my spine. It wasn't her voice; this was the same voice I'd heard calling to me as a kid.

Welcome to the Dark, Turner.

Chapter 26

Richard

The idea of spending his first Christmas Day back from Cambridge alone seemed ludicrous. Watching films on paid TV had spooked him to leave the house, to try and find something familiar to latch on to, anything to relieve the anxiety—and here he was at the gym. The building was cold inside, dead cold. The heating and lighting were off; everything was off, and no one was there. The gym's soul had escaped to brighter places. Had the Light Master abandoned it? Had he been discovered? Had people in pillowcases and torches come, as he'd said they would?

A stabbing pain in Richard's heart told him that the Light Master was never coming back.

He needed to think, to absorb this. He sat down in the centre of the mat and closed his eyes. Fi's face came to him, bringing a smile as he imagined her giggling at his lame jokes. They'd had a wonderful, unusually warm summer together. They'd seen each other almost every day, walking hand in hand along the Victoria Embankment, eating strawberry cheesecake ice cream—her favourite, and his. They lay on blankets in St James's

Park, and Richard tried to read *Cloud Atlas* whilst Fi interrogated him with quizzes from the latest *Bliss* magazine. They fed the squirrels peanuts and chunks of sandwich bread from their picnics, until the geese invariably launched a slow, silent invasion upon them. They talked about their plans for life, their distant careers, and their inevitable future together. They nuzzled, kissed, and held each other under cloudless blue skies. These moments were always followed by long, intimate afternoons, nights, and sometimes mornings.

When Richard visited Fi's home in a small village on the outskirts of London, her father initially offered a frosty reception, but he warmed up during one Sunday barbeque. Something Richard said seemed to change everything in an instant. He even insisted on being called Dad when he heard about Mr Turner's disappearance.

It was the most carefree and happy Richard'd ever been. He put the Light–Dark battle behind him and relaxed into this mundane life. James and the master had been wrong; Fi never asked even one question about his training after that first day. It was all he'd ever wanted; he was, finally, no longer a hero. What a wonderful world to live in.

But then Richard left for Cambridge and Fi for Bournemouth. They emailed and video-called each other every day for the first month or so. But slowly, the emails and calls became less and less frequent, until one week Fi stopped responding altogether. Richard had longed for her, but he'd eventually drawn back to his studies and the pain had eased, though it never completely ceased.

He opened his eyes. 'Golden Slumbers' by the Beatles floated in through a broken window, along with cold air that made him shiver and breathe out thick dragon's breath. He forced himself to his feet as if he were an old man. *I'll never find my way home. I am truly lost.*

The lights went out. Had they been on to begin with? Everything was black. Bees buzzed everywhere inside his head, swarming around Dad's disembodied face.

It's okay, son. Facing your demons is always hard.

And then Richard was back in the gym.

His pocket pulsated, and he pulled out his phone. 'Tom! You back in town?'

'Sure am. Beer?'

'Definitely.'

He slipped the phone back into his pocket.

Thanks, Dad. You're right, I will find my way home. Just not today.

He left the broken gym behind.

He thought about Fi many times over the ensuing years, about what might've happened if he'd done one thing or another differently.

Years later, he heard through the school grapevine that she'd moved back to her village after university and got back together with Bran. They settled in together at Fi's family home after her parents moved to California for their retirement, and they had two children, a boy and a girl. Richard hoped with all his heart that the two of them loved each other deeply and that she was truly happy with her life, because he loved her.

He never saw Fi again.

Chapter 27

Hero

Hero sat in Senate House amongst rows of mortar-board-wearing students like rows of penguins between their doting families. All except him.

I wish Dad could be here to see me. Or Mum. Or James.

Everyone chatted at a respectful volume as they waited for the graduation ceremony to start. He thought back to his first year here, when everyone had called him Richard. It'd been bliss. He grinned and looked around to see if he could spot any of his colleagues in the audience. But everything had changed in the middle of his second year. He'd been invited to make a speech for one of the equal rights councils and drew a standing ovation for 'The Future of Humanity'. Afterwards, he was on everyone's radar. It dawned on them that he was sitting on almost all of the councils. He'd stepped out of the shadows, and they had noticed his ability to inspire people to put aside their differences and unite behind the greater good, to do the right thing.

And then someone called him 'a total hero' during a jocular moment. His objection to the title had only made it spread faster.

He was once again Hero.

The low-level hum of whispers faded, and everyone stood up as the Esquire Bedells arrived, followed by the Vice-Chancellor, walking in procession towards the dais. The dull sound of bums impacting seats filled the hall as the audience sat back down. The university officers remained standing whilst the Proctors marched onto the stage. The Senior Proctor made a short speech welcoming everyone and then pronounced a couple of Graces, pausing between each.

'*Placet*,' replied the Junior Proctor, indicating that all was in order.

The Senior Proctor stepped forward to begin proceedings. '*Supplicant reverentiis vestris viri mulieresque quorum nomina juxta senaculum in porticu proposuit hodie Registrarius nec delevit Procancellarius ut gradum quisque quem rite petivit assequantur.*'

Hero scratched his nose impatiently. *Bloody Latin.*

'*Placet*,' the Junior Proctor said again.

Hero shifted in his seat and inhaled deeply. Then one of the Bedells led the Vice-Chancellor to the chair at the front of the platform. One by one, the students were called to the stage to receive their degrees. The parents of each student on stage clapped a little louder and more enthusiastically than the last.

The knot dropped in to see Hero as he lined up at the side. He walked onto the platform. The Praelector took his right hand and announced, 'Richard Turner.'

Hero stepped forward and knelt before the Vice-Chancellor.

The Praelector continued, '*Auctoritate mihi commissa*

admitto te ad gradum Economics and Computer Science.'

The modern subject sounded strange amongst the ancient language.

'*In nomine Patris et Filii et Spiritus Sancti.*'

The audience clapped, and his friends cheered loudly, but there was no enthusiastic familial support for him. The knot melted into a sagging pool of sadness hanging from his gut. He arose, bowed to the Vice-Chancellor, and descended the steps on the far side, exiting through the doctors' door to receive his degree.

It's been a hard three years, harder than anything I've ever done. Harder than even—

He still couldn't bring himself to think about the cause of all his troubles. The reason he couldn't connect with anyone, the reason he kept people at a distance and hid himself in plain sight. The reason the smell of bacon still made him gag.

There was silence on the stage for a moment. There were no more candidates. One of the Esquire Bedells called the congregation to order: '*Magistri.*'

Everyone stood. The Vice-Chancellor called an end to the ceremony: '*Nos dissolvimus hanc congregationem.*'

The procession of Esquire Bedells, the Vice-Chancellor, the Registrary, the Proctors, and the University Marshal left the House.

A jubilant hum of happiness fluttered in the air as the audience stood up and made their way outside. Unsure what to do, Hero ambled idly on the front steps. All of his friends were in small groups with their families, mums tidying collars and pulling little bits of fluff from the graduation costumes, dads proudly congratulating their sons and daughters.

Another four hours before the ball starts. What the hell am I gonna do? Guess I'll find a restaurant in Cambridge and eat, drink, and be merry on my own. Better go back to the hotel and change first. I don't want to look like a complete berk.

'Hey, Hero.'

He started from his thoughts. It was Eddie.

'Where're your folks?'

'I don't have any,' Hero replied as more of his friends drifted over with their parents in tow.

'I never knew that,' said Lucy, a pretty Asian girl with shiny black hair. 'Why didn't you tell us?'

'You never asked.'

'Oh mate, I'm really sorry,' Eddie said. 'All this time, we never knew.'

'It's fine. Don't worry about it.'

'What happened? With your family, I mean?'

'Well, my mum left when I was very young, about twelve. My dad disappeared one day, he said he'd return but never did. Then a few years ago, my brother and I had a big argument, and I haven't seen him since. You know, when I say it out loud, it sounds ridiculous, doesn't it?'

'It doesn't sound ridiculous at all,' Lucy said in almost a whisper. 'In fact, I think I speak for us all when I say it's the saddest thing we've ever heard. What're you doing later?'

He lifted his chin. 'I'm going to the ball. And you?'

'Yeah, we're all going to the ball—but first, we've got the graduation lunch. Aren't you coming?'

'I thought about it, but I didn't really want to be sitting on my own.' He smiled ruefully.

'You're joining us, that's what's happening,' Eddie said. 'That's okay, isn't it, Mum and Dad?'

'Sure.' They nodded in unison.

The world blurred as tears welled in his eyes.

'Hero.' Lucy put her hand tentatively on his shoulder.

'It's . . . it's this year.' He sniffed loudly. 'It's been so hard, and I've had nobody . . . to go to in the holidays . . . I'm so alone.' He dabbed at his eyes. 'And you guys, that's the nicest thing anyone's ever done for me.'

Lucy wrapped her arms around him and hugged him tightly.

Eddie threw an arm around Hero's shoulders too. 'What are you talking about? It's been a hard year, Mr First-Class Honours Guy.'

Shit, I've been too good. They've noticed. 'Sorry, I'm being a complete sap.'

'Don't be silly, you're not being a sap.' Lucy linked her arm with his.

'Come on, mate, let's go and eat,' Eddie said. 'I'm starving.'

As they entered the immense marquee for the lunch, they passed a gleaming Steinway & Sons grand piano. Hero found himself drawn to it as the needle of a compass is drawn to point north. He ran his fingers over the polished ebony surface and drew the tips over each of the curves, as if caressing a naked woman. The minor-key melody of 'Fi's song' rolled through his mind. The cool ivory of the keys against his skin gave him goosebumps, as well as unwelcome memories that threatened his fresh composure: playing with James.

His soul folded in on itself, drawing the air out of his lungs. After James left, every piano reminded Hero of their good times together and how much he missed his brother.

Lucy drew near. 'Are you okay?'

'I used to play piano all the time,' he lamented.

'Really? I'd love to hear you. Would you play for me now? Musicians are very sexy, you know.'

He smiled distractedly, his fingers drawn again to the keys. He yearned to make them dance and sing for him.

'I can't,' he said, pulling back.

'Why not? Please?' she begged.

'I just can't. The last time I played, it was with my brother, before he—' He drew a deep breath. 'I miss him.'

'Oh, I'm so sorry, I didn't mean to . . .' She caressed his arm maternally.

He ripped himself away from the magnetic field of the piano. 'It's okay, you didn't know. Let's get back.'

The rest of the lunch passed merrily, with the graduates chattering about their three years studying together and their plans for the future. Many of them had received offers to work in the City. Hero had already signed a contract with a company called BloomBox, a financial media firm. Others had decided to take a year to travel the world 'whilst they were still young,' and a few others were going on to a PhD.

At the end of the lunch, the friends temporarily disbanded. Hero went back to the hotel to get ready for the graduation ball that night.

Beautiful ball gowns whirled like dervishes of gold, white, and black, connected to tall, handsome penguins as if their shoes were tied together.

'You know, you look really good in a tuxedo,' Lucy cooed. She stroked Hero's jacket with her palm. 'I love these silk lapels. So smooth.'

'Everyone looks good in a tux,' he countered.

'You look better.' She grinned, her perfectly straight white teeth blending with her pale skin, which always appeared to have a purple tinge.

'Thanks. I love your dress. Did you have it made?'

'Yes, back in Hong Kong.'

'Of course. Kowloon?'

'How did you know?'

He smiled. 'I didn't. That's the only district I know.'

She blinked a couple of times as if clearing her vision.

What's she looking at?

'So?' she said expectantly.

He returned her gaze with a squint of confusion.

Her purple tinge deepened. 'Are you going to ask me to dance?'

'Oh.'

How did you miss that? Berk. 'It would be my pleasure.'

He bowed theatrically and held out his hand, palm up. She took it in her glove.

'I see what you mean about silk,' he said.

They joined the synchronised couples in the waltz that was just starting.

'You're a good dancer,' she whispered as they twirled in three-four time.

'Only because you make a good partner.'

She sighed. 'I wish I was.'

The band swung brightly into the next song, and Hero leaned forward. 'Sorry?'

'Oh hell, this is my last chance.' She stood up on tip-toes and pressed her lips against his. She moaned against his lips.

'Last chance'—that's exactly what Fi had said. He pulled her closer.

She pulled her face a few inches back. 'Mmm, you're very a good kisser.'

He glanced over her shoulder. A man who'd apparently eaten one too many Mars bars was glaring at them—was that Martin? *I'd almost forgotten about that guy. Tit.* Sometimes, long ago during training, he'd imagine bumping into the little bully again, and the candle flame itch would flicker.

He whipped back to Lucy with what he hoped was a confident swagger. Her eyes were welcoming pools that invited everything. He smiled grimly. *I can't do this, I can't do this again. I got lucky with Fi—she understood me from the moment we met. How am I gonna get out of this?*

He could feel Martin's eyes boring into his back. It wouldn't be so hard to hand her off, really. Could he play that card?

Sap.

They danced slowly, noses caressing, lips so close that they could feel each other's breath, until the music stopped. He cradled her in his arms; she sighed.

'I don't want to let you go,' he whispered.

212

'Then don't.'

'But I need the toilet.'

'Oh, okay.'

'I'll be right back.'

He studied her face for a few seconds. *These are the moments to remember.*

He smiled and walked towards the bathroom, but he went right past it, out into the dark night. The sounds of the party faded behind him. *Don't look back.* The loneliness grew even as he quickened his pace. *There's nothing there. No monsters under the bed.*

His heart accelerated to match his pace as a strange sense of being followed dawned. *Don't look back.* His skin prickled against his stiff dress shirt. *Oh, sod it.*

He spun around. Nothing.

He wheezed slightly, his heart still pounding, his skin still bristling. *But there is something there.* Stepping forward with trepidation, he peered into the shadows, waiting for his eyes to adjust, hoping to glimpse what it was.

He called out into the night. 'It's okay, I won't hurt you. You can come out.'

An overwhelming sense of familiarity washed over him.

'James?'

Nothing. Shadows upon shadows.

He glanced back at the ball, now silent with distance, and smiled ruefully. *Goodbye, my friends.* He resumed his solitary midnight journey.

This time, he did not look back.

Chapter 28

Turner

I watched Hero as he danced with her, that petite Asian girl. He couldn't see me, of course—no one could. But then that was always my trick.

He didn't seem to have made any effort with her. *Learned some new tricks, bruv. Good on you.* He appeared almost surprised to be dancing with her. There was a guy watching the two of them intently. I'd seen that look before: Bran. This could be interesting. There might be an opportunity here.

Then he strode out of the venue and away from the ball. I followed. *What're you doing? Get back in there, bruv.*

He never looked back, but he was twitching. Nervous. What was he up to? He stopped and looked right at me. Had he detected me? He edged closer, one small step after another. He must've been only two metres from me, but he didn't seem afraid. Did he know I was here? Could he sense it was me?

'James?' he called.

Interesting. I slipped back into the darkness to hide myself from him.

Perhaps I'd found his weakness at long last.

Chapter 29

Hero

'Welcome to Saxon Goldberg, Mr . . . Turner.' The smartly dressed HR rep was squinting at Hero's recently printed ID badge.

'Good morning and thanks.'

She smiled. 'Please, help yourself to coffee.'

'And biscuits, I hope?'

'Of course. The induction will start in ten minutes.' She turned. 'Welcome to Saxon Goldberg, Mr . . .'

Her voice melted into the soup of nervous chat from the other new entrants. Hero ambled towards the coffee and biscuits. The smell of coffee always reminded him of Dad.

Best not get emotional right now.

He helped himself to a cup of coffee and a chocolate digestive biscuit.

'Hi, I'm Steve.'

A short, plump, slightly balding man to his right was helping himself to four biscuits.

'Richard.' He held out his palm.

'Where were you before here?' Steve asked as they shook hands.

'BloomBox. I joined there straight out of uni.' Five long years at BloomBox. He and Tom had had some raucous whisky- and beer-filled times until Tom'd accepted a job in Japan. It made sense—Hero had teased Tom about how he only liked Asian women, which he always vehemently denied, of course. Good ol' Tom. *Come back soon, mate.*

'Good firm, but hard to work for, I heard. Is it true you only get twenty days' holiday there?' Steve asked.

Hero grinned. 'I didn't find it that hard, but you're right about the twenty days. It's gonna seem like school holidays again coming here.'

'Which uni did you go to?'

'Cambridge, and you?'

'Oxford. I can tell that we're going to be mortal enemies already.'

'Well, it'd be rude not to be. What did you study?'

'Computer science. You?'

'The same, although I also did economics. Is this your first firm, then?'

Steve shook his head. 'I was at Morton Associates for five years, decided it was time for a new challenge, and heard this is where the best of the best come.' He smiled as if to add 'although we both know that isn't true.'

'Okay, everyone, please make your way to the main seminar room and take a seat,' called one of the HR reps. 'We're about to start.'

Hero and Steve joined a slow-moving line of smartly dressed people shuffling into a large amphitheatre, where a projection screen on stage was already showing the first slides of the morning. The rhythmic movement of the line brought back images of a music video Hero had seen when he was a teenager, something about masks. Then it struck him: Pink Floyd's 'The Wall'.

It was as if everyone there were wearing a mask, but not like the pig masks in the video. It was the eyes—he'd seen the look before in James, when they were younger and James had saved him from those bullies. The whites of his eyes had disappeared, and for a moment, he'd looked like a monster.

A small shiver snaked down Hero's back.

He sat next to Steve about halfway back and looked over the itinerary whilst the last few people filtered in and found seats. The induction proceeded much as expected, beginning with an introduction to Saxon Goldberg and praising the new employees for the wise choice they'd made. This was followed by introductions to HR and compliance, contact numbers and procedures, and a one-hour session on sexual harassment.

Next, they got a virtual look at the subsidised gym, recently refurbished. Numerous photos showed changing rooms decked out with mahogany lockers, granite flooring, and sturdy benches. There were banks of running mills, cycling and rowing machines, and a myriad of equipment for weightlifting. And as if that wasn't lavish enough, there was even a twenty-five-metre pool.

Hero stretched and rubbed his palms against his thighs with anticipation. *I'll definitely be signing up for that. It's breathtaking, much nicer than the—*

Got to look good for the girls, bruv, he heard James say in his mind. James wouldn't have lasted two minutes in this place without provoking a sexual harassment case.

The last two sessions of the day seemed a little odd. The first covered the culture of Saxon Goldberg. They explained how most people who joined the firm found it difficult to adjust, but if you could hang in there, you eventually would.

How strange. I didn't need cultural training for BloomBox—or Cambridge, for that matter. Surely if people have difficulty adjusting to your culture, doesn't that mean your culture needs to change? Unless the assumption is that their culture's the best in the world. What kind of people would think that?

Finally, a speaker arrived to talk about reputation—specifically, that of the bank. 'Whenever you write an email or leave a voice message, imagine how it would look on the front page of a newspaper.'

Why on earth would that be a problem if you're doing the right thing? Unless you're not. Unless you're the Da—

He forced his thoughts back to the session, which was concluding to a round of applause. The new employees were directed back to the coffee area behind them.

Hero leaned close to Steve as they shuffled forward. 'I don't understand that last thing. Why would you need to think about what you're writing in an email? Surely if you're always above board, then there wouldn't be an issue?'

Steve smiled curiously. 'You've never worked in an investment bank before, have you?'

He shook his head.

'Well, don't worry about it. You'll get there. Everybody does, like lambs to the slaughter.'

In the coffee area, they joined queues in front of a desk staffed by HR reps. They only waited about two minutes, such was the efficiency of the operation.

'Name?'

'Richard Turner.'

'Turner . . . Turner . . . Ah yes, report to the third floor. Someone will be waiting for you there.'

'Thanks.'

He walked towards the lift.

'Hey, Richard,' Steve shouted after him.

He glanced back.

'Stay in touch on email. Surname's Johnson.'

'Will do.' Hero waved.

He crammed himself into the lift with as many other passengers as would fit, forced his hand to the side, and pressed the button marked three. The doors closed. His stomach lurched as the lift began to descend to the next stage of his life.

Chapter 30

Hero

'Get your hand off my arse,' said one of the passengers behind Hero in the elevator.

The lift fluttered with nervous giggles.

'That'd better be a gun in your pocket, mate,' fired back one of the girls.

The lift erupted with laughter.

This is brutal.

The elevator stopped at every floor as they descended. At each stop, the door opened and a few people got out. By the time the number three came up on the display panel, Hero was the only one left.

The doors opened, and he stepped out. The lobby was deathly silent. Hero's stomach tensed. *Not felt that in a while.*

'Mr Turner?' asked a young, curly-haired woman.

'Yes.'

'We've been expecting you. Please, follow me.' She took out her ID card. 'Got one of these?'

'Yep, right here,' he said, holding up the one around his neck.

'Try swiping in on the pad over there.' She pointed at a card reader to the side of a set of opaque glass double doors. 'Let's just check it works.'

He did as he was asked, and the doors unlocked with a clunk. As she pushed one of them open, they were hit by a wall of sound. Before him was a huge open-plan office with row after row of people looking at screens flickering with numbers and charts. People were shouting information to each other, asking and answering questions, calling prices across rows or the entire floor. Wherever a pillar held up the ceiling, screens clustered around them showed various channels of BloomBox TV reporting on one of the world's markets.

Christ.

'Welcome to the trading floor,' his escort shouted over the din. 'It takes a bit of getting used to, doesn't it?'

She grinned.

'I'm glad it's not just me,' he roared. 'For a minute, I thought I was going deaf.'

They rounded a corner, and the noise dimmed slightly.

'And here we are,' she said. 'This is your manager, Justine Honce.'

What? He hid his amusement under an aggressively friendly smile.

'Heeey, Richard, great to see you finally,' she said, standing up from her desk, upon which sat a small Louis Vuitton bag. Her eyes were oddly dark and narrow, out of sorts with her long blond hair. *Textured, as Toni and Guy might say.*

He swallowed the laugh forming in his belly. 'Great to be here finally.'

'Come on, I'll show you to your desk. Then let's meet the team.'

Impressively efficient.

His desk wasn't much to behold. It was exactly the same as the desk at his previous office: three screens, a keyboard, a mouse, an office desk, and a pedestal, all in bureaucratic grey. *Scientists at office manufacturers have discovered the most boring colour possible, the one that sucks out your soul as you look at it. And that's the colour they use for furniture.*

As Hero met the various teams in the office, he had the strange feeling he was at a Disneyland resort. Everyone and everything were brick-for-brick perfect copies, a perfection that gave them away as fake. 'The Wall' echoed in his mind for the second time that day.

Only two people looked as if they weren't wearing masks but rather showing their true selves. The first was a beefy, barrel- shaped man who carried himself like a wrestler.

'This is Frank Bosch, head of sales trading,' Justine said. 'You'll likely be working closely with him.'

'Nice to meet you,' he said in a broad New York accent.

Here's a man who likes his steaks. 'Likewise.'

'Call me Bosch.'

She pointed to the man standing next to Bosch. He was tall and imposing—well built too, his shoulders wider than his hips.

'And this is Samir Blagg. You won't work directly with him, but you may need to provide him with information from time to time.'

'Information'? Sounds ominous.

'Hi, Richard.' He held out his hand. 'Just call me Sam.'

'Hi, Sam.'

'I heard what you did over at BloomBox. Impressive.'

'Thanks.'

'Does it really work off the Fibonacci sequence?' Sam asked.

'Yes and no. You have to combine it with—'

Bosch held up a hand. 'Does it make money?'

'Should,' Hero replied.

'Good, 'cos our bonuses depend on you—so no slackin' off.'

Justine stepped in. 'Okay, Bosch, thanks for the pep talk.' She turned to Hero. 'Right, so here's your desk. We've put some reading material there to get you up to speed.'

Hero sat down in his executive office chair and began the bizarre ritual of trying to keep his eyes open whilst reading reams of in-depth procedural documents. *I'm going to need matchsticks for my eyes.*

'Hey, Hero.' A disembodied voice floated above the back- ground din.

He peered over the top of the document he was reading. It was Bosch, looking directly at him.

'Yeah, I'm talking to you.'

'It's Richard, actually,' he replied, setting the papers on the desk and standing up.

'Really? I have a friend over at BloomBox who says your name's Hero.'

His neck burned at the delight in Bosch's eyes. He could see how this was going to pan out—the same way it had all those other times. *No point in fighting it.* He sat back down and picked up his document; as he did, he noticed that everybody had frozen.

He spun around—there was Sam Blagg with a hand outstretched towards him. He instinctively brought up his arm to block.

'Wow, fast reactions.' Sam staggered backwards.

He forced a smile. 'If you say so.'

'I do. I used to box quite seriously. That was quick.' He regarded Hero suspiciously. 'Anyway, just wanted to say ignore Bosch. He's always like that.'

'I'll take it under advisement. How seriously did you box?'

'I used to train with Team GB. I nearly went to the Olympics.'

'Wow, that's really good.'

'Thanks. Fancy sparring some time?'

Hero chuckled. 'No thanks, mate.'

'Come on—you'd be great with reactions like that. How did you get that fast, anyway?'

'I used to do martial arts when I was a kid, but I don't fight anymore. So no thanks.'

His eye was drawn away from Sam towards a corner of the room. It was nothing more than empty space, really, but there was something odd about it. The shadows appeared to be darker there than anywhere else on the floor. People rushed about their business without paying any attention to it.

Below the raucous noise of the trading floor, he heard a quiet voice: *Welcome to the real world, Hero.*

He looked around, but there was no one there.

The first two weeks in the office had passed without incident. Hero glanced at his digital watch: 15:42. He stretched. *I'm going snow-blind. I need a coffee.*

'Hey, Sam,' he called. 'Wanna grab a coffee?'

'Not right now, mate.'

He got up and began walking towards the kitchen. *Coffee, coffee, coffee . . .*

'Hi, I'm Catherine. You're new here, right?' said an American voice to his right.

A young woman in her twenties offered her hand. He obliged with a handshake.

Her eyes. What colour are they? Hazel? They're yellow, almost orange. They're so warm. Beautiful. Innocent.

'I joined a couple of weeks ago. I'm Richard.'

She pulled backwards slightly, surprised.

'What?' he asked.

'Oh, it's nothing. I thought your name was Hero.' She giggled, causing her chestnut hair to flutter in waves all the way down to the bottom of her back.

'Bloody Frank Bosch—I hate that guy.'

'I think it's quite cute.'

The warmth of her eyes relaxed him. The redness under his cheeks faded. 'That's something, I guess,' he said with a smile.

'Hey, Hero, are you going to do any work today?' Bosch bellowed from a couple of rows away. 'Haven't you got to save the world or something?'

A ripple of laughter broke out around the office.

'Bugger off, Bosch.' Hero turned back to Catherine.

'I'd better get back to work—but first, coffee. Want one?'

'No, sorry, I don't drink it.'

'You can drink tea if you like. That's also legal, if perhaps a bit immoral.'

'What?'

Swing and a miss. 'Sorry, it's something my dad used to say. He wasn't much of a tea drinker.'

'Right.' She forced a smile.

'Well, maybe I'll see you later.'

'I hope so.'

This time, her smile was completely natural.

Chapter 31

Turner

Once I'd made the Decision, I knew I needed to leave my old life behind and go somewhere no one could find me. It was much easier than I'd expected. I simply hid in plain sight. I moved out of my old apartment and into a gleaming new duplex penthouse near to Wapping Docks. So close. The Light Master would never look there.

I soon felt at home in my new address and often strolled through the deserted city by night. That evening, I was standing on the bridge near Tobacco Dock in the moonlight overlooking the canal. The old clipper ship loomed forebodingly in the darkness, and the water twinkled like liquid silver as a gentle breeze rippled the surface. An elderly man was walking his dog along the pavement at the side, ambling comfortably as his pet ran around sniffing various walls and posts.

Three youths burst from under the bridge and pushed the old man backwards.

'Give us your money,' the leader demanded.

The man seemed dazed, confused by the words.

This should be interesting.

The three youngsters each pulled out kitchen knives, the kind used for cutting up vegetables. They aimed the blades at the man's neck, waggling them up and down.

'Last chance, old man. Give us your money. Now.'

There was just enough light on his face for me to make out the terror in his eyes, so wide they reminded me of two cherry-topped pies.

He patted himself down, distractedly searching for his wallet. He found it in his inside pocket and tried to pull it out, but in his panic, it became stuck. He tugged more urgently until it burst free.

'And your watch.'

The old man dutifully took it off and handed it over.

The leader stuffed the items in his pockets, lurched forward, and plunged the knife into his victim's chest. The old man's expression changed from terror to surprise, as if he couldn't believe that he now had four inches of metal buried within him.

'Come on, stick 'im,' the aggressor cried.

His two friends took turns burying their blades into the man's flesh until he fell to his knees and toppled like a giant, proud oak.

When the leader turned and noticed me, he nudged his mates with his elbow. They regarded me with the predatory eyes of young sharks, dead and unfeeling. Animals. Then they walked calmly away, back under the bridge.

The old guy coughed and spluttered. An expanding pool of claret blood dripped over the quay edge into the canal. Nothing could save him now, poor dog. Perhaps in the next place, he would find a better home.

I continued on my way. My penthouse apartment was in one of the new builds nearby.

Not twenty metres along, I saw them loitering in the shadows. I couldn't see their faces, but I knew it was the same three. They walked into the light of the street lamps and stood in my path.

'Evening, lads,' I said nonchalantly.

'You got the time, mate?' he asked.

'No, sorry.'

'You're wearing a watch.' He pointed to my wrist.

'So are you,' I replied with a smirk.

'Give me your watch,' he ordered.

'I don't think so.'

He pulled out his knife. It still had dark red streaks on it. 'Give me your watch.'

An effort to be more sinister? As if that were necessary when you had a knife in your hand.

'You wanna be careful what you do with that thing.' I pointed at his knife hand. 'It looks like you've cut yourself.'

'That's not my blood—but it could be yours,' he sneered with a psychotic smile.

The coldness emanating from my soul made me feel as distant as if I were having an out-of-body experience. I wondered what it must be like to be a normal person in a situation like this, to feel genuinely scared—no, terrified—for your life.

'You know,' I said lightly, 'I'm feeling charitable tonight, so I'll give you five seconds to piss off, kid. After that, it will be your blood.'

He lunged for me, but I'd already dilated time and idly stepped to one side.

'One,' I reminded him.

He took a sideways swipe. I ducked. 'Two . . .'

He swiped and lunged. I coolly avoided the lethal blade.

'Three . . . four . . . five . . .'

He thrust towards my eyes. I grabbed his wrist and twisted until I felt a satisfying snap. He squealed. His grip on the knife released, and I relieved him of the burden of his weapon, then kicked his ankle. The loud *crack* startled his accomplices and a gaggle of geese that squawked their way into the night sky. He fell to his knees.

I moved on to his accomplices. I sliced the wrist of the first one and then, in a single sweeping movement, carved his nose clean off. It flew through the air like a tiny, wingless bird. I spent no time at all on the third, simply severing the carotid artery with a single slice. Blood arced gloriously into the air. Time dilation always makes that look so beautiful, like some horrific piece of art at the Tate Modern.

Having dispatched his comrades, I returned to their leader as he was attempting to crawl away on his knees.

'Hello again,' I whispered into his ear.

'Please,' he murmured.

'What?'

'Please don't kill me.'

'You beg me for mercy?' I brought the knife up towards his eye.

'Please let me go.'

'But you didn't show that old guy any mercy.'

His cornea popped as I slid the knife slowly into his

eye. He jerked violently as the knife reached into his brain, then collapsed in a lifeless heap. A heap of steaming shit.

And then a voice was shouting inside my mind, so real I might have sworn I could hear it outside my ears—most disturbing, because it sounded like me: 'Do you have any idea what you're asking me to do?'

Chapter 32

Turner

Back home, I poured myself a big glass of whisky and turned on the TV, then settled in the lounge downstairs to watch the Japanese market open report on BloomBox. I hadn't relaxed for more than a minute or so when I became aware that one corner of the room was becoming darker. It grew progressively gloomier until it was virtually sable. I watched with suspicion, at the ready, always ready to fight when in the company of wolves.

Blond on black. Everything about her was striking. She was like lightning; she woke you from your daydream, brought you to attention with a snap.

'Come with me,' Sophie beckoned. 'Come.'

I got up and went over to the darkened corner. The shadows extended around me, and my apartment faded until I stood in the umbra, with Sophie next to me.

'We call this the Dark Corridor.'

A new room came into view, and we walked forward until we were standing in another luxurious penthouse. I glanced out of the window and saw a line of yellow taxis.

'Where are we?'

'New York.'

'How?'

A regal English accent rang out behind me. 'The Dark Corridor can take you wherever we need you.'

I turned around. The man in the corner was in his fifties, distinguished and cold. He wore the seemingly obligatory black suit, but in contrast to Sophie, he had ordinary grey hair.

He stepped towards me. 'Hello, Turner, I've been waiting a long time to meet you.' He smiled, but there was real malice there.

'And you are?'

'The Dark Master.'

I nodded slightly in acknowledgement. 'Ironic. You're an Englishman in New York, and the Light Master is an American living in London.'

'Why is that ironic?'

'Wouldn't it be easier to stay in your home coun—oh, I see.'

'Yes, Turner. As you've now experienced, location is of no importance for us.'

'Most unfair,' I said sardonically.

Sophie and the Dark Master both grinned. He gestured for us to sit on the black leather sofa, striking against the white decor of the place. Very clean lines.

'So.' He settled opposite us in a similar armchair. 'To business. What're we going to do about your brother?'

Why were they so interested in him? It should be me they were talking about, not him. 'What do you mean?'

'He's dangerous to us.'

But Hero was clean. I knew that; they knew that.

Leave the guy alone. I straightened up and shrugged. 'He's out now, isn't he?'

'You know he won't stay out.'

I held his gaze. Of course I knew. My brother was a prick—he didn't want to be in the Light, but he couldn't stay out of it, either. But we couldn't interfere with the Clean; those were the rules.

'He said he doesn't want to kill anymore,' I said levelly. 'He said he's staying clean. We can't touch him till he gets back in.'

'We can touch him. Everyone's touchable.'

Paedo. I sniggered like a schoolboy, and the Dark Master raised his eyebrows quizzically.

'Talking about touching boys,' I said. 'It made me laugh.'

'Right. Well, Turner, this is serious. We're talking about how we're going to kill your brother.'

Whoa. I didn't like my brother, not after he turned his back on me like that, but I didn't want him to die.

'Has that focused your attention?' he asked condescendingly.

'That's breaking the rules. You'll burn if you do that.'

'We have ways around the rules.'

'I thought the rules were unbreakable. Created by God. Or whatever.' I always liked to be sarcastic about God when talking about the Game.

'Very droll, Turner. We have ways.' He sounded grave.

I'd heard that they could do this, even though it's against the rules, but I felt they were underestimating him—and me, for that matter. 'I don't think so.'

'What do you mean?' He crossed his legs and tapped his finger on his mouth.

234

'You say you have ways—but honestly, I don't think you do. If you've been watching him—and I'm sure you have—then you know how fast he is. He's faster than a bullet. He's certainly faster than any of us. So if you're serious about neutralizing his threat, the only way to do that is to hope he stays clean—or, if it doesn't break the rules, to keep him clean ourselves.'

'Hmm.'

I shrugged, feigning nonchalance. 'Your call. Try it. See what happens.'

'And how would you propose to keep him clean?'

'Why are you asking me?'

'Don't try to play me, Turner. How would you keep him clean?'

I breathed out heavily. 'Look, I could only draw on my experience from when we were kids. We'd have to watch him. I doubt we'd need to watch 24/7, possibly not even every day. Anytime he gets near to helping someone, we could step in and avert it.'

The Dark Master looked at Sophie in a way that made me sweat on the inside. I had to sell this; otherwise, I wasn't getting out of there alive.

'Okay, it's a bit more complicated than that,' I added.

'You don't say.'

'I don't want to give all my secrets away, all things considered.'

He laughed, a deep, chesty guffaw. But whilst he was clearly amused, his laugh lacked depth. It lacked soul. The smile faded from his face. 'I'd start, if I were you.'

And so I did. 'The trick is to think several moves, as I call them, ahead.'

'Explain.'

'I can't explain how, but I can see a chain of events triggering each other like dominoes falling.'

'Uh-huh.'

'If you could see how the dominoes were set beforehand, and you could remove one of them at just the right moment, then you could stop Hero from even getting close to helping someone. For example, there used to be a girl at his school who was besotted with him. I got her to look the other way—well, for long enough, anyhow.'

'Good, good.' The master nodded dismissively. 'Turner, I'll let you in on a little secret: what you've just told us is no secret.'

'What?'

'We all know this. We wanted to see if you knew.'

'Oh.' A bead of sweat ran down my forehead. I refused to touch it.

'Don't be embarrassed.' He smiled. 'The fact that we all know what you do doesn't mean we can do it. Some of us can, of course. But you are by far the best we've seen at this, and that's really important to us.'

I smiled weakly.

'So how would you do that for Hero, especially now that you won't be able to talk to him?'

I folded my arms across my chest. 'That does complicate matters, but only slightly. He always ignored my advice, anyway.'

We all laughed.

'I'd do what I did before. Find the important domino and remove it.'

'Good. That's your job, then: keep Hero clean.'

'Oh.'

I really thought he'd assign me something more grandiose like starting a war or something. To be honest, I had no idea what the Dark actually did. Sure, I knew they were selfish, but surely that would make the entire human race Dark—even Hero. Was it really the case that choosing not to save people when you knew you could made you Dark?

The Dark Master rubbed his hands and moved to look out the window at the lights crawling past below. 'Don't worry, Turner, that's not the only thing you'll be doing. You're gonna be a busy boy. We've got big plans for you in London.'

I hoped that they might feel moved to share them at some point. 'And what happens if I fail? To keep him clean, I mean?'

They exchanged a look that sent a shiver down my spine. I'd heard how cruel the Dark were, but I'd never really been afraid. Up until now, no one had ever been close to my skill level, except the Light Master in the early days, and this was a new feeling. I kind of liked it.

'Let's cross that bridge if we come to it,' he said. 'Sophie will look after you and teach you how to use the corridor.'

She nodded silently, reverently. She'd already opened the Dark Corridor; that corner of the room was black. She beckoned for me to follow her.

'Turner?' the master called. His eyes were dark, as if the whites of his eyes had been enveloped by his pupils. 'You don't want to fail us.'

A shadow fell over the room.

Chapter 33

Turner

BloomBox TV was still blaring the latest financial headlines as we stepped into my apartment. Sophie turned
around without warning, catching me off guard, and I
nearly folded myself into her lips. She didn't flinch, her
eyes inches from mine, her nose just millimetres away.
I could feel her heat radiating onto my face. When she
opened her mouth to say something, her breath tingled
against my cheek.

God, you smell good. I felt myself get a little hard
and took a step backwards to avoid embarrassment. I
looked her up and down with elevator eyes. 'I have to
say, you do look good in black.'

She rolled her eyes. 'Really, James? Is that the best
patter you've got? You're gonna be single for a long
time, if it is. You should've gone with how I smell.'

Whoa. I'd forgotten she could read my mind.

'I can't read your mind. You're predictable, that's all.
You're going to need to work on that.' She shrugged.
'Shall we get on?'

'Sure. Coffee, tea . . . whisky?' I grinned and raised an

eyebrow. 'Actually, you're probably more of a Lambrini girl.'

'Just coffee, thanks.'

I poured a couple of cups from the evening's brew, and we sat on the sofa. My heart accelerated in anticipation of what I was about to learn. I wasn't certain if I was excited or afraid. She was inside my head. I had to think what to do, be careful about everything I said.

'The first thing you've gotta realise is that we don't invite everybody to meet the Dark Master,' she said. 'You're in a very elite group.'

'I feel honoured.' I nodded primly.

'This is serious, Turner.'

'I'm sure it is. And I'm still waiting to hear what it is. So either tell me, or stop wasting my time and get out. I've got things to do. The markets are in motion, and I need to earn some money.'

She pulled backwards, blushing imperceptibly. 'Wow, you actually surprised me there. Well done.'

I held her gaze as steadily as I could. *Get out of my head. Let's spend some time in yours.*

She shifted uncomfortably in her seat. 'Have you ever heard of the Illuminati?'

'Oh God, don't tell me that you're the fabled Illuminati? Shall I put on my tinfoil hat?'

She chuckled. 'No, we're not—'

'Oh, good.'

She frowned. 'They work for us.'

Intriguing—but I wasn't giving up so fast. I sighed. 'Tinfoil hat time. So we've been around for at least three hundred years, then?'

'The Light and Dark have been around a hell of a lot longer than that. You see occasional mentions of us in all sorts of ancient texts.'

'So whose side are you on?'

'All sides. We play each side off against the other.'

'You're responsible for the deaths of millions of people?'

She laughed hard. 'So that's where you draw the line, is it? You're fine with inserting a knife into some kid's eye, but this is too much for you?'

'It's just the sheer scale of it.'

She pushed my jaw back up and closed my mouth. 'Welcome to the big leagues, Turner. And whilst we're on the subject, now that you're one of us, you've got to stop with the killings. One of our principal rules is that we operate in complete silence. We don't go around blowing shit up, killing people in broad daylight, all that Hollywood jazz. We get the Clean to do that. So those three kids you killed? You've got to stop that. If you don't, we'll burn you.'

I tried to gather my thoughts. Everything seemed so far away. *Focus. Don't let her get to you.* 'What exactly is it that you do?'

'We make sure that power remains in the right hands.'

'Which is?'

'Ours, obviously.'

'But why?'

'Because people are stupid. They don't know what's good for them.'

'And we do?'

She walked to the window and glanced at the people

below, going about their business in the early hours. The orange glow of the lamps outside made her look unwell. 'Because we can manipulate time, people like us have higher IQs than anyone else by the time we're fifteen years old. We couldn't let the Clean run things. It'd be total mayhem.'

'And the Light? Presumably they disagree?'

'We keep order by permitting them just enough to survive. If we gave them more, it would fall apart very quickly. The Light believe that everyone should be able to choose their own paths. The thought sends a shiver down my spine. Their original goal was to help humanity get to that point, and then the world would be better off without either of us. But as you've seen, they've pretty much given up on that.'

'And that's why you want my brother out of the Game?' Naive Hero. How little he knew.

'He does worry us. He's different. He could've renewed their hope. But so long as he's out, we're fine. Don't underestimate how important that is to us.'

'Don't worry, I won't let you down, o ye of little faith.'

She turned towards me and tilted her head, the way an owner looks at its dog sometimes. 'Oh no, I have complete faith in you. The question is do you?' She paused to look at her watch, a gold Patek Philippe Nautilus. 'I've got to be going soon. Let me show you how the corridor works.'

I stood quickly. I'd been looking forward to this.

'And then we have an assignment for you.'

But I already knew what it was. I'd always known.

Chapter 34

Turner

I peered through the Dark Corridor at the Light Master in his gym. He was sitting in the centre of the mat, legs crossed, surrounded by candles. No doubt his eyes were closed to aid his meditation. Although he wouldn't be able to see me in the darkness, I knew that he would already sense that I was watching him. I'd only been with the Dark a few months, but I'd always known it would be me that faced him, even back when he was still training me.

I took a deep breath. *Here we go.*

The gloom of the Dark Corridor extended into the gym and surrounded the master. The candles flickered and slowly faded to black.

'Welcome back, James.' I couldn't see his face, but it sounded as if he was smiling.

'It's good to be back, master. You know why I'm here.'

'I taught you well,' he affirmed. 'You kept your promise.'

I strode towards him, raising my sword high above my head.

'I won't fight you, James.'

'Then, you will die.' This was way too easy. I brought my sword down to his neck.

At the last second, his sword flashed over his shoulder and blocked my attack. He leapt up and spun in a vortex of wind, holding me at bay.

This was more like it.

I brought my sword back to a defensive position, mirroring him. 'I thought you said that you weren't going to fight me?'

'I lied.'

'Quoting Hollywood B-movies again, are we? Well, I can't say I'm disappointed. I've been looking forward to this for a long time.'

You stupid old bastard.

I feinted to attack. He twitched a defence but wasn't fooled. He lunged towards my heart. I rotated a parry, jumped forward, and landed my elbow to his mouth. Damn, missed his nose. I sliced his chest and arm as I pulled away. He staggered backwards and smiled, teeth stained with blood. His white suit now included a red sash.

'Give it up, old man, and drop your weapon. I can make this painless.'

He raised one eyebrow.

'Well, almost.' I smiled. 'It's your call. But I'll slice you up piece by piece if I have to.'

He brought his fingers to his mouth, scooped up some of the blood, then licked it. 'Mmm, delicious.' His expression would've made Ted Bundy proud.

My nerves twinged with a kick of adrenaline. I grinned in response, then clenched my teeth. Our swords ferociously clattered again and again, sparks flying out in all directions, reminiscent of a Victorian foundry. We were snarling at each other like rabid animals, foaming at our mouths.

His defence dropped just an inch. This was it—my opening. I reversed the sword and swiped towards his neck. He ducked and sliced across my leg. A trick.

'You've still got a lot to learn, young man.'

'Enjoy it while it lasts.'

I reached down with my free hand to inspect the wound. Seizing the opportunity, he swung his sword high and brought it down like a sledgehammer. I countered to the throat. He reversed his attack to parry. I dipped my shoulder into his ribs and barged under his arm. Staggering backwards, he swivelled his sword in a protective arc across his body to mirror my position.

'Good move,' he said through a cough. Blood trickled down the side of his mouth. 'You've learned a few new tricks, James.'

I must've broken his rib. Good. 'No, you're just past it, old man.'

He chuckled and beckoned me with his free hand.

But I didn't approach; I flashed my sword in and out. His ear went flying into the night. He staggered back, a little aghast. But his determination and courage returned quickly, and he came at me, feinting right with a deft swipe to the left.

Not this time, old man. I blocked his move with my sword inverted; without hesitation, I rotated it upwards.

His hand spiralled away into the air, freed from the arm from which it was born, his weapon still gripped within its grasp. The silence was broken by a thud and clatter as the lifeless objects fell back to earth. He looked at his arm, aghast, as if expecting to see his hand still attached. Then he crumpled to his knees, head bowed, shoulders rising and falling with the tide of his breath.

'I told you I'd slice you up if I had to, didn't I?'

He didn't look up or speak or tremble.

'Lift your head,' I ordered.

Languidly, he raised his head until our eyes met, his unwavering gaze defiant.

I placed the tip of my sword underneath his chin and pushed until it drove through the top of his head. I left the blade buried in its new home, turned, and walked away. I didn't look back.

The Dark Corridor opened before me; behind me, the Dark lit up with the burning body of my former master. I felt the shock wave of the corpse's explosion against the back of my neck as I exited the corridor into the real world. I'd learned long ago not to hang around after one of these fights. I liked bacon, after all. And I wanted to keep it that way.

Chapter 35

Turner

I was restless, so I got dressed and went downstairs to watch the midnight bulletins on BloomBox TV, see what was happening in Asia right now. I sat down on the couch.

'Busy night?' Sophie's soft American voice floated through the darkness of the room.

'Hmm. Busyish.' I glanced in her direction.

The darkness dissolved behind her, revealing her in the usual all-black suit.

'You still have energy?' she said with a smirk.

'I always have energy for you, Sophie.'

She slowly approached. What was she up to? Her cheeks were translucently rosy, and her eyes shone as if covered by a film of silver. I became aware of coolness on my forehead—sweat? And my heart was thumping. What was going on?

She walked all the way up to the couch, then straddled me so that she was sitting on my thighs, knees resting on the couch. Heavier than she looked.

'Not too heavy for you, am I?'

'No,' I croaked sarcastically.

She grinned, caressing my chest with her dark velvet fingernails. My nipples hardened almost instantly, giving me a small shiver.

She leaned towards me. 'What are we going to do with all that energy, then?'

I felt her warm breath on my mouth, as if magnets in our lips drew us together. I leaned forward to meet her. Her full lips brushed mine, and my muscles came alive with fire. My heart lurched. I wanted to be inside her.

I put my hand on her waist, gently stroking upwards towards her breast. Much more than a handful there.

My hard-on was trying to tear through two layers of fabric. I pushed up against her.

'Oh James, you really are a bad, bad man.' She slipped backwards off me and knelt between my splayed legs. Her hands made their way down my chest and over my stomach to the bulge between my legs, gently rubbing as she deftly pulled off my trousers. I closed my legs to help, then opened them again for her to shuffle forward, drifting her hands along my inner thighs.

I flinched as her thumbs lightly caressed my balls. She nudged her lips within millimetres of my head; I could feel the humidity of her saliva before she began planting infinitesimally light kisses, starting at the top and moving down. She opened her mouth, and I gasped as she took my balls inside, swirling with her tongue, then pulling back and kissing them with soft, full-lipped kisses. She looked up through her lashes with eyes that were dark and filled with desire. Without breaking that gaze, she smiled and dragged the tip of her tongue all the way back to the top, then opened her mouth greedily. I moaned as she closed her bright red lips around me and fucked me with her mouth.

'Oh God.' I pawed at the sofa, trying to grab hold of something, anything, but my fingers slipped against the leather surface. 'I'm gonna come.'

She drew back and sniggered. 'Already, James? Is this your first time or something?'

I couldn't believe she was laughing at me.

'I'll let you cool off a bit,' she purred, standing up and peeling off her black jacket.

I stood up and pulled off my T-shirt, leaving me completely naked.

'Let me help you.' I moved towards her, gently kissing her as I unbuttoned her shirt and slid it off. I glided my fingertips around to her bra clasp, which I opened with a single snap, then guided her backwards towards the sofa.

She sat down and leaned back, breathing heavily. I kissed down her cheek, her neck, and her chest until I reached the very top of her nipple with the tip of my tongue. She moaned in appreciation and slid her hand around to the back of my head, pulling me in more tightly. My tongue traced its way across her stomach, past her navel, down to the edge of her trousers. I undid them and eased them off, revealing a pair of lacy black knickers. Not much to them at all. *That's my girl.*

I pulled them down and smiled at what I saw.

'You like?' she asked.

'Definitely. I don't understand what's with all these girls ripping out every last hair.'

Softly, I kissed around her groin. I licked up the inside

of her thigh, and she arched her back as the tension mounted. She gasped loudly as I pushed my lips against her warmth and then licked slowly all the way up and down, again and again. She had the other hand around the back of my head now too, pulling me closer still.

My hard-on raged to new levels. I slid my hands from her waist to her breasts and gently circled her nipples with the tips of my fingers.

'Yes,' she breathed.

I pushed my tongue up to her clit and circled it. Groaning, she thrust her hips towards me. All I could see, all I could breathe, all I could taste was her. Bolts of ecstasy shot through me. I was going to come. I darted my tongue in and out of her, occasionally taking a long stroke up and down her sweet spot.

'Yes,' she screamed, 'like that.'

I continued darting my tongue, again and again. She started to shudder, groaning and screaming. She arched her back, shuddering violently, and then fell back, still moaning, writhing.

My muscles, my skin were on fire. Every molecule, every atom seemed so real. I straightened my back, pulling away from her.

'Wow, you're so gorgeously wet,' I murmured.

'Mmm, you're good at that,' she said with a smile. 'You're *definitely* doing that again.'

'You're so delicious, I could do that all night.'

She patted the spare space on the sofa. 'Come here.'

I sat down next to her.

'Well look at you, big boy.' She grinned, hauling herself onto her knees and straddling me. Without taking her eyes off mine, she kissed me softly and positioned me underneath her. I felt her hot wetness brushing against my tingling head. She eased her hips downwards as I moaned at the slow agony of her tease.

She let out a satisfied groan when she finally had all of me inside her.

No condom?

'Don't worry, James.'

She must've felt me tense up.

'That's it. Relax.'

She pressed her lips against mine as she eased up and down, her liquid silk enveloping me. The tingling sparked from the head and shot down into my balls, then everywhere else. I was being electrified in the most ecstatic way.

'Oh God, you feel good,' I whispered.

Every part of me was on fire. My whole body was singing, screaming, crying. *No, no, don't cry. Don't be a sap.*

'Give yourself to me, James,' she breathed.

'I'm all yours. Take me.'

She quickened her pace, thrusting herself upon me again and again.

'Yes,' she screamed, reaching back and gently stroking my balls with her fingertips.

'I'm gonna come inside you,' I groaned, shaking.

'Yes, come inside me. I want you inside me.'

The fire within me exploded like an atomic bomb. I melted, gushing, and became one with her. I gave myself to her; she owned every part of me.

And then I was back on the sofa. Sophie had collapsed

on top of me, with me still inside her, our arms wrapped around each other, holding on for dear life. I wanted to sing, I wanted to shout, I wanted to cry. I knew I could do none of these things.

Not in front of her.

'That was amazing,' she whispered into my ear. 'It seems we've found your area of excellence, James.'

I was falling into a dark bottomless hole, barren and isolated.

'We're going to do that again and again and again,' I whispered back. There seemed to be a hollowness to my voice.

'Yes, we are.'

She purred as I held her tightly with one arm and ran my fingers up and down her back.

I awoke. Sophie had gone, and the apartment felt empty. I felt satisfied yet desolate. Within me boiled a strange sickness, a coldness in my stomach. I was still shaking, buzzing.

I put on the news, partly to see what was going on in the world but mostly to distract myself from my inner isolation. Some part of me had been stolen, ripped away. I felt as though I'd been raped, but not in my body.

In my soul.

Chapter 36

Hero

Hero sat in front of his computer. His body felt sapped of energy, as if he'd been for a run, even though he'd been sat down for the past twelve hours—such was the effort required for his job. He glanced up at the clock in the centre of the trading floor: 6:30 p.m.

Only one thing for it: gym.

He logged out, gathered up his gym bag, and made his way to the lift. A number of people waited, chattering jubilantly about the night ahead. Thursday was the new Friday.

The virtual tour in the induction hadn't done the company gym any justice at all. The changing room smelled of sandalwood, the granite floor greeted his bare feet with warmth, the locker doors felt chunky to the touch. He went through to the main cardio area, catching a whiff of chlorine en route. Even the cardio room offered faint hints of roses.

Just a run tonight, I think. I'll warm up with an easy 5K and then jog home.

'Mind your head,' called a voice from behind.

He spun around. Flying towards him was a boxing

glove attached to a short, tubby arm—Kevin Burns, one of the traders who worked for Bosch. Hero had spoken to him a few times about trading strategies.

Hero twisted and blocked the playful punch with his elbow, then slapped Kevin's face with the back of his hand. 'Don't be cheeky.'

Kevin recoiled. 'Christ, that was quick. Have you thought about sparring with Sam?'

Hero glanced upwards into the other room. About twenty or so people were sat in a large circle, in the centre of which Sam and Bosch circled one other, ducking and weaving and throwing the occasional punch.

'Fighting's not my thing,' he said, looking back at Kevin.

'Could've fooled me.'

'I'm gonna take a run. Have a good evening, mate.'

Miraculously, a couple of running machines stood available. He stepped onto one at a walk and climbed quickly to a steady ten kilometres per hour.

'Wow, that was fast.' Catherine stood at his elbow.

It's her. His legs hollowed out. 'Oh, hello. What was fast? You mean with Kevin just now?' He pointed over his shoulder with his thumb.

She nodded. 'How did you do that?'

'It was nothing, really. I did martial arts when I was a kid.'

'So what're you training on tonight?'

'Just warming up. Doing a 5K here and then running home. And you?'

'The same really, just a jog. Where's home?'

'I live in my family home near Westminster.'

'You live with your parents?' She couldn't resist a smile.

He smiled back. 'I haven't seen my parents since I was a kid. Or my brother, for that matter.'

Her smile faded, and she bent over to fiddle with a shoelace. 'Sorry, I didn't mean . . .'

'It's okay. Where're you based?'

'I'm a little bit further over in Fulham.'

'Well, if you're feeling ambitious, once we're done here, you're welcome to join me in a proper jog.'

She stood back up with a grin. 'Sure, why not?'

Just like that? 'Great. Do you run a lot?'

'Yeah, I've always been into cross-country. I'm planning on doing the London Marathon next year.'

This could get interesting. 'Did you get a place? I heard it was really difficult.'

'Yes, I got a charity place with Cancer Research.'

'Well, sign me up for sponsorship.'

'Thanks.' She gave him a friendly wave and headed towards her own machine.

Catherine breathed comfortably next to Hero as they jogged westward along the embankment. Small boats and barges loomed in the shadows on the river, whilst the Victorian street lamps cast pools of light on the pavement. The night was clear and cold, the stars twinkling above the halo of the London lights. Illumination from the nearby apartment blocks reflected in swirling patterns on the ripples of the Thames.

'I love this route home,' Hero remarked.

'It's pretty,' she said.

Big Ben towered above them in the clear night sky as they arrived at Westminster Bridge.

Hero motioned off to the right. 'Well, I'm gonna head up there, past Parliament Square. I guess you're going to carry on straight ahead?'

'Yep, see you tomorrow.'

'Definitely. Er, do you fancy getting lunch tomorrow?'

She smiled and plucked away a strand of hair that had stuck to her lips. 'That'd be nice.'

'I found this place that I think you might like. They do tea and scones and other things.' He smiled in a way he hoped was charming. 'It's very English.'

'I'm sold. See you tomorrow.'

She moved ahead with a little burst of speed. He slowed to a stop and watched as she disappeared into the busy London night.

Shall we meet at the exit at 1:00?

The email from Catherine had arrived in Hero's inbox that morning, provoking the knot that was now drilling his stomach into submission. By the time he made his way to the exit at the appointed hour, she was already waiting for him.

'Sorry, I hope you haven't been here long. The weather's not too good, I see.'

'It's fine, I just got here. You Brits, always talking about the weather.' She snorted.

He led the way along the Strand. 'Indeed we are. The finest chit-chat in all the world. We basically invented it.'

'You're crazy.'

'So soon? I thought it'd be a few weeks till you

255

noticed.' He grasped her elbow and cut into a side street.

'You're obviously in a good mood too.'

'Here we are,' he announced.

'BB Bakery,' Catherine read as he held the door open. 'Chivalry's not dead after all.'

'Sir, madam,' said a waitress with a pleasant smile.

'A table for two, please,' Hero said.

The waitress showed them to a small, elegant table by the window, saddled on either side with beautifully upholstered high-backed chairs. The smell of cakes, coffee, and tea mixed with the agreeable chatter of the patrons. The waitress handed them both a menu.

'I think I'll have an afternoon tea,' he said to Catherine as she studied her menu.

'Sounds delicious, but then maybe soup and a scone— and a cake,' Catherine said with a grin. 'Everything looks good—but yes, afternoon tea, why not?'

She placed her menu on the table and looked around curiously at the charming drawings on the walls. 'This place is so cute. How did you find it?'

'I walked past one day from work and thought it looked nice.'

'You'd never been here before then?'

'Honestly? I've been coming here every day for lunch since I arrived at Saxon Goldberg.'

She raised an eyebrow. 'Really?'

'Yep.' He signalled to one of the waitresses, who promptly came to the table. 'Hi, Martina, can you tell my friend how often I come here? She doesn't believe me when I say it's every day.'

The waitress chuckled. 'He really does. He's our regular. Are you ready to order?'

'After you.' He gestured to Catherine.

'I'll take an afternoon tea.'

'Same for me, please,' he added.

Martina scribbled the orders into a notepad and left.

He turned to Catherine. 'This is my little oasis of tranquillity in the violent sea of hot air that is investment banking.'

She giggled.

A few minutes later, a cake stand piled with a variety of sandwiches and treats arrived, accompanied by two pots of tea.

'Whoa, that's a lot.' Catherine grabbed a sandwich. 'You don't eat this every day, do you?'

'Of course not. I have to watch my figure.'

She smiled over the top of her sandwich. They ate for the most part in silence. Hero had been ravenous all morning. He scoffed his food, barely taking a breath. *Probably the extra training. Ever since I met you, I've been in the gym every day.*

'So where're you from originally?' he asked.

'New Jersey.'

Hero couldn't stop the smirk that darted onto his face.

'It's not all like on the TV.' She sounded defensive. 'Where I'm from is actually really nice.'

He nodded. 'I know, sorry.'

'I grew up in a lovely house out beyond the suburbs, went to private school, and then ended up going to university in Tennessee.'

He raised his eyebrows. 'Why Tennessee?'

'I love barbecue.'

Hero nearly spat out the tea he was sipping. She joined him in a grin.

'And so you came to London because you love . . .?'

'Tea, of course. But I've always wanted to come. England seemed so cute.'

'And now I assume you've discovered it's not all Downton Abbey,' he said with a wink.

'Indeed.' She chuckled, but then her mirth faded. 'What happened with your family?'

He shifted uneasily in his seat. *How much should I tell her?*

'My mum left my father, brother, and me when I was about twelve. I never spoke to her again. I don't know what happened.' He took a deep breath. 'My dad left when I was eighteen. All I had was a note saying good-bye. He said he'd come back, but he never did. A few days later, my brother and I had a huge argument, and he disappeared. I've not seen him since.'

He blinked at the assortment of cakes.

'It must've been very difficult for you.' Her hand appeared amongst the cakes as she reached for his.

He looked up at her eyes, and a forlorn smile appeared on his lips.

'I lost my sister to cancer when I was younger,' she continued. 'We all watched as she slowly faded away. It was very painful.'

'I'm so sorry.'

They regarded each other in an easy silence.

'It's okay,' she said. 'It was hard, but I found a way

to deal with it. Now I do what I can to ease the pain for others.'

'I wouldn't expect that from someone in investment banking.'

'I'm not really sure I fit in, to be honest.'

Hero realized his mouth was slightly ajar. This woman pulled him towards her like metal to a magnet. *I haven't felt that since—*

He didn't want to think of her name for fear of jinxing what he had in front of him.

'What are you thinking about?' Catherine asked.

'Something you said reminded me . . .' He looked out the big window and into the distance. Then he blinked and turned back to Catherine. 'And that's why you're doing the London Marathon?'

She nodded. 'I also help out at a local hospital from time to time.'

He gripped her hand in response. They seemed to be caught in a small bubble of their own reality.

He sucked in his breath. He hadn't accidentally stopped time, had he?

But everything seemed normal. They were merely engrossed in each other's presence. What a wonderful, fresh development this was.

'Well, this has been different,' she eventually remarked with a smile.

'Yes, it has. I've enjoyed it,' he said softly.

'Me too.'

They let go of each other's hands and sat back to enjoy lighter conversation whilst sharing a well-decorated Belgian chocolate cake.

'Will you join me again?' he asked finally.

'Here for lunch? Every day?'

'Well, yes, possibly—but it wouldn't matter to me if we were here or in a greasy spoon. So long as I'm with you, it's fine by me.'

Catherine squinted. 'That's really corny.'

'Maybe. But it's also true.'

She tilted her head flirtatiously. 'Look, a few of us are meeting after work tonight for drinks . . .'

Join us.

Hero went as stiff as the candle flame that first time. He hadn't heard those words since—

'. . . join us?'

He caught his breath and shook the ice caught in his limbs. 'Oh, of course. Sorry, it's just for a second, I thought—It's nothing.'

'What?'

'Don't worry about it. It's in the past now.' He stood up and motioned to the doors. 'Shall we?'

He dropped some cash on the table, placing a teacup on top to hold it still. He chuckled. *Join us.* The words that had brought such horror and misery now brought him joy.

Chapter 37

Turner

And so I resumed my day job of following my brother. I watched from the shadows as he came out of Saxon Goldberg with a girl and they went to lunch at a local teashop. There was something in him—the way he looked at her, that nervous smile of his. I'd seen it before.

Fi.

Well, well, bruv. Your inner sap has come bursting out yet again—and we have a winner.

As they walked back from the shop, I could see his hand reaching towards her, trembling, but never actually touching her. *Always respectful. You total girl.*

I was going to need to follow this one. I needed to make sure she was on the righteous path.

I waited for them to round the corner, then turned the other direction and strolled away.

Later that day, I waited outside Saxon Goldberg for her to come back out. I suppose I could've tracked them both inside, but it seemed pointless. Their work was always rather dull. Instead, I could watch all of these terribly important people busying themselves along Chancery

Lane, each one with a story they'd love to tell but no one wanted to hear.

I had to wait quite a while. She eventually appeared at the doors at around eight o'clock. Why did these people work such long hours? Surely they couldn't be that efficient by the end of it. Then again, I suppose I worked a twenty-four-hour shift.

And so it began, a private game of cat and mouse, although only one of us knew it was happening. I followed her from the office to Blackfriars tube, a crush of stressed people with the same air of self-importance as the Chancery Lane crowd. These people had their heads so far up their own arses that I was surprised they didn't collapse in on themselves to create one of those micro black holes.

Down we went into the hell's kitchen that was the underground at this hour. The District line. Westbound. Jammed into some loser's armpit. *You need to use deodorant, mate.*

The temptation to use the Dark Corridor was overwhelming. I mean, I was on business, after all. But I had to resist. It would raise too many questions, and in any event, I needed to study this one. Understand her. Understand how she'd got inside his head.

What did we think, then? Chelsea? Too rich, surely? She was only young. Fulham, then? Yep, ten pounds on Fulham. She got out a book to read, and I managed to get a quick peek at the cover. *Jane Eyre*. Of course. What a cliché. I bet she rode horses too.

I looked around the carriage as best as I could with so many people. Everyone to a man or woman was reading or looking at their phone. I was the odd one out, nothing to do except watch her without looking and mentally catalogue the delicious aroma of sweaty bollocks. I checked more than once to make sure I hadn't accidentally dilated time; to my dismay, I had not. At times like this, I wished I could compress time too. Why was it only one way, anyhow?

Hell finally ended as she got up at Parsons Green. Fulham—what did I say? I squeezed myself out of a different door like an oversqueezed blob of toothpaste. The old tube station hadn't been renovated since the war, and like all stations in London, it smelled of week-old piss.

It was already night, so I needed to keep as much distance as possible; women always seemed to be alert to being followed or any weird behaviour from guys. Couldn't blame them, I suppose. With the rare exception of those who'd been trained, most women could easily be overpowered by almost any man. A place like London must seem terribly frightening to them in even the most mundane of circumstances. Didn't excuse their rudeness, though, or their stupidity in almost all other situations.

Left again, off the main road, and we passed by the pastel terraced houses that are endemic in Fulham. I was able to blend into the thinner crowd headed the same way off the tube, less than ten of us left. She slowed, searching through her cavernous bag. I slowed my pace to match but realised it'd soon just be the two of us, so I carried on walking past her. Once I was far enough along, I blended into the shadows—easy enough with my black suit.

She found her keys and glanced up. She looked nervous, scared, as if she knew she was being watched. She looked directly at me, and for a moment, I thought I'd been rumbled. Then she shrugged and turned towards her pastel pink house.

I used the Dark Corridor to peek inside, hoping to get some clues about her life and her weaknesses. Had to be careful not to disturb anything, not to mention being seen. Her place was exceptionally tidy. OCD tidy. I couldn't have handled a girl like this. I'd have got on her tits, and not in a good way. One good thing about the OCD was that it made it easy to rifle through everything. I just had to remember exactly where it went; someone like her would have noticed immediately if something were out of place.

I moved upstairs to her bedroom. She was there, getting changed into some old clothes.

Marks out of two—I'd give her one, bruv, and another one.

Again, she stopped and looked around, clearly spooked. Goose-bumps appeared over her porcelain-white arms and shoulders. She was detecting me. She was one of us. She just didn't know it yet.

How very interesting, bruv.

She went downstairs with me in tow, picked up her bag from the kitchen table, slung it over her shoulder, and hurried out. She turned left up towards the main road at quite a pace, which made it easier to hide from her. She waited at the bus stop heading towards Chelsea and Sloane Square beyond. It wasn't long before a bus came, and she hopped on. I took the Dark Corridor directly upstairs, right at the back. Using it like this was quite odd; it gave me a strange sense of separation from the world and that none of what I was doing really mattered.

The ride was brief, and she got off right outside the Chelsea and Westminster Hospital. She crossed the road and went inside to the first floor, the children's ward.

A woman behind the desk smiled. 'Hey, Catherine, how are you this evening?'

'I'm good, thanks, Sarah. You?'

'Good, good.'

'And how's Danny?' Catherine asked.

'The same little rascal he always is.'

'How're my little ones this evening?'

'Still bad, I'm afraid. Little Rachel was asking after you today.'

Catherine's demeanour changed, and the room went with it; somehow it seemed a little colder. 'That one really breaks my heart.'

'That's why the children's ward is the hardest to work on.'

She nodded. 'See you later. Have a good night.'

'You too.'

Sarah reached across and pressed the button that unlocked the double door to the ward, and Catherine went inside. She walked down the long corridor and turned into a single patient room.

A small, pale girl lay prostrate with all manner of tubes and wires poking into her arm. Even though she was clearly gaunt, her shaven head made her cheeks look round.

Catherine knelt at the side of the bed and sandwiched the girl's hand between both of her own. 'Hey there, you. How're you today?'

'Not so good,' Rachel said. 'I feel so tired all the time. And I hurt.'

'Where do you hurt, sweetie?'

'Everywhere. In my legs, my arms, my chest.'

Catherine squeezed her hand a little.

'I'm going to die soon, aren't I?'

A forlorn expression crept into Catherine's eyes.

'It's okay, I know. I'm okay with it,' Rachel said calmly. 'Do you think there's a God?'

The room was dark except for the bedside lamps, which made it easy for me to open up the Dark Corridor wherever I wanted. I changed my position so that I could see both of their faces. Small rivulets crept down Catherine's face. She kept her head bowed, trying to hide it from Rachel.

'Don't cry, Catherine. It'll be okay.'

Catherine sniffled. 'I do think there's a God, but it's hard sometimes to have faith.'

'I think there is too. Soon I will be with him and the sun will be shining and I won't hurt anymore and I'll be playing with all my friends.'

A part of me hoped she was right. I'd thought many times about who invented the rules. Maybe all of this had been invented by God. But then I thought about the horrific nature of what we do. It couldn't have been so.

'Would you read me a story?' Rachel asked.

'Of course.' Catherine went across to a bookshelf and started looking through the books.

'Read me the one about the poor girl that goes to the ball and becomes a princess.'

'Cinderella?'

'I like that one.'

Catherine riffled through until she found what she was looking for and pulled it out.

'Once upon a time, there was a kind young girl . . .'

Rachel listened intently. About halfway through, at the point where Cinderella was dancing with the prince at the ball, she broke in with a whisper. 'That would be heaven for me, dancing with a handsome prince, wearing a beautiful sparkly blue ballgown that whirled with my every turn, my long blond hair fluttering with every step. That would be perfect.'

Catherine put her hand over her mouth.

'Why're you upset? It will be so beautiful.'

Catherine nodded. 'It is.'

I gulped, stifling a storm of my own. They were both right: it would be beautiful. I'd seen it before. The way she described it reminded me a little of Hero's graduation ball.

But this was no time to be sentimental.

Catherine wiped her face with her sleeve and carried on with the story. Rachel rolled onto her back and closed her eyes, I assumed in order to better imagine herself as Cinderella. She soon fell asleep.

Catherine closed the book, tidied the bedclothes a little, and kissed Rachel on the forehead. 'Good night, sweetie, sleep well.'

I followed Catherine as she said goodnight to all the nurses and doctors. Everyone seemed to know her. I

267

could see why she and Hero liked each other; they were practically the same person. It made me wonder if someone I felt pulled towards would ever see something they wanted more of in me.

She left the hospital and got back on the bus headed back towards Parsons Green, but instead of going home as I'd expected her to, she got off after Fulham Broadway, crossed the road, and headed down North End Road before turning left into Dawes Road. Finally, she turned right and headed straight into St Thomas of Canterbury Church. She made her way to the front pew and knelt on a cushion to pray. Her murmured words echoed around the dimly lit church.

There was a squeaking of a badly oiled door hinge at the front of the church, and a man in casual clothes appeared. 'Hello, Catherine, what're you doing here so late?'

'Good evening, Father. It's Rachel again.'

She obviously came here a lot. I shrugged. It'd be hard on anyone.

'I see.' The priest nodded sagely and sat down next to her. 'I know that whole episode has been very hard on you. So what happened this time?'

'Today she asked me if I think there's a God. I told her yes, obviously, and then she told me how she thought heaven might be for her.'

He raised his eyebrows, encouraging her to go on.

'It was Cinderella.' She smiled gamely, but her voice broke. 'She was so right. It *would* be beautiful—heavenly, even. It was heartbreaking. I've been crying ever since.'

She started to cry again. 'I've read her that story so many times. She really loves it.'

'I understand, my child.'

She cried harder. 'But I don't have the heart to tell her she won't go to heaven.'

He frowned. 'Why do you think that?'

'She's not Catholic.'

He blew a deep breath of relief. 'That's not correct. She will go to heaven, even though she's not in the faith.'

'Really?'

'Of course. She's a child, an innocent. God's not unjust, not irrational about this. He wants us to be good people. She's never had the ability to be Catholic; she was born into the wrong family, perhaps. But don't worry, Catherine, she's going to be okay. She'll get to be Cinderella.'

'Born into the wrong family'? Dickhead.

Catherine sobbed for a while longer, her head in her hands. I noticed that the priest remained respectful and didn't put his arm around her for comfort.

'His ways are unknown to us, but I'm sure whatever happens will be for the best, in the end,' he soothed.

This was amusing. Here was a good Catholic asking God and a priest for answers, and all the while, she had a dark angel on her shoulder, watching her every move.

'Thank you, Father,' she said with a smile. 'You've really helped.'

'That's what I'm here for. You know you're always welcome here, anytime.'

She smiled wearily and shuffled to the exit. From there, she returned home, ate her dinner in silence, and cried herself to sleep.

After all that excitement, I paid a quick visit to Hero to make sure he wasn't getting himself into trouble. He seemed fine, so after a few hours' sleep, I returned to watch Catherine to see what a new day would bring.

She awoke before dawn. Her first stop was again the church, where she attended the first service of the day along with a smattering of other people. Oh, Christ— she wasn't only Catholic, she was devout. I wondered if she was a virgin too.

Good work, bruv.

I followed this little bird for a week, and it was the same every day like clockwork. Although she didn't always go to the hospital, she went to church even at the weekends and never took a sip of coffee, much less alcohol. She wasn't crazy in any way—well, apart from religion, obviously—and she kept herself healthy. No vices.

No way for me to get to her.

Finally, I decided to go back to the hospital to try to find out more about the little girl. It had been the only time I'd seen even a chink in Catherine's armour.

Rachel's mum arrived in the evening to chat and read her a story. It wasn't so different from Catherine's visit. By the time she left, she still had hope in her eyes. *And it's the hope that kills you.*

I thought about it for a moment: the little girl slowly fading away, her heart monitor slowing, slowing, and then level, nothing but a monotone, her hand falling limp over the edge of the bed.

I fell in behind the mother. This might be the chance I needed to keep Hero on the straight and narrow.

Chapter 38

Turner

At least Rachel's mother lived within walking distance. I didn't think I could've handled another tube ride. And unlike Catherine, Rachel's mother didn't stop on the way home to have a chat with God.

The small terraced house was off the North End Road, small and dank. It seemed devoid of life, as if it were spiritually connected to Rachel, slowly being drained of its energy until the bitter end. I saw from some letters on the coffee table that her mother's first name was Sally. I looked around Sally's home from the shadows. As she was downstairs in the lounge, I started in the bedrooms. It was safer this way.

The main bedroom was quite ordinary, yet there was a feeling of something missing. It took looking through the wardrobe before I realised what it was: there were no men's clothes here. In fact, there was no sign of any man here at all. It made me think of the 'extra' space I kept in my wardrobe at home.

I walked down the hallway to the next bedroom. Pink wallpaper, teddy bears spread over a puppy-dog duvet cover, ready to greet their owner. *Sorry, guys. She's never coming back.*

Something poked through the shroud surrounding my soul. Was this sadness?

I barged through to the bathroom. Just one tooth-brush and all manner of washing products surrounded the bath, but nothing a man would use. I wondered why he had left. And when. I opened the door of a small cabinet hanging on the wall. Toothpaste. Medicine. Prozac. She was truly alone.

I decided to watch Sally downstairs; she wouldn't be able to see me, of course. She was sat on the sofa rocking back and forth, looking at her phone. She looked as though she wanted to call somebody, but she kept changing her mind.

But then she did it. She pressed Call.

'Hi, it's me. I don't know, I just wanted to talk. I saw Rachel . . . She's in a bad way, Michael, you really should go and see her. I don't think she's going to be around for long . . . I know, I know, you don't want to know. But I think we should talk. It's difficult for both of us, you know, not just you . . . I know what you said. It's just that she made her peace with God today. You're her father. You should go and see her whilst you still can. You'll regret—'

She took the phone from her ear and stared at it. From where I stood watching, I saw a single fat tear land on the screen.

That answered that, then. I guess he hadn't been able to handle watching his daughter like that, nor the guilt of abandoning his family, so he pretended they didn't

272

exist. Sort of like I pretended the person I wanted in my own life didn't exist. Except they never went away the way we expected, did they?

I stared at her a while longer as I thought things over. I could see the dominoes forming into a line. She was alone, and she had nothing to lose. She was perfect.

Now that I had things sorted, I couldn't stand to watch this anymore. I needed to get out, clear my head. Coffee—perfect. I knew this great boutique coffee place on the North End Road. I used the Dark Corridor to exit into a nearby alleyway and then walked the rest of the way. It would be nice to have a cup of good coffee to mark my next decision.

To mark what I was going to do with Catherine.

Chapter 39

Turner

The coffee place was small, but at this time of the night it was only half full, mostly with people who'd been out drinking and wanted to finish the night off in a classier way. I went to the counter and asked for my usual.

'Grande Americano, black.'

'Anything else?'

'No, thanks.'

'That'll be two pounds seventy, please.'

I handed over the money, collected my drink, and found a quiet corner to sit in and think things through. I found myself thinking about Sally, all alone at home. How could her husband abandon her like that, and his own daughter, in their time of need? Of course it was difficult when you knew your child was going to die—but it's family. You don't abandon family. What a bastard. He was lucky I didn't know who he was; otherwise, I'd have been tempted to show him just how disgusted I was with him. Although Sophie would've been displeased with me if I had.

'You don't abandon family, eh?'

I sighed into my cup. I'd abandoned my own brother,

hadn't I? My heart panged with guilt. *Haven't felt that in a while.*

I blinked as my awareness returned to the coffee shop, and I realised I was staring at an attractive red-haired girl with alabaster skin and deliciously red lips. Even though she sat square on to me, her head was twisted away to a blank wall. What do you suppose was the difference between somebody who hadn't noticed you and someone who was deliberately ignoring you?

She was looking nervously at me out of the corner of her eye.

God, you girls really are so pathetic.

My smirk broadened to a grin and then to a chuckle. I looked around the place: mostly surreptitious couples, perhaps friends, or people who'd met that night. One Italian guy was doing his level best to seduce the girl he was with in the most gesticulative manner possible.

I looked back and caught the girl's eye. I smiled ever so slightly, and she returned it with one of her own and then looked down at her coffee.

You don't need to give me any more signals than that, love.

I ambled across to her table. She looked up as if I'd somehow surprised her. Seriously?

'I'm sorry about staring just now,' I said. 'I've had quite an unusual night, and I was just thinking about it. I was a million miles away.'

She idly swirled her coffee cup. 'That's okay. What was so unusual?'

I sat down in the chair next to her. 'A friend of mine's

daughter has cancer; looks like she's not going to be around for much longer. It's very sad.'

Just talking about it brought back anger, a tight feeling seeping into every part of my body. I wanted to take it out on someone—and who better than some poor, unsuspecting girl?

Her expression changed to one of real surprise and pain. 'Oh, I'm so sorry to hear that. It must be very difficult.'

'It is—but if it's okay, I'd quite like to be distracted away from it. How was your night?'

She told me about her evening out with the girls. I didn't really listen; I was on autopilot, thinking about Sally, Rachel, and Catherine. Besides, when you've seduced as many girls as I have, they all seem to merge into one. How very boring.

We got in a cab and went back to my place. I decided not to do the clichéd thing of kissing her in the back seat; instead, I teased her a little by putting my hand on her knee. Always better to let them wait, make them beg for it. In the lift to my penthouse, I slid my hand onto the small of her back. She reciprocated by putting her arm around me. We wasted no time in going straight upstairs to the bedroom.

I held her from behind and slowly kissed her shoulder and neck, then turned her around and softly brushed her lips with mine, caressing her face. Then I slipped off her dress and planted warm kisses down her naked body. I took her panties in both hands and slid them to the floor before standing up again, fully clothed, in front of her exposed body.

276

I stroked my hand across her breasts as I circled behind her. Then, I ran my hands down her sides, one hand continuing between her legs whilst the other moved back to her breasts.

'Give yourself to me,' I whispered. 'I want every inch of you.'

I turned her around, looked into her eyes, and brought my finger into my mouth so I could taste her.

'Sit down on the bed,' I ordered.

She sat down and watched with greedy eyes as I slid my jacket off and unbuttoned my shirt. Her mouth opened slightly as the light cast shadows over my smooth, well-trained pecs and washboard stomach. I undid my belt, unbuttoned my trousers, and slid everything off with my boxers in one movement.

She bit her bottom lip seductively as my hard-on sprang towards her. She snaked her arms around me, and I pulled her head towards mine, kissing her hard. Then I pushed her backwards so that she was lying on the bed. She moaned as I licked slowly downwards across her nipple, then her stomach, and then slid my tongue between her legs.

'Yes, keep going,' she breathed.

God, I loved doing this. I teased the end of her clit, circling it again and again. She ground her hips against my mouth, and I felt her sliding further and further towards climax with every moan. She shuddered as her essence liquefied into mine.

I pulled back. 'Get on your hands and knees at the edge of the bed.'

She rolled over, got up onto all fours, and shuffled

backwards to the edge. She looked vulnerable. I hoped she felt vulnerable. I went around the bed to one of the drawers on the other side, pulled out a condom, and stood in front of her. We looked at each other as I rolled it on; she licked her lips and smiled.

I went back behind her, grabbed her hips, and pulled her back onto me. We both moaned as I speared into her.

'Fuck me, James.'

I bent forward, sliding my hands to her shoulders and pushing her head down towards the bed. She groaned with ecstasy, knotting the duvet in both hands. I slapped her ass as hard as I could. The sound was so loud that it echoed.

'Oh God, yes, spank me.'

'Yeah, that's it—take it, you dirty bitch.' I drove into her, spanking her again and again.

'Yes! I'm coming!' she shouted, hands clenching even tighter, her whole body bucking, swaying, and shuddering.

Seeing her twitching and moaning uncontrollably pushed me over the edge. I tumbled into that deep pit, pinning her most vulnerable places against mine and groaning loudly as my mind shattered into a million pieces.

I collapsed on top of her, kissing her shoulders and neck again. We lay like that for a while, our bodies intertwined, savouring the feeling of each other's warmth. For the moment, I enjoyed holding her in my arms, before the detachment and numbness crept back once again.

The semblance of a life now forgotten.

*

She came down the stairs fully dressed. 'What're you doing down here?'

'I had to do some work. Must've fallen asleep on the couch.'

'Fancy coming back to bed?'

'Sorry, no can do. I need to get to the office.'

What office? I stood up and went across to meet her halfway.

'Well, thanks for the spanking last night.' She grinned wickedly.

I smirked.

'God, you're good at that. I don't think I'll be able to sit down today—I'm completely red.'

I nodded, enjoying the mental image of my red handprint on her pale skin. She leaned in and brushed her lips against mine. They felt warm, comforting.

I needed that, some semblance of humanity.

'Will I see you again?' she whispered.

I opened the door. 'I'll call you.'

She looked at me for a few moments and then left. I watched her walk to the lift with her head bowed, then I quietly shut the door.

Chapter 40

Hero

Six o'clock came around in what seemed like seconds. Hero had spent the afternoon dreamily thinking about Catherine whilst scrolling his mouse up and down in the same window, pretending to work. He was brought back with a start as most of the co-workers around him stood up, laughing and joking, Catherine amongst them. She looked over at Hero and smiled nervously.

'Where're you all headed off to?' he called across to them.

'Just next door, The Cheshire Cheese,' Kevin called back. 'You coming?'

'Sure.' He locked his computer and hurried to join them.

The pub was one of the oldest in London. It still had wooden beams and whitewashed walls from the medieval era. Hero paused inside the polished double doors. *Smells like it hasn't been cleaned since then, either.* The place was packed with revellers looking to wind down or at the very least distract themselves from their stress.

He weaved his way through the crowd, popping out at the bar and luckily catching the eye of the barmaid.

'Are you being served?' she asked.

'No, can I get a double Glenmorangie, please?'

'Any ice?'

'One cube, thanks.'

Drink in hand, he went to find his colleagues. Sam, Bosch, and Kevin were engaged in a lively debate about football. Kevin had supported Arsenal since he was a kid; Bosch, being American, had naturally adopted Chelsea; and Sam argued the case for Liverpool's all-time greatness.

'Who's your team?' Kevin asked Hero.

'I don't really have one. Sorry, I'm more of a rugby man.'

'Really? You don't seem like the type,' Bosch said rather mockingly.

He shrugged. Most of his mind was engaged in finding Catherine using his peripheral vision. He dilated time a little to help. *A little bit selfish, maybe, but I doubt the Dark cares about something so trivial as this.*

His breath caught in his throat when he found her. He recognised her from her long chestnut hair, which she was playing with. He slowed time a little more and strained his eyes till they felt as if they might pop out of their sockets.

Oh God, no.

She was talking to a good-looking guy about her age who was standing with his hips thrust forward in that slightly bizarre, overconfident pose that young men always seem to adopt when they're trying to seduce women. *Until they know better, as James might say.*

'Are you in there?' Sam was asking, snapping his fingers in front of Hero's face.

'Hmm?'

'You seem a little distant.'

He gaped at Sam. *I can't watch this. I need some air.* He made his excuses and slipped out of the side entrance to the beer garden as inconspicuously as possible.

He was alone; the last remnants of February had bled furiously into March, dropping the temperature, keeping everyone inside. The door squeaked slowly to a close and echoed around the paved space. Though fairly large, the garden felt claustrophobic due to the press of tall buildings all around.

I really thought—you idiot. Why would she?

He paced around the courtyard, breathing in the cool night air and breathing out mist. He sipped his whisky in the hope of easing his tightened chest, but his claustrophobia heightened as if the buildings were edging towards him. He perched on an irregular stone wall capped by what would become flowers in a few months. He could barely breathe.

Maybe I should go home, leave them to it. Maybe it's for the best. I mean, she'd never understand.

The door squeaked open.

'Hey,' Catherine said as she walked over. 'Are you okay?'

'Yeah, yeah, fine. I just needed some air.'

She remained silent, regarding him.

'I wasn't sure if I'd get to speak to you tonight, and when I saw you with that guy . . . I don't know. I felt a bit jealous.'

'What guy? Ali?' She cocked her head.

'I don't know his name. Anyway . . .' He shrugged.

282

'Why would you be jealous?'

His face burned. 'I don't know. It's just . . .'

She stepped a little closer. 'Just what?'

He steeled himself and looked her in the eyes. 'It's just I really like you.'

She smiled. 'Oh, I see. It's okay. I didn't want to make it obvious in front of the others.'

She leaned a little closer, their lips millimetres apart. He ached to feel them pressed together.

'What's going on out here, then?' a voice called out.

Catherine stepped back and collected herself as Bosch, Kevin, and a couple of other guys filed out into the courtyard, grinning like schoolboys.

Hero plastered a smile on his face as Bosch pounded him on the back.

Oh God, so close. Please don't let this be like Fi. Don't do that to me again.

Chapter 41

Turner

I rolled onto my back and stared at the concentric circles of light made by the bedside lamps. She lay next to me, her body still hot from exertion, her hand on my chest, her dark red lips nibbling my shoulder.

'What are you doing to me, James?' she murmured.

My throat wouldn't open. I was still pulsating like the core of a nuclear reactor. She caressed my chest a while longer.

'I've got to go.' She rolled lithely out of bed.

Of course she did.

She stood at my feet, her wondrous skin still rosy, almost translucent in the ambient light. She was almost alien to me—the sort Captain Kirk would have taken a fancy to, no doubt. I swore she did this to frustrate me when she left my side.

She picked up her black blouse from the floor where she'd discarded it so hastily, such was her fervour for me.

'This Catherine girl interests me,' she said.

Just as I'd thought. 'Been following me around, have you?'

'Don't flatter yourself.' She buttoned herself up, never taking her eyes off me.

'Why does she interest you?'

'I know we spoke about keeping Hero out of the Game, but we could use her to get to him. He'd be a very useful asset.'

Shit. I didn't want him joining the Dark, messing things up for me like he did when we were kids. My next words needed to be spot on.

'I don't think he'd compromise his values like that.' That much was true.

'Are you sure about that? Guys tend to get a bit crazy when they're in love.'

Was she talking about me or my brother?

'Do they,' I said flatly.

Her piercing blue eyes studied me as a butcher might cattle. 'They do. We've done this before, a long time ago. There was a member of the Light a lot like your brother, a man of very high moral value—one of the best there ever was, actually. We wanted him from the moment we saw him. He was always on the edge between Light and Dark, but he just wouldn't budge to our side.' She took a deep breath. 'Then he met a woman, fell in love, and stupidly wanted to stay clean. We saw our chance to get him.'

'Well, that wouldn't be your decision to make. It'd be his.'

'Would it?' She raised her eyebrows, then began hunting around the bed like a poacher in the long grass. 'Ah, here they are.' She picked up her lacy micro-knickers. I was never sure why she bothered with such a small thing at all. Perhaps her trousers chafed without it.

285

'What did you do?' I asked.

'We took his wife. After that, he was a good little boy.' She grinned. For a moment, I swore there were shark's teeth in her mouth.

'But you can't do that. You get burned for that, by God or whatever!'

'Oh, James. Sometimes I wonder whether you're really one of us at all.'

What was she talking about?

'There're many ways to skin a cat, as you say,' she said.

Or indeed anything else. The words floated in my head, but not in my voice—the Light Master's.

I sat up in bed. 'I still don't think Hero would go for it. Remember? He saved that obnoxious boy Bran despite his feelings for Fi.'

'Good point. So what's your plan? The same thing you did to Fi?'

How long had they been following me? My whole life? 'I don't think so. Catherine's Catholic.'

She gave me a blank look.

'No premarital sex, remember?'

'I see. Well, we can't have him protecting her. It's too dangerous. You'll have to kill her.'

Hearing it put so nonchalantly was a sledgehammer to the skull, even though it was exactly what I'd planned. She never minced her words; that's why I loved—

I pulled a pillow close and nodded. 'What was so great about him?'

'Hero?'

'No, the guy who used to be in the Light.'

'Oh. He had a way of saying things to people. His

words wormed into your head, and they'd pop up again and again at moments when you had a big decision to make. He could turn any man from Dark to Light. That's why we wanted him.'

'Or any woman.'

She sat on the bed and twisted around. 'He tried, but he couldn't turn me. Instead, you could say that I turned him . . .' There was an intensity in her gaze as she chuckled. 'I even gave him a pet name: the Turner.'

'The Turner?' I pulled the pillow casually into my lap, another layer of safety. 'Anyone I know?'

'I don't think you've met him.' She leant over me. 'And you should be glad of it.' Her breath entered my mouth, stirring me again.

She was deliberately not telling me something.

'Don't worry about Catherine,' I said. 'I'm on it.'

'I know.' She caressed my face as her lips lingered against mine for a glorious moment. 'Thanks for tonight. See you soon.'

She opened the Dark Corridor and evaporated into it. I collapsed and rolled over onto her side of the bed. Her perfume was the sweet embrace of heroin, agonisingly short of the high. The silence of the room closed in around me, oppressing me, pushing my head further into the suffocating goose down. Only the light from the bedside lamps kept me from diminishing to nothing. I did not switch them off—for days.

The Light Master's voice echoed around me as if I were on the edge of sleep, with that disconnected feeling of being at the bottom of a well and the whole world continuing at a distance without me.

There're many ways to skin a cat, as you say—or indeed, anything else.

She couldn't possibly have meant who I thought she meant. Could she?

Chapter 42

Hero

It was Tuesday evening, and Hero felt as if he'd got nothing done. Thank God his trading strategies were all automated. He'd spent every waking moment since Friday thinking about Catherine, his heart screaming. Everything about her seemed perfect. Her lips. Her eyes.

Her soul.

They hadn't met on Monday for lunch. She'd said something had happened at the hospital and she didn't want to talk about it. He found himself trying to snatch glances at her without being caught, not by her but by the ever-present Bosch and company.

What were the chances of finding someone so selfless in the world of investment banking? The bank participated in many charity programmes, he'd discovered, but the people who operated them had a strange attitude, as if they were doing penance for crimes committed—past, present, and future.

Catherine sees who I am, the way Fi could.

'Hey, Hero,' someone bellowed, yanking him from his thoughts.

He blinked over at Kevin. 'What's up, mate?'

'A bunch of us are going out to eat tonight. Do you wanna come?'

He thought about it, blowing out his cheeks. He wanted a quiet night in. He was exhausted from the sheer noise of the day, the hustle and bustle and the gut-wrenching intensity of his thoughts and feelings for her.

Kevin leaned in. 'Catherine's going to be there.'

Hero flinched at the mention of her name. 'That obvious, huh?'

''Fraid so, mate.'

He scrolled nervously up and down the page open on his screen. *I really just want some rest. But this might be a chance to finally kiss her.*

'Okay, what's the plan?' he asked.

Kevin smiled triumphantly. 'We're meeting at the Fifth Floor at Harvey Nic's at seven o'clock for a quick drink before we go to the restaurant. See you there.'

By evening, the spring rains had set in with a vengeance. The sound of splashing traffic and the old wood smell of new rain after a drought filled the air. One round of drinks, then they headed to the restaurant, an upmarket place in Knightsbridge called The Rib Room. They'd reserved a large table by the window, opposite a grand piano that seemed pretentious and out of place.

Hero hadn't played piano in such a long time; not since James. It'd been too difficult. But the urge expanded within him like steam in a boiler, trapped by the valve of his throat. He might explode if he couldn't play.

He asked a waiter if it'd be okay.

The waiter recoiled as if he'd never heard the words before. 'Of course. Please.'

Service with a sneer, so typical of London. Hero approached the piano with trepidation.

It's been too long, old friend.

He already knew what he was going to play. He thought back to the last time he'd played a piano—at home, with his brother.

Yes, it has. Bruv.

He breathed deeply and began.

He could feel James. It was as if his brother were there playing next to him. The icy chill of that sadness cooled the lava that tracked up into his throat.

Everyone in the room stopped eating; they turned to face him, mesmerised by the power of the music. He finished the piece and stood up. Stillness descended upon the room, the usual clatter of metal upon porcelain silenced. Then the shuffling of his feet broke the quiet, unleashing a crescendo of hands upon hands.

Hero looked around at the rapturous crowd for a moment, then bowed his head without acknowledging them and headed back towards his friends.

All those years, I've missed you. What happened? Where've you been? What're you doing now?

Outside in the rain, across the street from the restaurant, two eyes watched from the darkness of an alleyway. They were silvery with the cold of the air, steamy breath floating away in front of them.

*

'Excuse me.' A thick female Italian accent interrupted Hero's thoughts. 'That was beautiful. No one has ever played like that, not here.'

'Thank you.' He smiled at the waitress.

'What was it?'

'"Nuvole Bianche" by Ludovico Einaudi.'

'It was amazing. I'd love to hear you play more.' She handed him a folded piece of paper. 'My number. Call me.' Her head tilted away, her cheeks rosy.

'Oh, I see. Okay.' He stuffed the paper into his top pocket.

Opposite him at the table, Catherine smiled at him and winked. He couldn't stop looking at her. It was her twinkling eyes; they made his heart jump every time. A few drops of sweat arose along the searing heat of his hairline. It seemed as if time had stopped.

Careful.

Behind him, a bottle smashed against the floor. His skin prickled as a woman at the next table screamed.

'You killed my daughter,' snarled a woman's voice over his shoulder. 'She was all I had—now it's your turn.'

He craned his neck. A scruffily dressed woman stood behind him, training a gun directly at Catherine.

A Decision.

Instinctively, he slowed time with such intensity that his brain heated up. Everyone was frozen mid-sentence. Catherine had a look of horror in her eyes; the gun-woman, a transfixed expression of pure focus. Everyone else staring at the shooter, aghast.

The gunwoman was squeezing the trigger. In less

292

than a heartbeat, Hero poked his finger behind it to prevent the gun from firing. As he normalized time, he used his other hand to break her wrist with a loud snap.

Outside, the rain continued its clatter on the cars lining the street as a low-pitched murmur of voices blew down the alleyway. The glittering eyes faded to black.

Welcome back, bruv.

Chapter 43

Bertrande

When Bertrande and Ravenscroft arrived at the restaurant, the rain was still pelting down like shards of liquid metal. They'd managed to park right outside the entrance—another advantage of being a policeman.

'I really don't understand why we've been called to the scene to investigate this, sir,' Ravenscroft said. 'It's a petty gun crime. No one was killed, and the woman with the gun has been taken back to the station.'

'Apparently there's something unusual about it. Let's find out.' Bertrande pushed open the car door. 'Better run—don't want to ruin your suit.'

'And I was just settling in to watch *X Factor*,' Ravenscroft mumbled.

'In that case, I did you a favour,' Bertrande called over his shoulder.

Mostly unscathed from the watery onslaught, they were met at the door by a smartly dressed elderly man.

Bertrande pulled out his identity card. 'I'm Chief Inspector Bertrande. This is Sergeant Ravenscroft.'

'Good evening, sir. I'm Jacques Dumont, the manager here at The Rib Room.'

The man's accent reminded Bertrande of his child-hood. He pushed that impatiently aside. 'Can you tell us what happened?'

They began walking into the restaurant.

'Well, I was in the office at the time.'

'So who did see the incident?'

'The maître d' saw the lady walk in with the gun.'

'Okay, let's start there. We'll need an office to con-duct the interviews. Can we use yours?'

Dumont pointed towards a door at the back of the restaurant. 'Of course, it's over there. You'll need to walk through the kitchen to get to it.'

'And the maître d'?'

'Marco—over there.' Dumont indicated a smartly dressed man surrounded by other staff.

'Thanks.' He nodded politely, then tipped his head towards the knot of employees. 'Ravenscroft, would you be so kind?'

The office was a small, windowless, dingy affair containing a wooden desk piled high with invoices and receipts. Bertrande sat down in the chair behind the desk, whilst Ravenscroft followed the maître d'.

'So, Marco, tell me what happened,' Bertrande said.

Marco gripped a bunch of his floppy black hair. 'That woman walked right in. Before I could stop her, she'd barged past one of the waiters, gone across to the table with all those people, and was pointing the gun at one of them. Then that piano guy took the gun off her.'

'How?'

He shrugged. 'I didn't see, sorry.'

'Okay, anything else?'

Marco shook his head.

'Can you show Ravenscroft who the woman was pointing her gun at, please?'

Marco nodded and left with the sergeant in tow. Ravenscroft returned a few minutes later leading a pale girl with sunken eyes. She was visibly trembling as Ravenscroft seated her in one of the chairs.

Softly does it. 'Good evening, I'm Inspector Bertrande. And you are . . .?'

'Catherine Kennedy,' she murmured.

'Well, Catherine, tell me what happened.'

She shook her head and shrugged. 'I can't tell you that much, Inspector. When the woman came in, she shoved a waiter out of the way and made him drop a bottle. Then she came over and pointed her gun at me.'

'Did you know her?'

'No.'

'You've never seen her before? Are you sure?'

'She looked familiar, but I'm certain I've never met her.' Her lips started to tremble.

Bertrande sighed. 'Well, did she say anything to you?'

'No. Yes. She did, actually. She said, "You killed my daughter—now it's your turn."'

He allowed the silence to lie fallow, unperturbed.

She shook her head again. 'Inspector, I've no idea what she's talking about.'

'Okay. And what happened next?'

'Hero took the gun off her. He took the gun off her so quickly that her wrist was broken.'

Ravenscroft sniggered.

'Thank you, Sergeant,' Bertrande reprimanded.

'Sorry, sir.'

'Hiro? He's Japanese?'

She smiled wanly. 'No, Hero. It's a nickname. His real name is—wait, I . . . I can't remember.' She sat back in her chair. 'Richard! It's Richard. Richard Turner.'

'Okay, how did he manage to take the gun?'

She looked puzzled. 'I don't know. I didn't see.'

'But you must've been looking right at him,' Bertrande said incredulously.

'Yes, but I didn't actually see him take the gun. It was like one second she had it, and the next second he had it and he was holding her wrist. She was on her knees, screaming.'

Ravenscroft and Bertrande exchanged glances.

'Right, then. Well, thank you, Catherine.' He turned to Ravenscroft. 'Would you show her back and then bring in this hero guy?'

Ravenscroft smirked, and Bertrande glowered at him again.

'Yes, sir. Sorry, sir.'

Chapter 44

Hero

Catherine fixed her eyes on Hero as she returned from the interview.

Looks like I'm up next.

The sergeant followed her out of the office. 'Mr Turner?'

Hero nodded.

'Follow me.'

He shuffled behind the sergeant into the office with his eyes down. *Keep calm.*

The man behind the desk half rose. 'Good evening, I'm Inspector Bertrande. And you?'

'Richard. Richard Turner.'

Bertrande blinked a couple of times. 'Well, Mr Turner, what happened?'

His grip tightened. *Keep calm. For God's sake, think of something.*

The inspector remained implacable.

'I was walking back from the piano to rejoin my friends at the table—'

'Oh, you play?'

He moved his lips in a smile that didn't reach his eyes. 'I haven't played for a long time. It was nice.'

'What song were you playing?'

'Einaudi's "Nuvole Bianche".'

'I have an old friend who used to love Einaudi. His music is very beautiful, isn't it?'

The inspector's smile seemed cautious, as if roping off a pothole, but Hero couldn't for the life of him think how what he'd been playing might be relevant. 'Very.'

Bertrande made a circular motion with one hand. 'Go on.'

'I was walking back to the table, and a waitress stopped me to compliment my playing. She gave me her phone number.'

Ravenscroft glanced at Bertrande and grinned.

'I'd barely sat down when all the guys at the table suddenly looked horrified. They were staring at something behind me. I looked over my shoulder, and there was a woman pointing a gun directly at Catherine. I think you just interviewed her.'

Bertrande leaned forward. 'Yes, go on. What did you do?'

Just tell the truth. 'I stood up and took the gun off her, then put her in a wrist lock.'

'How?'

Shit! What do I say? He blinked. 'I don't really remember. It all happened so fast, I didn't have time to think. I reached over, yanked the gun out of her hand, and put her into a wrist lock.'

Bertrande folded his arms and sat back in his chair. 'That's quite impressive, Mr Turner. You must be very fast.'

Does he know something? Impossible. Don't say a thing. Don't give anything away. He remained silent, unmoving.

'Do you have any army training?' the inspector asked.

Whew. 'I did martial arts when I was younger.'

'Where did you train?'

'Just a local gym, with my brother.' His chest tightened. *What did I say that for?*

Bertrande paused a moment, tapping his finger on his lips. 'Was he as fast as you?'

'More or less.'

'What was his name?'

'James.'

Bertrande's eyes flickered.

He knows something. I'm sure of it. 'What?'

'When did you last see your brother, Mr Turner?'

Hero turned his face away. 'Not since I was eighteen. We had a huge argument, and he stormed out. He disappeared. Do you know my brother?'

'No,' Bertrande said nonchalantly.

Bullshit.

He looked back at the inspector. 'Is he in trouble?'

'No.'

The two men held each other's gaze in an awkward silence.

'Mr Turner, why do people call you Hero?'

Eh? Strange turn.

He bowed his head with a wry smile. 'They told you, did they?'

'It came up in conversation.'

'The name's followed me around ever since school.

300

I've never really understood the charm of it for other people. Why do you ask?'

'No reason—it's just an unusual nickname.'

'And a very annoying one.'

They all sniggered together.

'Okay, Mr Turner, you may go,' Bertrande said.

Hero slid his hands down the thighs of his pants, discreetly wiping the sweat from his palms, shook hands with the officers, and turned to go.

At the door, he glanced back over his shoulder at Bertrande. The two policemen were chatting sombrely; Bertrande glanced up and held Hero's gaze.

He's going to come after me, isn't he?

Chapter 45

Bertrande

One by one, Ravenscroft showed in the patrons for Bertrande to interview. They all said the same thing: the woman came in and pointed the gun at Catherine, and then Hero disarmed her, although no one could actually describe how he did it.

The policemen stepped out of the office into the main restaurant.

'Okay, all of you, we're finished,' Bertrande called out. 'Have a good night.'

The crowd murmured in relief, and people began gathering their belongings and slipping out the front doors.

He leaned close to Ravenscroft. 'I see why they call him Hero now.'

'Why?'

He nodded across the room. 'Look at him.'

The young man was busying about with a look of real concern for Catherine, who was shivering as if she were freezing cold. He was handing one of her friends some money for a cab to take her home and look after her for the night.

Ravenscroft gave Bertrande a questioning look.

'You wouldn't expect that from a banker, now, would you?'

He nodded politely at a last knot of people near the doors and gave a final glance at Turner.

You don't remember me, do you, Richard?

Chapter 46

Bertrande

The woman waiting in the interview room looked frightened, desperate. As he and Ravenscroft sat down opposite her, Bertrande opened the folder he'd been carrying. It was a report of the evening's events and the interview that'd already been conducted with her.

'You've waived your right to a lawyer. Are you sure about that?'

She nodded.

'I just want to talk to you. I read over the interview notes from earlier tonight, and I wondered if you can help me fill in some blanks.'

She nodded again, though she was visibly shaking.

'It's Mrs Pearce, isn't it?'

'Yes.'

'Well, Mrs Pearce, what's all this about then?' He smiled and tilted his head.

'I wanted to kill her. It's as simple as that.' Her voice was robotic.

'Why?'

She shuffled in her seat and looked down at the table

for a moment, then back at Bertrande. 'Like I said before, she killed my daughter.'

Bertrande and Paul exchanged glances.

'And how did she do that?'

'She gave her the wrong medicine.'

'How d'you work that out?'

'There was a guy. He told me.'

How long would this hold up? Bertrande got up suddenly, startling the others, and began pacing up and down his side of the table. 'So some guy tells you that someone you've never met killed your daughter, and you believed him?'

'No, it wasn't like that. He was a doctor. He was the one who agreed to get her the new drug.'

What?

He stopped pacing. 'Paul, come with me.'

Ravenscroft picked up the report, and they left the room.

'What's she talking about? There's no mention of any new drug or anything like that in the patient notes.'

'Honestly, sir, I don't know.'

'But the girl did get better for a while. What was her name?'

Ravenscroft consulted the papers in his hand. 'Rachel, sir.'

'And then suddenly Rachel got worse?'

'Yes, sir.'

'I mean, that would fit with what she's saying.'

The pair stared at each other for a moment.

'I have to say, sir, I've seen a lot of liars in this business,' Ravenscroft said. 'I'll tell you something, she isn't one. She believes what she's saying.'

Bertrande grinned. 'I agree. I'm glad you're working with me, mate. You're a good copper. Come on.'

They went back in and sat down again.

'Mrs Pearce, can you tell me about this doctor?' he asked, as if enquiring about a friend.

She shrugged. 'He was nice.'

Bertrande let the silence grow.

She shook her head. 'He was good-looking. I think he had a beard or stubble. It's strange, I can't really remember. I don't really care what he looked like. He had this new experimental drug that could save my daughter—my baby.' A steeliness hardened in her face, then softened again. 'He offered it to me—he showed me Rachel's charts, he explained that she had no chance except for this. That was nothing I didn't already know. Then he showed me the results from this new drug. They were amazing.'

'That sounds as though it must have been an expensive proposition.'

'No, no, not at all. That was the thing—he didn't want anything for it. He wanted to help. I had no reason to doubt him. Why would I doubt a doctor in a hospital?'

Bertrande shifted in his seat. 'That's fair, I guess. And you agreed to use the drug?'

'Of course I did. I had nothing to lose. He didn't promise me anything, but what little hope he offered—it was something.' She put her head in her hands. 'It was more than we had before.'

Bertrande waited patiently until she wiped away her tears. 'And then what happened?'

'Well, Rachel started to get better. The speed was

incredible. We all thought she'd make it. But then she started to get worse—and again, the speed of it . . . She was gone almost before we had time to say goodbye. The doctors couldn't understand. They were testing her blood all the time, but they couldn't work out what was happening. It wasn't until it was too late that Dr Gilmore realised that that girl, that stupid girl, had been giving Rachel the wrong medicine.'

'Dr Gilmore?' he asked. 'That was this doctor's name?'

She nodded through clenched teeth.

'Okay, thanks. And I'm sorry for your loss, ma'am.'

They prepared to leave the room again. 'You know, ma'am, what Dr Gilmore told you is impossible.'

She stared back at him.

'No hospital—or doctor, for that matter—would ever allow an untrained person like Catherine to handle medicine of that nature. I'm sorry, but whatever happened, that wasn't it.'

She whimpered a little as she started to weep again.

The two officers walked quickly back to their desks. The floor was deserted, the silence broken only by the hum of the vacuum cleaner pulsating backwards and forwards. The night crew were already in.

Bertrande closed the glass door to his office. There was no way around it. 'Right, Ravenscroft, let's find this Dr Gilmore guy, then. We need to be quick on this.'

'It's gonna be a long shift, isn't it, sir?'

'I'm afraid so.'

'Shall I get the hospital on the phone, sir?'

'If this doctor is real and he's broken the law, no. I'd like to surprise him.'

Ravenscroft dropped into his chair. 'You don't think he's real?'

At the desk opposite, Bertrande tapped in his password and started scrolling through his emails. In a browser window on his second monitor, he navigated to Chelsea and Westminster Hospital website and searched for 'Gilmore'.

'I think it was one of the other doctors covering themselves, but you never know. He could be real—or it could be something much more sinister.' *Would a doctor really experiment on patients? Would an entire hospital?*

Ravenscroft nodded distractedly, pounding away at a computer keyboard that was at some risk of being buried by any of the stacks of files piled around it. 'What do you mean?'

Bertrande tapped his finger to his mouth. 'We're almost certainly going to have to talk to their security to find out who this guy is, aren't we? Let's take another look at the file and see if we can work out when this Dr Gilmore should've been there.'

'I've got it up on the screen now, sir.'

He came around the desk and peered at the monitor. 'So when did Rachel start getting better, according to the doctor's report?'

Ravenscroft pointed. 'That was around February, sir, looking at this. It's as you said. You can see that the doctors actually thought she might make a full recovery at one point.'

'And when did she start getting worse?'

'About a month later, give or take.'

'And can we cross-check that against the dates when Mrs Pearce was there?'

'We'll need to use their system for that, sir.'

Bertrande drummed his fingers on the desk. 'Actually, do give them a call, but only ask them about Mrs Pearce. Get them to email across her entry and exit times.'

The thrill of the chase still excited Bertrande even after all these years. He didn't like that he enjoyed it either, he wished he wasn't needed at all. So much darkness in this world.

Ravenscroft replaced the receiver. 'They're sending it now. We should have it in the next ten minutes, I guess.'

He nodded.

'Coffee?'

'Sure. Canteen?'

By the time they returned with their drinks, the email from the hospital was waiting. Bertrande scanned the list of entry and exit times. *And now a night of good old-fashioned detective work. Dr Gilmore, whoever you are, if you've done what I think you have, I'm going to nail you, you bastard.* Mon Dieu, *I sound just like—*

He set his coffee on the desk and reached for his coat. 'Can you print that for me? I think it's about time we visited the hospital.'

Chapter 47

Bertrande

Everything was surgically clean at the Chelsea and Westminster, to be expected, the usual white and blue NHS colours everywhere and dreary, tired green lino floors. They took a lift big enough for a bed up to the first floor. The corridors were empty. Visiting hours were long over, with only the staff left and those in the emergency wing on the other side.

'Good evening, gentlemen,' said the receptionist. 'How can I help you?'

'Good evening. I'm Inspector Bertrande, and this is Sergeant Ravenscroft.' They showed their identity cards. 'We were hoping to talk with Dr Gilmore, if he's available.'

'Doctor who?' She giggled at the way it sounded. 'I'm sorry, it's just I've literally never heard of Dr Gilmore.'

They didn't have time for this. Bertrande glared at her. 'Can you check?'

She clicked open a document and scrolled with her mouse. 'I'm sorry, there's no doctor at the hospital by that name.'

He pressed his lips together. 'Okay, we need to talk to your security.'

'I'll have them come up straightaway.'

He shook his head. 'Just tell us where they are. We need to go to them.'

She stood and pointed across the way. 'They're in the basement. Take the lift down there. You'll see the signs in front of the lift.'

'Thanks.'

In the security room, they were met by an imposing middle-aged woman. 'What can I do for you gentlemen? Are you lost?'

'Good evening, madam.' Bertrande brought out his identification.

Her eyebrows went up. 'Is there a problem, Mr Bertrande?'

'We have a suspect who's saying that she spoke to a Dr Gilmore at this hospital in the children's ward. We've been up there, and they've said he's not on the system. We'd like to see if we can identify him from your security footage.'

'Of course. It might take a bit of time to get that sorted. Do you know what dates and times you're looking for?'

Ravenscroft handed over the printout. 'It'll be any one of these between this time here and this one here.' He pointed to the entries and exits columns.

Her eyes widened. 'That's a lot of footage. We'll have to put that on a hard drive for you.'

Bertrande tried to disguise his impatience. 'Is there any way we can see it now, please? It's important.'

'Erm, I guess I could set you up on a monitor over there and we could go through the footage.' She pointed to the far end.

The three of them walked over and sat down.

'I'm Ellie, by the way,' she said, extending her hand.

'Call me Bertrande,' he said.

Ravenscroft was already settling into his chair. 'And you can call me Paul.'

Ellie showed them how to use the control to follow Mrs Pearce's visits through the hospital.

They sifted through all the dates and times on the list. There was Mrs Pearce, arriving at reception, walking down the corridor to Rachel's room, going in, talking with her daughter, and then leaving the way she came. Sure enough, during another visit, one of the doctors came into the room and started talking with Mrs Pearce.

'Freeze that!' Bertrande said as the doctor faced the camera.

Ravenscroft captured the shot. 'Ellie, can we get this as a picture on email?'

'Press the Print Screen button.' She pressed the key, and a little text box opened up asking for a place to send it. 'Now put in your email address, okay?'

'Thanks.'

'Anytime, honey,' she said, touching his arm.

The security room became darker and quieter as the depths of night drew in and lights were switched off to conserve energy, until all they could hear was the faint hum of the computers.

It took over six hours to review all the footage. They identified only six people who'd been in Rachel's room and spoken with Mrs Pearce, two doctors and four nurses.

Bertrande pushed his chair back, bleary-eyed. 'Right, then, so this is the lot?'

Ravenscroft wiped his hand across his face as if to clean off a film of tiredness. 'Yes, sir. As far as I can see, this is it.'

Bertrande had seen something else, but he didn't want to tell Ravenscroft. Was the young sergeant ready for this? Did he suspect? Even with all his experience, Bertrande couldn't bring himself to believe that someone could be so callous. He needed to confirm it wasn't true.

He stifled a yawn. 'Let's get some sleep. I'll meet you back here at nine thirty. The shift'll be changing, and with any luck, we'll get to see all six at once. We'll see if we can find out who this Dr Gilmore really is.'

'Right you are, sir.' Ravenscroft lurched to his feet.

'I'll call us a couple of cabs—this one's on me.'

Chapter 48

Bertrande

Bertrande entered the hospital at exactly nine thirty the next morning. Ravenscroft was already waiting.

'Exactly on time, sir.'

'Never keep people waiting, Ravenscroft. Always remember that. It'll hold you in good stead.' He took a breath. 'Come on, let's get to it.'

The hospital manager, Sarah Furness, greeted them and showed them to a small office. She took the list and agreed to send in the staff, starting with Dr Phillimore, who was looking to get away quickly.

A few minutes later, there was a knock, and a bespectacled woman with blond hair tied back in a ponytail appeared from around the door. Bertrande noticed that she had kind eyes, the sort of eyes that children would immediately trust.

'Dr Phillimore, is it?' Bertrande said.

She nodded.

'Please, take a seat. Have you ever worked with Dr Gilmore?'

She settled on the edge of her chair. 'No. In fact, I've never heard of him. Or her.'

'Hmm.'

'What's all this about?'

'I need to ask you a few questions about one of your patients, Rachel Pearce.'

She wearily unwound her stethoscope from her neck and slipped it into one pocket of her white coat. 'Oh. That was such a sad case. We really thought she was going to make it, and then . . .'

'Why do you think she got better, in those final days?'

'Honestly, we don't know.'

'Doesn't that worry you?'

She looked slightly affronted. 'Yes, of course it does, especially as we searched for a very long time.'

'Searched?'

'We ran blood tests and full toxicology screenings to try to explain how she was getting better, but there was nothing, nothing at all, let alone anything unusual.' She sighed. 'If only we could have found something. Imagine what we could've done with that.'

Pain washed over her face before it returned to the expressionless façade it'd been before. Years of watching children die did that to you, and he understood all too well. He'd had some very hard-to-stomach cases involving little ones. He swivelled side to side in his chair, then leaned forward. 'So you're not aware of anybody administering an experimental drug to her, for example?'

'Of course not, that's absurd—and illegal, I might add.'

'Is it? I mean, if there's no hope, and the parent and child agree, surely that would be fine, right?'

'Still illegal, I'm afraid, but you're right, it poses a serious ethical question for us doctors.'

'Would you be tempted?'

She squinted at him, trying to read his intentions. 'I think that would depend. If it was completely experimental, then no. But if there were good results attached to it, I might be inclined.'

They sat in silence for a moment, staring at each other. The air seemed as thick as Greek yoghurt.

'But, as I said, I didn't. And in any case, there's no such drug.'

Bertrande caught her gaze. 'Let's just say there was a drug, a miracle cure for cancer. How would you administer it to a patient like Rachel?'

'That'd depend on what the drug was, but the most obvious way would be to inject it into her drip.'

'How long would it take to work?'

'Again, that would depend on how it works,' she replied, tapping her foot.

'Give me a ballpark.'

She glanced at her watch. 'If it's in the drip and it's rewriting the cell structure, about two or three weeks. But that's just a guess.'

Bertrande smiled warmly. 'Okay, thanks. You may go.'

She stood up.

'You don't have any holiday plans, do you? In case we need to speak to you again.'

She frowned and narrowed her eyes. 'Are you saying you think someone used an experimental drug on Rachel, and that's why she got better?'

He watched her carefully. 'I'm not saying that.'

Her face went blank, as if she were fixated on some faraway object beyond the walls. 'And what happened?

The drug didn't work? The drug stopped working?' Her expression changed to one of abject horror. 'They stopped the experiment? Midway through? Listen, if somebody in this hospital is illegally experimenting on patients, I need to know.'

Bertrande forced a smile.

'Have a nice day, Doctor.'

She glared at him for what seemed like eternity, then wheeled about and left.

As the door clicked shut, Ravenscroft leaned forward. 'Dr Phillimore?'

'And?'

'Dr Gilmore, Dr Phillimore—they're kinda similar.'

'Mrs Pearce said she spoke to a man. Not sure if you noticed, but Dr Phillimore's a woman.'

Ravenscroft laughed. 'Of course. But even so, is that really a coincidence?'

'I doubt it.'

'Right.'

Bertrande glowered at him incredulously. 'First rule of a con artist, Ravenscroft: choose a name that's similar to one that people already know and trust.'

'Yes, of course,' Ravenscroft nodded. 'Sorry, sir.'

'Don't worry about it. Everyone's allowed a lapse, especially after the night we just had.'

The rest of the interviews proceeded in much the same way. No one had heard of Dr Gilmore, and all were shocked and confused at the idea of the use of experimental drugs in the hospital. They were staring glumly at each other in the empty room when Sarah Furness returned.

'I've rechecked the records, and there's definitely no Dr Gilmore, but I'm sure you already knew that,' she said snippily.

'Yes, we gathered,' Bertrande said.

'I heard that you have some concerns about the use of experimental drugs?'

'I don't, not anymore. In fact, I'm fairly certain I know what's going on, and it's nothing to do with anyone at the hospital, you'll be pleased to hear.' He sat back in his chair and let out a sigh full of the fatigue of terrible knowledge.

'Would you like to elaborate, Inspector?' she asked.

'No, I would not. As I said, it's nothing to do with you.'

She shrugged and left.

'Would you like to elaborate for me, sir?' Ravenscroft raised his eyebrows.

He rubbed his forehead. Images of past cases flitted before his eyes. His conclusion was becoming unavoidable. *I can't believe you would do such a thing. Please don't be—*

'Sir?'

'We need to look at those videos again. And this time, we need to look very, very carefully.'

'What're we looking for?'

'Anything, no matter how small, how insignificant. If it seems even a little bit strange, we need to note it.'

'Stop!' Bertrande yelled.

Ravenscroft hit the Stop button with a slap as Ellie surged across the room towards them. Bertrande had told her that she didn't need to stay while they reviewed the footage yet again, but the investigation seemed to have caught her imagination.

'Go back. I mean, forward. You know what I mean.'

Ravenscroft smirked. 'Right you are, sir. Here we go.'

'As slowly as possible.'

'Got it.' He feathered the rotary control.

'There!' Bertrande burst out again.

Ravenscroft stopped the video at night-time in Rachel's room. 'What? I don't see anything.'

Bertrande scrutinized the scene. He'd seen this before, but he had to be certain. 'Can we compare that to the same time on the previous day?'

'I'm not sure,' Ravenscroft muttered. 'Ellie? Can we snapshot one frame and compare it to another?'

'I don't think so, hun.' She stared at the screens, considering it for a few more moments. 'Actually, if you press Print Screen, you could move it over to that second monitor there and then scroll to the next frame on this one.'

'That's perfect.' He winked.

'Anything for you, hun.' She returned to her desk, whistling on the way.

'Can you see the difference?' Bertrande demanded.

'Honestly, other than Rachel's position on the bed, nothing.' He stared at the screens, frantically looking between the two. 'I guess that snapshot's a little bit darker than this one on the live video.'

Bertrande slapped both palms on the table emphatically. 'Exactly.'

It was good to confirm his suspicions, but he knew

319

it was about to get a lot more difficult. It was time for Ravenscroft to know the truth. He needed to see it.

'I'm not sure I understand, sir.'

'I'll explain later. Right now, I want you to go back to where we were and watch everything that happens whenever Mrs Pearce is in the hospital but she's not with her daughter.'

They began the tedious process yet again. They'd gone back about a week when Ravenscroft stopped the footage.

'There.' He pointed at the screen. Mrs Pearce had stopped in the corridor and appeared to be having a conversation with someone just out of the frame.

'Well, she's obviously talking to someone, and then . . . I guess she must come . . . in here?'

'And?'

'Who she talking to? It's a shame there's no camera in here.'

'Exactly.'

Ravenscroft gave him a look of anticipation.

'I saw a case like this a few years ago,' Bertrande said. 'A guy was killed in Westminster tube, murdered in the middle of the day right in front of a bunch of witnesses, but when we looked at the footage, he couldn't be seen.'

'What do you mean?'

'The exact point at which the man was killed was out of sight of all of the cameras, and the man that the witnesses described couldn't be seen entering or exiting the area.'

Ravenscroft stiffened and jerked his head back. 'What are you saying, sir? He's invisible?'

He gave the sergeant a withering look. 'The witnesses didn't describe anything unusual, so he's not invisible to people. But he can't be seen on camera.'

Ravenscroft laughed raucously. 'Please tell me you're not gonna say he's a vampire.'

'Vampire? You owe me a pint, Ravenscroft.'

Ravenscroft pushed back his chair and looked at his watch. 'Lunchtime, sir—I thought you were never gonna ask.'

Chapter 49

Hero

Who will they send?

Hero's bowels felt like water the following morning as he got into the lift. Three smartly dressed women poured in next to him, excitedly chatting. They seemed to be fighting a fashion challenge every day. He was relieved he only had one suit.

Who will they send?

' . . . apparently pulled a gun. Just like that.'

'Which floor?' he asked as he pressed three.

'Eight, please. That's unbelievable.'

'So how did he get her?'

The doors slid open, and Hero rushed for the double doors at the end of the empty lobby. They opened on the usual wall of noise, but after a few seconds, all that could be heard was BloomBox TV and the occasional tapping of keyboards. Hundreds of eyes turned his way, and there came a dull, thunderous sound as people across the floor began to stand up and clap.

He froze in the entry area. Everybody was facing him; the applause was for him.

Who will they send?

He turned, thinking he'd make a tactical retreat to the restroom, when his eyes caught someone still sitting, her head down.

Catherine.

He walked straight over to her, not looking at anybody else. As he drew nearer, she raised her head, her eyes glimmering with unshed tears.

'Hi,' he said with a smile.

'Hey.'

'How're you doing this morning?'

'Okay, I guess. Had a nightmare about—'

He put his hand on her shoulder. 'It'll be okay. BB Bakery later?'

'That'd be nice.'

'You look like you need it.' He smiled again and started towards his desk.

'Hero?' she called after him. 'Thank you. For last night.'

He nodded and continued to his desk.

Sam skidded around the corner. 'Hey, blud. I heard about last night.'

Has anyone not heard about it?

Sam clapped him on the back. 'How did you do it?'

'Do what?'

'Get the gun?'

He gave Sam a weak half smile. 'I don't know, I just did. I had some training when I was younger.'

'Yeah, but even so, that must've been *intense*.'

Hero busied himself turning on his computer and preparing his desk for work, but Sam kept talking.

'No seriously, that must have been some shit to see.

I can't believe I missed it. I'd love to see you train. Can you show me?'

'Not really.'

'Oh come on, blud,' he pleaded.

'Nah, mate. Sorry.'

Sam leaned over his computer. 'How about a few rounds in the gym, just you and me?'

'Oh mate, come on, seriously? You know I'm not into all that.'

'Just this one time, so I can see your speed.'

He sighed heavily. He could probably use the practice.

Who will they send?

'Okay, okay, if it'll shut you up—but only if it's just you and me. No one else there, right?' He pointed at Sam, emphasising his demand.

'You got it.' Sam clapped him painfully on the back. 'After work? Six thirty?'

Hero rolled his shoulders to shake off the sting of his skin. 'Fine, see you then.'

'You were right, I really did need this.' Catherine sipped her peppermint tea. The warmth of it must have been working, because her face was becoming rosier. She'd looked pallid this morning, even whiter than the sandwiches taking up half of the table.

The morning had crawled by. Hero had jumped and looked over his shoulder at every little sound. But so far, nothing. Of course it wouldn't happen at work.

'You're becoming an honorary British woman,' he said in jest. 'A good ol' cup of tea can solve any problem.'

'I can't stop thinking about it.' She was sniffing more food than she was eating.

Hero was wolfing his down as per usual; he would need all his strength for later. 'Understandable.'

She looked into his eyes. 'How can you be so calm?'

'I had a different upbringing, I guess. Very little fazes me.'

'Perhaps, but I don't think that's it. There's something about you.'

'What do you mean?'

'I don't know exactly. Like how did you get the gun off that woman?'

He slowly put down his cup. 'The question is not how, but why?'

'I don't follow.'

'Of course you don't. I don't normally help people, not like that. There're going to be consequences.'

'What're you saying?'

He glanced around them. 'I can't explain everything right now, but this might be the last time I see you.'

'What? Are we breaking up?'

He took her hand in his and held it gently. 'No, Catherine. I've never felt like this before. Every day I'm excited to come to work, and it's because of you. Every time I see you, my heart does a little twist and I feel better. I thought I knew what love was, and then I met you.'

Her face turned crimson, but she gripped his hands more tightly.

'That's why I saved you. Because I couldn't bear a world without you in it, no matter what the cost.'

'What does that mean?' she said.

'Something the inspector said, I don't know. But I've got a bad feeling. We'll see. And then maybe . . .'

Who will they send?

He drew in a deep breath. 'Anyway, we need to get back.'

They gathered up their things, and Hero left twenty pounds for the bill.

As they started for the door, Catherine said, 'Can I see you after work tonight? I don't want to be alone. I feel so vulnerable.'

He wrapped one arm around her shoulders. 'I'd like that.'

The sun had burned through the morning gloom, making their return to the office pleasantly warm.

'I've got to spar with Sam after work before we can go this evening,' he noted with some annoyance. 'Can you wait for me until after that? He's been on at me to fight with him since I started working here. And after last night, he's been non-stop about it, so I thought I might as well do it, if only to shut him up.'

'Can I come?'

He scrunched his face. 'Hmm, I don't know.'

'Please.' She nudged him with her elbow.

'Okay, then—but only you.'

Hero looked up at the digital clock in the centre of the trading floor: 6:15 p.m., the perfect time to stop. Just enough time to get to the gym and change. Sam had left some time earlier, saying he needed to warm up to have any chance at all, and the floor had become eerily quiet. He collected his kit bag and made his way towards the elevators. There was no one in the lobby, either.

Where the hell is everybody?

The sound of the lift doors sliding open reverberated, startling him. His hair prickled at the sight of the empty cabin. What the hell was going on? The lifts were normally bursting at the seams at this time of day. The soles of his shoes echoed on the floor with each step as he stepped into the lift and pressed B. The gears whirred into life, the motor emitting a constant hum as he descended.

He went to shift his kit to the other hand, but it wasn't there. *I could've sworn I picked it up.* He looked down by his feet. It wasn't there.

And then he smiled forlornly at what he saw instead. *Of course.* His suit had turned white. In his hand was a razor-sharp sword. *They always come for you when you're alone.* His stomach imploded as the whirring gears were replaced by a low-pitched murmur of a thousand voices.

Brace yourself, bruv.

The walls of the lift seemed to be mirrors facing each other, disappearing backwards into an infinite fractal darkness. His heart accelerated as the darkness enveloped him, dragging him through the back wall of the lift. He let his muscles relax except for his grip on the sword, which tightened.

The winds dissipated, the voices subsided. *It's true, then. The second time is easier.*

The familiarity of the voice that spoke from behind him sent a bolt of lightning from his neck to his groin.

'Hello, bruv. Long time no see.'

Oh God, no.

Chapter 50

Bertrande

The two officers ambled outside the hospital.

'Where shall we go?' Bertrande asked.

'It's the King's Road, sir, I'm sure we'll find somewhere.' Ravenscroft shrugged.

'This way.'

They turned right out of the hospital and strolled down the road.

'It was more of a rhetorical question, Paul—and whilst we're having pints, don't call me "sir". Call me François.'

Ravenscroft smiled dubiously and then pointed. 'There's a pizza place just there. It's a chain, so the beer probably won't be too good.'

'You English and your beer. It always has to be perfect. Anyway, we're still on duty.'

Bertrande's stomach took a long, loud growl in appreciation of the welcoming oregano and tomato sauce aroma hanging in the air. Ravenscroft glanced across and smirked. Brightly clothed tourists chattered loudly about the sights they'd seen that morning.

'Could we have somewhere quiet, at all?' Bertrande asked the waiter at the entrance.

'Not sure about quiet at this time of day, but I think there's a place free at the back.' He showed them to a booth in the corner at the rear of the restaurant. 'Best I can do, sorry.'

'It's perfect,' Bertrande said as he sat down. Time to let everything go for a few precious moments.

Ravenscroft slid into the booth opposite him and pushed the menu aside. 'I already know what I want.'

'Me too.'

He folded his hands on the table. 'Can I speak frankly, sir—I mean, François?'

'With me, always.'

'Yeah, but I mean without reprisal, no matter what I say?'

'Like I said, I always respect honesty, regardless of the content.'

Ravenscroft shifted uneasily in his seat. 'Who—'

'Have you decided, gentlemen?' the waiter asked.

'Calzone for me, and a Coke please,' Bertrande said.

'And pepperoni for me, and orange juice to drink, please.'

The waiter scribbled the orders and left.

'You were saying?' Bertrande said.

'Who exactly do you work for? 'Cos it isn't London Met, that's for sure.'

Bertrande tilted his head. *Let's see how smart you really are.* 'How do you work that out?'

'When you first joined us from who knows where, it was like you'd dropped in from outer space. I was immediately partnered with you, told to drop everything I was working on. Not that I mind. It's just not normal.'

Bertrande smiled.

'And then we started investigating these very odd cases, all seemingly unconnected—but I get the very distinct impression that they are connected, and you know exactly how.'

Very smart indeed. Good. That's why I picked you.

'And when I say odd,' Ravenscroft continued, 'I mean just plain weird. Do you remember that guy in the high-rise, the one with his heart cut out and left in the bin?' His expression grew pained. 'In all my life, I've never seen anything like that.'

Bertrande took a deep breath and let it out slowly. 'The question you should ask yourself, Paul, is if you think you were assigned to me by accident.'

Ravenscroft didn't react.

I bet it crossed your mind. 'We've had our eye on you for some time now, Paul.'

Ravenscroft swallowed hard. 'Who's we, exactly?'

'I work for London Met most of the time. For example, remember that case on the train?'

Ravenscroft nodded. 'Who could forget?'

'That was a normal investigation. But occasionally I work for . . .' He shook his head imperceptibly.

Ravenscroft's eyes lit up. He got the message: 'not here'.

'And so how have you found the investigations so far?' Bertrande asked.

'Interesting, they're very interesting. But I really think it would help if I knew who or what it is we're looking for.'

'What if I told you—'

'One calzone, sir. One pepperoni. Orange juice. Coke.' The waiter left with his huge tray.

Bertrande took an enormous bite of his folded pizza. He needed it. 'Sorry . . . hungry . . . no breakfast.'

Ravenscroft took a slice, eating the pointy end first.

'What if I told you that there are people in this world that are very different from you and me?' Bertrande took another mammoth bite.

Ravenscroft rolled his eyes theatrically. 'I thought you said not to mention the V word again. I don't want to owe you yet another pint, do I now?'

Bertrande grinned. 'We're not talking about vampires.'

'Now you owe me a drink, sir.'

Time to get serious. 'These people—and we're pretty sure that they are people—they're fast.'

'So's Linford Christie.'

'We think these people are so fast that that's the reason they can't be seen on video. In fact, they're faster than a bullet.'

Ravenscroft muttered something about Superman, obfuscated by another mouthful of pizza.

'Superman's invincible, Paul. These people aren't. That guy in the high-rise, he was one of us. He was on the force. We'd kitted him out with a new weapon, a high-velocity rifle.'

'I don't think that's technically new.'

'This one was. It was like nothing you've ever seen. That rifle could propel bullets at Mach nine. You need eight weeks of training to use it.'

Ravenscroft whistled through his teeth.

'Yeah, that fast—but it still wasn't fast enough. He

found his target, locked on, then the radio went dead. By the time our guys got there, he was pretty much as you and I saw him. Of course the clean-up team had removed the gun before we arrived, but you get the idea.'

'So who the hell did that? *What* the hell did that?'

He pressed his lips together. 'We think it's all the same person, a gentleman by the name of James Turner.'

'Where've I heard that name before? Wait a sec—that guy's brother from last night? What was his name again? Richard? The hero? Richard Turner?'

Bertrande nodded, chewing more calzone.

Ravenscroft's mouth opened with shock. 'Hold on, hold on—and Hero's girlfriend was Catherine . . .'

That's it, Paul, connect the dots.

'. . . and Catherine used to work at the hospital, seeing Rachel'—he sucked in a breath—'who started to get better, we think, after being administered an experimental drug by this unknown Dr Gilmore.'

Nearly there.

Ravenscroft's eyes darted back and forth. 'Dr Gilmore is James Turner—Hero's brother.' He took a big swig of juice, then leaned on the table, his hand covering his mouth.

Here it comes.

'You think he did it deliberately.' His eyes were hollow with realisation.

So the pattern was clear to him too. 'Rachel gets worse, dies. Her mother, on the advice of Dr Gilmore—James Turner—blames Catherine and tries to kill her. And Hero stops Mrs Pearce.'

Ravenscroft took another giant gulp of his juice. 'But why?'

'Good question. Any thoughts?' He leaned forward, resting his chin in his palm. *Let's see how far you can go. How useful you'll be to me.*

'Richard said they had a big argument, didn't he?'

Bertrande nodded.

'Revenge, maybe? But for what?' Ravenscroft stroked his chin pensively. 'He's fast—I mean, he stopped Mrs Pearce from pulling the trigger, took the gun right off her without anyone seeing it. That's gotta be fast. And what was it you asked him about? His training, with his brother?'

'Yes.'

'But who trained them, then?'

'Exactly.'

Ravenscroft looked stunned. 'Oh my God, they're not the only ones, are they?'

Bertrande's smile broadened. *That's my boy. Welcome aboard.* 'There're many people like Turner, but it's worse than that.'

'They're organised.'

'We think it runs like a company, or something along those lines.'

'Doing what?'

Bertrande sat back in his seat. 'Bad things, Paul, very bad things.'

'Hold on—no, I'm sorry, but that Hero guy didn't seem like the kind of person that would rip someone's heart out, at least not to me. So maybe killing Catherine would've been a punishment because he didn't toe the company line?'

'Maybe. But did you see his reaction when I mentioned

his brother? That was genuine shock. I don't think he's a part of them. You're right. He's different from the others.'

'If he's got that skill but he's not part of their company, then he's an outsider to the outsiders. He must know, surely?'

Of course he knows. That must be the worst part.

'So he's been keeping it a secret for years. Jeezuz.'

Bertrande washed down the last of his pizza with his Coke and dabbed his mouth with his napkin.

'Can you imagine what it's like? To have to think about everything you say before you actually say it? To think about everything you do before you do it, constantly double-checking yourself?'

'Yes, Paul, I can,' Bertrande said quietly, sitting back in his seat.

'It must be exhausting.'

'Yes, it is.'

Ravenscroft paused. 'You never married, did you, François?'

'I never met the right girl.' He smirked.

'It's a modern world now. People would understand, you know.'

'So what happened when you came out, then?'

'Oh no, I'm not—'

Bertrande put on a Noel Coward voice. 'Homosexual, dear boy? I believe it's called being gay, nowadays.'

Ravenscroft went bright red.

'I'm also a good copper, Paul.'

The two policemen held each other's gaze for an uncomfortable few moments.

His voice became earnest. 'I meant what I said. We've been watching you. You have the knack. You ask the right questions, and you find your way to the answers. Do you realise that you've been driving this investigation since the beginning? Sure, I've prompted you in the right direction, but you uncovered the evidence, and you worked out the relationships. Like I said, you're a good inspector.'

'I'm a sergeant, François.'

'Are you sure about that? No one else on my team is.' Bertrande smiled, biting his bottom lip. 'I'll tell you one thing. The fact that you and I are different, that we have a secret that no one else can know—it helps us understand the people we're looking for.'

Ravenscroft sat back, folding his arms tightly.

'I think people know, but because I never say anything, they let it go, happy to ignore it. The force has made progress since I joined, but it's still got a way to go. They're not ready for people like us to be rubbing it in their faces, as they might say. And the world is not ready for people like Turner.'

'Yeah, I guess you're right, sir.' He brought his hand to his mouth as he considered everything he'd heard. 'I'm on board, not so much because of your speech—well, a little, I suppose—but because since I've been on this case with you, and especially now I know what it's all about, for the first time since I remember, I feel that I'm making a difference.'

'Well, come on then. Let's catch a killer.' He stood up. 'And a hero.'

Chapter 51

Hero

'So? How ya been?'

James seemed jovial despite the sword glinting in an invisible light. Hero glanced around furtively, as if looking for the hidden camera on a TV show.

James raised his eyebrows, expecting an answer.

'Okay, I guess.' Hero shook his head. 'A-and you?'

'Good, good.' James nodded. 'Well, this isn't a game of Touch My Chin, old boy. Shall we?' He raised his sword. '*En garde.*'

'I can't fight you, James.'

'That's fine by me—an easy kill. I'll be home in time for dinner. I think I'll have myself a nice hot fried bacon sandwich, dripping with fat. Delicious.' He licked his lips.

Hero's stomach tilted upside down at the thought.

James raised his sword and brought it slicing towards Hero's neck. At the last second, Hero dilated time and brought his sword upright in defence. Their weapons clattered together, sending sparks flying into the darkness and scattering across the floor like embers from an open fire.

'So you managed to find yourself some balls after all.' James puffed his cheeks out.

The knot set up camp in the pit of his stomach. *Welcome back, old friend.* 'I really didn't think you'd do it.'

'Yeah, well, you never really understood me, did you?'

'I thought I did. I remember you protecting me, teaching me, just being there. What happened to you?'

'Those days ended, bruv, when you decided to be a tit.'

They began circling each other slowly. Hero couldn't believe it was happening. He wanted to be somewhere else. With Catherine. Anywhere. Why did it have to be like this? Was he really going to fight his brother? To kill? To mur—

'Because I wouldn't fight? Murder people?'

'It's not murder if they're evil.'

I used to think that. But it's not true. Surely you know that? He snorted. 'So you decided to join them?'

'If you can't beat 'em, join 'em—or is it "join us"?'

Hero shook his head. 'What the hell has happened to you?'

'*You* happened to me, dickhead. Why couldn't you just carry on being a tit?'

'What?'

'She was supposed to die.'

'Who?'

James glowered incredulously. 'Your fucking girlfriend. Why didn't you let her die, like you did the others?'

'What're you talking about? I didn't let anyone die.'

337

'Really? How many people do you think lost their lives because you refused to join the Light? Thanks to you, the Dark are all over it, and I should know.'

Hero's legs weakened and he staggered backwards, trying desperately to steady himself, but there was nothing to hold on to. *My choice didn't matter. It never mattered.*

'Now, I haven't got time for this.' James's lips curled, snarling. 'Fight me, or die.'

He swiped his sword across Hero's eyes, catching the bridge of his nose. Warm blood poured down over his lips in a torrent.

James didn't hesitate. He hurtled closer, eyes empty, lunging at Hero's midriff. Hero skated sideways, the sword nicking his hip. He hobbled further backwards, off balance, and cried out as his coccyx smashed onto the floor. James hammered down, and he rolled, the blade clanging next to his ear. He flipped up onto his knees as James's blade angrily sliced through the air again. He brought his weapon sideways in defence.

'Just die,' James screamed.

Maybe I should. I murdered them. I deserve to die.

A face entered his mind, its gentle warmth smiling upon his soul. Catherine.

I won't just lie down and die.

James brought his weapon down once more, but Hero pushed back, knocking his brother off balance. He rose to his feet and raged forward, his mouth foaming. James stepped back uncertainly.

Hero's sword crackled ominously as he attacked faster and faster. James ducked—a small hairline cut.

Hero pulled on time with every fibre of his being. He brought his sword down again, flecks of spit flying from his mouth and then freezing mid-air. Sparks scattered from the collision of the weapons and hung next to them.

James cowered as Hero hammered him again and again.

Hero pulled time again. His sword roared with a rumbling thundercrack as he smashed at James.

'Leave me alone! Just leave me alone!' he screamed above the din.

The air around them was becoming choked with crystallized sparks and smoke. Hero swiped at his eyes with the back of his hand. *What the f—*

Something was wrong. He backed away. James remained crouched, as shaken by the elemental anomaly around them as he was. Fissures appeared in the darkness like a delicate eggshell cracking around them, forming a lattice of lightning.

'What the fuck is going on?' James cried.

'What's the matter, bruv, don't have all the answers?' Hero asked mockingly.

James's eyes snapped back to his. 'You have come a long way, haven't you?'

As the fissures brightened, the darkness lightened to a grey silk sheet, and imprints of something else began showing through: hands, bodies, faces contorted with anguish. There came a low murmur of groaning voices. Wind rushed in around them, and the noise became unbearable. James began to rise to his feet—

Then silence.

They were back in the gym. Sam had stupidly invited everyone—Bosch, Kevin, Justine, so many—and they all stood staring, open-mouthed. How much had they seen? Hero searched their faces; it was impossible to tell. His eyes ranged across them until he found one who seemed unperturbed. Vibrant. Real.

Catherine.

Chapter 52

Hero

Oh God, no. I can't let her see me like this. What will she think? Will she ever forgive me?

'Fight me,' James ordered.

He whipped his gaze back to his brother. 'I don't want to fight you, James.'

'Still a complete tit, then.' James looked at his finger-nails as if checking for dirt.

'Look we're out of the darkness. Let's go home, forget all about this.'

'You think that's going to work?'

Hero bolted for the double doors, shoulder first. They didn't budge, and he bounced off and tumbled to the floor.

James flung back his head and laughed like Ming the Merciless.

Hero got back to his feet and dusted himself off. *Too good to be true.*

Behind James, Bosch had edged through the crowd. Hero glowered at him: *Don't do it, don't do it.*

But Bosch lurched forward and grabbed James's sword hand, trying to rip the weapon from his grip.

'Bosch, no,' Hero shouted.

James grabbed Bosch's wrist and twisted into the lock. Bosch fell to his knees with a yell.

Hero's voice was low and steady. 'He didn't know, James.'

'That doesn't matter.'

'Please, James, let him go.'

'Shut up, dickwad.' He turned towards Bosch. 'Do you know what I normally do to anybody who interferes with my business?'

Bosch shook his head silently, in too much agony to speak.

'I'll tell you. I rip their heart out of their chest and play football with it.'

Bosch cringed.

'But don't worry, I'm not gonna do that. Okay?'

Bosch nodded.

With a single swipe of his blade, James removed Bosch's head, sending it rolling along the floor towards Sam Blagg's feet. Sam staggered out of the way, and the head continued all the way to the wall. Blood pumped onto the gym floor from Bosch's open neck, as if someone had dropped an expensive bottle of wine.

A couple of girls whimpered. Catherine covered her mouth and half turned away, but keeping Hero in view, transfixed. He kept her in his peripheral vision whilst doing his level best not to look directly at her. Mustn't invite James to—

'Shut up, or you'll be next,' James shouted at the crowd.

There was a loud thud as Kevin Burns collapsed in a heap.

342

James turned back to Hero. 'Now, fight me.'

I don't want to kill you, man. The word was easier to think this time. It made him want to throw up. 'I can't do this, James.'

'Well, then, you're going to die.' He took in a short, sharp breath as if he'd suddenly remembered something. 'Oh, Fi sends her regards, by the way.'

His whole body reacted. 'What?'

'You know, I really liked her.'

'You spoke to Fi?'

'Oh come on, bruv, do I have to spell this out for you? Why do you think she stopped talking to you? You weren't the only one who could make her scream.' The edges of his mouth formed the smallest of smiles. His eyes twinkled.

Hero couldn't believe what he was hearing.

'Although I have to say, your new girl is really nice. Such innocent eyes, don't you think? Don't worry, bruv. After you're gone, I'll look after her.' He turned and found Catherine amongst the onlookers and winked.

Shut up! Stop it. Shut UP! Hero's sword hand twitched. His whole body twitched with electricity; he felt invincible.

But James wouldn't stop talking. 'You know what I really like about sweet girls? It's when you finally break them, that look in their eyes. Hunger, pure hunger. You know they're going to be total sluts, fulfilling all your needs and loving every minute of it.' He nodded back at Catherine, his eyes pure black. 'I'm going to enjoy every inch of this one—and she's going to enjoy every inch of me.' He laughed psychotically, unhinged, like a cartoon *Bond* villain.

343

Hero's head snapped up, and James came into sharp focus. A Decision. A genuine Decision. Whoever this was, it wasn't the loving brother of his childhood. He imagined the light in Catherine's eyes fading as his brother had described. *I won't let you do this*.

His spirit ignited—not a fire, but a nuclear bomb. He slowed time as hard as he could and took a vicious swipe at his brother.

Parried.

He reversed and slashed again.

Parried. But James was open.

Hero spun inside James's defensive zone, smashing his brother's sword with a hammering blow. James's weapon hurtled through the air like a javelin and buried itself in the wooden floor, swaying to and fro.

Without hesitation, Hero whipped his blade to his brother's heart and plunged the blade all the way through, pinning James to the wall.

Someone screamed in the crowd behind him.

'Why?' Hero lamented as he staggered a step closer to his brother. 'Why did you do this? Why, why, why?'

James's eyes glazed over.

His brother was gone to a better place—he hoped. He already felt as though he'd been disembowelled, but if this was anything like before, he knew the truly harrowing part was about to begin.

James's body began to quake.

Hero stood transfixed as the fire moved up James's arms, legs, and body, engulfing him in flames. James was trying to scream; blood gurgled in his throat and spurted out of his mouth, which had begun to glow from the fire. The stench of burning flesh seared the air.

Hero's sword clattered to the floor, echoing across the gym.

The hot winds became stronger, and flames swirled around James's body. Hero backed away gingerly.

'Run, brother,' James croaked.

He turned to discover everyone's eyes transfixed on him in horror.

'Get down,' he shouted.

But nobody moved. The howling wind was now accompanied by the low-pitched groans of a thousand voices within. He ran towards the group.

'Don't just stand there—get down, now!' he screamed.

He dropped to the floor and rolled as the explosion hit, the force of it flowing over the top of his body. He continued back up to his feet and sprinted for the door. There, he paused to survey the prostrate crowd. One person was looking back at him: Catherine.

Her eyes pleaded with him to stay. He could hear her voice in his mind: *Please don't leave me.*

He looked back for an eternal moment. *But I must.*

Chapter 53

Turner

I found myself in a bright place, the inverse of the darkness—the purest white, everywhere. A figure walked towards me, and as he got closer, I recognised him. It was the Light Master, dressed in white from head to toe.

Was this a Justification?

'Welcome to the Light Room,' he said.

I nodded admiringly. 'You know, being God suits you.'

'I'm not God, as you well know.' He gestured around us. 'In here, the Dark can never come because there're no shadows. There's no darkness. We can talk freely.'

Wait a second. I remembered this—this happened a long time ago. I'd walked into the gym one afternoon, and no one had been there except the Light Master in the centre of the mat. He saw me and immediately placed his finger over his lips to signal me to keep quiet.

What's going on?

He beckoned to me, turned, and headed towards the lift; I followed silently. The doors closed behind us, and as the master placed his hand on the lower section of the button panel, it scanned him. The lift descended for what seemed like an eternity. Where was he taking me? Hell?

Finally, the doors opened into a room of brilliant, endless light. I wondered if it might make me go blind without shades, but the master didn't offer any, so I assumed it must be safe. We went in. The doors closed behind us, sealing themselves so completely that I couldn't see where the exit had been. The entire room was featureless, giving me the eerie feeling that I was floating in pure white light.

'Welcome to the Light Room, James,' the master said. 'In here, the Dark can never come because there are no shadows. There is no darkness. We can talk freely.'

Had he already said that? It sounded different now.

I grinned and played it off. 'It's dark in my ass crack.'

'Well, you be sure and tell me if there's a Dark in there, then.' He chuckled, but it faded faster than it had come.

His eyes seemed to become darker, and he leaned closer and closer to me. 'By now, I'm sure you've worked out who your mum and dad were?'

Chapter 54

Bertrande

Bertrande's nostrils twitched as he and Ravenscroft walked through the Saxon Goldberg gym, their shoes clipping on the granite floor. Bertrande peered inside the yoga room. *Sandalwood. Classy.* It almost felt wrong to enter with his shoes on.

'What the hell happened here?' Ravenscroft asked.

One white wall had obviously been blackened by fire, another a Picasso smeared in deep red. At the centre of the ruby tornado was the outline of a body. Bertrande's and Ravenscroft's footsteps made a hollow echo on the wooden floor as they walked across to inspect the spreading pool of blood leaking from a headless body.

'Okay, so this is new. My guess is this is the work of James Turner,' Bertrande said. 'Let's find out.'

They trundled back to the main cardio room, where all the witnesses had been gathered together. Bertrande eyed up a particularly cocky man who looked like a boxer.

'You.' He pointed to the man. 'Let's have a chat.'

They settled down in a small administration office outside the gym.

'What's your name?' Bertrande asked.

'Sam. It's Sam Blagg.'

'So what happened?'

Blagg scratched at his stubble. 'Hero and the other guy appeared in the gym.'

'Appeared?'

Blagg nodded. 'From nowhere. They argued for a moment, and then Bosch tried to stop them, and the guy—'

'Which guy? Hero?'

Blagg shook his head. 'The other guy. The one in black.' He stared right through Bertrande. 'Oh God, Bosch . . . What are we going to tell his wife? His parents? His kids!'

'I'd leave that to us,' Bertrande said, rubbing his temple. That was still, by far, the worst part of this job. Well, that and discovering the tiny, limp body of a—

'You know, it's weird. The two of them looked very similar, except one was in white and the other in black. And it happened so fast. For a moment, it looked as if Hero was fighting himself.'

'The guy in black, did he have a name?'

'No. Wait.' He frowned. 'Yes, Hero called him James.'

Ravenscroft and Bertrande exchanged a glance.

'And then?'

'Hero killed him. Stabbed him through the heart with his sword.' He looked away. 'And then the guy, James . . . exploded.'

'Exploded. Right. What did Hero do after that?'

Blagg's head seemed to be retracting into his shoulders. 'He disappeared.'

349

'Disappeared.' Bertrande nodded. 'Did you film it? With your phone?'

'Yes, a few of us did, but—'

Bertrande shifted forward in his seat.

'It's really weird.' Blagg licked his lips. 'None of us got a clear shot.'

'Show me,' Bertrande said.

'You don't believe me.' Blagg pulled out his phone. 'You think I'm making this all up.' He began searching for the video.

'Not at all, Mr Blagg. In fact, I'm certain that you're telling the truth. Because if I were going to make up a story, that would not be the one I'd go with.'

Ravenscroft choked back a snigger.

Blagg placed his phone on the desk in front of Bertrande and pressed play. The screen showed the back of someone's head, whilst in the background some people talked inaudibly. Then there was a commotion. The camera shook and appeared to fall sideways before refocusing on several people lying on the floor.

Mon Dieu! Comme d'hab.

'I was sure I had a clear shot.' Blagg shrugged.

'You said others made videos as well?'

'They're all like mine: out of focus, off to one side . . . One didn't even record at all.'

'Thanks, Mr Blagg, you may go,' Bertrande said.

Blagg shuffled out like a dog with its tail between its legs.

The two officers stared at each other in silence.

'Like I said, not vampires.' Bertrande waved his hand dismissively. 'It's not that we can't record them. We

350

actually have footage of James Turner. It's that they're always off-camera or out of focus when they're doing something interesting.'

'Well, James Turner's dead. What next?'

'We need to find Hero. And we need to do it quickly and quietly.'

He adjusted some stationery lying on the grey desk so that they were arranged in a row, in order of size. He tapped his finger on his lips. 'I've got an idea. Come on.'

Chapter 55

Hero

Bertrande's gonna be after me. They're all gonna be after me. It's just like they said, people with torches coming to take me away to some underground bunker so they can run tests.

With time still dilated, Hero pounded down the Strand towards Westminster.

I need money, I need clothes, I need transport and a place to stay—not home. That's the first place they'll look.

He spotted a cash machine on the opposite side of the road near the Savoy and crossed over, winding in and out of the motionless traffic. There would be limits on how much he could withdraw on a single card. He'd have to use all his accounts.

He put his first card into the machine, but it jammed halfway. He tried forcing it a couple of times, but it wouldn't go.

Of course, the time dilation. None of the machines will work.

He normalized time and jumped as everything burst into life, like walking out of an air-conditioned building into the Texan summer heat. He fed in his five cards, one by one, each time withdrawing the maximum one thousand pounds. He put the cash in his pocket and turned to hail a cab.

Got to be careful, don't want to get mugged. Wait a second—no one's going to be able to mug me. Actually, I'll dilate time and walk home. I'll get there faster.

London fell silent again. The once-animated crowd were now perfect waxwork statues, frozen in time like those poor souls at Pompeii. The scene looked like a 3D photograph with no speed streaks around the moving objects. It reminded him of a zombie movie he'd seen some years before, with one difference. In the movie, London had retained its characteristic qualities: the sounds of lapping waves on the Thames, the gentle breeze moving the trees that lined the embankment. But here, the atmosphere was not only silent, it was oppressive. It felt like a weight pushing on his eardrums. It was suffocating.

He'd never dilated time this long before.

It was surprisingly difficult to walk around the busy streets like this. In normal time, people and vehicles would have created tangled currents within a sea of humanity, but with time dilated, the world was static. Bumping into anybody in this state could seriously injure them or worse.

He weaved in and out of the living statues. *I wonder if I age compared to everyone else when I dilate time like this. I don't think so; otherwise, I'd already be seventy years old.*

In the end, he found it easier to walk in the road

between the pavement and the stationary cars. After what seemed like an eternity, he arrived home. His energy drained out like dirty water.

Maybe I'll get my head down for twenty minutes and refresh. His head sagged. *Can't risk it. Got to get on. Bertrande will be all over me like a rash.*

He dragged his heavy limbs up the stairs to his bedroom, where he ransacked his wardrobes and drawers like a burglar searching for jewellery. Instead of valuables, he scooped out the essentials and threw them into a large suitcase: underwear, jeans, T-shirts, jumpers, couple of jackets, toiletries. That should do it. He started to close the case, tossed in a couple of pairs of trainers, and then began zipping up the case again.

Car keys—what did I do with those? Where, where . . .

He stopped himself and took a deep, cleansing breath. *God, I'm stupid sometimes. I've got all the time in the world.*

He walked calmly to the set of drawers and opened the top one. Sure enough, his shades and his car keys stared back at him. A pang of excitement and fear flashed across his chest as he remembered where the car was parked.

At the front door, he took a final look back at the house that had been with him all his life. *Goodbye, my home, my childhood memories. Fi.*

Chapter 56

Turner

I remembered the day I came home and found Dad waiting to tell me Mum was gone. That look in his eyes—I'll never forget it.

'I always wondered what happened to Mum. I take it she lost, then?'

'Your mum wasn't one of us,' the Light Master said. 'But she did lose, in a manner of speaking.'

'And Dad?' I smirked, though I didn't know why. 'I can't imagine it. He was always so tame.'

The Light Master frowned. 'You don't know what happened to him, do you?'

'I always guessed that he was one of us. I suppose he helped somebody, Justified, and wasn't good enough.'

'Oh no, he was good enough. That's why the Dark wanted him.'

'What?' I exclaimed, my stomach doing somersaults.

'Are you sure you want to hear this?'

'That's what we're here for, right?'

He recounted the tale of what happened to Dad on that morning they'd come for him.

'So? What happened after he got in the car?' I asked.

'Well, that's the thing, James. He didn't get into the car.'

I waited patiently.

'He killed those two guys—well, I say "killed". Pulverised would be closer to what he actually did.'

I squinted, confused. 'Wait, we're talking about the same guy here, right?'

He nodded.

'My father being John Turner, right?'

He nodded again.

'I can't believe my dad would've done that.'

'I guess you've never seen him angry. That's why he kept on telling you not to go down that path. He didn't want you to have the same life he had.'

I was transfixed. I wasn't sure if it was the effect of the endless light in that place, but the master seemed to waver in front of me as if he were underwater.

'Your father was light for many years.'

'You know, him being light kinda makes sense.'

'Not is. *Was*.'

I took a step back; my body was rigid. 'My dad's dark?'

'He's interesting, is what he is. He was always a maverick. He didn't care about anything. He did what he wanted, when he wanted.' The master shrugged. 'Until he met your mum. Then he stopped—he stopped everything. You see, suddenly he had something to lose.'

Mum!

I gasped for air. 'What do you think happened to her?'

He blinked at me in the light.

'Mum's dark too?' I cried incredulously.

'No, I told you, she was clean, completely clean. In fact, she had no idea about your father, not until—'

My heart was pounding in my chest. For so many years, I'd thought she'd abandoned us, but now I suppose I'd told myself that lie to make things easier. I'd imagined she was a member of the Light, had Justified, and lost.

Now I was about to find out what had really happened.

'She was kidnapped, James.'

'That's impossible. The Dark aren't allowed to do that. We can't touch the Clean—that's the rule.'

He shrugged. 'They didn't, technically. There're many ways to skin a cat, as you say—or indeed, anything else.'

His words hung in the air.

'What do you mean, "or indeed anything else"?'

He looked deep into my eyes, but gently, almost tenderly. 'Are you sure you want to hear this, son?'

I nodded, gulping hard.

'Your dad received, I'm led to believe'—he sighed—'body parts.'

My mouth bobbed open and closed like a goldfish as I snatched at the air for breath; in the end, I screamed.

It was lucky there were no walls in that place, or there would've been a hole in at least one of them. I paced up and down, walking in circles, I'm not sure how long for. My mind wandered, and I felt weak.

And then everything became hazy, and I found myself back in my flat. But not just anywhere. I was in my secret room—the one I'd kept hidden from everyone, even Sophie.

Chapter 57

Hero

There it was, the old gym, looking uncared for, unlived in. Dilapidated.

Hello, old friend.

Hero surveyed the tarmac that had once been used for parking cars, now overgrown with weeds poking up through cracks. His eyes traced across the windows, some broken, others boarded up with aged wood, the surrounding brickwork faded by sunlight.

I guess it couldn't hurt to take a look for old times' sake.

Surprisingly, the front door was unlocked. He slipped inside. It was just as he remembered it: the training mat, the Light Master's office, the meditation room. This was the place that had changed the course of his life; in some ways, this place was the source of all his pain and all his joy.

A thick layer of dust puffed up as he moved towards the centre of the mat.

I'm proud of you, bruv. His brother's beaming smile at Hero's qualification drifted through his thoughts. Poor James.

What happened to you? Where did you go so wrong? Why did you go Dark?

He choked and coughed, partly because of the dust but mostly because of tears caught in his throat. He'd almost destroyed the gym that day. The Light Master had been shocked at the extent of his abilities to stop time. *What was it he said? 'That was redemption, James'—something like that. I wonder what he meant?*

He shrugged and made his way off the mat towards the master's office, leaving footprints in the dust behind him like newly fallen snow. He swept cobwebs from his face as he entered the stale office. The large wooden desk and black leather chair were still there, almost unrecognizable under a shroud of dust. He wondered what'd happened in this place of choices since he'd left. His stomach twisted. He could hardly bring himself to think about it. About the Light Master.

I bet it was James who . . .

As soon as the thought entered his mind, he knew it was true. Seeking to distract himself from such horrors, such betrayals, he opened the top drawer in the desk. There was an assortment of biros, clips, and papers inside. Nothing interesting. He closed it and moved on to the second drawer, where he was greeted by a collection of unknown keys. He poked through them with his finger, which instantly turned black.

Something caught his eye on the desktop. A piece of paper. Whereas everything around it was buried in dust, the note was completely clean. Although it was upside down, Hero immediately spotted what it said: JAMES, followed by his old address.

359

His stomach twisted again, but this time from excitement.

James's old apartment—he couldn't have, could he?
It couldn't hurt to check.

Chapter 58

Turner

Was this happening before or after the Light Room? I think after the Light Room, but before now. It was becoming confusing.

I was taking something out of my safe—my chess set. It was a truly beautiful piece of art, a replica of the Strasbourg chessmen. Each piece had been hand-crafted from rosewood and mahogany; the board itself was made from alabaster squares with dark walnut burl around the edges. I set the board on the table in the centre of the room and laid out the pieces to start, the pawns dutifully ready to sacrifice themselves, the kings and queens brooding over their strategies.

But it wasn't their strategy. It was mine.

And so I sat down to play my game. How did one win at chess? At any war, for that matter? Strategy and tactics. First, I needed a strategy, and that meant I needed to understand my opponent. I needed to know their mindset, how they would react. I needed to find their weak point or their blind spot. Everyone had one, and for some reason, they couldn't help telling you what it was. You just had to listen.

What was it that he wanted?

Let's find out.

'Pawn to queen bishop three,' I said out loud, moving the piece as I'd directed.

Immediately, my mind flooded with images. I was there again, watching him, waiting for him to tell me. I thought I knew what his secret was.

Let's see.

'Queen to queen rook four. Check.'

I must've pushed at least ten girls towards him, but he never even seemed to notice them; they sure noticed him, though. Then a new one came along, all on her own—organically, one might say. I smirked at the idea. I watched as that Asian girl flirted with him for three years. He never made a move, but she never gave up. I watched as she lost patience and grabbed him at their final party, before my spirit dissolved like an aspirin in water. I watched from the bushes as he walked out of the ball and left all his friends behind.

I did not expect him to do that.

'White king refuses early queen's gambit,' I said, sighing and sitting back in my leather office chair.

Maybe I was wrong. I needed to restrategize, I guess. The moment replayed in my mind again and again; it almost made me sick. But I'd confirmed one thing. Something about his eyes. There'd been a look there.

An idea flashed past me, still just beyond my horizon. In my mind, I saw his eyes, close, so close he nearly caught me watching him. I tapped my finger on my lips. Then the idea's fullness filtered through like the early morning sunrise.

I was right. He had a weakness. The Light Master was wrong about him; he did want something, although I suppose in a way you could say that he wanted nothing, it wasn't really true.

And that was it, wasn't it? I just needed to wait. This could take a long time.

I leaned forward towards the chessboard again.

Chapter 59

Hero

He turned around to face the gym as he left, a little out of respect but mostly from sadness.

James's old apartment was only a short walk away. He dilated time again and started the journey back towards his childhood.

The place was familiar, but somehow different than he'd expected. Everything looked clean from the outside, the hedges still well-trimmed. He rooted around in the bush for a few moments before he found the familiar rock. He lifted it up; underneath, buried slightly in the dirt, the glint of two keys.

Surely not?

With trembling fingers, he inserted the key and turned it. *Click*. The door swung open, and he went inside and up the stairs to James's apartment. Second key. *Click*. The apartment opened itself with a creak.

Welcome home, bruv.

The place didn't have the same musky smell of the gym. It smelled clean, of air freshener and floor and furniture polish. Hero went through to the kitchen. Everything was tidy; there was no dust anywhere. He looked in the fridge. There were fresh fruit, vegetables, and meat inside.

Surely he couldn't've been living here? Right under the master's nose—and mine.

He went into the lounge, remembered the conversation about the Decision they'd had there. He remembered sleeping on the couch there after his first fight and how they'd got drunk on whisky first in the local pub.

Bacon. His stomach tightened.

He slowly climbed the stairs to the bedroom and office. The place was looking a little worn, but it'd definitely been lived in recently. The bedroom was as he remembered: wardrobe along one wall, bed facing out from the other. He slid the wardrobe door sideways; the internal lights came on, and he gasped. Inside, James's black suits hung neatly in a row next to a set of white shirts; beneath, his shoes sat on the rack.

Definitely been living here. Wow.

He closed the door and turned away. The bed was right in front of him, inviting, drawing him closer. The day had been long. He'd fought and killed his brother, then fled the scene, fled from Bertrande. He'd dilated time for so long that his brain had overheated to the point of cooking itself.

I'll just lie down. A couple of minutes couldn't hurt.

He kicked off his shoes, climbed onto the bed, and closed his eyes.

He was looking through a window into a café. Was it BB Bakery?

Catherine was inside, drinking tea and eating cakes.

He was pressed up against the window shouting to her, trying to get her attention, but she couldn't see or hear him.

'Fancy a game of football, bruv?' said a voice from behind.

He spun around; it was James. He glanced down at the football his brother was kicking around. It was a giant beating heart with blood squirting out onto the grass.

'You've got to wake up and smell the bacon, bruv,' he said, still playing keepie-uppie.

When he turned towards Hero, his eyes were ablaze with swirling, hypnotic fire. 'Help me, bruv.' A burbling scream emanated from his lips, and blood sprayed out from his mouth. 'For God's sake, wake up!'

He opened his eyes and sat up with a start. His skin was cold with a thin film of sweat; his shirt stuck to his clammy belly. His heart was pounding in his chest, while outside, spring rain hammered noisily against the window like marbles smashing a metal tray.

I need a shower.

He swung his feet to the floor and nearly crumpled, so weak were his legs from the efforts of his nightmares. He looked at his watch: just after nine o'clock, but the date had changed. It was morning.

I've been asleep for fifteen hours. I guess I needed it.

His heart leapt to a new danger.

Bertrande.

He bounded across to the window and peered out into the street. Nothing.

366

He switched on the shower and undressed whilst it heated up, leaving his clothes in a pile away from the reaches of the pouring water. He stood under the water-fall for a long time, motionless except for his bobbing mouth, occasionally turning around to heat up his other side. Repeatedly, he let the water pour into his open mouth and fill it before spitting the contents into the plughole. Finally, he motivated himself to laboriously clean his body and hair. His brother's minty shower gel and the soothing heat of the shower invigorated him, and by the time he got out, he was whistling to himself. He towelled himself in front of the bathroom mirror, chortling at the array of James's hair products staring back at him.

Vain until the end, eh? I suppose you always were the better-looking one.

The smile faded from his face, and he tentatively reached for the tube on the end. He teased the product into his hair, trying to remember how his brother last looked without thinking about the fight.

That's about it. His hair was standing on end. There was a strange beauty in its asymmetry, and the product had made his hair look a little darker. He grinned as he went back through to the bedroom with the towel around his waist, slid open the wardrobe, and began searching through the various drawers to find some underwear.

He shuddered as he realised that his brother had prob-ably worn the pants and socks he was sliding into only a couple of days earlier. It seemed so close to his skin, so personal. He opened the suit and shirt compartment and selected one of James's outfits, completing it with a pair of shoes. Everything was as perfect a fit as if it'd been tailored for him.

Very strange. I was sure he was bigger than me.

He closed the wardrobe and observed himself for a few moments in the full-length mirror.

A wicked smile appeared across his face. 'How *you* doin', buddy?' he said, parodying his brother's voice. His grin widened, and he raised one of his eyebrows. 'Do you have a pair of balls?'

He turned sideways on and pointed at his reflection like his brother had when they were kids. 'You need to grow a pair.'

His joviality vanished the instant his face morphed to his brother's in the mirror.

What the f—

He blinked deliberately to clear the disbelief from his eyes. He was himself again. He stared into the mirror, breathing heavily, wearily.

What have I done?

He reached slowly towards the glass. Thinking. Hoping. *If I could touch James, maybe he wouldn't be dead. Maybe I wouldn't've kil—*

He watched himself shudder as tears streamed down his bright-red face. He dropped to his knees. 'Please,' he whispered. 'Please don't be dead. Please be a nightmare.'

The pain rose up in a tidal wave; he held his breath, trying to stop it from escaping. Lightning sparked randomly in all directions from his heart, searing paths through his soul.

He broke into sobs. 'I'm sorry, I'm so sorry.'

368

It felt as if something were stuck in his throat. He ran to the toilet and let out all the pain, the anger, and the bile. His volcanic stomach erupted again and again until all that he could do was retch dry, acidic air.

Come on, pull yourself together, bruv.

He gripped the porcelain bowl and took back control of his bodily functions, forcing the fire back down his throat. He rested his clammy forehead on the backs of his hands and closed his eyes.

'Why? Why did you do it? Why did you join them?' he murmured. 'You were a good person. What happened to you?'

He opened his eyes again. He felt better. The volcano had been calmed, and he felt refreshed. He looked at his watch; it was midday. He'd been out for two hours.

Slowly, he got to his feet, steadying himself on the toilet, then went to the sink to wash the foul-tasting acid from his mouth. He ambled down the stairs to the front room and crashed down onto the sofa, letting out a huge sigh.

He groped for the remote on the coffee table. By now, his face was bound to be on every news channel in the UK. He flicked between the channels until he found the news. Nothing. There was no mention of Saxon Goldberg throughout the entire programme. How was that possible?

Bertrande was absolutely on top of it. He knows something, I'm sure of it. He's trying to find me.

His stomach growled. He needed to eat; he'd not eaten since yesterday breakfast. He found some cereal in a kitchen cupboard. He took milk from the fridge and smelled it. Still fresh.

Weird.

Back in the lounge, he sat down in the chair with his breakfast. He could stay here. They'd never find him here. Maybe that's why James had been here recently, come to think of it. To hide from Bertrande.

If it worked for him, it could work for me.

He sat back in the chair and stared out the window. If he was discreet and had all his food delivered, he could stay here forever. But he'd have to give up—

He folded his arms tightly across his chest against the drill-like pain and closed his eyes. All he wanted to do was sleep, sleep until it was all over and everything was better. His stomach grumbled impatiently, wondering what the hold-up was.

He opened his eyes. The room had become strangely dark. He reached for a lamp on a table nearby and pressed the switch, but nothing happened.

Oh, what.

He put the bowl down and studied the lamp. The plug was lying uselessly next to the socket. He got down onto his hands and knees, plugged it back in, and creaked up to a stand again.

Click.

It was the sound of the tumbler of a safe dropping into place. He tried again. Nothing. He flicked the switch next to the socket.

Clunk.

He tugged on the socket and the door opened, revealing a safe with some papers inside. He took them out and settled back into the chair just as the sun came back out, its rays penetrating the room.

The Structure of the Dark. This had to have been written by James. It gave a detailed description of how the Dark were structured and how they operated, along with grave concerns that if a powerful member of the Light such as Hero were to help the Clean in a particular way, he could completely dismantle the Dark's operations.

He wasn't that powerful. And he was no hero, either. *Even in death, James, you mock me.*

Up until that stupid moment when he'd saved Dad's coffee cup from falling and earned his stupid nickname, life had been simple. Naive. Fun. *If Mum and Dad could see us now, James, what would they think of us? Who we are? What we've done?*

He brought his knees up and squeezed tight with his arms, trying to make himself the smallest ball possible. *I'm sorry, James, but I didn't want any of this. I just wanted to be left alone, to fall in love.*

He turned the page. Dust suspended in the shafts of light dangled on the ends of invisible wires. Everything stopped. One word on the page stood out.

Catherine.

James had written a detailed plan on how they could use Catherine to lure Hero to the Dark.

Oh, James. I'd never turn.

He nearly threw the diary across the room. James had concluded that if Hero wouldn't turn, they'd have to kill Catherine and anyone else he fell in love with to prevent him turning back to the Light. Then, as if being beaten against the ropes was not enough, James had landed a final haymaker to the jaw: *Catherine is one of us*, he had written. *She would be a useful asset if we could get her to join us.*

A roar echoed from the pit of Hero's stomach with such violence that he thought he might have ripped open his throat. He hurled the cereal bowl at the far wall. Its life ended as it splintered into a thousand pieces and tinkled onto the floor. Its cornflake entrails slowly followed suit.

He paced about the apartment like a caged animal, finally ending up back in front of the wardrobe staring at his mirror image. He couldn't fathom how many people must've suffered at the hands of those bastards, living with the terrible knowledge and constant fear of the inevitable 'Thunderdome', having their hopes and dreams ripped away from them—and for what? The greater good?

There're no sides. There's no good and bad, just Decisions made by people. Real people. He leaned forward with his hands either side of the mirror and rested his forehead against the cold glass. *They'll never leave me alone, will they? They'll always be coming.*

White porcelain decorated with rivulets of blood flashed across his mind.

That's what you were trying to tell me, wasn't it, James? All those years ago in the bathroom, when you talked about the terminator people. You knew. Even back then.

Hero's warm breath clouded the reflection in front of his eyes as he steadied himself.

I can't let them kill her. Even if that means I have to give her up. Even if it means I have to die.

He thought about it, considered what it would be like to find his way up onto the roof above James's apartment, close his eyes and easily, almost leisurely, fall forward into a wonderful cloud, a wonderful soft bed in which he would sleep for eternity.

They would just turn her.

For a moment she was standing in front of him, but different—her innocent eyes pure black, like James's.

The breath from Hero's nostrils blew misty circles on the glass as the image cleared. *There's no way out. I have to stop you. I have to stop all of you. I have to get to her before they do.*

'And now I know how,' he murmured.

He straightened his back and dusted himself off, mimicking James again. 'I've finally grown a pair of balls, bruv.' He grinned and winked.

The reflection became hazy, as if his eyes had lost focus. For a moment, James himself stared back at him.

'Run, brother,' he whispered.

Chapter 60

Turner

I found myself somewhere completely different, West-minster tube station. It was a swelteringly hot day in London, and the humidity in the tube was predictably suffocating, as if breathing through one-day-old wet gauze. Why was I here? How did I get here?

I made my way down the stairs from the District line towards the Jubilee line; the escalators were out of action, as the station was being remodelled for 'greater efficiency'. The air was prickly with expectation. Perhaps I was picking up on some unknown frequency of the mind, or perhaps subconsciously I could see the hairs on people's necks standing up.

The whole stairway was blocked by London commuters who, defined by their impatience, had become edgy with being forced to wait an extra few seconds for no good reason. What was the hold-up? I found the cause about halfway down: a family of four travelling down the stairs, the two parents trying to guide their crying son, probably about four, with the older daughter one step behind. They laboured under the usual parental burden of bags, a pushchair, and toys. In typical haste, the other Londoners had been pushing past the youngest, weakest link, causing him to scream with fear at the oncoming herd of elephants. The father was shouting to his son that if anybody else tried to push past, they'd be getting a punch. The bastard looked right at me for a moment.

No one told me what to do. And no one threatened me with violence. A small smile crept onto my lips, and my heart accelerated with mischievous delight. I pushed my way through the gridlocked crowd and shoved past the young boy.

Incoming.

The guy lashed out with a pathetically weak punch. I didn't even need to dilate time to block it and push him off balance. He rolled down the last few stairs like a fully laden beer barrel and came to a stop sprawled over the floor. For a moment, everyone froze—and it wasn't even me doing it.

I bounded down the steps, hauled him to his feet, and put him in an armlock. He squealed at the unexpected pain.

'What do you think you're doing?' I asked.

He looked up at me out of the corner of his eye; he could barely turn his head for the agony.

'You can't go around threatening to punch people who don't do what you say. You understand that, don't you? I mean, who do you think you are?'

'My son was scared,' he moaned. 'People kept knocking into him as they pushed by.'

'And you thought violence was the answer?'

Something unusual about the guy's family was pinging

375

at my awareness. I looked them over more carefully and quickly spotted what it was: the wife was wearing sunglasses. Inside the dark tube.

'Do you always think violence is the answer?' I repeated.

He froze at the new implication.

With time slowed, I looked more closely at his wife. Around the edge of her shades, sure enough, a bruise. The daughter bore faint finger marks on her neck, and the son had a pale bruise on the side of his face. I eased time back.

I remembered searching the internet for help and ideas back when I was trying to figure out what was wrong with my brother. I hadn't known he was being bullied. The answer had jumped out at me from a forum about child abuse, a post from a woman who worked in child services. She said you didn't get accidental bruises on a child's face. It wasn't possible.

A cold stillness descended on me, on the entire station. *Did I just dilate time again?*

I hadn't. But the hesitant looks of the scurrying Londoners skipped across me with terror. Could they sense it? Is that why everyone was on edge? All this time, somehow, they'd known what I was going to do?

'Do you love your wife?' I enquired at last.

He nodded, the whites of his eyes gleaming in the dull, almost translucent strip lighting.

'Tell her, then.'

His eyes darted back and forth.

'Look at her and tell her you love her,' I ordered.

He looked at her with a pleading look. 'I love you, Chris.'

'And your kids. Tell them.'

He attempted to face his daughter and winced. I released my grip just enough.

'I love you, Cassie,' he said through a sob.

He turned again to the young boy who had, perhaps inadvertently, started all of this. 'My little Ollie, I love you so much.'

So how did he do it? He obviously loved his family, so how could he hurt them? My thoughts bounced around in my head. There was a familiarity to the words that made me feel a little queasy. Was I the same as this guy?

I wrapped my arm around his neck and, dilating time just a tad, pulled upwards. The snap attracted screams from the gathered audience, and I added my own, but the shrillest was his wife's. It echoed in my head, but fading, fading, as if I were coming out of a dream.

Chapter 61

Hero

Hero gagged at the thought of getting inside the lift outside James's apartment. He turned to take the stairs at the side. *I need the exercise, anyway.* His back straightened a little with each step down, as if a weight were being removed from his shoulders. At the last step, he stretched to his full height, filled his lungs to capacity, and slowly exhaled. He'd only felt like this once before, with Fi.

He was free.

Silently, he moved through the lobby with purpose and out into his new world. The brightness of the sun blinded him momentarily. *A new day, a new man.* He paused a beat, allowing his eyes to adjust. *A normal day.*

Men in suits of grey and dark blue rushed past with strained faces. Women in designer outfits teetered by, balanced precariously on high heels. The traffic hummed with a cacophony of engine pitches.

He started towards the kerb, his eyes fixed on a black cab halted at the traffic lights.

How will I find her? Without being caught, that is. Surely they'll be watching Saxon Goldberg. I don't know where she lives. I could hide, follow her from work. Would have to be careful.

The cab was still stuck at the lights.

Perhaps I could sneak inside. Would have to get past security. Or wait outside, see if she goes to Starbucks—no, wait, she'll go to BB—

The cars had gone static. They were silent. The once-bustling businessmen and -women were frozen in time.

Hero slowly slid his eyes left until they strained. There it was, a small slug of metal hanging in the air like a wasp made of steel. The sting from this insect would've been fatal. He bent backwards just enough and gently allowed time to slip free again. He followed the path of the bullet as it silently made its way past his eyes.

Would've been a good shot.

He followed the trail of the bullet back up to its source. About two hundred yards away at the top of a church clock tower, the telltale glint of a lens reflected momentarily in the morning sun.

In a church, no less—these people have no shame.

A small fire ignited and fizzed down his internal fuse wire, then exploded in rage. As everything around him remained still, Hero started towards the church.

Kill him.

The voice wormed its way into his ear. A candle flame. An itch too deep to scratch.

Do it, the voice repeated.

Heat infused his chest. So this is who they'd sent, a mere human sniper.

'Sunray One, this is Sunray Two. Target lost, over.'

Hero inched silently towards the prostrate sniper.

The radio crackled. 'Sunray Two, this is Sunray One, please elaborate, over.'

'Target disappeared, repeat disappeared, over.'

'Evacuate your position immediately, repeat, immediately, and proceed with extreme caution. Shoot to kill is authorised if resistance is encountered, over.'

'Roger that, Sunray Two out.'

Kill him, came the whisper again.

He pictured it in his mind. He'd heard stories about this before, from the Light Master. Stories about how the Dark dealt with the Clean when they interfered like this. They punched a hole right through the chest and ripped out the heart. It was allowed.

His heartbeat quickened with excitement as his muscles prepared for action. He felt good. He felt sexy, smooth as silk.

The sniper shifted positions, preparing to stand up. Hero noticed a photograph next to his hand: the gunman with a woman and two children, a boy probably about eight years old and a younger girl. Presumably his wife and kids. *Just a normal guy doing his job. What would his family do if he was gone? If I killed him?*

His stomach and lungs contracted to the size of marbles. He shrank back around the corner, retreating. *What was I about to do just then? Kill that man, take him away from his family?* He hardened himself against the malign influence. *Family, that's what I want. And Catherine. I've got to find her.*

And I've got to stop those voices. I've had enough.

380

Chapter 62

Turner

I was still screaming.

'Are you okay?' The master was staring at me.

I was back in the Light Room again.

Perhaps my mind had whisked me away. Perhaps it couldn't take the knowledge of what it was being asked, so it escaped somewhere. My future? My past? I was no longer certain exactly where I was or what I was doing. My mind was shrinking like a balloon with a tiny puncture.

I fell silent, stunned.

'That was your dad's reaction,' the Light Master said at last.

I shook off the fading memory of that shrieking woman, letting it melt into the bright light of that place.

'What did he do?' I babbled.

'He did the only thing he could do, James. He did exactly what they asked him to.'

'Which was?'

'He went Dark like a good little boy and did what they asked.'

I was collapsing inwards on myself. I felt desperate,

but I didn't know what for. Air? Something. Anything to hold on to.

For the first time, I realised that I really missed my mother and father.

'I can't be certain, but if I know your father, he would've carried on looking for her until the bitter end.' The master hung his head. 'And it would have been very bitter.'

'But surely they would have monitored him?'

'Of course, but he was very good at disguising his true intentions. He was like you, James, and'—the master smiled, his eyes glinting—'he was like your brother. He was fast, very fast. And he had real empathy, but he was dangerous with it. You couldn't predict what he was gonna do next. I guess that's why your mum fell in love with him.'

'And she tamed him.' I managed a grin, but it morphed quickly to dismay as I remembered the small packages Dad occasionally received and the haunted look in his eyes as he opened them. He never showed anyone the contents. I could not imagine the horror of receiving a loved one's finger in the post. Or worse, an eye. They wouldn't dare, surely?

Dad's demeanour after Mum left now made a lot more sense. It'd made sense to my childish mind that he missed her, but I also felt betrayed that she'd abandoned us. Still, I'd always felt there was something more. I saw it in his eyes. Imagine that: every day, worrying about the person you loved most, each day losing a small piece of that love, a piece of your humanity extinguished— until, what? What would be left? Nothing. Nothing but darkness.

'I see you're still thinking about what they might have done to your mum,' the master said.

My guts wanted to heave. The blinding lights in there made me sweat, gave me a feeling of having nowhere to go, nowhere to hide. I closed my eyes to shut it all out. It didn't work.

Dad's words, 'Girls will be the end of us all,' took on a more lugubrious tone now. He had died, on the inside, because of her. Because of love.

Sophie—

'She's still alive, that's for sure,' the master said. 'They wouldn't dare kill her, and they wouldn't do anything really serious to her, either. The minute they touched her with that sort of intent—well, I can't imagine what your father would do. Tear the world apart, probably. That's what you should really worry about, the mess he would make. The mess he'll inevitably make, given this unceasing pressure.'

'So what? Let him go after them. Let him make a mess.'

'You don't understand. Like I said, he's unpredictable. He'll do whatever it takes to get her back. He won't care about anything else—but afterwards, maybe he'll stop.'

'So?' I shrugged.

'It's up to us to stop the Dark and . . . Let's hope that your father doesn't—excuse me, isn't forced to'—the corners of his mouth drooped with disgust—'get in the way.'

I shook my head. It was all too much to take in. I'd always known that our goal would be to wipe out the Dark, but I'd never thought about Dad like this, or Mum.

The strategist in me kicked in. 'So what's the plan?'

'I don't think it's an accident that your dad has disappeared at this exact moment. At the same time that Hero Justified for the first time.'

I brought my hand up to my mouth, considering what he was saying.

'For years, the Dark have been monitoring you and your brother because of your father. I suspect they've surmised—correctly, in my opinion—that Hero's the only one that can beat *her*.'

Chapter 63

Hero

'Hi—David, isn't it?'

'Yes,' Hero replied, 'and you're George, right?'

'That's me. Come on in.' He beckoned. 'Let me show you the room.'

Suitcase in tow, Hero followed George along the hallway to the bedroom that would be his home for the next week. He'd found an advertisement for it on the internet.

'Double bed, desk—perfect.' He could hide here another week, at least. 'I'll leave my bag here, if that's okay?'

'Of course.'

He rolled his case into the corner of the room.

'We share a bathroom.' George led Hero along the hallway. 'Here it is.'

'Nice.'

They carried on to the lounge and kitchen, a combined room dominated by a massive television.

'How big is that screen?' he exclaimed.

'Sixty-five inches of pure entertainment,' George said with a grin, picking up the remote.

The TV sprang into life at his command.

'And a reminder of today's headlines, in an extra-ordinary U-turn, the prime minister announced earlier that the government will be doubling the funding for the NHS and education . . .'

'Oh yeah,' George said excitedly. 'Have you seen this?'

'No, what's going on?'

'All us doctors and nurses are getting a pay rise, that's what.'

Hero feigned surprise. 'Wow, what brought this on?'

'I don't know, but to whoever did this, thank you.' He powered the TV off with satisfaction.

A warm feeling spread across Hero's chest. They would never know what had transpired behind the scenes, all thanks to his brother. It was exactly the kind of thing James said affected the Dark in a massive way. He'd even lined out the details using the example of a young cancer patient at Chelsea and Westminster Hospital. *I wouldn't have figured out the first thing about how to accomplish something like this without his report. And as for the Dark Corridor . . . Wow.*

'Actually, we're all going out for a drink to celebrate tonight. Do you want to come? There'll be a few nurses there,' George said with a wink.

'Sure, why not? I could do with a drink.' 'Excellent. Get yourself ready by six, and we'll head out.'

Thursday night in London was the usual brawl at the bar, thirsty customers desperately trying to get served and exasperated bartenders trying to attend to their needs but failing miserably.

'Finally! Pint for you, whisky for you.' George handed the pint to his colleague Max and the whisky to Hero.

'Cheers,' they all said in union.

'I think you've got no bar presence, mate,' Max said mockingly to George.

'Well, I'm glad he took his time,' Hero said. 'I'm absolutely smashed already. How the hell do you guys pack so much away?'

'Trust me, Dave, if you saw the things we see every day, you'd drink just like us,' Max said. 'You've got no idea.'

Hero sniggered. *No, Max, you've got no idea.*

'What?' Max asked.

'Nothing. I was wondering what it is you see every day.' Hero threw the last of his whisky down his throat. 'Well, lads, that's quite enough for me. It's been a long day, and I need to get some sleep.'

'So soon? Are you sure we can't tempt you into one more, one for the road?' George begged.

'Sorry, guys, I can't keep up with you. You're too much for me.'

'Well, I think a couple of the nurses are going to be disappointed,' George said with a nod of his head towards the other table. 'They've been eyeing you up all night.'

'Tempting—but no, not tonight. I've gotta get my head down.' Hero stood up. 'Besides, it's you they're looking at. You're the dashing doctors, after all.' He winked, then squeezed his way through the heaving mass of tipsy revellers like a salmon trying to swim upstream.

The cool night air was refreshing on his face. Guys were

chatting loudly with drunken deafness, and girls were giggling in little groups under the orange glow of the street lamps. Hero dragged his weary body in the direction of his new place, not far behind a solitary girl in a short skirt and sleeveless top tottering along ahead of him. *Bloody hell, she must be cold*. She seemed to be a little edgy, looking over her shoulder without making it obvious that's what she was doing.

The air felt thick with boozy humidity. The whisky had made his mouth numb. He crossed over the road. *Don't want her to think I'm following her. Must be bad enough walking home alone as a girl in London, anyhow.*

From a darkened alleyway between two houses, two disembodied arms wrapped themselves around the girl and dragged her backwards into the darkness. Her muffled screams failed to perforate the atmosphere.

What the hell?

London froze silently under Hero's command. He crossed back over the street and contemplated the scene before him. The man was using his weight to hold the girl against the wall, one hand over her mouth and the other on his zipper.

You piece of shit.

London came alive again as he smashed his palm into the rapist's cheek. The force snapped the man's head to the side; his legs buckled, and he dropped to his knees. Hero moved in instantly, wrapping his hands around the guy's throat.

Do it.

He wanted to throttle this trash. To teach him a

lesson. *I am your judgement.* He felt like he had as a kid during his first candle session.

'Please, don't,' the guy croaked.

'You want mercy?'

'Please.'

Hero nodded towards the girl. 'You weren't going to show her any mercy, though, were you?'

Eyes round with panic, the man grabbed Hero's wrists and struggled to push them away. Hero rotated out of the guy's hold, snapping the clutching fingers as if tearing a chicken leg away from the carcass. He increased the pressure of his hands around the rapist's neck, pushing his thumbs into the exposed windpipe. It started to collapse. A pleasant warmth emanated from somewhere inside him—pleasure.

The muffled scream of the girl behind him jolted him back to reality. He shoved the man roughly backwards to the ground.

'Next time, I won't stop,' he snarled. 'And I will be watching you.'

He stepped away.

'Have a good night,' he said to the girl, who was still flushed, her hands over her mouth in shock. He walked away.

'Excuse me,' she called.

He looked back over his shoulder.

'Would you walk me home? It's just, I don't feel very safe, not after . . .' She pointed at the prostrate man.

'Where do you live?' These people were exhausting. He wanted to get some sleep. Maybe the Dark would take him and Catherine; then they could be selfish together. He stifled a snigger.

'Not far. About half a mile that way.' She nodded in the direction he'd been headed.

'Okay, lead the way.'

Each of them studied the tarmac in great detail as they continued the journey in silence.

'Thank you,' she said at last, 'for what you did back there.'

'You're welcome,' he said, smiling. It was nice to help. He'd never really turn.

'It was so fast—and you came out of nowhere.'

'So did he.'

'Well, I'm glad you did too.'

He glanced at her face. 'Can I recommend that next time, you consider taking a cab home—or perhaps wearing more clothes?'

She swerved away from him a little. 'Oh no, you're not one of those people, are you? One of those God squad types, always telling women what to do, what to wear.'

He chuckled and shook his head. 'Not at all—quite the reverse, in fact. I think women should be able to wear whatever they want and not live in fear just for walking home from the pub. That'd be a great utopian world, wouldn't it?'

She was looking at him somewhat incredulously.

'But we don't live in that world,' he continued. 'The one we live in is so far from that, you wouldn't believe.'

'Wow, where did you come from? It's like you dropped right out of the sky.' She abruptly stopped. 'Well, here we are.'

'Saved by the bell.' Hero snorted a laugh.

Her eyes twitched nervously.

'Well, have a good night.' He turned to walk away.

'Wait,' she called.

'Again?' He smiled.

'I feel I owe you. I can't just let you walk away. Can I maybe buy you a cup of coffee or a drink some time?'

'Honestly, you don't owe me anything.'

'It's just that I never met anybody . . .' She turned and began trudging up the steps.

'I'm sorry,' he called after her quietly. 'You're lovely, but my heart belongs to someone else.' *And I have to get to her before they do.*

She turned around. The street was empty. She hesitated on the step, poised to go back into the street to investigate, but instead opened the door and went inside.

Chapter 64

Hero

It was a bright spring lunchtime in the City. Summer seemed to be coming early. The smells of hot sandwiches and noodles drifted along the pavement as Hero cautiously approached familiar surroundings. He silenced London into a waxwork pose and took a walk along Carey Street until it joined Chancery Lane. To the Saxon Goldberg offices.

He studied the suited male and female mannequins that littered the pavement, some mid-stride, others with mobile phones glued to their ears. He wove in and out amongst the empty cars parked opposite the offices.

What's this? Two people sitting in this one. He couldn't quite see who it was due to the sun's reflection from the windshield. He edged closer to the driver's door.

Bloody Bertrande. And what was the sergeant's name? Ravenscroft.

Hero backed up slightly, looking up and down Chancery Lane.

Impossible to get inside in normal time without their seeing; they'll be on me in half a minute. My badge probably won't work, anyway, if they're looking for me. I could use the Dark Corridor if—no, not for me. I could stop time, but is she ready to see that? I'll have to wait here, wait till she goes for a cup of tea.

His emotions collapsed at the thought of their tea-shop escapes from the lunacy of investment banking. He drew a steadying breath, then headed for the pub across the street. He strode into The Knights Templar and straight through to the toilets before allowing London to live and breathe again.

When he was done, the bar was starting to fill up with office workers demanding lunch.

'What can I get you, young man?' the grey-haired bartender asked.

'Can I get a latte, please?' he replied.

The bartender busied himself with the coffee machine.

Hero picked up a spare newspaper sitting on the bar. Useful as cover.

'Two fifty, please.'

A freshly made latte slid before him with a small clatter. He paid, made his way into the least conspicuous corner, and pretended to become absorbed with the newspaper whilst looking out of the window for any signs of Catherine.

He didn't have to wait long. His insides lurched, causing him to spit out a mouthful of coffee. He pushed his seat back, ready to stand up. *Hold. Let's see what Bertrande does.*

A couple of people by the bar were impatiently eyeing his table. He ignored them. The doors of Bertrande's car opened on either side, and the two policemen got out. They kept their distance, but as he'd expected, they were following Catherine.

He abandoned the newspaper and stepped out into the heat, ensuring that a decent gap remained between him and the police. As they followed along behind her, he realized that her route felt familiar to him. She was taking them to BB Bakery, their old haunt.

The policemen took up a place by the window in the Mexican restaurant opposite.

Bertrande, you are a pain in the arse. I'm going to have to deal with you. Hero parked himself in a sandwich shop a bit further along and watched Catherine through the windows. She was sat at a table on her own, drinking her usual peppermint tea and eating a mountain of sandwiches. She looked outside forlornly, her eyes occasionally tracking someone—in each case, a single man.

They all look a bit like me. She's searching? For me? Then his hope plummeted. *Look how lonely she is, how unhappy. I did that to her.* He couldn't watch the pitiful scene any longer. Besides, he was feeling uneasy, as if he were being observed himself. Bertrande and Ravenscroft were out of his line of sight, but he couldn't shake the feeling that dark eyes were tracking his every movement.

He hoped it was time already. *I've helped enough people by now; they must be about to come.* The thought of Justification held no fear for him. *What could be worse than killing your own brother?*

He left Catherine and the officers behind and retraced his steps, walking past the gothic architecture of the old County Court. The white stone was blotchy with mould, nature at its best, but the high, pointed arches gleaming with small panes of glass, the huge old oak doors, and the intricately sculpted gothic flowers retained their ancient beauty in spite of it. He paused to marvel. He really should have taken more time to enjoy these wonders whilst he still had time.

Onwards to Portugal Street. He turned right on The Kingsway, forcing himself to keep close to the traffic. The police always looked for people trying to hide right next to the buildings, and Bertrande wouldn't be the only one looking for him. It was better to hide right out in plain sight.

A commotion erupted ahead. A woman cried out as she was shoved out of the way by a well-dressed young man with short hair and bright blue eyes. The man was running hard in Hero's direction, weaving in and out of the pedestrians, who were doing everything they could to clear a path for him.

A woman burst out of the All Bar One, glanced up and down the street, then pointed directly at the running man.

'My handbag!' she shouted. 'He stole my handbag. Somebody stop him!'

Hero barrelled the thief backwards against the nearby wall. The man slid towards the pavement like a defeated cartoon villain, blood dribbling from the corner of his mouth.

'That handbag doesn't suit you, mate,' Hero whispered, bending down to pick up the thief's lost bounty.

The thief looked up in surprise, an expression which quickly morphed into another, more familiar one.

'I know you're thinking about getting revenge,' Hero said, 'but you won't. I promise.'

He turned his back on the man confidently and handed the handbag to its rightful owner with a bow of his head. 'I hope this is yours; otherwise, I owe that man an apology.'

She giggled, bringing her hand over her mouth. 'Yes, it is—my life's in this bag. Can I buy you a drink? Just to say thank you.' Belying her words, her smile was enigmatic.

'Thanks, but I need to get home. Have a good night—and be more careful with your life there, eh?' He nodded towards the handbag and grinned.

As she went on her way, he glanced around, searching for his favourite stalkers. All clear. He sighed and turned back the way he'd come.

I can't carry on like this—I need to talk to her. I need to get to her before they do. I'm sorry, Mr Bertrande, but you've got to go.

Chapter 65

Turner

'The Last Dark?' I asked.

'You'll get to know her as Sophie,' the Light Master said.

Sophie. My insides hollowed out at the mention of her name. Had I met her before this moment, or after? I mourned for the unknown girl.

The master looked at me with a shadow behind his eyes, and I knew he'd been burned by her, badly. 'You'll understand, the first time you meet her. She has a way of getting into your head, finding out what you want, and giving it to you.'

I gave him my best cocky smile. 'Why would that be a problem? Sounds like quite a nice thing, if you ask me.'

'Because it comes at a price that will always be higher than you can afford. And therein lies the problem for you, James. You want too much.'

I sputtered and then clamped my mouth shut.

'Rule number two, James: never lie, especially to yourself. You know that. We both know that you've always wanted to be the hero.'

My head dropped, but I smiled to myself.

'And I'm sorry, son, but you can't be the hero. She'll smell it on you a mile away, and she'll destroy you with it.'

'I doubt that,' I said with a grin.

He looked me up and down. 'You know the worst thing about it? You'll actually want it to happen. You'll will it. And that's where your brother comes in.'

I lifted a hand questioningly. 'I'm not sure I follow.'

'I think you do.'

That feeling of desperation descended upon me again. I knew something was coming, but whatever it was, it was just beyond my sight. What exactly was I going to have to do?

'Your brother's the only one that can end this war because he doesn't want anything. No one can manipulate him, not even you. That's why he nearly beat you. Your tricks don't work on him. And neither will hers, although in some ways, maybe they already have.'

'You've lost me.' I shook my head.

'Your brother's Justification. It was a farce. They sent one of the easiest people they had, a real novice, about as green around the gills as they come. I don't know what happened, but I think your brother is going to stay clean.'

'What?' I erupted. 'That yellow-bellied piece of sh—'

'And that reaction right there'—he pointed at me—'is how Sophie will rip you to shreds.'

He watched me try to swallow my rage. 'You care about him. That's why you're going to turn him back to us.'

'Oh?'

The master remained unmoved. I could see, beyond his eyes, a spreading shadow. Something was wrong.

He studied me a moment longer. 'You really don't follow me, do you?'

We studied each other in silence for several more moments; it seemed to last for eternity. Then suffocating darkness descended as I realised what it was he was suggesting.

'Oh no,' I groaned. 'No, no, no, no—'

'This war has to end, James, and your brother is the only one who can do it.'

I studied his face.

'But how?' I knew how. I just didn't want to believe it.

He raised his eyebrows.

I opened my mouth to talk, but there was nothing.

'You're going to have to be the bad guy,' he said finally. 'You're going to go dark.'

There was a finality to those words. I'd always known that I'd be dark one day, ever since I'd first heard that beautiful voice calling me, but I'd always resisted. Even now.

My head dropped. 'I wouldn't even know how to be one of them.'

'Don't lie to me. We both know you've thought about it. Be yourself. You'll do fine.'

I'd never been told how it worked for the Dark. What would I do? Would it hurt?

'H-how?' I stammered in the end.

He looked confused.

'How do I join them?' I asked, regaining my confidence.

He nodded and sagely stroked his grey beard. 'You don't join the Dark. The Dark come for you, and you let them take you.'

'But how? Why?' My stomach growled, a bowling ball resting on my bowels.

'It's been a long time. The way to darkness changes for different people. In your case, I think you're going to have to destroy the thing you love. You're gonna need to walk away from your family. Your brother. All of us.'

And there it was, the bombshell I'd known was coming, that'd made my lungs snatch at air from the first moment I'd started thinking about all of this.

'I'm sorry, James, but you're important to them.'

'So?'

'They'll send the Last Dark. You're gonna have to bring your A game. You're gonna have to forget about him.'

'But I'm all he's got. He needs me. I can't abandon him.'

'I'm sorry, James. There's no other way. There're always sacrifices in any war, and I'm really, really sorry, but this is the first sacrifice that you're gonna make, not the last.'

We studied each other in silence.

I forced myself back. 'How do you know all of this?'

That shadow darkened his face again, but this time, the darkness seemed more part of his essence, like a black oil stain on the road.

I recoiled. 'You're joking. You? I can't believe it.'

'Believe it, James. Once upon a time, I was Dark.'

'What happened?'

'Your father happened. He saved me.'

'How?'

'That's another story, son, one we don't have time for right now.'

'But Dad? He made you switch back.'

'You could say he showed me the light,' he said with a wry smile.

I sniggered. I knew I shouldn't, but I couldn't stop. The snigger became a guffaw.

The master joined me, but the mirth soon faded. 'No one with true remorse is ever beyond redemption. That's what he said to me, James.'

A small tear trickled down his face. I'd seen this before. But when?

'Do you want to know why they're called the Dark?' he asked.

I nodded.

Chapter 66

Hero

It'd been a long day. Hero'd had two fights with the Dark, the first time he'd had more than one battle in the same day. They weren't held in the darkness anymore, not since—he still couldn't think about what he'd done. Now the battles happened in the real world, in quiet places like empty warehouses. It'd become vaguely amusing how reality changed to contrive the circumstances. In between duels, he'd helped a couple more people—nothing particularly serious, just street crime. Even the ways in which he helped people were becoming more and more trivial.

They must be getting desperate by now.

When he wasn't fighting, he was thinking about her. He needed to see her. It was driving him crazy that the Dark might be making their move at this very moment. He needed to keep her in his sight, make sure she wasn't alone.

But he'd have to deal with Bertrande to do that, and what could he say? 'Oh hello, Mr B, yeah, I can stop time—thought you should know. Oh, err, and in front of a crowd, I stabbed my brother through the—'

He retched.

But there was something about that guy, as though he knew something. Maybe they could work together, solving crimes. It all seemed so comic book, like Batman. Hero grinned as he imagined how he might explain things in a gruff voice. The master's words reverberated in his mind: *You don't want that kind of attention, son, trust me.*

He dragged his weary body back from the supermarket, where he'd picked up some food for his evening meal. The night was drawing on, and the street lamps had already lit up. The atmosphere felt close, as if he were breathing through a mask over his face. There was a ridiculous number of people out. It was Friday and that meant lots of drunk, excited Brits. Tired of dodging through the boozy crowds, he turned down a deserted side street. His footsteps clicked on the pavement like a movie about a deranged killer in which he was the victim. *If anyone came after me, they'd find that I'm the killer.*

The idea spooked him so much that it took him a moment to realise he really was being followed. He glanced around surreptitiously. The street had taken on a listless quality, as if the colour had been drained out of the buildings. He felt his grip change; looking down, he saw that he was no longer holding his shopping, but a sword.

What the hell? I'm right out in the open. There're people, right there.

'In here,' called a voice to the side, its owner clearly German.

He swivelled his head. The Dark stood there, black suit and black shirt as usual. Her long, dark hair fluttered as she beckoned.

'You're joking, right?'

'No, please.' She gestured for Hero to come inside.

'After you. Keep where I can see you, and keep your sword down by your side.' He levelled his weapon at the Dark.

'Okay, okay,' she replied, holding her sword impotently downwards and trapping the door open with her foot.

'Go on, keep going.'

They both inched inside, the Dark backward and Hero forward, scrutinizing each other. The corridor opened out into a large expanse, a nightclub that'd long since gone out of business. The wooden floor creaked beneath their shoes, echoing in the cavernous room as they took up their places opposite each other.

'I won't fight you,' she said at last.

'That's not possible. Only one of us can leave, you know that.'

'I know, but you've decimated us. I've been waiting for it finally to be my turn. I've always known that I can't beat either of you. I want you to make this painless.' Her mouth twisted. 'Please don't let me feel myself burn.' Her wide eyes glimmered in the shards of light coming through the windows from the street lamps.

His stomach twisted into the ever-present knot.

'What do you mean, 'either of us'? My brother's dead.' *I killed him.* 'I thought you knew that—and anyway, he was one of you.'

404

'I'm not talking about your brother.' Her sword clattered to the floor. She marched forward and dropped to her knees. 'Please, don't make me burn.' Tears dripped down her face, emulsifying with the dirt on the wooden floor.

She must've known it would end like this eventually.

'How do you want me to do this?' he asked.

'I think it's best . . . if you just remove . . . my head,' she said through quiet sobs. 'I shouldn't feel a thing.'

Did she really deserve this?

Those with true remorse are never beyond redemption, a voice whispered in his ear.

He ducked involuntarily—the voices again. He straightened up, composing himself. *No one deserves this, this Game. It has to end.*

'What are you doing?' she cried. 'Why are you waiting? Why are you making me suffer like this?'

Hero looked down at her. She was just a girl—a girl wearing normal clothes, prostrate and quivering like a penitent monk before God. *But I am not God.*

Those with true remorse are never beyond redemption, the voice breathed again.

He stood rigid, didn't react. His sword blinked away; nothing, the sword wasn't there. He checked his clothes; nothing white.

Those with true remorse are never beyond redemption.

His response floated from his mind: *You can be redeemed? I didn't even know that was an option.*

But the knowledge of it sunk in. His eyes welled at the simplicity of it.

Of course you can. We all have a choice. And it's ongoing.

'I think you've been redeemed,' Hero announced at last.

'What?' she mumbled, head still bowed.

'Look at me.'

She shook her head, her hair tumbling over her face.

'Look at me,' he repeated.

She drew up her head. Her burning eyes met his.

'Look,' he said, pointing at his hand. 'I have no sword. Look at my clothes. Look at your clothes.'

She hoisted herself up, glancing between them. 'I don't understand.'

'I don't know what you did as a member of the Dark, but you've been redeemed.'

'Thank you!' She threw her arms around him, burying her face in his chest. 'Thank you, thank you, thank you.'

'Don't thank me,' he replied teasingly. 'I was going to kill you.'

Her eyes flicked to his face and upon seeing his grin, she erupted with nervous laughter.

He brought his hands up to her face, stroking her cheekbones with his thumbs. 'Listen to me: you've been given a second chance. Use it. Get out of this Game, stay clean, and do something good with your life. As yourself.'

'I will. I've only just met you, but you've already changed my life. Who are you?'

'I think you know who I am.'

The answer floated in the air like a balloon that'd

freed itself from its owner. She spun around. There was nothing except darkness and dust.

Those with true remorse are never beyond redemption. Maybe Bertrande would understand.

Chapter 67

Turner

The Light Master began pacing up and down the room. He seemed to know instinctively where the unseen walls were.

He puffed his cheeks out, then said, 'You don't lose your humanity all at once. It's more like you start out in a room with hundreds of lights and with each selfish, perhaps even shameful, act—each time you turn a blind eye to someone's else's selfish or shameful behaviour— one of those lights goes out. One by one they go out, and with them a small part of you dies, until one day, you find yourself stranded in abject darkness. Alone.'

He stopped pacing and faced me forlornly. 'The funny thing is, at first, it's great. You actually enjoy it. You can do what you want, when you want. It's all just for you, for your own ego.' His smile faded. 'Perhaps if you're lucky, you get to stay like that, but that wasn't the case for me. It started as a feeling that something in my life was wrong. I found it more and more difficult to carry on doing the things that I was doing for the Dark, so I did them less and less. I was worried that they'd burn me. Perhaps in some ways, what happened was worse.'

'What?'

'Your father came. I expected him to kill me—I was genuinely shitting my pants. I'd heard the stories. He didn't just kill people; he annihilated them.'

I recoiled at the idea that my dad could ever be like that.

Sensing my disdain, the master tilted his head and smiled. 'He saved me. He brought me out of the darkness, showed me I could be a good person. He even showed me how.'

'That doesn't seem so bad,' I said.

The shadow appeared over his face again. 'Perhaps. But now I get to live with the guilt. Not a day goes by when I don't remember. And now, James, it's your turn.'

I stood there trying to clear my lungs as though they had water in them. I knew it was true. It was my turn, and I knew what it meant.

'If I do this—if I go Dark—you know what they'll ask me to do, right?' My eyes were now as haunted as his.

'We all knew what the price of ending this war would be, son.' He sighed with resignation.

'I don't want to do this,' I babbled. 'I don't even want to think about doing this. I don't want to—'

If I didn't say it, maybe it wouldn't happen. Won't have happened.

'Don't worry, son. You'll win.'

I gaped. 'You can't do that. They'll know if you let me.'

'Oh no, James, I'll be fighting for my life all the way—you're gonna have to earn it—but you'll beat me anyway. You're better than me.' He grinned.

I swallowed again and again, but my mouth was parched. I licked my lips. My chest tightened; I couldn't breathe.

'There must be another way, a better way, surely? I bet I can beat her—I'm sure I can, no one beats me. Well, except maybe Hero, but he's clean. What is it about him, anyway? Is he a better fighter than me?'

He shook his head.

'Faster?'

'You can't beat the Last Dark, James. He can, but you can't.'

I gritted my teeth in frustration.

He rubbed a hand over his bare, shiny head. It was strange to think I'd gradually seen him go bald since— well, I didn't really know if it was 'since' or 'until' anymore, but seeing him bald was damn strange.

'I suppose it's not that you can't, but you won't,' he said. 'You won't want to.'

'Why?' I cried. I couldn't wrap my mind around what he was telling me.

'I know you don't believe me, son, but I promise when the time comes, you'll understand. You'll have to trust me.'

Wait. When he said something about walking away from it all, surely he hadn't meant—

Chapter 68

Bertrande

Bertrande sat in the car parked in front of the Saxon Goldberg offices, as had become their routine, tapping his fingers on the steering wheel in time to the radio. *Van Halen—this takes me back. Before j'ai trouvé ma voie.* He reached down for more coffee. Stalking was thirsty work—the car reeked of the stuff, not to mention the numerous pizzas. Ravenscroft was watching a You-Tube comedy clip on his iPhone.

Bertrande checked his watch, then held his chin and tapped his lips. 'Keep your eyes peeled, Paul. She should be out in a minute. Off to lunch for one.'

'Why d'you think she does it, sir?' Ravenscroft asked, putting his phone away. 'You think it's something they used to do together?'

'Whatever it is, it's heartbreaking to watch. She looks so . . .'

'Sad, sir?'

Bertrande nodded mournfully. 'It's more than sadness. It's love—real love.'

'You think, Mr Bertrande?' a voice behind them asked.

Bertrande and Ravenscroft snapped around. Richard Turner sat in the back seat.

'Oh Christ, where the hell did you come from?' Bertrande cried as Ravenscroft fumbled with his door handle.

'It's okay, I'm not going to hurt you,' Turner said. 'Also, I've locked the doors.'

Ravenscroft reached into his jacket pocket.

'Don't go for the radio, and don't go for your gun. Otherwise, I'm gone. And that's if you're lucky.'

'And if we're not lucky?' Ravenscroft pulled his hand slowly away from his jacket.

'I'll rip your hearts out first.'

They put their hands in the air.

'Put your hands on the dashboard,' Turner said. 'There's no need to be dramatic. Or uncomfortable.'

They did as he asked, and all paused for breath.

'Why're you following her?' Turner asked at last.

'We're looking for you,' Bertrande answered.

'Well, you're not looking very hard. I've been watching you two watch her for the past week from that pub over there. Quite a sad sight, isn't it?'

Bertrande lifted his chin a tad. *Don't be too familiar, but be firm.* 'I guess. But enough chit-chat. Who the hell are you? And what the hell is going on?'

'You wouldn't believe me if I told you.'

'I think you'll find we probably would,' Ravenscroft said.

'I need you to stop following her,' Turner continued.

Bertrande twisted in his seat and looked directly at Turner with an unwavering gaze. 'I'm sorry, Mr Turner, but we need you to come with us.'

412

'I think you realise you can't make me do that.'

'Yes, that's why we need you to come willingly,' Bertrande said soothingly, using all of his negotiating prowess.

Turner looked down at his hands, nodding his head, weighing the pros and cons. 'I'm at the end of the line with all this, I really am.'

'We can help you, Mr Turner,' Bertrande said. 'You're not alone in all this.'

'It's funny, I've been thinking about coming to speak with you. I thought maybe I could help you. And now that I'm here, you're offering to help me. I suppose I should be laughing at the irony, but I'm not.' His face took on a pained expression. 'I'm alone. I always have been. I understand it now. This has always been down to me.' He looked at Bertrande with burning eyes. 'And I'm sorry, but you can't help.'

'You don't understand, we know about you guys,' he replied. 'We want to help you. You've done nothing wrong.'

'Apart from killing my brother, you mean. That was pretty wrong.'

'Was it? How much do you really know about him? You told us you hadn't seen him for years.' The young man's heart must be breaking. 'We've been following your brother for a while now. Someone had to stop him.'

'So you think the death sentence is appropriate, then?'

'I won't lie, we don't know everything, but it seems as if there's not much choice with you guys. Look, all we want to do is talk, to understand you.'

Turner's head drooped as if he'd been broken. 'Okay.

Next week. I'll talk to you, maybe even help you—but I need you to stop following her.'

Bertrande exchanged a glance with Ravenscroft. 'How do we know you'll keep your word?'

'You don't. You're gonna have to trust me. But you'll have to do a whole lot more of that if I do come with you.'

'He's right about that,' Ravenscroft added.

'Okay, Mr Turner, but I can't call everybody off,' Bertrande finally said. 'The best I can do is give you tomorrow lunchtime; we won't watch her at the bakery. Deal?'

He smiled. 'Deal. Out of interest, why didn't you slap my picture all over the press?'

Bertrande tilted his head. This boy really needed their help; he had no idea what was going on. He really wasn't one of whatever his brother was.

'We want to help you, not arrest you. We didn't want you to run.'

'So what was that sniper all about then?'

'Sniper?'

'Yeah, in the church near my brother's place. Tried to kill me.'

'That wasn't us. I don't even know where your brother's place is.' He kept his eyes wide, free of guile. *But I'd very much like to know.*

Turner remained stony-faced.

He doesn't believe me. How much does he believe of anything, I wonder?

'It wasn't us,' Bertrande said. 'But I'll find out who it was.'

414

'Okay, I believe you. I'll see you next week.'

He started to reach for Turner's arm to stop him, then carefully put his hand back on the dashboard. 'Why next week?'

'Don't know. Just a feeling.' Turner scooted across the back seat and opened the door.

'How will we find you?' Bertrande called.

He leaned back into the car. 'Don't worry about that, Mr Bertrande. I'll find you if I'm still alive.'

'You've got another fight, haven't you?'

'I don't know. Maybe. Something's coming. Something bad.'

He closed the door with a clunk.

Bertrande and Ravenscroft peeled their hands from the dashboard, leaving sweaty palm prints that gleamed in the sunlight.

'Why did you agree to that?' Ravenscroft exclaimed.

Bertrande beamed at him. 'Nice to know my acting is still in good shape.'

Ravenscroft wore an expression of complete befuddlement.

'You've a lot to learn, young man. That boy needs us, he really does. We're still going to watch her. We'll just do it from a little further away. And if we can, we'll follow him.'

'How're we going to help him?'

'I don't know. But he needs us, I do know that.'

'But I don't understand. Why don't we arrest her and wait for him to come to us, now we know he will?'

Bertrande sighed. 'I want him to trust us. He doesn't know he can; he doesn't know who we are. Let's not give him a reason to run. Just like you and me, that poor boy has been alone his whole life. He doesn't know how much he needs us.'

'You're not worried about having your heart ripped out, then, sir?'

'We both know he won't do that.'

Ravenscroft pursed his lips. 'He's not like that, is he? He's good.'

'Good? Do you think that's how they look at it?'

'I don't know.' Ravenscroft shrugged.

Bertrande nodded slowly. 'But yes, Paul, he is—as you say— good.'

He was very good indeed.

Chapter 69

Turner

'What are you asking me for? "Walking away", "destroying him" . . . Why won't you just say it?'

The Light Master smiled to acknowledge that I'd finally caught up with the true horror of the plan.

'But you said he's staying clean, that none of us can touch him.' My words dissolved in front of me as I said them.

There're many ways to skin a cat, as you say—or indeed, anything else.

I was floating. This wasn't real. Couldn't be real.

'You won't be able to do it directly,' he was saying. 'You'll need to use other methods, other people. The Dark will suspect you from day one. They will be watching you.'

'Do you realise what you're asking me to do?' My disembodied voice again, but this time it'd come from my lips. I screamed my own reply with all the air in my lungs. 'You're asking me to fuck up his life.'

And then the redness receded, replaced by a sickening feeling that I was drifting over a waterfall with no hope of redemption. I spoke quietly, breathlessly. 'And it's not just that. You're asking me to give my life—and not just my physical body, which is of course inevitable—but everything that I am, everything I love, everything I stand for. You're asking me to fuck up his life so badly that he decides to rejoin the Light and go after the Dark. You're asking me to destroy him. And me.' I looked at the invisible floor. 'I'm sorry, I can't. I love that guy. You can't ask me to do this. You've got no right.'

I screamed again at nothing in particular, just noise booming out of my lungs. I needed to get it out, to be heard, to be released.

'James,' the master said gently, 'look at me.'

The invisible walls were closing in. The light in that place was suffocating me; I felt sick. I squeezed my arms around myself.

'You're the only one who can do this,' he said simply. 'If you don't do this, everything is lost. We'll lose our humanity.'

My body slumped, energy trickling out of me in the same way as a solitary tear trickled down the master's face.

I remembered where I'd seen that before: on myself, when my brother . . . our fight . . .

I was whisked away again.

Chapter 70

Hero

Hero looked at their translucent reflection in the glass of the opening door. Their eyes met, the door to their favourite haunt froze halfway open, their eyes locked in an invisible embrace.

He gasped. Had he stopped time like the old days with—?

She blinked once, then again.

No.

She remained motionless, blinking at him. People in the shop had begun to turn around to see why she was holding the door open—was she coming or going?

She can see me.

He forced a smile. She didn't respond, just stared. He scampered across the road, holding her eyes. She turned around quickly to face him, letting the door close behind her. *This is it, my chance.*

'Hi,' he said as he approached.

Her expression changed to a look of horror. 'It *is* you.'

'It is.'

'It's just, when I saw you just now . . . you look like . . . Oh my God, that guy was your brother.'

'Yes, he was.' *Was. I can't believe he's gone. Gone because of me.* His chest ached again, but he was becoming used to it ever since—

Her eyes roamed over him in shock.

'Oh,' he said, pointing to his hair, 'I changed my hairstyle.'

'And your clothes.' She delicately brushed the black Italian wool lapel. 'Nice suit.'

He gently touched her elbow. 'Please don't drink tea alone today.'

'It's funny, I always felt you were with me. You'll join me?'

'Yes, but not here. Come with me.'

'Why not here?'

'You're being watched.'

Her eyes widened. 'Who? The police?'

He nodded.

'They're still watching me after all this time?'

'They really want me.'

She hesitated.

Maybe I was wrong. 'I'm sorry, there're no more chances. I have to go. They're still watching—they said they wouldn't, but I know they are.' He turned to leave.

'Okay, okay,' she said. 'I'll give you ten minutes to explain. That's all, though, so talk fast.'

Oh, thank God. That's all I have anyway. Bertrande is no doubt 'en route', as he might say.

He guided her to one side of the bakery as patrons pushed irritably by. 'I always loved your smile. It's my favourite thing about you. It's what I always remember.'

She raised her eyebrows. 'Ten minutes. Talk fast.'

420

'Erm.' He'd rehearsed this so many times, but in the moment, it was different. 'Well, so, what happened after the, uh—'

'After what, Hero? After you killed your brother?'

Her tone tore at him. 'I had to kill him. I didn't want to. I had no choice.'

'I mean, he was saying some pretty nasty stuff,' she said, 'but that was like something out of a horror movie.'

'I don't even know where to start with all this. You won't believe it even if I tell you.'

'Try me.'

He glanced nervously about. Nobody around them seemed to be listening, but that didn't mean they weren't. This just wasn't something to be confided outside a bakery, of all places. 'To tell you that, I'd have to tell it to you from the beginning.'

'Okay, what're you waiting for?'

He tried not to jump as a car honked in passing. 'Explaining this is going to take time. I need to get out of London—like I said, Bertrande is right on top of me. I need to go somewhere quiet. I know a place in Devon I can go. I'd really like you to come with me and I can explain all of this on the way.'

She folded her arms across her chest. 'No. You're gonna have to tell me something first. And anyway, I've got to get back to work.'

'My car's parked nearby. If I can convince you by the time we walk to it, will you call in sick and join me?'

'Hmm. I'm not gonna say no, but I'm not saying yes. Now talk.'

'Let's go,' he said, grateful to be moving again.

421

She walked by his side as he led the way.

'What do you want to know?' he asked.

'Everything. Why were you fighting? Why did he explode?'

'Explode, burn—it's what we do when we die in battle.'

'Whoa. "We"? "In battle"? What're you talking about?'

'I'm like my brother.'

'What do you mean? You're not human?' Her tone became sarcastic. 'Are you a vampire? Is this like *Twilight*?'

'Don't be silly. Of course I'm human.' They stopped outside a multi-storey parking garage. 'And please, don't ever use the T word with me again. There's no such thing as vampires—although I do look good in black, don't you think?'

She giggled.

'In here.' He opened a side door to the garage. They were hit by the acrid smell of petrol overlaying the dank musty stale water.

'So what did you mean about you and your brother?' she asked, hurrying after him.

'Do you trust me?' He cringed as his voice echoed.

Tyres squealed on another level as they weaved in and out of parked cars.

'You know, it's strange, but I do. You did save my life, after all.'

He stopped before a car with wide, sweeping sills and a long bonnet that made it look as if it belonged in a museum, except that it was obviously recently built— modern, even.

'This is my car.'

'Seriously? Whoa. Who are you, Bruce Wayne?'

His head drooped.

She tilted her head. 'Sorry. You kind of are, Richard, aren't you? And you never wanted it.'

At the sound of his name from her lips, he shook his head, clearing the tiredness from his eyes, and smiled. 'My dad bought it for me. A parting gift, I guess.'

She ran her fingers over the smooth, dark blue curves of the sill. 'What kind of car is it?'

'It's a Morgan Aero 8.'

'I love the design. It's very art deco, isn't it?'

'My dad said it would be the offspring of sex between a car from the nineteen twenties and one from the early noughties. He was a good man.' He laughed nostalgically, then cleared his throat and took a firmer stance. 'And now I'm going to show you something, and it's going to disturb you.'

She raised her eyebrows and smirked.

He snorted. 'Not that.' He pulled out his wallet and put it in her hand. 'Hold this. And give me yours.'

She hesitated.

'If you wanna see this, you're gonna have to trust me.'

She pulled out her purse and handed it over.

'Ready?'

She nodded.

He raised one eyebrow, smiled, then nodded towards her hands, signalling that she should look again.

Her purse was back in her own hands.

Frowning, she looked up. Hero was holding his own wallet.

'What the—' She started to grin, but her mirth morphed into panic as it dawned that she and Hero were standing in one another's places. 'How did you—'

He turned his wallet over pensively before slipping it back into his pocket. 'I told Bertrande I'd hand myself in next week. He says I've done nothing wrong, they want to help me. I wanted some time away from everything, from the constant hustle and bustle of London, to think, and . . .'

Should I tell her how I feel? He sighed through his nose, his teeth gritted.

'What?' Her face flushed.

'I've never told anyone about myself, much less shown them. But ever since I first met you, I've kinda trusted you—and I know you feel the same. I want to explain. Everything, all of it, now. But we need to go.' He looked at his feet and shifted awkwardly. 'And I also wanted to spend some time with you, just me and you.'

But she was already stepping backwards. 'I want to come, Richard. I've missed you. But you killed a guy—your brother—and now all you've done is show me a parlour trick. An impressive one, sure, but a trick nonetheless. I'm sorry, but no.' Her shoes echoed as she headed for the exit.

She's right. I need to really show her.

He caught up to her. 'Okay, okay,' he said gently. 'Hold my hand.' He held it out as if asking for a dance at a ball.

She recoiled. 'Why?'

'You said you trust me. Do you?'

She took his hand. 'So?'

424

'I'm going to show you how I see the world. Don't let go, okay?'

He led her outside to a London that was lifeless once again.

Her eyes darted between the statues lining the streets, one of which was caught gulping back the last of her coffee. A pigeon was floating mid-swoop, aiming for a French fry that thought it had escaped the fate of its friends.

Right outside the door was a young man, his hand raised in a greeting that had been cut short. And the oppressive silence.

'What's going on?' She asked, her voice wavering.

'This is how I see the world.'

She relaxed a millimetre. 'It's . . . it's beautiful. Like a dream.' She gazed at Hero with a soft look, then turned her attention back to the man, lifting a finger to poke him.

'Don't. You could kill him, if you do.'

She stepped backwards, and her heel caught on a crack in the pavement. She toppled into Hero's free arm; he saved her just as he'd saved Dad's cup all those years ago.

'I've got you.' He didn't move, just held her and stared.

'What're you doing?' she asked.

'I'm burning your face into my mind.'

'Why?'

'Because in a moment, I'm going to let go of your hand and from your perspective, I'll disappear. But I'll never forget you, Catherine. I hope you'll never forget me.'

He began to release her hand. *Goodbye, my love. I hope they don't come for you.*

'Stop!' she cried, gripping hard. 'I'll come. I'll come. There, I said it,' she said, her voice an emotional sing-song, 'I'll come.' She smiled nervously.

He smiled back and released his grip on time. London roared to life around them. 'Okay, then. Let's go to Devon.'

Chapter 71

Hero

'Where exactly in Devon are we going?'

The V8 engine purred through chrome side exhausts as Hero wormed through the meandering London traffic towards the motorway.

'Lynmouth. It's about four hours away. My family owns a small cottage and some land down that way. It's a lovely place, hidden away, and it's in my mum's maiden name, so I don't think we'll be followed. Sorry, it's the only place I know I can go.'

'No, it's fine. It sounds very romantic. I really love your car, by the way.' She stroked the polished walnut dash.

'Girls and cars,' he said teasingly. 'It's always funny.'

They fell silent again. Catherine looked out of the window, seemingly lost in faraway worlds.

He tried to focus on the road.

It's only a matter of time before she starts asking all the questions, and I have to answer them. I'm tired of hiding who I am, being careful what to say, what to do, how to act, thinking about everything right down to every single word in every single sentence. I'm not just tired anymore—I'm exhausted.

He shifted the chrome gear lever, and the engine note deepened.

I have to open up to somebody. I hope she'll understand. I'm sure she will; she's come this far. Why would she come to Devon if she wasn't prepared to accept me? Especially after seeing what I can do with her own eyes.

The sun finally peeked out from behind the grey clouds, creating a pleasant warmth on his face. He pulled down the sun visor.

'Are you going to tell me, then?' she finally burst out.

He was as ready as he ever would be. 'Ever since I was a kid, I was fast. Not just a bit fast, very fast. Faster than anyone else. Faster than anyone could believe. My brother was the same.'

'So you're fast. Big deal. That wasn't what I saw back there. What was that?'

She doesn't mince her words, does she? I like that. His throat thickened as she continued to stare at him dubiously. 'I can slow down time. Sometimes I can almost stop time itself.'

She looked at him with utter incredulity. 'What's that expression you Brits use? "Behave"?'

He sniggered. 'Think about it for a second. Think about what just happened.'

'It was beautiful. I—' Her expression turned to shock. 'No wonder.'

'What?'

'No wonder you were able to stop that woman with the gun. And when you fought your brother—it was so

428

fast. And then in the garage . . . So why did you fight your brother?'

'Because we have to make a choice. All of us.'

'What do you mean, "all of us"?' she asked slowly, almost begrudgingly.

'It's not only my brother and me. There're many of us. I don't know how many, but it's a lot.'

'That's impossible. Surely we would've seen you by now—you know, normal people?'

'We're trained from an early age to hide ourselves. And besides, reality changes so we're never seen using our ability, not on any camera, not even a painting.'

She turned away then, looking out the window, and he wondered if he'd lost her.

'You know,' she finally said, 'some of the people at work swore that they'd filmed your fight, but there was nothing on their phones. In fact, there was no evidence anywhere.'

He nodded.

She gave him a long, suspicious look. 'Go back a bit. The choice. What choice?'

'Whether we want to use our abilities—'

'—for good or evil?'

'It's simpler than that, actually. It's whether we use our abilities to help others, to help ourselves, or not at all.'

'Then why do you fight, if it's a choice?'

'That's something you'd have to ask them.' He flexed his fingers around the steering wheel. 'The people like my brother.'

'The ones who choose to help themselves?'

He nodded. 'We call them the Dark.'

'Hmm, and what—'

'We call ourselves the Light.'

She fell silent, winding her hair around one of her fingers.

'It sounds strange, I know. I had these conversations myself when I found out. These names were created thousands of years ago, so you can't blame us for that. All we know is that if the Light want to use their abilities to help people, then they have to fight the Dark for the right to do so.'

She looked less puzzled than put out. 'So the whole time we've known each other, you've been having secret duels with the Dark?'

'That battle was the first I've had in years. In fact, it's only the second time that I've ever fought.'

'So you can stop?'

'Of course. Every time you fight, you choose again. I chose—'

'Oh God.'

Here we go.

'It was me, wasn't it?' She brought her hands over her eyes. 'Because you saved me from that woman. You had to kill your brother because you saved me.'

She peered out from between her hands at him. He turned his eyes straight ahead, concentrating on the road.

'I'm sorry, I'm so sorry.' It sounded as though she was beginning to cry.

'It's not your fault, Catherine.'

'It is,' she wailed. 'Because you saved me from that woman.'

He reached across and gripped her hand tightly. 'It

430

isn't. You didn't know, you didn't choose. I knew, and I chose.'

She was in full meltdown mode now. *I really don't want to do this. We need to get out, get as far away as possible from London, from Bertrande. From them.*

'There's a services coming up,' he said, 'and I'm going to pull over. I need some fuel, anyway. This car drinks the stuff.' He pulled the car off the motorway and parked. 'Tea?'

She was still shuddering. She nodded, eyes burning red. He walked around to her side of the car and helped her out of the low seat, then wrapped his arms around her. She reciprocated, and they remained in the embrace until her trembling finally ceased.

'I'm okay now,' she said.

Inside, they ordered a tea and coffee and found a quiet corner.

She blew onto her tea to cool it. 'So you've had this gift since you were a kid?'

He nodded, carefully sweeping scattered granules of sugar into a neat line on the square mahogany table top. Anything to keep away from the thoughts of Bertrande's inevitable pursuit. *Must act normal, mustn't spook her.*

'How did you find out? I mean, it wouldn't be the most obvious thing, would it?'

'I had it for years and never realised. I guess it must've been really strange for my family to see it. I'm surprised they didn't say anything before.'

'Before what?'

He took a large sip of coffee, slurping a little. 'When I was at school, I was bullied pretty badly. My brother

James saved me. He was always training at this gym, and I thought maybe it could help me save myself.' He wiped sugar from his hands on the green upholstery.

'And did it?'

He nodded. 'That's where I learned about my ability.'

'So he wasn't always dar—selfish?' She painted on an overly bright expression, trying to cover up the ugly word she'd almost used.

'No, that's the thing. I remember him as being funny, protective—and annoying. But then after my first fight, he disappeared. I've missed him for so long. I just don't understand.'

She reached across and stroked his forearm. 'Why would he leave you like that?'

'Because I wouldn't fight.'

'But why?'

'I don't know—and I guess now I never will.'

She watched him intently as they sat in silence.

'So why did you stop helping people, when you could do so much good?' she finally asked.

'You saw what happened to my brother when I killed him. I . . .'

His eyes welled. He was too choked up to continue.

'It's okay,' she said. 'Tell me when you're ready.'

But we need to go! Get out, get away! He sipped his coffee, trying to melt away the lump in his throat. 'When we die in battle, we burn from the inside. He set on fire. Did you see the agony on his face?'

She paled.

'And then we explode.' His voice caught. 'Catherine, I didn't know it would be him I'd face.'

They sat blankly across from one another, unable to respond further to the horror his life had become.

He finally sat back. 'How could I carry on helping people when I knew what the price would be? I couldn't bring myself to do it. It surprises me that anyone can.'

'You helped me.'

'When I saw the gunwoman there and realised she was going to pull the trigger, I couldn't imagine a world without you in it. There was no price higher than that for me.'

Catherine looked into her teacup, her face tinged with scarlet. 'But wouldn't that be a selfish reason to use your power?'

'It's a fine line that we tread. But yes, and I think the Dark have been trying to turn me ever since. They can do that if I'm selfish.'

She jerked backwards. *Oh shit, she's gonna run!*

'I didn't turn, I didn't,' he said, panicked, 'but it was close.'

She relaxed again. 'At least you're not a liar. It must be difficult, with all that power. I don't think I could handle it.' Couldn't she? James said she was one of us. She leaned back in her seat. 'Where did you guys come from?'

He couldn't help smiling. 'We're from London. I told you that. We're not aliens.'

She smiled back. 'No, silly, I meant in the gym. At work. We were all waiting there for you to arrive for the match against Sam, but then you and your brother appeared from nowhere.'

'I see. Yes, that's difficult to explain. I'm not sure

433

what happened there.' He drained his coffee and made the paper cup the victim of mindless wringing in his hands. They'd got to get on. *They're coming, I can feel them*. 'When we fight, it's in a place that's pitch-black except for the fighters. We're lit up with a spotlight or something. I was travelling down in the lift—'

'You mean the elevator.' She grinned, alleviating the gravity of the moment.

'I was travelling down in the lift,' he repeated carefully, grinning back, 'when I heard my brother's voice behind me. And then we were in the darkness, ready.' He thought for a moment. 'It's funny, really. Ever since then, we've been fighting out in the open. It's as if my brother and I broke the system.'

'What do you mean, "ever since"? How do you know?'

'Something happened to me after—'

After I killed my brother. He saw his brother as a kid, standing tall, saying, 'I'm your Huckleberry.' He hadn't really said it, of course, but he could have. *Ah, James. I love you, man. The world is a complex place. Sometimes I even think I should join them. Maybe my life would be easier. Better. Is that why you joined? Please don't let it be because of me.*

'I realised that sometimes you have to do bad things in order to do better things. All I wanted was a normal life. I thought after I made my choice to stay clean that they'd leave me alone. But all this time, they've been watching me, interfering in everything I do. They need to be stopped. Both sides. The war between them needs to end. Humanity needs the opportunity to dictate its own fortunes—without people like us.'

434

Catherine reached across and took his hand in hers, gazing at him unwaveringly. He returned her scrutiny with a smile.

I love you.

'I really think I'll lose myself with you,' he whispered.

Her smile grew wider as she caressed the back of his hand.

He sat up and tugged down his cuffs. 'Anyway, I'm really sorry you had to see all those watery eyes. I just need to grow a pair—my brother always used to say that.'

She took a last sip of tea. 'No, it's okay. This is . . . I don't know. It's weird, Richard, it's like I've always known you. I've always known about this. And when you showed me the world, frozen . . . I had a dream when I was a young girl—it was exactly the same. So I knew I had to come.'

Back on the road, with the car's monotonous, low hum taking precedence over conversation, Catherine's head started to bob. 'I'm sorry, Richard, all this has exhausted me. Do you mind if I take a nap?' Her head sagged like a daffodil in a drought.

'Not at all. We've got a way to go. Get some sleep.'

She closed her eyes and rested her head against the tan leather headrest. Within minutes, she was snoring.

I know how she feels. Sometimes I wish I could forget my worries and sleep the rest of my life away.

Lynyrd Skynyrd's 'Free Bird' came on the radio. *I'm not walking away this time.*

He changed the channel.

Chapter 72

Turner

I returned directly to Sophie's penthouse on the Upper East Side overlooking Central Park. She was waiting for me, swathed in black from head to toe. She never wore anything else when she was with me. I perched awkwardly in one of her elegantly positioned Le Corbusier armchairs and stared at the pristine books on one of her bookshelves. I'd never seen her read any, but I presumed that she did.

'Bad night in London?' she said.

I nodded.

'He's back, isn't he?'

I nodded again—it was best to say nothing at times like these. I knew she knew. They always knew.

'How the hell did that happen? You had one job to do.'

'I did what I said I would. I tried to kill Catherine. He wasn't supposed to be there. I thought I'd taken care of him, but one of his friends convinced him to go. She was supposed to die.'

Her head drooped and her whole body sagged, a demeanour that I'd never seen on her before.

'It's me, isn't it?'

I didn't really need to ask. I'd always known it would be me who'd face him, even though I'd never really thought about it. Perhaps I'd always assumed that I'd lose, although I never had before. But seeing her like this made me remember, for the briefest moment, the sight of Hero at the end of my sword instead of the end of my finger. I gasped.

She raised her head, but at first she wouldn't look at me. Her eyes darted back and forth, pretending to look everywhere but me. Finally, she gave me her full attention. 'Are you ready?'

'As I'll ever be.'

'Then we should make the most of the twenty-four hours.'

This would ordinarily have been the point when she grabbed my hand and led me to the bedroom, but instead she gravitated towards me and wrapped her arms tightly around me, her head pressed deeply into my chest. I'd never seen her like this before. It was hard to accept. Was she manipulating me? Trying to ensure my loyalty?

This time was different. We faced each other, slowly removing each other's clothes with none of the usual tearing, as I walked her backwards to the bedroom. She didn't close her eyes, nor did I. I hovered above her. Our lips gently brushed as we gazed at each other.

I've never felt so close to another human being. In those moments, those final beautiful moments, we liquefied in each other's arms; we became one. Images filled my mind as I filled her body. I saw her childhood, everything that happened to her that made her who she was. She was just a little child, trapped. I could have helped her if I'd stayed, if I'd won. But now I was trapped too.

Oh God, what had I done?

Afterwards, she rolled onto her side away from me. She usually left after a couple of minutes, but this time she stayed. I remained perfectly still, hardly daring to breathe. The bed quivered. Was she crying? Had I made her cry? Had I hurt her? Impossible. What should I do next? I swallowed hard. I wanted to tell her what I'd done, about everything. I wanted to make her feel better.

I put my hand on her shoulder. 'It'll be okay. I'll beat him, I promise.'

She pulled me closer and hugged my arm tightly.

'Please don't leave me, James. Everyone in my life seems to leave me. And you, you're—' Her whole body shuddered as she gasped. 'I . . . I . . .'

Say it. Please say it.

Maybe I should've said it. To help her. But what if this was a game, another one of her tricks? But what if it wasn't?

I could make a life with her. All I had to do was kill Hero. And after all, I'd never lost.

It was lunchtime, but I didn't want to eat anything. Sophie walked through to the lounge and stood in front of me in all black, her face expressionless. They always wore black when they were on business. And she was always on business with me.

'It's time.' Her voice was ominous, sombre.

438

I brought my hand up to her face. Our eyes met. My heart lurched. Her beautiful blue eyes always did that to me. I never wanted it to end, but I knew it would one day. And that day was today.

'You've made a real difference to me,' I said. 'Before you, I was numb. I felt nothing. But whenever I see you, I feel different. I feel something. I think I . . . I—'

'You're not going soft on me, are you?' she said.

I recoiled, then looked her up and down with a sad smile. *I'll miss you.* 'You know, you always did look good in black.'

I turned and marched to the door. Like a good little soldier.

'James?'

I looked back.

'Please come back. I—I want you to come back . . . for me?'

She had a look in her eyes that I'd never seen before. All of this was new. Was it sadness? Love? Was she capable of that? Was she capable of love? Or was this another one of her games?

I went out into the corridor, closing it quietly behind me. Then I turned back to the door and put my finger-tips against it, caressing downwards slowly.

'I love you,' I whispered.

Why was it so hard to say that to her face?

My stomach tightened.

Did she love me?

I guess I'd never know.

I stood upright, faced the far end of the hall, and began the inevitable march of the damned. Far ahead of me, I heard the fluorescent lights go out with a click. Then the next lights, then the next. The clicking drew closer and closer; my skin bris- tled. The corridor receded into the distance, leaving a small pinhole of light like an old tube TV switching off.

The light expanded outward again towards me. There he was.

Hero. He was expecting me.

'Hello, bruv,' I said. 'Long time no see.'

Chapter 73

Hero

'Wake up, sleepyhead.' Hero gently shook Catherine's arm.

She languidly opened her eyes. The car purred up the lane towards a thatched cottage that had been kept in its original condition.

She sat up. 'Wow, this looks like those cottages you read about in fairy tales, like Hansel and Gretel. You're not really a witch who's planning to eat me, are you?'

'Well, I'm not a witch, anyway.'

'Oh, you Brits and your innuendos.' She giggled, winding her hair around her finger again.

'You're so cute when you do that,' Hero said with a smile. 'Come on, let me show you around the gingerbread house.'

They walked through the place, what dim light they had provided by a full moon. They carefully removed the off-white dust covers as they went. Catherine spluttered when they were too fast with one that smelled unlived in—not quite dank, but getting there.

He gathered it into his arms with an apologetic look. 'I don't think any of the family have been here since I was a kid. That was the last time we all went on holiday together.'

She looked out the window at the car in the gravel driveway, hemmed in by mossy walls wrapped in places with ivy. The river sloshed a few hundred yards away. She craned her neck upwards. 'It's a beautiful night, so clear. You can see all the stars.'

'It's still quite warm,' he said. 'Shall we take a walk?'

'Yay.' She squealed and danced out into the night, seemingly without a care in the world.

Oh, shit. She was alone. He sprinted after her, his heart pounding.

'Are you okay? You look flushed,' she said.

He tucked her hand into his elbow. 'Let's go, then.'

They walked into the forest alongside an irregular stone wall that had been subjected to too much Devon weather. The river frothed and swirled on the other side. As they went deeper, the trees dulled its sound, replacing it with the rustle of leaves shivering in the wind. The round moon peeked through the canopy, lighting their path as the scent of sharp pine and earthy moss invigorated their senses and the wings of the birds they disturbed flapped and clacked above them.

Hero slid his hand down to hers and interlaced their fingers. Her grip tightened around his, and the energy in his legs emptied. Wobbling slightly, he slowed and placed a hand on a nearby tree to steady himself. The warmth of her gaze burned into his head.

'It's so beautiful here,' she whispered. 'And so quiet.'

'I guess you do get used to the noise of London.'

'I could live here, I think.'

'Me too. It gives you time to reflect upon yourself and life in general.' He shifted uncomfortably under her gaze. 'Follow me. We can see the stars over there.'

They walked a short distance to a clearing, where the night sky opened before them like a black sheet sprinkled with fairy lights.

'Look.' She pointed into the sky, her mouth open in delight.

A thin, arcing line dashed across the dark expanse.

'A shooting star! Make a wish, make a wish,' he chanted.

They bowed their heads, eyes closed. When he opened his eyes, they were facing each other. Her hazel eyes glowed in the moonlight that filled the clearing with a silvery mystique. He felt drawn to her. He couldn't resist this mesmerising power anymore.

He edged closer and put his hand on her waist. His heart fluttered like a butterfly's wings.

Butterflies. That's exactly what this is.

They inched together until he could feel her soft breath against his mouth. His face flushed, and his lungs went into breathless overdrive. Their lips gently brushed. She leaned in to him, her heart pulsating against his chest. The radiance of her body enveloped his, but it was more than that. His tension dissipated as his essence joined with hers. God had reached into them and liberated them from their solitary prisons. They'd grown wings and were floating, as one, upwards into the night.

'I found you,' he whispered. 'I don't believe it, but I found you.'

'I found you too. I'd almost given up. I thought you didn't exist, but here you are, right in front of me.'

Now their lips were touching, lightly at first, and then their souls were melting together. For a moment, Hero thought he could hear angels singing. Their love became a newborn star, lighting an infinitesimally small section of the night sky before exploding and fading back into the darkness from which it came.

Chapter 74

Turner

I saw myself in the darkness opposite my brother, our swords at the ready. And then I was myself again, looking through my own eyes at my own flesh and blood. My own brother.

It was all like a dream, but I know it was real. I remember it.

I felt seething anger at him, and contempt. He was pathetic. My skin was sweaty with prickly heat. Every nerve in my body danced to the same tune. I was going to kill him, and I was going to enjoy it. I was going to enjoy watching him die slowly on the end of my sword.

I could be with her. I could be happy.

Couldn't I?

Was I allowing myself to be deluded? Was I deluding myself? Could she ever love me, really, the way I loved her?

Would I save my brother the way I was supposed to? Be a good little boy like they wanted me to be?

Fuck them. They didn't own me. I wasn't their toy. I was my own man. I did what I wanted.

And just like that, the darkness filled me again like a

good Scotch, its warmth seeping into every molecule of my body. The simple choice: her or him? Who should I save? Could I defeat Hero if I really wanted to? Did I really want to?

I could let him win.

But I wanted her. I wanted a life with her. Would she give me that, though? Could I really have that with her? I saw her face, in my mind, smiling. I yearned for her; I ached to hold her in my arms again, to have her hold me back. To lose myself with her, once again.

If I beat Hero, would she give herself to me?

I contemplated the question for an eternity. The lights went out. I was back in the darkness, alone. Dad's disembodied face appeared.

'Don't go down that path,' he said. 'You're better than that.'

And I was back in the gym, a frozen moment within a frozen moment. But I knew what he told me was true. I didn't think she would.

I miss you, Dad.

I heard the reply: *I miss you too.*

Was that his voice or mine?

My grip on the sword loosened. I couldn't let it go—that would be too obvious—so I parried a couple of times. I allowed my brother to spin inside my defensive zone. I could've stopped him—perhaps not easily, but I could've stopped him.

Then he swiped across my line, and in that moment, I let go. I realised what was going to happen. This was it. My death. My brother was going to kill me.

Time slowed down in a way that I'd never experienced

before. I saw him swivel his sword over the top in his signature move, bringing the blade tip to my heart and driving forward. I sank to my knees. It actually didn't hurt as much as I'd expected. Drowning on my own blood was a little more disconcerting. And then the fire.

At first it felt like heartburn. I guess that's exactly what it was; my heart was on fire, my soul was on fire, slowly spreading, consuming every last part of me. I said my final words to him, words of warning, words that would echo between us across the ages: 'Run, brother.'

A single tear. I remember the way it almost hurled itself to the floor.

Somehow I knew that I was still in the gym, pinned to the wall by Hero's sword, but I was also somewhere else, a small, dark, contracting universe just for me. I was back in my secret room.

I made the final move. 'White king moves to protect queen.'

A forlorn smile passed over my lips.

'Checkmate.'

I slouched back in the chair, all those people's images burned into my mind.

Catherine. Perfect. One of us, just as Fi had been. And so she had to die.

That had always been his weakness. The Light Master was wrong. It's not that Hero wanted nothing; it's that he wanted to disappear. His desires in life were always more mature than mine. All he ever wanted was to meet his 'one', fall in love, and vanish. That's why he'd come to the gym as a kid. He didn't want the training; he wanted people to leave him alone.

And now they would.

I'd thought I was doing the right thing. I wanted to help the Light, to help humanity. I did what I had to do, and I got him back in the Game. But how many lives had I destroyed doing it?

I'm sorry. I'm sorry, all of you. I know you can't hear me, and even if you could, you wouldn't forgive me, but I'm sorry all the same.

'I need to confess,' I muttered. 'I killed a child, a little girl. Her name was Rachel.'

Please don't let me die like this. Please don't let me die in the darkness.

Chapter 75

Hero

They stood grinning at each other like lovestruck teenagers.

'That was the most beautiful thing I've ever experienced,' Catherine breathed.

Hero was still panting. 'I think my heart exploded. That was better than sex—I didn't think that was possible.'

She held him closer, their lips centimetres from each other. 'I wouldn't know.' Her face grew a little pinker than usual.

Hero gaped, partly in disbelief but, if he was honest, mostly in relief.

'I'm Catholic.' She looked down, seemingly hiding her eyes from him.

He caressed her glowing cheek until she looked up and smiled. 'I've only ever had one serious girlfriend.'

Now it was her turn to stare.

'The only girl until now that I ever loved was at school,' he mused. 'But your kiss—it was like we were the sun.'

'As if we were the boiling light, as one with each other, with everything.'

He looked at her, drawing every moment in as if it could last forever. *But it could. I could make that happen.*

'I am absolutely, one hundred percent head over heels in love with you, Catherine,' he whispered.

She purred, snuggling up against him, and touched her fingers to her lips with an almost imperceptible sigh. 'Hey, when did you change your jacket? That outfit suits you.'

'What do you mean? I didn't—'

He was wearing a white suit. 'Oh shit!'

He dilated time and leapt away from her, circling his sword defensively. Ahead of him amongst the trees, the shadows became deeper and started to lengthen. A figure appeared, her long blond hair contrasting against the blackness.

He normalized time.

Catherine hurried to him. 'What is it? What's going on?'

'Look there.' He thrust his sword in the direction of the shadows. He pushed her back with one arm. 'Keep behind me, Catherine—actually, can you stand over there, please?'

She edged to one side. 'This is one of them, isn't it?'

'Yes, so please, you need to go. Do you remember what happened to Bosch?'

Horror washed across her face in a slow-moving wave. She stumbled over a small tuft of grass and crashed onto her bottom.

He looked frantically back towards the shadows.

'It's nice to meet you at last, Hero.' Her eyes were inches from his.

'Christ!' He staggered backwards, nearly tripping over himself.

'A word of advice: never normalize time in our presence,' she said. 'You know, you look a lot like your brother.'

Her lips trembled almost imperceptibly. Did she know James?

'We're the last of us, you know,' she said.

'You're the Last Dark?'

'That is my name.'

'And me, I am the Last Light,' he murmured.

'No, there is one more of you. He used to be with us—or so we thought.'

Her blond hair fluttered over her black-clad shoulders. It was like seeing lightning. She moved so quickly she appeared hazy, yet she seemed like white porcelain when she was at rest.

'Not what you were expecting?' she asked, her lips a deep scarlet.

Hero's brain couldn't focus on anything else for a moment. 'I—I guess I expected someone ugly. A man.'

'Of course you did.' She let out a sarcastic little laugh, as if she'd heard it hundreds of times. 'I don't know what you and your brother did, but the darkness is broken. We've been fighting our most recent fights out in the open.'

'I know,' he said. 'I was there, remember?'

'Are you tired of all this, Hero? You look tired.'

He took a step backwards. *I am, I really am. I never wanted any of this. All I've ever wanted was to live a normal, happy life away from everyone and everything.*

451

She looked him up and down, one eye squinting slightly. 'It's true what they say about you. You make me want to be honest, to confess. And I think I will.' She paused, breathing heavily. 'I'm tired of this game, Hero. I don't want to play it anymore. I'm tired of all the killing. I don't think anyone even knows why we fight anymore.'

Wow, she's just like me.

'I was just a little girl when I first started the Game.'

'I was just a small boy.'

'You know, we always wanted you, Hero. Ever since you were a kid.'

'I know. I felt you. But you could never turn me.'

She nodded. 'It's a shame. We're not as bad as that old man told you. And it's not as if you've never been selfish, is it?' She glanced at Catherine and smiled ruefully. Her eyes shimmered in the moonlight. 'I had that once, what she has with you—and you have with her.'

'What happened?'

'You took him from me. I didn't know it before, but without James, I have nothing to live for anymore. He was the only one that ever understood me.'

She might as well have stabbed him.

'And she's not the only one, is she?' Her voice grew higher, tighter. 'You did the same with Fi. With your school. With Cambridge. Even in your career—your whole life.'

What had he become? The very thing he had always feared?

'Just admit it,' she screamed, 'if not to me, then to yourself—you've always been one of us.' She calmed down. 'It's funny even saying that. In the beginning, there was only one side. The old man never told you what Justification was really for, did he?'

His mind was spinning. He couldn't grasp anything real anymore.

'We could have been one big happy family, but instead, you chose to take everything from all of us. Maybe you'll be the next true Dark Master. It suits you.'

He was one of them—no, he was worse. He'd deluded himself all these years. He was a monster. He always had been.

'Let's get this over and done with, shall we? This war needs to end.' She dropped to her knees in front of him. 'Please make this painless. I don't want to burn. I'm terrified of that.'

Those with true remorse are never beyond redemption.

He raised his sword, ready to end the war at last.

A gust of wind whispered past his ear: *Run, brother.*

What?

Run, came the wind again.

Instinctively, he dilated time almost to a dead stop and jumped backwards, rotating his sword defensively. There was a clang of metal as swords clashed together; the Last Dark had thrust her sword where Hero had been a moment earlier.

She looked up at him through her lashes like a psychopath in a horror movie, a flicker of a smile at the edges her mouth.

'You nearly got me, you really did,' he said. 'I can see now how you took my brother from me, how you've

453

taken so many lives. But you didn't know I could stop time, did you?'

'Of course I knew,' she replied flatly. 'Why don't you try doing it again?'

He slowed time. Nothing happened.

Oh—

He concentrated, his brain burning. Nothing. He couldn't dilate time any further. His stomach slowly squeezed in on itself and the knot reappeared, as it always did when he was in trouble.

The Last Dark rose from her knees.

Chapter 76

Turner

I was surrounded by light again. I was back in the Light Room.

'What was that?' the master said.

I looked him in the eye. My innards felt as though they were collapsing under the weight of my guilt.

'I killed a child, a little girl,' I repeated. 'Her name was Rachel.'

'I know.'

'I didn't kill her,' I said. 'I murdered her.'

'You didn't. You just didn't give her the medicine. You didn't help her when you could have.'

'It's the same thing. I could've saved her, and I didn't. I murdered her.' I looked down at my feet and felt something inside me implode.

When I raised my head again, the Light Master was gone. I was alone in the Light Room, but only for a moment. A blurry image flitted past, and I heard a giggling.

Oh, no.

She came into view wearing a blue Cinderella dress. Her beautiful long blond hair fluttered as she danced towards me.

She stopped and looked up at me with innocent blue eyes. 'Hello, Mr Turner.'

How did she know my name? 'Hello, Rachel.'

She looked exactly as she'd imagined she'd be in heaven. 'I'm going to a ball tonight, just as I always dreamed.'

'You look beautiful—absolutely stunning.' The smile trembled on my lips.

'Thank you.'

Those eyes continued to stare at me, shimmering in the unseen light. I reached towards her but stopped short of her arm. I dared not.

'I'm so sorry,' I said.

'Why?'

'Because of what I did to you. I killed you, and I'm so sorry.'

She stepped forward and put her hand on my shoulder. 'It's okay, Mr Turner. I understand.'

I dropped to my knees before her, my head bowed. 'I'm sorry. I'm so, so sorry.'

She patted my arm. 'You had an impossible choice, Mr Turner. Sometimes all you have are bad choices, but you still have to choose. No one in the world could've made this one but you. And that's why you were chosen.'

I looked up, confused.

She wrapped her arms around me, and I reciprocated, closing my eyes and holding her tightly. I needed to feel her warmth against mine; perhaps, somehow, her empathy might ease my pain, my guilt.

'It's okay, James, I forgive you,' she whispered in my ear.

The dam broke inside me. I shuddered as tears streamed from my eyes and became dark blue pools upon her gown.

'I'm sorry, I'm ruining your dress.' I was squeaking as if I were the little girl, not her.

'Where I'm going, it's impossible to ruin anything,' she said with a grin. 'Now, stand up.'

I couldn't do it.

'Stand up, son.'

Her voice had changed.

'Stand up, James.'

I got to my feet in front of the Light Master. He looked different than before, kinder.

And then I heard something I hadn't heard since I was a boy: the voice.

No one with true remorse is ever beyond redemption, it said.

'Welcome back to the Light, James,' the Light Master announced.

I looked at him with a confused frown. 'You didn't say that last time.'

'No, I didn't.' His mouth turned down in a look of sad acceptance.

'Oh. I see.'

'Welcome home, son.' He embraced me again more tightly.

Tears burned tracks down my cheeks, and I wrapped my arms around him as he wrapped his around me. I remembered now. All this time, I'd been dead, reliving my entire life in flashbacks. And everything I'd ever done, I'd done for my brother and for humanity.

457

I drew myself upright.

Come on, bruv. You can do this. I believe in you. We all believe in you.

We were surrounded by the brightest, most beautiful light I have ever seen. And then I was fizzing, every atom in my body effervescing like a soluble aspirin in water. Slowly, the atoms separated, and I dissolved into the light. I became a part of it.

And it was the most wonderful, joyful feeling that I've ever known.

Chapter 77

Hero

'You were never really going to end this war, were you?' he said.

She shook her head slowly with a rueful smile on her lips.

'Then, I'm sorry.' He raised his sword into position.

She responded in kind. Silent. Stoic.

'Don't be sorry,' she said finally. 'We're even now, as I'm sure you're already aware.'

Don't let her in your head. Wait for the move, just wait for the move.

He slowed time as hard as he could. It wasn't much.

Hopefully it's enough.

He watched her face and body intently, looking for any movement, any small twitch of a muscle or her eyes.

Nothing.

They circled each other slowly, eyes locked.

I won't attack first.

Nothing.

Catherine came into view behind the Last Dark; momentarily, his eyes diverted.

There was a crackling sound as her sword swept

459

through the air, biting through his ear as it passed. The pain was intense enough to remind him not to get distracted again. No matter how difficult.

Without pause, she thrust forward. He jolted sideways as her sword sliced through his suit and the upper layer of his skin. The fabric darkened with claret, as if he'd been at a raucous party and spilled wine on himself. The pain took his breath away.

He stepped backwards and tripped over a small stone. He rolled in reverse and sprang up as quickly as possible. The sword fizzed over his head, scattering hairs like dandelion seeds in the wind.

'You're smarter than I expected,' she exclaimed. 'I thought you'd be burning by now.'

Thoughts entered his head from all angles.

She's too good. She's too fast, too smart.

She tricked me, and now I'll end up like the others.

She's won.

Chess, whispered a voice on the wind.

He regained his footing. *A chess game. Yes. Be calm.*

His mind seemed to loosen a little.

Maybe I could slow time a little more.

He relaxed, trying to open his soul. He thought of Catherine's lips caressing his, the warm embrace of her spirit, her electricity. It surrounded him, infused him; energy screamed into the night sky once again, and it bought him a single moment. It was all he needed.

He replayed the last few moves.

Wait a second. What was that?

He played it again. It was her eyes. Her eyes flicked

460

in the direction she planned to move, and there were the smallest of ripples in her arm.

What if it's another trick?

Trust yourself, murmured the wind.

Hero faced the Last Dark. He tried to put the pain out of his mind and focus entirely on her. Her psychotic smile remained glued to her face.

Her eyes flicked.

Left.

He rotated his sword to the left. A second later, she swung her weapon.

Their swords clattered together.

Her eyes flicked again.

Down.

He inverted his sword, and there was a second clang as she attempted a double strike.

Thrust.

His sword grated as though he were slicing through crusty bread as it chewed into the bone under her arm. She squealed and staggered back into a nearby tree. Her sword thudded into the damp undergrowth of the forest.

'You were never supposed to be able to fight like this,' she cried in agony. 'You were like . . .'

Her lips took on the bittersweet smile of reminiscence. 'I missed you, James.' She raised her other arm towards his face and cried out in pain, then dropped it back to her side. Her eyes glimmered in the moonlight. 'Why did things have to work out like this?'

'I'm sorry, I'm so sorry,' he lamented.

He drew back his sword.

461

'You've got Hero's heart at last,' she whispered. 'It's what you always wanted, James.'

Hero tasted the salt of his tears as he thrust his sword through her heart.

She screamed as she was driven into the tree behind her, then choked as blood pulsated up her throat. It splattered out of her mouth and onto Hero's white suit. Her stare grew vacant, lost in the wilderness of the universe.

He reached to her, engulfing her cheeks with his hands, and brushed his lips against her searing forehead. 'I didn't want to do this, I really didn't. Goodbye.'

He didn't even know her name.

Sophie, her name is Sophie, the wind whispered.

'Goodbye, Sophie.'

Her lips were moving languidly. Was she trying to tell him something? He dropped his ear to her mouth, feeling her breath against his ear.

'What?'

She breathed louder, but he could only make out '—k you.' She opened her mouth in a gruesome smile, and he was hit by a shot of heat.

What the f—

Her eyes and mouth were searing white.

Run, brother, came the wind again.

A stifled scream came from beside the tree— Catherine. She was standing with her hands over her mouth, as if trying to catch her cries.

'Get down,' he shouted as he sprinted towards her.

He glanced back. Sophie had begun to shudder and was trying to scream, but her lungs were full of fire.

The wind swirled around her, accompanied by the low-pitched sound of a thousand whispers.

'Get down,' he shrieked. Time was up.

Catherine stood frozen.

He threw himself at Catherine just as Sophie's head tilted back and her mouth opened wide. The whispers were cut short in a glittering red and green explosion that shattered the tree into flaming spikes. The shock wave hit him in the back, launching him and Catherine into the air and sending them tumbling to the under-growth with a single, dull thud.

Chapter 78

Hero

Catherine lay beneath him. Hero felt strange, dizzy. He slid sideways off her, rolling onto his back. The grass beneath him was soft and warm. Every part of him pulsed with his heartbeat; somebody with a hammer wrapped in barbed wire was working a long shift on his head. The world was a mass of blurry blobs swimming to and fro in a thick fog. The white and black keys of a piano flashed before his eyes before the world firmly returned. Slowly, their edges began to sharpen and come into focus.

Catherine was straddling him, her smile beaming against the darkness. The moon behind her lent a bright aura to her head; she had become an angel.

A real-life angel come to take me away.

The world continued to sharpen around him. Everything seemed more real than usual—exceptionally real, a super-focused cartoon of its former self.

Catherine stooped down and gathered him into her arms, shaking with the excitement and adrenaline of what'd happened.

'You did it,' she whispered into his ear. 'The war's over. You're free.'

'I don't think so,' he said.

His lips trembled, but not with excitement.

'What do you mean?' she asked. 'That's what you said in the car. That was the last of them, you said. It's just you and me now. We can have a normal life. Together.'

'It is what I always wanted.' His breath rasped noisily. 'But I'm sorry, I'm not going to be free. She tricked me.'

She could tell that something was wrong. She pulled back and brought her hands up so she could look at them in the light; they were stained red.

His back felt warm and wet. A numbness was spreading throughout his body from his waist as blood the colour of deep claret expanded around his prostrate body.

'A fragment of that tree, I think.' He winced as he answered the unasked question. 'She got me to come too close. She tricked me.'

'No,' Catherine cried. 'Please don't leave me! I only just found you.'

But his eyes had closed.

Shiny black-and-white wooden keys whizzed in front of his face. He looked around. He was back at home, a kid on that day he'd been beaten up by Martin and his friends and James had come to rescue him. They were smiling and giggling from the errant 'Entertainer' that always amused him so much.

James was grinning at him. 'You see, bruv? Everything will be okay because we can always laugh together.'

'I've missed you, bruv,' Hero replied despondently.

James smiled enigmatically. 'Let's try something else.' He began playing 'Nuvole Bianche', as he'd done so many years ago. Hero dutifully joined in. He was whisked forward to that moment at the restaurant with Catherine when he'd played it on his own; this time, however, James was by his side.

He looked across at his brother. 'I always knew you were here with me. I felt you. As I feel you now.'

'You're weird—you know that, right?' James winked as they continued playing.

And then they were back at the piano in the house too, in both places at once, the two points in time channelled through the brothers, the piano, and the song. Something inside Hero came alive again, and he saw now it'd never truly been dead. It'd been throbbing in the background so long that he'd got used to it, but now he could see it for what it was. All those years, their connection had been a phantom limb, but now he could see they'd always been connected. They'd always been one person, helping each other whenever there was need.

The piece came to an end, and James put his arm around Hero.

I've missed you so much. But you never left me.

'I'll always be there for you, bruv, and you'll always be there for me,' James murmured.

And you were, weren't you? I never lost you at all. You were standing in the shadows, looking out for me like you said you would, all those years. I've always known.

Then he was in the bathroom, blood running from his lip into the sink. He looked up in the mirror at James, who was speaking to him: 'Sometimes you stand and fight. Sometimes you do nothing. And sometimes you run, brother.'

'We're not running anymore, bruv,' Hero replied.

'No one is, thanks to you. Was it worth it?'

'I'll miss her. I love her.'

'Me too.'

His smile broadened to a grin. 'But yes, it was. And now I'm coming for you, James. I'll see you again soon, to touch your chin.'

He chuckled, then winced as his body reminded him of the wooden stake. The cold Devon wind bit into his ears and neck.

James was gone.

'Oh God, that hurts,' he whimpered.

Catherine was still crouched over him, shuddering, tears streaming down her face and dripping onto his chest. He mustered all his remaining energy and raised his hand to her cheek, caressing it with his thumb.

'You're so beautiful.' He looked into her beautiful hazel eyes. 'Such innocent eyes. I would've enjoyed losing myself in them every day until the day I died. I guess I did.'

His arm fell limply by his side.

He began to feel as he'd felt when he'd kissed her before, as if the Creator were smiling upon him—a powerful, connected feeling of acceptance. With it came a beautiful stillness and relaxation.

'You're on your own now, all of you. Use your freedom well.' His breathing became shallow. 'I'll see you on the other side. I love—'

Catherine howled, shattering the peaceful night.

The moonlight bathing him seemed so bright; he couldn't see where he ended and it began anymore. Time stopped and then slowly reversed. His essence fizzed and fused with particles of light as they floated upwards into the sky, sparkling in the night's pale radiance.

Everything's okay, bruv. Everything's going to be okay.

Chapter 79

John Turner

John Turner's eyes burned as tears streamed down his face. Catherine bent over Hero a hundred yards away, well out of sight of his vantage point within the forest. Anger seethed behind his pain, finding its way to the surface, seeping through every pore.

He looked away from his son's lifeless body. Staring back from a few yards away was a grey-haired man with lines on his forehead as deep as the experience they betrayed. He leaned against the brown bark of an oak tree, his dark grey suit outlined in blue from the flashing lights on the road behind him.

The two men nodded at each other like old war comrades separated by the grotesque remains of a battlefield.

John lifted his chin.

Hello, old friend. I know what you want, but I'm sorry. Not this time. I tried to save them. The Dark took everything from me, for no better reason than who I was. What I was. And I destroyed them for it. There's only one left who means anything anymore, and I have to find her.

The man tilted his head to one side and frowned.

This time, we do it my way.

John looked back at the scene in the clearing. *They wanted me to turn? Well, now I truly have.*

Behind him, the shadows of the forest darkened, accompanied by the low-pitched murmur of a thousand whispering voices. He stood up before the shadows could envelope him and dissolve him to nothing.

My sweet little boy, I'm so proud of you. I'll see you again very soon. I'm sure.

Chapter 80

Bertrande

Bertrande stared across the clearing. Dressed in all white, the man was still difficult to make out in the darkness of the forest beyond, but there was no doubt who it was. Bertrande's mind snatched at fleeting images of his friend's son bouncing on his knee, giggling furiously as only children can: *Again, Uncle Bertrande, again, again!* The sounds of happiness echoed before fading, engulfed by history.

Their eyes met.

Hello, John. Bertrande held his gaze. His friend's eyes were pure black, his face an immobile mask of mourning.

Don't do this. Please, John. We can sort this out together, the right way, we can find her.

He tilted his head and frowned.

John?

His old friend nodded at him across the clearing. Bertrande returned the acknowledgement.

A barely audible groan rumbled towards him then, a thousand voices murmuring from beyond the battlefield. On the other side, his friend vaporised into the umbra.

Shit.
His head drooped.
The Turner's back.